A Lie
UNIVERSALLY
HIDDEN

Anngela Schroeder

AnngelaSchroeder-Author on Facebook.com

A Lie Universally Hidden

ISBN-13: 978-1537773377
ISBN-10: 1537773372

Cover Design: Shari Ryan at "Mad Hat Covers"
Formatting: Shari Ryan at "Mad Hat Covers"
Editor: Christina Boyd

Other books available by the author on Amazon:
"The Quest for Camelot"
"Affections and Wishes"
"Then Comes Winter"

ACKNOWLEDGEMENTS

This book began as a small kernel and grew into something I could never have imagined, with so many people who helped it along the way. It has been a tumultuous year, with our son's cancer diagnosis and treatment forcing us to reevaluate the focus of our lives. Writing became my escape; from something that I once enjoyed, to something I now needed to emotionally survive. A simple thanks cannot express the gratitude I have felt and still feel for the doctors and nurses who not only have taken care of our sweet son, but us as well, as we spent countless days and nights at the hospital. From late night candy pilfering, extra pairs of warm socks and the offer of warm hoodies, to encouraging me to get some rest mom, this book would not be possible without you: Laura (my Scottish Latina), Tiff, Rachel, Robyn (my boy's rock), Neil the Ninja, Luke Yoda (whose patience with multiple light saber battles helped us get through Christmas on the 4th floor), Carolyn (bat girl), Chris, Kris, Tina, Paul (the man!), Blanca, Consuelo, Tammy and Trish, Lisa, Renee, Johnna, Kelly, Shurpreet, and all those who I've forgotten to mention, as well as all our doctors Drs. K.J., S.L., A.R., S.A., and Dr. Annie. Thank you.

To those who have supported and encouraged me throughout this process, friends and strangers alike: the readers at fanfiction.net (your suggestions were appreciated and helpful), Patty (my other mother), Diana (who always gives such valuable advice), Kristin (my writing buddy), Kori (next time it'll make sense), Teresa (my kindred spirit), Sandra (she who has an estate now named for her), Becca (my other half), Kellie (my Fishy), Neany and Neuby (my unofficial mentors), Calamity Jane and Vanilla (who taught me to work harder for what I want), and all my students throughout the years, most recently my AP and Creative Writing classes (let's have a potluck to celebrate). My greatest appreciation to you all.

To my peers in this Regency world of writing: my gifted editor, Christina Boyd, who made my words sound more brilliant than I could have imagined, thank you is not enough. Your patience with my endless emails, messages, and questions have kept me afloat and encouraged my excitement at low moments; author Joy King, without whose confidence I wouldn't have taken the plunge on some of the most important steps in the writing world, or known some of the quirky ins and outs of publishing; Claudine from *Just Jane 1813* whose kindness and willingness to help me will assist my book in reaching so many more readers; my cover designer, Shari Ryan, whose patience with all my questions and suggestions would surpass my own, and whose last minute formatting skills saved my sanity and my Christmas turkey. Thank you all.

To my family who has believed in me and never imagined I couldn't fulfill my goals: my Sissy, MJ, without whom, I would not be able to function sometimes; my dear mother-in-law Mama Meg, who gifted me with her brilliance and more importantly, her #1 son; Beck-Beck and Lala, who cheered with me as MJ lost Mr. Darcy-victory was ours; my pesky brothers (Li Wilhelm, Gabeo, and Munchito) and their wonderful wives who support my most fantastical whims; my nieces and nephews who bring me such joy; my cousin Lisa Ann (my partner in crime, the Thelma to my Louise and the sister I never had); my sweet Daddy whose love and pride in me knows no boundaries—ana bahabek, Bayi—all my love, all my kisses; my dearest Mommy, the woman I was blessed with for 32 years to look towards as an example of all that was good (…if there is anything lovely of good report or praiseworthy…it was you!), my sweet sons, Mims, Little Fat Dumpling, and Chub-o-love, YOU ARE MY JOY! And finally, to my sweet Schro... as I sit here on the pink writing chair you bought me, typing away to my heart's content while you make breakfast for our brood, I am once again reminded how grateful I am that I turned my car around on a cold, March afternoon 17 years ago. You are my greatest blessing. I love you.

For Miss Tay. You're still making a difference, and your beautiful smile will live on indefinitely.

http://www.strong-as-steele.org

＄

This book is dedicated to my sweet son Timmy,
who has taught me over the last year what a true hero is.
Mommy loves you!
N.N.S.T.N.M.C.A.G.M.G.T.S. XOXO
#TimmyStrong

＄

PROLOGUE

Pemberley,
Derbyshire, 1794

"I would speak to you on an urgent matter. If you continue to persist with this charade, we must establish the future for Fitzwilliam and Anne."

"My niece?"

"Yes, your niece. I want your assurance that Fitzwilliam will marry Anne when they come of age."

Lady Anne sighed with both the exhaustion of her illness and the weight of her sister's demands. Her light blue eyes flitted around the room endeavoring to memorize everything that mattered to her in the world: the picture of Fitzwilliam hanging above the fireplace; the miniature of her dear husband on her bedside table; the silver rattle for Georgiana on the dresser; the view of the grounds of Pemberley through the window. All this she absorbed as she listened to her sister's prattling.

"I want you to promise you will speak to him about his responsibility to the family, to Pemberley, and to Anne."

"Catherine, Fitzwilliam is not yet twelve years old. He does not need to have it thrust on him by his dying mother that he should marry Anne. She is a fine girl but I want him to marry for love, not duty."

"And what if he does love Anne? What then?" Lady Catherine asked indignantly.

"She is a dear girl, and I am sure she will make a wonderful wife. If that is Fitzwilliam's wish, then that is what I wish for him."

"And yet...?"

"And yet, I do not want the last moments with my son to be those of guilt. Please drop this. Allow me that." She began to cough forcefully and her maid assisted her with a cup of water as her sister sat there unmoved.

When the fit was over, Lady Catherine said, "I see I cannot change your mind so I will move on to a different subject. My solicitor drew up these papers to ensure your inheritance from Father's estate will pass in trust for Georgiana. Fitzwilliam will be provided for by the Darcy estate. You owe this to your daughter."

"I believe my husband has taken care of this," she replied weakly, reaching for the papers.

"No, he has not." Lady Catherine placed a quill in her sister's fingers instead of the papers. "Sign there at the bottom."

She pointed to the lower portion of the paper as Lady Anne withdrew her hand. "I would rather George looked at these before I sign anything."

Lady Catherine bristled. "Anne, do you not trust me? I am your sister. Everything I do is for your benefit. Allow me this final kindness for you. While you have time."

A wave of uncertainty washed over her as Lady Anne Darcy, the mistress of the great estate of Pemberley, was once again reduced to a child by the mere tone of her older sister's words. "Very well, Catherine." She sighed and weakly scrawled her name across the paper. "Sister, I am tired. Please leave me to rest."

Lady Catherine rose quickly. "Very well. Goodnight."

"Please ask Hazel to come in?"

"Of course."

Her breath shallow, Anne Darcy waited as her trusted maid returned.

"My lady?"

"Hazel. Please take a letter for me."

"Of course, Your Ladyship."

"Once I have signed it, place it on my writing desk."

"Yes, my lady. How would you like me to begin?"

Lady Anne Darcy looked out the window feeling the regrets of a life unlived. Tears welled in her eyes as she began. "My dearest Fitzwilliam…"

CHAPTER 1

F itzwilliam Darcy looked out the window across the estate as the late afternoon summer sun began to descend behind the woods of Pemberley. Attempting to regulate his breathing, he gripped the windowsill to steady himself before turning to take in his surroundings. The golden light danced across the elegant room with the lavender walls complementing the darker plum of the canopy and drapes. The rich furniture brought in elements of nature, as did the painting of Pemberley's gardens hanging above the settee.

Yet, no matter the beauty of the chamber itself, he could not escape the obvious. The long-ignored scent of illness was now permeating the room of the only woman he had ever loved. He abandoned his post and walked tentatively over to where she lay. Her small frame seemed engulfed in the mahogany four-poster bed, the pillows and feather quilts swallowing her up. He gently sat down on the edge as she opened her eyes and slowly smiled at him.

"Fitzwilliam."

"Yes, Mummy," he said, trying to ignore the catch in his throat.

"Come closer, Son." She tried to move the counterpane but in her weakened state was only able to rest her hand on the covers. "I would speak with you." Her breathing was measured and she seemed determined to not allow the moment to pass before she imparted the words he needed to know.

Unable to speak, he anxiously leaned in closer fearing what she might say.

Lady Anne Darcy took a deep breath and began the speech he dreaded. "Wills, as much as you nor your father wish to acknowledge it, my days are coming to a close."

"Mum—"

"Please—" A fit of coughing caused young Darcy to rush to the end table and pour her a glass of water. He gently held it to her lips.

"Drink." His brown eyes took in her withered form. He realized her blue eyes, once filled with laughter, were now dull and tired. Her golden tresses, which before had shone like the sun, hung limply in a plait beside her. Her skin was pale, almost translucent, as she took a sip of the water through her parched lips.

He pulled the cup away and she smiled. "Thank you, Fitzwilliam. You have always been my joy." She grimaced as he plumped her pillows and straightened the counterpane before she continued. "Some mothers never understood. 'A child should be seen and not heard' or 'Nannies rear children, not mothers.'" She raised her hand with great will and touched his face. "They could not understand the love I feel for you, my sweet William. Since the moment you were placed in my arms, you have made me the happiest and proudest of mothers." A tear escaped and streamed down her cheek. "Your goodness and honesty are such examples to others. I am grateful our little Georgie will be guided by you. You will grow strong as your father—to be the master of Pemberley. Always remember who you are—and the people who came before you."

"Yes, Mummy." He could not stop his own tears and lay down next to her.

"There, there, my sweet Wills. There is no shame in crying." She ran her hands through his dark curls and wiped away his tears. "You know the love I have for you will not end in death. Know that I want you to be happy. Know whatever choices you make in life will be right for you. You have both duty to Pemberley and family. But, you also have a duty to yourself." He lay there as she began to weakly sing their favorite song:

"The pale moon was rising above the green mountain,
The sun was declining beneath the blue sea;
When I strayed with my love to the pure crystal fountain,
That stands in the beautiful Vale of Tralee…"

Her voice faded as she gently reached for his hand. "I love you, Fitzwilliam."

"I love you, too."

He snuggled closely to her until he could hear her heartbeat and the rasp of her breath. His heart was light in this almost perfect moment: to be alone with his mother before she left the Earth, drinking in her love and attention.

"Mr. Darcy. Mr. Darcy, sir, come at once. Lady Anne calls for you!"

George Darcy woke suddenly and rolled over in the darkness, struggling with the counterpane wrapped around his ankles. He heard the barking of his sister through the door leading to his wife's chambers and was at once running toward the clamor. Lady Catherine was already there, berating his beloved to find the strength to pull through.

Anne's eyes opened and closed slowly. "George, Fitzwilliam, Georgiana…"

"I am here, my love," George said tenderly, pushing past his wife's sister and placing a kiss on her wrist. "I am here."

Fitzwilliam rushed into the room, knelt beside his father, and laid his head next to his mother's small frame. "Mummy? Mummy, please stay. Please don't die!" His sobs were muffled in the counterpane.

"Oh, George," Anne said in a far-off whisper. "Tell Georgiana I loved her. Let her know of me—her mother—her guardian angel."

"Anne, my bride. Do not leave us. Dr. Griggs is arriving from London. Wait for one more day and all will be well. Please, my love. Try."

Lady Catherine was taken aback by the scene in the presence of the servants but held her tongue in respect of her brother and his impending grief. She turned her head to avoid the intimate exchange when she noticed a letter on her sister's writing table addressed to "Fitzwilliam" and saw the wax pressed with Anne's seal. Her curiosity piqued, she only wrestled with her conscience long enough to hear Fitzwilliam say, "Mummy, I will protect Georgie. I promise."

As Lady Anne Darcy breathed her last, Lady Catherine thrust her sister's final thoughts for her son into the sleeve of her own dressing gown. She pulled back her shoulders, raised her chin, and strode over to view her sister for the last time.

CHAPTER 2

Hertfordshire, September 1810

Sixteen years later

D
arcy placed his book on the seat next to him and stretched his long legs in the carriage while trying not to awaken his sister. The travel was comfortable but tedious through numerous counties and small hamlets to visit his good friend's leased estate. This was the second day of their journey, having rested the previous evening in their London townhouse, and he had been anxious to get on the road early to avoid the unusually wet September weather. Looking at his sister, he wondered if the sunrise departure had been too hasty.

But, there is little to be done now. Distance from my aunt was an immediate necessity. Bingley will be an enjoyable distraction.

Despite this truth, Darcy felt a pang of guilt. He found little pleasure at Rosings with Lady Catherine and his cousin Anne. His aunt was biting and cynical, hardly what he willingly subjected either his dear sister or himself to. His cousin, or rather his intended, had changed so much as they grew into adulthood that he hardly knew her. *When we were younger, I enjoyed Anne. Yet, as soon as Lady*

Catherine produced that letter from my mother, everything changed—for both Anne and myself.

That letter had reminded him where his duties and responsibilities lie, thus as he grew, he applied his life on fulfilling the desires of his mother. *I wish I could have spoken to Father about marrying Anne. Then, with Father dying five years ago...* He shook his head to concentrate on his current circumstances. *Yes, helping Charles with this estate will be a much needed distraction.*

He had received a barely legible letter from Charles Bingley a se'nnight before at Rosings asking for his assistance in determining if the estate he was leasing was adequate. Feeling a responsibility to his friend and needing an excuse to leave his aunt's home, Darcy began preparing for his departure. It was a delicate undertaking to convince Lady Catherine to relinquish her hold. For this first major decision in Bingley's life, Darcy would do all he could to properly guide him.

He looked out the window at the rolling hills of the countryside. The scenery was much different from the area he had left months before. The peaks of Derbyshire were far superior in his estimations to these simple undulations, but he could not deny their beauty. He wondered what this untamed countryside held for him for the next months while he helped Charles determine if this endeavor would be profitable.

He turned at the sound of his sister stirring only to settle back into a light slumber. *My dear Georgie. How this life of ours is going to change. I only hope what our mother wanted and planned for me will bring us both happiness.*

"Are we there, William?" she asked, opening her blue eyes and looking out at the passing scenery. They were the same eyes as their mother's and he believed that was one reason he loved and protected her so.

"Not quite, dear girl," he said tenderly. "John informed me with our early departure, we should arrive at Netherfield by ten. It will not be much longer now." He reached in his pocket and pulled out his watch to check the time.

At sixteen years of age, Georgiana Darcy had a becoming artlessness which could be attributed largely to her brother's protective nature. Her golden curls were pinned under her bonnet and a shy smile was present at the corners of her mouth. Fitzwilliam's worries as her guardian were seemingly unwarranted. She was a kind, gentle girl who understood her position and the necessary restraint and decorum required as a Darcy.

"This is the second time this year your holiday has been spoiled by my plans. First, you were set to go to Ramsgate when Aunt Catherine summoned us to Rosings for July and August, and now our trip to Dublin has been postponed because of my friend. I hope you do not hold it against me?"

"Wills, how can I hold anything against you? You are the best brother I could ask for, so loving and kind. I know whatever you decide is the absolute paramount for me. Like this carriage for instance. Had you chosen an inferiorly sprung transport, I would not be able to finish our gift for Mr. Bingley!" She grinned, picked up her sewing, and continued to embroider a sampler for his friend.

He smiled at her innocence and implicit trust in him and was grateful for his ability to protect her. He had only told her the partial truth about the earlier summer trip to Ramsgate. His cousin Colonel Fitzwilliam, who had shared guardianship of Georgiana with him since Darcy's father's death, had gained intelligence from one of his foot soldiers that someone with a close connection to the family had been awaiting her arrival in attempts to damage her reputation in a most reprehensible manner. *George Wickham.*

He unconsciously clenched his fists and took a deep breath at the thought of his childhood playmate and the realization of what might have occurred. Wickham had planned to abscond with his sister—and her dowry—and he would have been eternally connected to that blaggard. As disturbing, Georgiana's then companion, Mrs. Younge, was discovered to have been a friend to Wickham and privy to the plan all along. She was immediately dismissed from Darcy's employ and the threat of jail loomed over her head.

Colonel Fitzwilliam and he made the decision to keep their young charge in ignorance on the near catastrophe and direct blame for the missed holiday toward their Aunt Catherine instead.

"Besides, had our holiday not been cancelled, Mrs. Younge would have been unable to assist her family in their time of distress. I do hope her father has improved."

Darcy clenched his jaw in response.

"Yet" —Georgiana glanced at the sleeping figure next to her— "Mrs. Annesley has proven to be a reliable companion whose guidance in the month since she has been with me has been all that is proper."

"Was Mrs. Younge's guidance not?" he asked turning to face her.

She paused seeming to search for the correct words. "Mrs. Younge chose unorthodox methods which at times made me uncomfortable. However, I am sure she always had my best interest in mind."

Yes, I am sure she did. A scowl creased his brow before she continued along another vein, interrupting his ruminations.

"Do you think Netherfield will be as grand as Pemberley? I so want Mr. Bingley to love his home as we love ours."

His body relaxed as he forced Wickham and Mrs. Younge from his thoughts. "I am sure he will, poppet. But nothing could be as grand as Pemberley."

William slyly winked at his sister and turned his attention out the window and caught sight of a young woman walking along the road. Had Georgiana been paying attention, his quick intake of breath might have surprised her. There was a flush about the young woman's cheeks from her apparent exercise, and her skin glowed with a soft radiance. A shawl was draped over her slender arms and loose brown curls spilled from her bonnet. But it was her deep brown eyes with their thick lashes which arrested attention and held his gaze. She nodded at him with a slight smile and continued walking in the opposite direction.

"Wills…Wills?"

"Hmmm?"

"I asked what I am to do about Miss Bingley. I do not wish to seem ungrateful, but her attentions make me terribly nervous." His sister bit her lip, then immediately stopped.

"I will rescue you if her attentiveness becomes unbearable. I will always rescue you, sweetling. Never fear." He patted her knee and picked up his book to continue reading. But his mind could not focus on the printed words as his thoughts rambled back to the young woman he had just seen. A slow warmth began to spread in his chest as he saw her again in his mind's eye.

"Why do you smile so, Brother?" Georgiana teased setting down her sewing.

He shook his head. *You are promised to another. There is only one woman you need to think of from now on.* He shrugged.

"Oh nothing, darling. I am only thinking…"

"Of Anne?"

"Yes," he replied smiling. "How pleased I am knowing how content we will all be when she is well enough to set a wedding date."

His smile faltered and he returned his gaze out the window, wondering about the young woman. *There was something rather pleasing about her features…*

The carriage passed in the direction of Meryton allowing Elizabeth Bennet's smile to linger a bit longer at the memory of the handsome gentleman who had only moments before disappeared around the bend. The imposing chaise and four surely was heading to Netherfield Park which, according to her mother, had been let at last. Mrs. Bennet seemed to think it would somehow affect her daughters, though Lizzy could not see how. Their new neighbor, a Mr. Charles Bingley, had been in residence for a little over a fortnight and no one, save Sir William Lucas, had made his acquaintance.

"But, I guess that is the problem with being a man," she joked to no one in particular as she continued to walk on her way home. "You have too much business and no time for frivolity."

Truth be told, Lizzy was not out on a frivolous walk. She had been visiting a few of her father's tenants with Cook's weekly basket of sweets. They had been lovely visits: the Millers were expecting their third baby next month, and as ungainly as she was, Mrs. Miller was very hospitable; the Watsons were grateful for the cakes as it was little Sarah's birthday the next day; and the Reeds were happy for the book of poems offered to young Billy as he was preparing to leave for the continent. She adored their tenants and was grateful her father had always encouraged the girls to visit them regularly since their mother did not.

Lizzy sighed as she neared Longbourn, her family's estate. She loved her home, even with its once stately façade now somewhat faded by the sunlight. The footprints of generations of her father's ancestors could be seen throughout the grounds and buildings—the park, a small nod to the great estates of years past with its asters, sage, and daisies; the barn, expanded a half century ago to increase the livestock output; the watermill along the stream to help the Longbourn mill produce flour for its tenants and local markets. She shook her head at the disuse. Her father had no disposition to increase the holdings of his estate.

I do not understand why he is so hesitant to consider the estate as a business instead of solely as our home. As a woman, my training is limited, but even I see the benefit of using the land for our advantage. The commotion of her home suddenly brought her back to reality. Even from this distance, she could hear her mother and the din spilling from the house as preparations were being made for tomorrow's festivities.

"Jane… Jane!" wailed Mrs. Bennet. "Bring your dresses to me so that I may pick which one for you to wear. We must take advantage of every opportunity."

Upon walking into the house, Lizzy could not avoid the uproar. Her younger sister Mary was plunking away at the piano. The youngest, Kitty and Lydia, were arguing over ribbons. At seventeen and not quite sixteen respectively, Lizzy often wondered if they were too young to come out into society but could not begrudge their pleasure due to her lack of the marriage state. She walked down the hall and knocked gently at the door of her father's study.

"Enter." He smiled as she crossed the room and kissed him affectionately on the cheek. "Good morning, Lizzy. How are our tenants?"

Lizzy inhaled the scent of leather and tobacco which permeated the air. Even in fifty years, she knew when she smelled the two scents together, she would feel her father's presence. Light filtered in through the dark window tapestries and a low fire was smoking in the hearth. He motioned toward "her chair" and she sat down, raised her feet under her, and crossed her ankles.

"All is well, Father. Mrs. Miller's time is near. I must finish the christening gown I am making her. Hopefully they will be pleased even though I am not as proficient with a needle as Mary."

"My dear girl, your efforts are always appreciated by everyone who knows you."

Their conversation was interrupted by a screeching Mrs. Bennet. "Lizzy? Lizzy? Where is that girl? Hill!"

The obedient servant could be heard rushing down the hallway into the room. "Yes, ma'am."

"Has Lizzy returned? I must approve her gown for tomorrow evening. I do not know who will look at her with Jane at her side, but all the same, she must be presentable."

Her voice faded down the hallway, barking both orders at her housekeeper and more complaints about her second, oldest child.

"Ignore her, my dear girl. Your mother's in a mood which will not be squelched until her moment's greatest desire has been fulfilled." Mr. Bennet readjusted his glasses and smiled mischievously.

"Which is...?" Lizzy asked picking up her favorite copy of Wordsworth which her father left on the end table for whenever she joined him.

"To be introduced to the new master of Netherfield." His eyes danced as he slowly let the sentence roll from his mouth.

"Well, Father, can you blame her? A man with 'five thousand a year' is not a man to be trifled with. Not often does an opportunity such as this come to the neighborhood—nay, to a house with five unmarried daughters!" They both chuckled while Lizzy repeated her mother's words for the hundredth time that week. "And you, sir! Refusing to visit Mr. Bingley, therefore denying your daughters the opportunity to dance with him on the morrow? By that lone decision, casting us into the hedgerows upon your death? It is not to be endured!"

Mr. Bennet chortled again as Lizzy's laughter filled the room. "Yes, my dear girl. You are an observer of the folly of characters, like your old papa." He raised his eyebrows and leaned toward her. "We are blessed then to have incomparable examples daily in our realm."

As if on cue, frantic cries rang down the stairs. "Kitty, give that back to Lydia at once."

"But, Mama, it is mine. My aunt Gardiner gave it to me for my birthday last year."

"Well, it looks much better on your sister than you. You heard me, girl. Off with it!"

The sound of stomping feet and slamming doors followed this unpleasant pronouncement.

"As I stated—" smirked Mr. Bennet over his book "—incomparable examples."

Lizzy reveled in these moments with her father, passing a pleasant hour together quietly reading. The shadows in the room lengthened before a knock came at the door.

"Yes," said Mr. Bennet without glancing up.

Jane Bennet, a comely girl of two and twenty entered the room, quickly closing the door behind her and gliding over to the chair across from Elizabeth. Her father noticed her weariness and grinned.

"Have you been consumed in conversation about lace and other fripperies these sixty minutes, my dearest?"

"Yes, Papa," she answered patiently. "And Mama has been extolling the virtues of the art of the fan. I regret I lack the talent nor am I interested. However, she assures me the fan is a useful tool for a young lady, and I must practice most ardently before tomorrow night." She weakly smiled at Lizzy. "Would you not like to learn as well, dear Sister?" They both knew her answer and giggled.

"As you know, Mama does not believe that *anything* will induce a man to desire her second daughter, so you, my dear Jane, must endure all the attentions our mother is apt to shower upon you. I am only sorry I cannot relieve some of the burden for your sake."

"Ha! You are not!"

"You are right. I am not!"

Mr. Bennet looked at his favorite daughters, grateful that at least two of his offspring had some semblance of wit, common sense, and propriety. "My dearest girls, if I confide in you, will you promise not to tell your mother?"

They looked at each other with curiosity before Lizzy said, "Is this something you will tell Mama we have known all along, or shall that remain a secret as well?"

"My, Lizzy! That will depend if she is upset and I need to divert her attention to another." With no little amusement, he moved to the door to ensure their privacy and turned to his daughters. "Today, I have a notion we shall have a surprise guest at tea." His eyes glinted with mischief. He paused waiting for a reaction.

"Who, Papa?" Jane asked, clasping her hands.

"Mr. Charles Bingley."

"Father! How do you come to know this? We have not even made his acquaintance!"

"Maybe you have not, my dear Lizzy, but I called on him yesterday and asked him to come to tea this afternoon. He welcomed the invitation, although his sisters and his brother, are otherwise engaged. *That* should put your mother in a fine mood." He appeared quite satisfied with himself as he opened his book and leaned back in his chair.

"But, Papa," Jane cried. "Lizzy and I are already engaged for tea with Charlotte Lucas. We will not be able to meet him."

"Well, child, you must be off before he arrives or your mama will not let you leave. And as for Mr. Bingley, he will have to wait until tomorrow evening to match wits with you. I daresay twenty-four hours will have no effect on either your wit or your beauty and he will be as delighted by you then as he would today."

Jane colored at her father's rarely bestowed compliment.

"And, Lizzy," said Mr. Bennet pulling out a letter from between the pages of his book, "I received a note today from Mr. Hamilton inquiring after our family." He noticed the slight blush in her cheeks as he continued. "He is almost finished with his business in London and believes he will be back in town later this week."

"That is nice to hear, Papa."

With a twinkle in his eye, he pressed on. "Why he continues to write me, apprising me of his activities is beyond my understanding. Of what interest could it be to this household, I wonder? I am at a loss."

"Maybe he will be here in time for the assembly." Jane reached over and squeezed Lizzy's hand. "He is a superb dancer, and he always singles you out, Lizzy."

Jane's sidelong glance made her sister smile. There were many things in life that Lizzy was unsure of, none of which were the affability and charm of Mr. Hamilton, nor the constancy of his affections. James Hamilton and she had been playmates since childhood. His family had been tenants on the estate of Longbourn for fifty years. Lizzy had always held him in high regard but young James seemed to know his place. However, at the age of thirteen, he had been singled out by a distant aunt as her heir and had been removed from his parents' home and given a gentleman's education, first to Eaton and then to Cambridge.

Upon the death of his aunt several months previous, Mr. Hamilton had returned to Meryton and requested a private interview with her father. Though he had not divulged his wishes to Lizzy, she suspected he made his intentions known during that interview, as her father liked to frequently mention her childhood friend's reversal of fortune and tease how one day that might benefit her. Yet, she was unsure if childhood felicity would translate to matrimonial bliss.

"It is providential that his aunt died with no children and left him that small estate. I must say I have been impressed with how he has managed. I only wish I had the patience and youth to do something similar."

"Come, Jane." Lizzy interrupted her father before his teasing began again. "Let us go walk in the garden and imagine what this Mr. Bingley will be like. Our family will have the benefit of knowing him before we do, so we can only speculate. Now, I believe that he and his party will be short and balding with a horrid case of spots. Except for possibly one dashing fellow," she said dreamily as the door closed behind her.

"Charles, we have known each other for many years—and I consider you one of my closest friends—but if you expect me to seek out company like that again, Georgiana and I will not make ourselves available for your invitations any longer."

Darcy threw his gloves on the seat of the red damask chair in Bingley's study, then poured himself a drink. His temples were throbbing with the threat of a headache as he tried to purge from his mind the shrill voice of the woman whose house they had just returned from.

"Darcy, it wasn't entirely unpleasant," his friend replied with a weak shrug. Running his hands through his hair, he exhaled noisily.

"Not entirely unpleasant? It was worse than unpleasant! It was excruciating!" Darcy shook his dark locks, which had been loosed from the three-mile ride back to Bingley's estate. "I will admit, I hoped it would be pleasant company. A nice tea after a two-day journey. Meet your neighbors. The company of five alleged lovely, young women."

"Yes," Charles said, shaking his head. "That was a disappointment. The two who are supposed to be the loveliest were not even home. But, at least we will see them at the assembly."

"Assembly? Bingley, I will not be attending. Georgiana is not yet out, and I do not want to leave her here alone. No, after this disastrous experience with the Bennets, I believe I will sit here and read."

There was a knock at the door and not waiting for admittance, Caroline Bingley entered the room. The youngest of the Bingley sisters, she was the tallest of all three children which was accentuated by her propensity for the latest fashion of turbans with long plumed feathers. Her eyes looked first to her brother then settled on Mr. Darcy as if he were her favorite pastry.

"Did the Bennets impress you with their country manners, or was I correct, Mr. Darcy?" A wry smile played at her lips as she sat down on the sofa staring at his person. Her gaze had always unnerved him.

"No, you were quite right, Miss Bingley, and I think from this point on I shall accuse you of being a fortune teller." He bowed politely and turned to the window, looking out into the haze of the early evening light.

Charles walked over to pour himself another glass. "I will agree with Darcy that I was surprised by their lack of decorum."

"Lack of decorum?" Darcy barked, turning to face his friend. "The three daughters had no more sense than a hare, and their conversation was boorish…either sermons from Fordyce or red coats. For a man to allow his daughters to participate in such idle conversation and his wife to prattle on about the windfall of 'handsome young men for her girls since the arrival of the militia' was…preposterous!" He caught Miss Bingley's vindictive eyes. "Forgive me. The middle daughter, Miss Katherine Bennet, I will grant you, attempted some sound conversation and seemed affected by her mother's ill-manners, as did the one with glasses."

"No, Mr. Darcy. Do not attempt to soften your opinions on my account. I observed their vulgar behavior in the village two days ago and was grateful we had not been introduced so I might ignore them entirely. I am sure I quite agree with anything you say."

He knew that was more of compliment to him than a degradation upon herself, but he could not view it as such. He bowed and excused himself to find his sister before he went up to dress for dinner.

"And was he short and bald?" Lizzy asked her three younger sisters after she and Jane returned from Lucas Lodge.

Before Kitty could respond, Lydia interpolated, "No, Mr. Bingley was quite handsome with his blue coat and ready smile. He was charming and diverting and I think he fancied me."

"He has five thousand a year," said Mrs. Bennet, reclining on the couch and smiling brightly as she yawned. "How wonderful for our daughters."

"Mama, what would make you believe that? Did he come into Hertfordshire with a mind to marry one of us?" Lizzy asked, picking up her sewing.

"Do not be silly, Lizzy! But, how could he not want one so lovely? I believe he took a fancy to Lydia because he could not stop glancing at her throughout his time here."

"Mama, he kept looking at Lydia because her behavior was so deplorable." The Bennet ladies turned with surprise at Kitty's declaration. "She was naughty their entire visit. Why would Mr. Bingley, or that other fellow, prefer her over Mary or myself?"

"Other fellow?" Lizzy asked. "What other fellow?"

"Why would he not prefer me above all others when I am prettier and taller than either you or Mary!" Lydia exclaimed, ignoring Lizzy's questions. "Kitty, you have become quite dull lately, and I for one am not interested in listening to your whining any longer." Turning to her mother before she walked from the room, Lydia snorted. "I dare say I'll invite her to the wedding, but she shan't stand up as a bridesmaid."

The family was used to this behavior from Lydia and had even come to expect it, but to have the two youngest sisters at odds was not anticipated. Mrs. Bennet rose to follow her favorite child and appease the slight she had received.

"Now, now, Kitty," Jane cooed to her sister sitting down next to her and taking her hand between her own, "your observations do you credit. You are displaying the mind of a fine, young woman by refraining from the silly exchange Lydia was attempting to goad you into."

"Yes, Kitty. I am very pleased with your deportment," Lizzy said, resting a reassuring pat on her shoulder. "What has brought this turn about?"

Kitty thought for a moment and contemplated while the sound of Mary's piano playing filled the room. "I daresay it was from Mr. Darcy."

"Mr. who?" Jane asked surprised.

"Mr. Bingley's friend—a tall, proud fellow who was looking on our family with disdain. While Mr. Bingley was all affability, Mr. Darcy was evidently displeased with what he saw. You know how Mama can be, and Papa was more interested in silently watching the folly, so we girls were once again left to our own devices."

"Did he insult you?" Lizzy asked, her ire rising at the thought of the handsome man from the carriage looking down upon her family. *Handsome or not, who is he to pass judgment?*

"No, Lizzy, he did not," Kitty said twirling a loose curl around her finger and contemplating her words. "But, just being in his presence…" She looked up at her sister's startled expression. "It is not what you think. My heart was not taken by him nor could I have any feelings for him—how could I on this short acquaintance? But I evaluated our family through his perspective and realized I no longer wanted to be what he saw.

"Lydia wants a red coat—someone to flirt with. I realized that I want a man of merit, such as Mr. Darcy. Someone who will see the value of me and not as a mere object. If I have any hope of fulfilling that dream, I must alter my ways."

Lizzy looked at Jane blankly and then back at Kitty. Was this their sister who only last week plotted with Lydia to visit the officers' barracks before the men were dressed? What had become of this girl, and what were these magical powers this Mr. Darcy had to influence Kitty in this manner?

Whatever powers he possesses, I wish it were proper to somehow thank him for his unknown act of service.

CHAPTER 3

"Three months," Darcy said slowly reading the letter from his aunt for the hundredth time since its arrival. He was unable to believe the time had finally come to take his bride. *A Christmas wedding during the merriest of seasons. Ironic.* "In three months, the dream of my mother will finally be fulfilled." *Not your dream, Fitzwilliam?* He picked up his morning coffee and looked out the window. He knew the answer to that. *I will honor the memory of my mother and stay resolute to the duty of both Georgiana and my mother's namesake.* He tried to hide a hint of mirth as he laughed at the irony that his future wife was named for the only woman he had ever truly loved.

"Love." He sighed absently, tapping his fingers on the glass pane. "I will never know love, not real love as my parents did." For a moment, the choices he would never make, would never be allowed to make, ran rampant through his mind before they were pushed aside. *But, my devotion to Pemberley and Georgiana are all I will need to be happy. Eventually, Anne will produce an heir, and then he will add to my felicity.* He stretched the emotional exhaustion from his muscles and crossed to the desk to finish a letter to his steward before making his way downstairs.

Though impolitic, he had remained in his room as long as possible for he had not the energy to fend off the overtures of Miss Bingley. *That woman knows I am promised to Anne, yet she insists on continually attempting to draw my favor.* He shook his head at her machinations. *If not for Bingley… But, now with the wedding date set, her actions and words will not do.* Fitzwilliam finished his letter and firmly closed the door behind him on the way to his friend's study.

⤚⤙

"Miss Elizabeth Bennet?"

Lizzy looked up from the rows of ribbons and lace with curiosity. Jane and Kitty had accompanied her to Meryton on the special demands of their mother to find the "perfect ribbon" for Lydia's dress. The favored child had pouted all the previous evening that Mr. Bingley would not give two straws for her if she did not have new embellishments for her gown, and with the possibility of losing the attentions of a man worth five thousand a year, Mrs. Bennet had dispatched three daughters to rectify the situation.

Lizzy did not recognize the lady as any of her acquaintances from Meryton yet smiled at the elegant stranger before her. "Yes, I am Elizabeth Bennet."

"Pardon my impertinence, but I heard the shopkeeper address you and wanted to make myself known. Allow me to introduce myself. My name is Caroline Bingley, this is my sister Mrs. Luisa Hurst, and this is Miss Georgiana Darcy. Your father made my brother's acquaintance a few days ago at Netherfield Park. I determined that would do for an introduction."

"Oh, yes, my father conveyed how much he enjoyed meeting Mr. Bingley," Lizzy said, setting aside the millinery and curtsied prettily. "My family had the pleasure of taking tea with your brother and Mr. Darcy yesterday. Unfortunately, my sister Jane and I were away." Lizzy turned to Jane and said, "May I present two of my sisters, Miss Jane Bennet and Miss Katherine Bennet?"

"Miss Darcy was eager to make the acquaintance of a gentleman's daughter as we will be residing in Netherfield until the Season. And after their meeting with your family, I am certain Charles and Mr. Darcy will encourage the connection with a genteel family such as yours amongst so many rustics."

Lizzy wondered at Miss Bingley's declaration. *An odd attempt at veiled insolence?* She also had a slight inclination the lady was mocking her. Instead, she turned her attentions to Miss Darcy. A petite, timid-looking girl of about sixteen. She had golden curls and large, clear blue eyes that were veiled behind long lashes. Her disposition seemed the opposite to that of her companion and Lizzy deemed she would like her at once.

"My father spoke very highly of your brother yesterday, and I am pleased to have met you. I do hope we will meet in company more often. Have you been in Hertfordshire long, Miss Darcy?"

"Only but a day," she whispered, looking up through her lashes. It seemingly pained her to speak and Lizzy could see her expression toward Miss Bingley was more of intimidation than companionship. "My brother and I arrived yesterday morning."

"And how are you finding Netherfield, Miss Darcy?" asked Kitty. She stepped forward and smiled encouragingly.

"Very well, thank you." Miss Darcy looked up, offering a genuine smile to Kitty. Forcing her voice to increase in volume, she shakily continued. "This shop is very quaint. It very much reminds me of the shops near my home."

Miss Bingley snickered before interrupting with her nasally voice. "These country villages are idyllic. Though the people are lacking in refinement, present company excluded of course, Miss Elizabeth. I do find the estate lovely. But Meryton is a curious little town in which to take a holiday."

Lizzy arched her brow. "Yes, we rustics are honored by your condescension and welcome you to our county. Hopefully, you will find respite here and entertainment before the delights of the Season whisk you away." She smiled sweetly and turned once more to Georgiana. "Miss Darcy, might we have the pleasure of your company this evening at the assembly?"

Georgiana shook her head sadly. "I am not yet out, so my brother and I will remain at Netherfield."

"Your brother will not be in attendance?" *If he is the same man from the carriage, it will be a sad evening indeed.*

"No, he is not one for balls and parties but would go if not for the worry of leaving me alone. He takes prodigious care of me." She smiled brightly, and Lizzy was slightly envious of not having such a brother of her own.

"And I will be staying with them as well," Miss Bingley interjected. "I could not bear to leave my dear Georgiana alone at the house with no female companionship. We will make quite a merry party."

Lizzy noted that Miss Darcy seemed both surprised by the revelation and not particularly pleased. They chatted a bit more about the Darcy's journey into the country before Miss Darcy excused herself and made her way over to a display of fine ribbons. Kitty soon joined her. They were engrossed in Kitty's one-sided conversation together while her own conversation with Miss Bingley was quite stunted. After an inelegant moment of silence, Miss Bingley curtseyed, joined Miss Darcy, and gently encouraged her to make a selection so they might depart.

Miss Darcy smiled at Kitty and said, "Thank you for your suggestion, Miss Katherine. I will inform you of how the ribbon matched my bonnet next time we meet."

"I hope to see it!" Pleased with her new acquaintance, Kitty curtseyed as the Netherfield party prepared to leave.

After the group exited the store, Jane rapturously said, "Were they not lovely! Miss Bingley was so kind with her attentions to Miss Darcy and Mrs. Hurst's gown was exquisite. I do look forward to meeting with Mrs. Hurst again tonight at the assembly."

Kitty agreed with her eldest sister, emphasizing the genteel manner of Miss Darcy, but Lizzy was not convinced. "Save Miss Darcy, I believe they are more pleased with themselves than what they see!"

"Oh, Lizzy, that cannot be true. I am sure they are all kindness. Why look at Miss Bingley! Willing to sacrifice a night of pleasure to stay at home to keep her young friend company. Is that not kindness itself?" Jane's large hazel eyes looked at Lizzy for confirmation, not believing her sister would have misjudged even that simple act of friendship for anything less than authentic.

"Yes, Jane." Lizzy took her sister's hand as they left the store after making their purchases. "It is kindness indeed." *And even I might be so kind as to sacrifice an evening to stay in company with such a handsome man!*

∽

"Oh, Fitzwilliam, the Miss Bennets were wonderful. So attentive and kind. Very solicitous and ladylike."

Georgiana was anxiously leaning forward on the sofa in her brother's sitting room while he put his book aside. "And where did you meet them?" Upon hearing the name "Bennet," Darcy's eyes became steely and his jaw clenched. *I believe I made my feelings about that family very clear to Miss Bingley last evening and do not understand why she exposed my sister to their uncouth behavior.*

"…and Miss Katherine Bennet was so thoughtful to offer her advice on a ribbon I was considering for a bonnet. She suggested blue, as it would match my eyes and she was right, dear Brother—it was the perfect choice."

He had not seen his sister so animated since before they arrived at Rosings and visited Aunt Catherine. If these Bennet women could do this for her, maybe they were not as vile as he originally believed. *Maybe it was Aunt Catherine's letter which had put me in high dudgeon! Well... Their mother and at least one sister are quite gauche.* His thoughts were once again interrupted by her next words.

"…and Miss Elizabeth Bennet stated she believed she saw our carriage arrive as she was walking home from visiting her father's tenants yesterday morning…"

"Miss Elizabeth Bennet?" A pair of bewitching eyes flashed in his memory and a smile pricked at the edge of his lips. "Pray, tell me about these Miss Bennets." He hoped she did not recognize his eagerness.

"Brother, Miss Elizabeth is lovely. I know the servants have mentioned Miss Bennet as a great beauty—and she is uncommonly pretty—but Miss Elizabeth has a charm about her which I cannot describe." Georgiana took a deep breath and slowed her rambling speech. "It is not only her physical beauty which is so appealing, but she also draws you in with her friendliness and sincerity. I felt myself at ease in her presence. But what impressed me the most was she was so patient and did not wince at Miss Bingley's… condescension."

His thoughts were lost in the description of this maiden. "What did she say?" Darcy asked, returning to the present and concerned about the vulgarities Caroline Bingley was capable of and seemed entitled to bestow as a member of the upper class.

Georgiana shook her head. "Forgive me, Brother. I am not trying to gossip."

Darcy looked at his young sister's blue eyes and sweet countenance. How like their mother she was! "Poppet, never be afraid to tell me anything you wish. I will not judge you. Now," he said, sitting next to her on the couch, "what did Miss Bingley say?"

"In her way, she insulted the village and its people. While attempting to appear to exclude the Bennet family from her avowals, I know her protestations were not genuine. I was embarrassed."

And this is the example my sister has before her?

"But Miss Elizabeth made Miss Bingley feel the sting of her own words."

"How so?"

"I cannot replicate it. Suffice to say, Miss Bingley will not likely spar with Miss Elizabeth Bennet ever again!"

∽

"…and so if the offer still stands, Bingley, I will accompany you to the Meryton assembly tonight."

Fitzwilliam Darcy grinned as he remembered the conversation with Bingley that afternoon in the music room while Georgiana played the pianoforte. She had smiled over her music knowing he wished to avoid being in the house alone with Caroline Bingley. Georgiana had assured him she would retire early and not be bothered by the familiarities of Miss Bingley and encouraged him to join his friend.

"Darcy, that is capital!" Bingley had declared, grinning widely. "And why the change of heart, man?"

Darcy had glanced at Caroline's ashen face. "Miss Bingley has been so gracious as to stay and chaperone Georgiana that I determined I must go out into society and see for myself if I can recommend you to settle here."

He chuckled at the thought as his valet, Briggs, straightened his coat and meticulously tied his cravat.

"Is that too tight, sir?" he asked his normally controlled master.

"No, that will do, Briggs. That will be all." *I must seek out this Miss Elizabeth Bennet and thank her for the kindness she showed my sister today.*

CHAPTER 4

E lizabeth Bennet smoothed the folds of her muslin gown as she observed those about the room. The blend of music and laughter could be heard throughout the assembly hall as young and old, neighbors and acquaintances took pleasure in each other's company. Drinks flowed and young ladies waited eagerly for a partner to single them out. Unfortunately, on this particular night, partners were scarce so many remained disappointed.

"Lizzy, you look lovely tonight," said Charlotte Lucas, Lizzy's good friend and the eldest daughter of Sir William Lucas. "That color is becoming on you."

"My dear Charlotte, you must have heard Mama declare how this cream-colored frock makes my tanned skin look like a farm laborer! I am sure she would wish me to hide in the house all day and not ramble through the countryside where the sun is apt to spoil my skin. But" —she whispered, dropping her voice an octave lower and conspiratorially leaning in toward her friend— "we both know that is not the *only* fault she finds with her second oldest child."

Both girls giggled at the obvious favor which Mrs. Bennet showed to both her eldest and youngest. Looking about the room and spying both sisters, Lizzy shook her head at their differences. Both were dancing with young officers from the newly encamped militia. Yet observing Jane, it was obvious she was a polished, young woman. She was attentive to her partner's conversation, smiled, and replied when needed. While Lydia...

Lydia is pride personified. Her loud, impertinent speech and her indelicate comments are shameful. It is evident she needs no more punch!

Charlotte gently rested her hand on Lizzy's arm. "No one would think any less of you or Jane because of the actions of others." Her attempt at a smile was interrupted by the fading sound of the music as the doorway filled with four strangers.

The moment of awkward silence before the music began again conveyed so much on the faces of the unknown guests. Charlotte whispered each of their names to Lizzy. "You have already met Mrs. Hurst who is married to that shorter gentleman in the wine-colored coat."

He looks like he's been in his cups since this morning.

"...the smiling fellow is Mr. Bingley..."

A pleasant gentleman with a ready smile. No, Lydia will not do for him, but Jane...

"...and the taller, austere man with the blue coat is Mr. Darcy of Derbyshire."

...who does not look as if he desires our company. But, he is just as handsome, if not more so, than when I saw him in his carriage.

With all her prejudiced notions from the words of her family set aside, she appraised his mien. His broad shoulders fit his blue coat perfectly. His brown hair was neatly styled, but a stray curl escaped and lay decidedly on his brow. His strong jaw and noble profile were such that she had never witnessed in a man before and she felt her breathing increase.

Mr. Darcy's gaze, which had been roaming the room with indifference, alighted on her. She felt conscious of his eyes on her cream-colored gown with its gold brocade ribbon that she knew displayed her figure well and she could not help but brush one of her loose curls away from her eyes. Yet for all her discomfort, she could not look away and cursed the flush that was overtaking her cheeks.

The change in his countenance was evident as his features softened and his eyes lit up as they met hers. Her blush deepened at being caught staring at his fine person, and she turned, attempting to hide her embarrassment, as Charlotte's sister Maria came bounding up to them.

"Charlotte, have you ever seen such a fine lady?" Her rapturous delight did not go unnoticed by Mrs. Hurst whose consequence seemed heightened by the flattery. *Once again more pleased with herself than what she sees. So glad Miss Bingley is not in company this evening. But poor Miss Darcy!* Lizzy was lost in her thoughts as Mrs. Bennet hurried toward her from across the room.

"Elizabeth, make haste! Your father is to introduce you and Jane to the two fine gentlemen just arrived. Although Mr. Bingley must be destined for Lydia and Mr. Hamilton has his sights set on you, Mr. Darcy is still an eligible match for dear Jane. Be pleasant and do not ruin the chances of happiness for your sisters! Come girl, make haste. Make haste!"

Lizzy colored once again and lowered her head at the volume of her mother's speech. Surely not only did those in close proximity but also those at the door must have heard her pronouncement. She looked up to see the once friendly smile of Mr. Darcy now replaced by disgust at her mother's humiliating performance. Her shame was great but as she was familiar with such exploits at the hands of her mother, she defiantly raised her head and met Mr. Darcy's eyes.

Lizzy drew herself to her full height to show she was not intimidated by this man as her mother marched her daughters toward the party from Netherfield.

"Mr. Bingley, Mr. Darcy, you have already met my wife, and may I present my two eldest daughters, Miss Jane Bennet and Miss Elizabeth? My younger daughters you see about the room in varying degrees of entertainment."

Lizzy glanced sideways to see Mary reading her sheet music, Lydia chasing an officer, and Kitty speaking with Maria Lucas. She curtsied deeply as Mr. Bingley and Mr. Darcy both bowed.

"Mr. Bennet, what a pleasure to see you again. And the Miss Bennets. How lovely to finally meet you," Mr. Bingley said, not taking his eyes from Jane. "Our sisters told us of the pleasure they had in making your acquaintance this morning in Meryton. We quite anticipated making ourselves known to you this evening."

"Thank you, sir." Jane lowered her eyes from his gaze before looking back up through her dark lashes.

"Is Miss Bingley not in attendance this evening?"

"No." Mr. Darcy stepped forward. "She stayed at Netherfield to keep my sister company."

"Ah, yes. That is very generous of her." Lizzy curtseyed to Mrs. Hurst and her husband as they retreated to the punch bowl without a word of welcome. Not to be deterred by their lack of manners, she turned back to her party. Mr. Bingley was smiling unabashedly at Jane who did her best to disguise her own pleasure. Mr. Darcy seemed to notice it as well and cleared his throat to break Bingley from his spell. However, that was unnecessary as Mrs. Bennet likely felt that she could no longer leave her daughters to their own devices if she were to obtain a wealthy son-in-law.

"Mr. Bingley, what a lovely coat you have. It is obviously made at one of the best shops in London. We are not used to seeing such fine, young men in Meryton, and we thank you for your attentions to our girls."

Mr. Bingley stumbled over what to say at such a speech but should not have worried as Mrs. Bennet continued to fill the awkward silence. "Jane, thank Mr. Bingley for his attentions."

"Mama," Lizzy said under her breath as Jane looked away mortified.

Mr. Darcy froze and Mr. Bingley awkwardly smiled at such demands as Jane was seemingly reduced to a child. "I said, thank him for his kind attentions, dear!"

Her father enjoyed observing the follies of his wife unless it brought obvious pain to his two favorite daughters. To Lizzy's relief, he reached for her mother's arm and excused them to the other side of the room. "Let us go and thank Lady Lucas for the invitation to her party."

"I already did," cried her mother, struggling to release her arm as she walked through the crowd.

After another awkward moment, Mr. Bingley cleared his throat and asked if they enjoyed their tea the previous day with Miss Lucas.

"It was lovely, thank you." Jane breathed deeply, steadying the flutter in her voice. "We were only disappointed to have missed the opportunity to make your acquaintance."

"But now that we have all met, all is well," Bingley said, grinning.

While Jane and Mr. Bingley conversed about the local country, Lizzy caught Darcy's eye.

"Mr. Darcy?"

"Yes, Miss Elizabeth." Upon hearing her name on his lips, she found it took all her power to concentrate on her own words and not his eyes.

"I wanted to thank you, sir, for something of which you are unaware." He raised a curious brow as she continued. "Your visit to our home yesterday had a most unexpected effect on my younger sister, Kitty. She has proclaimed to alter her behavior and behave with more decorum. For that, *this* older sister is grateful." He followed her gaze toward Kitty, who was now dancing and smiling up at a young gentleman. "I am not sure if it is noticeable to someone who has only met her once, Mr. Darcy, but your conduct toward my family the other day compelled Kitty to reconsider her behavior."

"Miss Elizabeth, I apologize if I was in anyway insulting to your family. I was merely distressed by a letter I received earlier that morning upon our arrival in Hertfordshire. I should not have been in company. Please allow me to express my regrets if my actions troubled your sister in anyway."

She was amazed at his divulging such personal information. His tone was still one of refinement and dignity but there was a sense of contrition as well.

"Oh no, sir, no matter the mode of your conduct, its unintended censure produced most pleasing results. I admit any slight on my loved ones might usually be met with my general spite and prejudice but I find I quite welcome these signs of improvement." They both looked again at Kitty before Lizzy continued amiably.

"I had the pleasure of meeting Miss Darcy this morning in town. If I may say, what a delightful sister you have! Amidst her reserve and intelligence, there is an air which bespeaks gentle manners and a kind heart."

Mr. Darcy seemed pleased to hear his sister spoken of in such an affectionate way. "I must agree with your observations, Miss Elizabeth, but I may be accused of being too biased in my praise, and therefore any argument I would make in congruence with yours would be discounted." He smiled and Lizzy laughed at his ready wit while Bingley's voice carried over their conversation.

"Do you dance, Miss Bennet?" Mr. Bingley extended his hand and Jane nodded an affirmation. In the next moment, he led her out onto the dance floor.

Lizzy had looked away from Mr. Darcy, not wanting him to believe she was hoping for a partner, when Mrs. Hurst came up behind him and said, "Now Mr. Darcy, I am sure you do not intend to dance tonight for we do not want Miss de Bourgh to receive word that her betrothed is courting another."

Her insipid laugh made Mr. Darcy flinch, but Mrs. Hurst was too simple-minded and her husband too drunk to notice his glare. However, Lizzy was neither and she turned her back in embarrassment for both Mr. Darcy and herself.

Darcy gasped and when Lizzy looked up at his face, she saw his features become rigid. Lizzy followed his gaze onto the dance floor where she discovered her youngest sister dancing with a good looking, young officer she had never seen before. He was tall and had a charming countenance. Lydia's laughter could be heard above the din.

Lizzy's shame at the antics of her family were short lived, however, as the gentleman Lydia was dancing with seemingly recognized Mr. Darcy. His features registered alarm for a moment before a sly, impudent grin slipped across his face. She immediately felt cold at his expression.

Whether Mr. Darcy discerned Lizzy's concern or not, he bowed to her before excusing himself. Even with his departure, she had noticed the rapid change in his countenance and knew there was more history between these two men than one might uncover in one evening.

Lizzy smiled at Jane and Mr. Bingley on the dance floor before making her way toward an empty chair beside her sister Mary. She sat undisturbed for a quarter of an hour when she saw Mr. Darcy return to the room and look toward where they had last spoken.

She wondered at this man, whose grim visage seemed to relax when he finally saw her. His hint of a smile, however, disappeared as he stopped suddenly while making his way across the room.

"Miss Elizabeth Bennet?" came a male voice from behind her.

Peals of Lydia's laughter permeated the room. The young officer that the youngest Bennet had been dancing with had returned to partner her again, and although he seemed to be aware of her youthful zeal, he also seemed to enjoy her impropriety. James Hamilton looked at Lizzy with understanding and then to the opposite side of the room at her youngest sister.

"Miss Elizabeth," he said, breaking into her thoughts, "I hope you are not overly troubled by your sister's behavior. Remember, those of us from Hertfordshire have grown immune to her lively manners, and although some might see a lack of decorum, both Miss Bennet's and your character would never come into question."

"How very gallant of you, James Hamilton." She smiled at her childhood friend and wondered at how those same sentiments spoken twice to her in the same evening did little to suppress her shame. Lizzy shuddered as another squeal came from her sister. Turning toward the door, she witnessed Mrs. Hurst looking on with repugnance.

Oh, Lydia. I hope your behavior does not ruin the newly budding hopes of your eldest sister. Lizzy glanced over at Jane and Mr. Bingley. They were once again lost in conversation.

Mr. Hamilton excused himself to refresh his drink and procure refreshment for her. *He is charming. Charming and pleasing to look at.* Lizzy was studying his imposing height and musing how his straw colored-hair only added to his fine person as he was approached by Sir William Lucas from across the room. His easy smile and good-natured laugh at the elder man did him credit. He looked up and caught her gaze, and he grinned in a most becoming way.

She felt herself blush, embarrassed to have been caught staring at a man twice in the same evening. *There are many women of my acquaintance who would be overjoyed with the attention which Mr. Hamilton has shown me. I do enjoy his company but…*

Lizzy liked James Hamilton; she always had. However, with the possession of his aunt's estate, and his unspoken pursuit of her as the possible mistress of Ashby Park, she had realized immediately she did not love him. *As a friend, yes, but not in a deeper sense of the word.* She had grown up in a house minus love and respect, and she had vowed her world would not be like that of her parents. *But, I care for him, and a deeper affection could grow…*

"Miss Elizabeth? Are you parched?"

Lizzy looked up at the outstretched arm of Mr. Hamilton. "Pray, excuse me. My mind was wandering at the delights of the evening." After a sip of punch, she asked, "And how did you find London, sir? Was your business completed to your liking?"

"Not completed but satisfied with the progress. But, I need not worry you with business dealings or the world of figures. Tonight, your lovely mind should be engaged with the dances, beautiful gowns, and lively conversation. Indeed, might I have the next dance?" His blue eyes sparkled at her as a pleasant smile spread across his lips.

"I would be delighted. However, I suppose you know me well enough by now, Mr. Hamilton, to realize that gowns and balls only serve to enhance the purpose of entertainment," she said impertinently. "It's the follies and vices of others that bring me much diversion."

"As you say, Miss Elizabeth." He smiled at her jest in a way that should make her swoon.

It should. As he took her hand in his hand as the next set formed, she was struck by her discovery. *But it does not.*

The candles cast a warm glow throughout the assembly hall and Miss Elizabeth's light laughter wafted across the room toward Darcy. He took another drink and tried to listen to Mrs. Hurst's prattle while he studied Miss Elizabeth. He had already ignored the advances of a number of desperate mothers and their daughters. *There is one benefit to being betrothed.* With the sound of Miss Elizabeth's voice in the air, he realized there were also dangers. *Now, if only Miss Bingley had not volunteered to stay with Georgiana, I would have already safely retired for the evening with a good book.*

He had had an industrious evening avoiding scheming mothers, observing Elizabeth Bennet, and keeping an eye on the one person who had darkened his life these past five years. He made his way slowly toward Bingley to inquire when they would depart.

"Oh, la. What a disaster!" Lydia Bennet squeaked as her punch spilled from her cup and down the front of Darcy's coat.

"Do not trouble yourself, Miss Lydia. The loss of one dinner coat will not affect Darcy."

"Wickham," Darcy said through clenched teeth as he took the outstretched napkin from Mrs. Hurst and quickly began wiping at the red stain. "I see you have once again ingratiated yourself into local society." He pointedly looked at Miss Lydia who had escaped, unconcerned with the damage she had wrought.

Wickham bowed slightly. "I see you are as you ever were." His words settled in the air before continuing. "And what does Meryton owe the pleasure of Fitzwilliam Darcy's arrival? Purchasing a smaller estate closer to Rosings for the eventual union with Miss de Bourgh? Attempting to see how the lower society lives? Or—" he whispered, leaning in so only Darcy could hear him "—following me to ruin my chances of happiness as you always do?"

Darcy stiffened and met Wickham's unwavering look before slowly spitting out his words. "You do well enough on your own. You obviously need no help from me." He rose to his full height and looked down upon the man before turning on his heel and walking toward the balcony.

Unbeknownst to Mr. Darcy, Lizzy had seen Lydia's reckless behavior and had excused herself from Mr. Hamilton's attentions to apologize to Mr. Bingley's guest. She had stopped, shocked at the exchange between the young officer and Mr. Darcy, and waited a few moments after the latter had made his way onto the balcony before making the decision to follow him outside.

It was a brisk, autumn night and the moon shown full in the heavens. He was at the far end of the balcony leaning against the railing, looking out across the moonlit field and did not hear her approach.

"Pardon me, Mr. Darcy?"

He started at her voice and turned abruptly. The anger in his eyes quickly dissipated as he corrected his posture and politely bowed. "Miss Elizabeth. May I be of some assistance?" His voice was guarded and his furrowed brow seemed to be weighted with worry.

"No, it is I who hope to be of assistance to you. If not assistance, at least to remedy a wrong." He looked at her quizzically as she continued. "I sought you out to beg your forgiveness for the indignity you suffered at the impropriety of my youngest sister. Please accept my sincerest apologies."

Darcy attempted to repress his frustration. *Will I never cease to be rid of Wickham and his interference in my life?* He shook his head. "Miss Elizabeth, please do not trouble yourself. The act was unfortunate but not malicious, and as you might have heard from that man, the loss of one jacket is nothing." Though he attempted to soften his words with a smile, the last was spoken with thinly concealed venom. "Forgive me, Miss Elizabeth. It is but a small matter which has been unexpectedly resurrected, much to my distaste."

"Then I shall leave you, sir, and not trespass on your privacy."

"Not at all." He reached out to stop her, then pulled his hand back before she saw his gesture. "I would enjoy finishing our conversation so as to remove the unseemly event from my mind."

"Of course. I would be delighted." Instead of putting his troubled mind at ease, her smile forced his thoughts in another direction.

"Miss Elizabeth, if I may be allowed to thank you for your attentions to my own sister this morning. Georgiana is extremely reticent amongst strangers. I confess that is a trait she and I both possess." He paused in thought. "However, I have not seen her so animated in many months as I did this morning when she returned to Netherfield from her excursion."

"I thank you for the compliment, sir, but must admit it was by no design of mine. Your sister is a most pleasant girl."

They allowed another lull in their conversation as the notes of a reel reached them and she instinctively began to tap her toes to the music.

"And how do you like Hertfordshire, Mr. Darcy? Do you find the manners refined enough for your taste? I can only imagine our country displays are much less polished than in London."

"Miss Elizabeth, you forget that I myself am from the country. I find Hertfordshire charming as far as I have discovered, a little limited in worldly pursuits, but nothing to dismiss it as a pleasant location. I think Charles would do well to settle here."

She seemed to almost bristle at his comment but must have realized the scope of his knowledge and experience. He was not slighting her little village, only pointing out the obvious differences. Yet, he could not ignore the archness of her tone.

"And what of your home county? Is it also limited in its worldly pursuits?"

"Derbyshire?" He tried not to smile at her pique. "Of course, Derbyshire has the grandeur of the Peaks, the beauty of Dovedale, as well as incomparable hunting. But nothing gives me greater pleasure than retiring to Pemberley."

"And have you recently leased your estate?"

"Oh, no." Darcy chuckled at her allusion. "Pemberley has been in my family for generations. I inherited both the responsibility for it and everyone who resides there five years ago upon the death of my excellent father."

He did not intend to say as much but it was obvious she felt the mortification of her words, and she hastily began to apologize. "Mr. Darcy, it seems as if all the Bennets have designs to make your evening unpleasant. I shall leave you to your own thoughts before I offend you once again."

"There was no offense, Miss Elizabeth. However, I would not force your obligation to stay and talk to me if you did not wish it." *But I hope you do!* Her smile was disarming, and he felt an unexpected tightening in his chest. "If I may, might I make a suggestion? Would you find yourself willing to bring your sister Miss Katherine Bennet to Netherfield for tea in two days if my sister were to extend the invitation?" Hoping to not appear too eager, he continued. "I believe Georgiana would benefit from the company. And if you feel your sister is attempting to practice more genteel decorum, I believe both would benefit from the acquaintance."

"Sir, I believe that is a wonderful plan. When Miss Darcy extends the invitation, I am sure Kitty will be overjoyed at our machinations." Miss Elizabeth laughed, and Darcy smiled at the sound of it.

He leaned against the balustrade as they continued to speak in the chill evening air. Firelight from the torches sparkled in her eyes that expressed so much and yet so little. Darcy was impressed with the list of books which she had most recently finished, as she seemed fascinated with his propensity for Shakespeare. They were comparing each other's favorite poems when their discourse was interrupted.

"Miss Elizabeth. There you are. I have been quite concerned not knowing where you had run off."

"Mr. Hamilton, I beg your pardon. May I present mister…"

"Darcy!"

"Hamilton. How are you, old man?"

Miss Elizabeth's mouth was agape before Mr. Hamilton turned to her. "Beg pardon, Miss Elizabeth. Darcy was a few of years ahead of me when I was at Cambridge and belonged to some of the same societies on campus. He and I were in different circles socially, but academically, I was his superior. Isn't that right, Old Man?"

"Now, James, I do not know if I would go that far!" Darcy smirked at his younger friend. "We definitely shared some interesting times, though. What are you doing in Hertfordshire?"

"My estate, Ashby Park, is on the outskirts of the county. I am here checking on the tenants before I leave for London tomorrow to try and finalize my aunt's will. She's been gone almost a year and I am trying to get it in proper order to move on with my future plans."

Darcy noticed Hamilton look openly at Miss Elizabeth as she turned her head away from his watchful eyes. A sickening feeling turned in Darcy's stomach when he realized he could never have the joy of marrying someone like Miss Elizabeth. She was from a small estate, he had been witness to that himself on the visit with her father; she did not dress in the newest fashion, nor did she follow the behavior of most ladies in the ton. *What do I care of her small estate or fashion sense? Her lack of simpering discussions of lace and balls—how refreshing! I am Fitzwilliam Darcy, the master of Pemberley. I can choose my own bride.*

Anne is your bride! said a voice in his mind, which sounded uncommonly like his aunt Catherine. *Remember your duty and obligations to this family, Fitzwilliam! Above all else comes loyalty!* the voice continued.

How much easier the idea would be if he were away from Miss Elizabeth's presence. Her artless vivacity was rarely encountered in any young woman of his acquaintance. Her archness and wit made him anticipate every word from her mouth, even on this brief acquaintance.

"Tomorrow, eh? Bingley is getting a hunting party together on the 'morrow, and I am sure you would be welcome."

"Charles Bingley? I have heard of him but have never met him." He cleared his throat and looked over Miss Elizabeth's head toward the ballroom. "I might be able to delay my trip a day or two, as Sir William also extended an invitation for his gathering in two days' time. However, who else would join us? Not a certain gentleman I saw dancing with Miss Lydia Bennet...?" His eyebrows were raised in question.

"Absolutely not!" Darcy bristled at the idea and Hamilton put a hand on his shoulder to calm him.

"Sorry, old friend. I had not known for sure if you had seen him."

"He approached me. I would never have come into the country if I had known he would be here, but I also presume we will associate in much different circles. With his presence, I might alter our travel plans and leave sooner than expected."

"Well, on that revelation, I am displeased and feel I must postpone my trip if you introduce me to Mr. Bingley."

"Of course, I see him talking to Miss Bennet. Shall we go in now?" Darcy instinctively raised his arm to offer it to Miss Elizabeth. He put it down quickly before she accepted Mr. Hamilton's arm—but she had noticed his blunder. He felt his face color, but his embarrassment turned to a very different emotion as she looked up at him through her feathery lashes and smiled.

"Thank you, sir," she mouthed to him as Mr. Hamilton whisked her back into the assembly room.

Why is what we cannot have what we most desire? he asked himself, following her with his eyes.

CHAPTER 5

I t had been many years since she had been inside Netherfield, yet
she had not expected to see the house as altered as it was from
when her childhood friends, the Carltons, had lived there. *It feels like
a museum*, Lizzy mused while taking in the stately surroundings.

Although the Bingleys had only been in residence a short time,
Lizzy recognized but a few pieces of Carlton furniture, and the art
which had hung in the library, painted by Lady Carlton's mother, had
been replaced with landscapes of exotic lands. The numerous
candelabra lighting the sitting room, as well as the impeccably liveried
servants in wigs, was so unlike the Netherfield she remembered as a
child. Caroline Bingley obviously knew what she was about as
mistress of the estate and Lizzy's surprise at a person her age having
so much wealth astounded her. However, she quickly shook off her
discomfiture and politely continued her conversation with Miss
Darcy.

Lizzy and Jane had received a written invitation the morning after
the Meryton assembly from Miss Bingley asking them to dine at
Netherfield after the men returned from their day of sport. Mrs.
Bennet was in raptures and the girls were not ignorant of the honor

being shown. Great care was taken with their preparations for the evening.

In guarded amazement, Lizzy noticed Miss Bingley studying her from across the room. Lizzy had not minded though. *This is not a test for me but for my sister. I am only grateful Mr. Hamilton was included in the party so that by obligation, I would be able to accompany Jane.*

However, it was increasingly apparent that Miss Bingley did not look favorably on her sister's friendship with Charles Bingley.

"And your uncle's home is in Cheapside?" asked Miss Bingley.

Lizzy stirred from her own private musings to keep a protective watch over Jane as the men had not yet returned from their after-dinner port in the library.

"Yes, he is in trade," Jane said softly, not meeting Miss Bingley's gaze.

"That is capital," said Mrs. Hurst with a twitch at the side of her mouth. Both she and Miss Bingley rose and walked to the other end of the parlor to take a turn about the room, leaving Lizzy and Jane alone with Miss Darcy.

Miss Darcy blushed for her new friends, but this emotion was short-lived as Lizzy turned her attention to Miss Bingley.

"I understand, Miss Bingley, that we share a commonality," she said as she rose to pour herself a coffee from the sideboard.

"Delightful. And what pray tell can that be?" asked Miss Bingley with a smug expression.

Lizzy slowly took a sip and glided back to her seat holding Miss Bingley's attention. The door from the hallway opened as the men spilled into the room and she smiled sweetly. "We both have family in trade."

"Family in trade?" asked Bingley jovially as he sat down on the seat next to Jane. "Yes. Not all of us can be born into privilege, eh Darcy? Some of us have to make our fortunes." Miss Bingley gasped at her brother and Mrs. Hurst lifted her chin.

He shrugged his shoulders and turned back to Jane while Miss Darcy looked at Lizzy with hero-worship.

"Well played, Miss Elizabeth," Miss Darcy whispered behind her glass of punch. "Well played!"

Darcy was the last to enter preceded by Hamilton who made his way toward the empty seat at Miss Elizabeth's left. Hurst immediately reclined on the divan and began to nod off, and Darcy took the only other seat available—to the right of Elizabeth Bennet.

He had come to an understanding with himself while out with the men shooting. She was forbidden for so many reasons not the least being his own betrothal to his cousin Anne. Looking at his friend James fall into such easy conversation with her, Darcy was surprisingly jealous. However, he knew his feelings must be ignored and turned to Georgiana, avoiding any eye contact with Miss Bingley. He said in hushed tones, "I am pleased you invited Miss Katherine Bennet for tea tomorrow. You are becoming quite the hostess."

"Well, Brother, it is so much easier when I am comfortable with the people I am hosting. Miss Bennet, Miss Elizabeth, and Miss Katherine are all such admirable girls. True, as Miss Bingley likes to point out to me," she said, dropping her voice an octave lower, "they are not accomplished in the sense of the ladies in London. But they are all so pleasant company and I feel that they truly like me for me and not for…" She paused, glancing up to catch Miss Bingley watching her. As a practiced smile spread across Miss Bingley's face, Georgiana nodded at her and continued. "Well, not liking me for…" She paused once again and looked at Darcy apologetically.

"Your wealthy, unmarried brother." He grinned and reached over to place his hand on hers. "Do not fret, sweet, little sister. I can always tell those who genuinely enjoy your company and those who have other aims. My attentions will never be wrongly placed."

"Nor can they be, William. You are to marry Anne." She smiled sweetly at him but not before she saw his frown.

"You are right, my dear. I have forgotten myself."

"What have you forgotten, Mr. Darcy? I find it hard to believe you capable of not being meticulous about every detail of your life."

He took a deep breath before turning to face Caroline Bingley standing directly in front of him with a cup of coffee in her hand and a cloying smile.

"I thank you, Miss Bingley but I am not inclined at this moment."

"But what is it you have forgotten, Mr. Darcy. May I ring the butler?"

"No. It is only that I have heard how lovely Miss Elizabeth Bennet's voice is and was hoping my dear sister would accompany her on the piano?" He turned to Miss Elizabeth who was speaking to Hamilton. "What say you, Miss Bennet? Will you not sing for us?"

Miss Bingley colored at the loss of Darcy's attention and returned the cup to the buffet. Miss Elizabeth raised her gaze to meet his. "Mr. Darcy, I assure you, you have been given false information. My singing is hardly what you are accustomed to hearing." He began to protest, never taking his eyes from hers when she said, "However, if

Miss Darcy will do me the honor of accompanying me, my performance will sound infinitely better."

Miss Darcy looked up shyly. "I would be delighted, Miss Elizabeth. What would you would wish me to play?" Miss Elizabeth took Georgiana's arm, encouraging the shy girl. As they sat down at the pianoforte chatting, Miss Elizabeth's laughter echoed through the room.

"They make a pretty pair, eh, Darce?" asked Hamilton, leaning in confidentially. "I haven't seen your sister in several years. I think it was shortly before your father's death when he brought her to see you at school. She has grown quite lovely."

"Yes, quite right. It has been above five years." They both smiled and sipped their drinks as the object of their conversation spoke with great animation to Miss Elizabeth. "I know next summer when she comes out I will be fending off the suitors daily." Darcy swallowed before adding, "And what a stroke of luck for you to grow up with someone as spirited as Miss Elizabeth. You are a fortunate man, James."

"That I am, friend. I did not believe the possibility of her to be in my grasp. But with my aunt not having any heirs and taking me on as her own when I was thirteen, my circumstance changed. I have dreamt about her since we were children." Hamilton laughed softly. "Darcy, even you, a man with quality women thrown at you for years must recognize that Miss Elizabeth Bennet is enchanting…"

Enchanting…that is the perfect word for her.

"Not only is her personal character desirable, but her manners make everyone at ease. She is a treasure buried in this provincial town of Meryton. I am only too grateful that no wealthy gentleman has come to steal her away from me." Hamilton chuckled at his own joke and continued with a lowered voice. "She does, however, have a level of impertinence which is a degree too severe for many. I hope she might grow out of her willful streak and will bridle that aspect after we are married."

"Is she a horse you hope to break?" Darcy took a deep breath and shook his head. "She is a remarkable woman. Her manners are pleasing. Her sense of humor and wit lively. And her intelligence superior. Do not break her spirit, Hamilton. You will not find another like her." He turned to look at Miss Elizabeth sitting with his sister at the grand instrument. *Her figure is lovely, her laugh is melodious, and I could look into her eyes forever.*

"You may be right, Darcy, but with her lack of connections and dowry, I cannot expect others to forgive her indelicacies. Yet, I do recognize I am a blessed man. Rather, we have both been blessed. Are you not to marry your cousin?"

"Yes, Anne." Darcy shook his head to remove the image of Elizabeth from his mind. "It is official then? Am I to wish you joy?"

"No, not quite yet. I go to her father tomorrow to request a courtship."

"A courtship. If you have known her for so long, why waste your time with a courtship and not just marry the girl? Hamilton, if I had a woman as lovely as Miss Elizabeth, I would secure her so that no man would come lay claim. Of that, I assure you!"

"Yes, but I want to have Ashby Park completely ready for its new mistress and will need several months more. Besides my mother always said, 'Long courtship, short engagement.'"

"Your mother was a wise woman." Darcy looked up and caught Miss Elizabeth studying him. She quickly dropped her gaze and blushed as Georgiana began playing a Scottish folk song. *Very wise, indeed.*

⁓

"It was a lovely tea. Thank you once again for encouraging your sister to invite us."

Lizzy leisurely walked one of the meandering paths of Netherfield Park alongside the prominent figure of Fitzwilliam Darcy. The early autumn weather was quite fine and the group of young people decided to take full opportunity of it. Jane and Bingley, as well as Kitty and Georgiana, walked ahead of them, which left her alone to talk with Mr. Darcy. Lizzy delighted in pointing out some of the prospects she remembered from her youth with the Carlton girls, and he seemed interested in her recollections.

"I am grateful Miss Bingley allowed Georgiana to play hostess while she is in London."

"Yes, as am I." With his eyes forward, he cleared his throat and turned his attention to the foliage around them. "This tree we are coming upon is the one a ten-year old Miss Elizabeth Bennet fell out of attempting to win a dare, you say?"

"Yes, this is the one." She laughed. "I realize now it was very unladylike, but I had to prove to young Henry Carlton and James Hamilton that just because I was a girl did not mean I was incapable!"

"No one having the privilege of knowing you could find anything wanting. You seem to be a force, Miss Elizabeth. One of which the likes of many, including myself, have never seen." He tipped his hat to her and allowed a deep chuckle to roll from his throat as Lizzy knew she must be pink at his praise.

They continued on in silence for a few minutes before she attempted more conversation. "And your home? I understand from Miss Bingley your Pemberley is far superior to any in comparison."

He clasped his hands behind his back and cleared his throat. "Miss Elizabeth, if I may be so bold as to caution you against believing everything Miss Bingley offers up as fact. She often elaborates to…to…to give an air of superiority…to me…where none is needed. She means well" —he rushed on, obviously not wanting to insult a lady— "however, the life I live is much simpler than she would have it portrayed."

Lizzy sighed with mock solemnity. "Sir, I am now at a loss. I have heard such different accounts of your character as to puzzle me exceedingly. If you say I am not to believe Miss Bingley, then I confess, I know nothing about you, other than what I have observed on my own and what Mr. Bingley has implied."

"Oh-ho. What have you observed of me? I am curious about your perceptions."

She pursed her lips together in concentration and stole a glance at his fine physique beside her before beginning. "I have noticed, Mr. Darcy, that you are a very good sort of brother. It is obvious you love your sister dearly, and she returns that affection whole heartedly. You are a good friend. Mr. Bingley thinks very highly of you and seems to value your opinion above all others, seemingly even his own. You are a reserved man," she said thoughtfully. "You have very decided ideas about propriety and responsibility which could be called admirable…"

"And anything else?" He stopped to look at her. The corners of his mouth twitched as he waited for her next pronouncement.

"You have a very relaxed countenance when you are left to your own thoughts."

"Indeed! And Bingley? What have you learned from him?"

She took a deep breath and slightly raised her chin, attempting to stop the color which was threatening to creep up her neck. "It has been said that you have a good seat when riding."

He let out a rich laugh. "Interesting, Miss Elizabeth, but might I suggest—" a dimple appeared in the corner of his mouth "—in the future, take the words straight from the source? Other than testimony regarding my excellent seat, of course."

Lizzy's blush deepened as she attempted to force the vision of Bingley's contribution from her mind. Clearing her throat, she finally responded. "I do believe that is sage advice, sir. Advice which I will heed. And so, from your own lips, please enlighten me on Pemberley."

They walked along companionably as Mr. Darcy imparted much about the home he loved, its surrounding woods, and a few improvements he was implementing to increase crop production.

"I am sure you are unaware, sir, Longbourn is entailed away from the female line."

"That is most unfortunate for a family with only daughters."

"Yes," she replied with a laugh in her voice. "We are to starve in the hedgerows if you ask my mother. However, the young man who will inherit the estate is coming at the end of the next week to stay with us, and dear Mama plans on showing our home to its maximum advantage."

"I am certain that will not be an impossible task. Longbourn has some very charming attributes."

"Very pretty, Mr. Darcy. Thank you," she said taking his hand as he helped her over a fallen log. "But, I am afraid we often romanticize our own homes and are disappointed when we see them through other's eyes. As you have seen, Longbourn is not as grand as Netherfield but there are characteristics which I love with all my heart."

"Such as?" He clasped his hands behind his back and continued to walk beside her.

"In the springtime, our orchard produces the most fragrant blossoms promising delicious plums and peaches in a few, short months. Many a day little Lizzy Bennet had a stomach ache from over indulging." He laughed at the picture she presented. "It has a floorboard which creaks outside of the sitting room that when my sisters or I were younger and reading novels, we had time to hide them before Mama came in." She ran her hand through fragrant daphne, letting the scent drift on the air. "But my favorite are the grounds. I have spent hours walking the well-known paths of my home, recognizing the new buds in springtime and knowing where the first frost will hit in winter. Could another person truly love my home as I do?"

He stopped walking as they came to a meadow and he looked out over the prospect. "Miss Elizabeth," he said gently, "like myself, you too are part of where you have come from. I would say, no, the young man fortunate enough to inherit your home will never love it as you will. *That* is what makes Longbourn a home and not just an estate: the people residing inside and the dreams they have. He may not appreciate it as you but he might come to love it. Surely his children will. They will grow to see the beauty and tramp through the woods you love so dearly."

A feeling of warmth rushed through her as she realized that he understood and must feel the same for Pemberley. "I believe you must be correct, sir."

As they continued their ramble, Lizzy spied Mr. Darcy through the corner of her eye and scrutinized his fine person once again. *I like the way his eyes seem to sparkle with mischief while he maintains complete control of his mien. Such a very handsome man with his tanned skin and wavy, dark locks. That one lone curl keeps licking at his forehead.* She stifled a giggle as he pushed it under his hat brim for the third time.

"I believe you are laughing at me."

"No, sir. Not at all. I was laughing at that curl that keeps escaping." Her eyes met his and held longer than they should before she looked away. With rapid speech, she began to stammer. "That puts me in mind of a most pleasant thought. Might I wish you joy, sir?" A shadow seemed to pass across Mr. Darcy's face before he checked himself. "I heard Mrs. Hurst say you were engaged to be married to a Miss de Bourgh. Might I also ask when the event is to take place?"

His shoulders tensed and his voice seemed stilted. "Yes, thank you, Miss Elizabeth. It is to take place in three months' time."

A strange feeling swept over her at his reply. "That is wonderful news. Is she a very accomplished young lady? That must be where Miss Darcy finds her example."

"Unfortunately, Anne does not have a strong constitution, therefore, she does not play or sing." Further along the path he professed, "I believe her painting and drawing is very limited as well."

"Oh, then she must be a great reader or master of foreign languages…"

"Truthfully, no. She speaks a little French, yet even less Italian." Mr. Darcy seemed to realize too late he had confessed all the obvious deficiencies of his intended and his voice trailed off into silence.

Noticing his introspective turn, Lizzy interpolated, "Oh. But. Does speaking Italian or French truly make one woman accomplished?" She continued in her attempts to put him at ease. "In my opinion, a woman worthy is not one who plays the pianoforte or draws exceptionally well. In fact, an accomplished woman uses her intellect and natural goodness to put others at ease and, if I may be so bold, to help her husband with his responsibilities. Now, with that in mind, I am certain your Miss de Bourgh will do an admirable job." She sighed feeling regret—but for what, she was not quite sure. Yet, she was rewarded with the seldom bestowed dimpled smile upon Mr. Darcy's face as he turned to her.

"Thank you, Miss Elizabeth. It is a rare young lady who fails to take the opportunity to recommend themselves to the other sex by undervaluing another." Lost in thought, they passed over a small bridge and coming around the far end of the lake, Mr. Darcy said, "My engagement with Miss de Bourgh is of a peculiar kind. It was the express wish of my dear mother. I could never disappoint her memory."

She could not explain it, but it felt more like an apology than a conversation. "Quite commendable. A mother is a son's first love, just as a father is a daughter's. It takes a truly great man to adhere to the responsibilities which he could easily brush aside." Her voice caught a little, and once again, she knew not why. She believed in her statement, but... *I think it is unfair that Mr. Darcy is to be engaged to a woman he had no choice in marrying. What about love? Admiration? He has the means to choose. He is a man entitled to freedoms...*

Lizzy unconsciously stopped in the middle of the path, warring with her thoughts.

Darcy's brows knit together as he gazed at her. "Miss Bennet? Are you unwell?"

She began walking again and dismissed his concern with brief smile. "No, no. Pray, excuse me, Mr. Darcy. I was wool-gathering. What were you saying, sir?"

"I was speaking of James Hamilton. And should I wish you joy?"

"No, Mr. Darcy. As of now, there is nothing to declare."

He wondered if he saw resignation in her posture, an uncertain wavering which could be construed as hesitation.

"He is a good man. I was impressed with his knowledge of agriculture and estate management when we were at Cambridge together. He seemed to quickly understand concepts which many of us in the same courses had been exposed to at a much earlier age. And even then, some of his peers still had difficulty with comprehension."

"He is a good man, I agree. I believe my childhood friend has grown up quite admirably!"

Enjoying the silence for a moment longer, they continued companionably on their walk, crunching leaves underfoot until their path crossed a small stream. Looking ahead, Darcy noticed the rest of the party had already traversed the obstacle. He walked three paces until he was standing atop a slight rise by the water's edge and extended his hand to her.

"Miss Elizabeth? If I may…?"

Her teasing smile made his heart thump in his chest. "Mr. Darcy, I appreciate your gesture but have been wandering these woods since I could wake before the servants and slip out Longbourn's doors." Her light laugh flitted in the air as she stepped past him on the rocks and stopped mid-stream.

Darcy chuckled. "Then maybe it is I who should ask for assistance?" He watched her nimbly maneuver across the slick stones without soaking her boots, all the while marveling at her abilities. Darcy could not look away from the pretty picture she made, breathless from her exertion. *Though she be but little, she is fierce*. He continued to watch her, waiting until she reached the shoreline before moving himself, when a step from her destination, a small cry came from her lips.

Darcy looked up just in time to reach out and catch Miss Elizabeth as she fell toward the water.

They stood their awkwardly for a moment, her light and pleasing form pressed against his chest while he attempted to balance on two stones. He finally exhaled, and looking her directly in her eyes, he hoped those windows to his thoughts did not betray him. "Miss Elizabeth. If you would allow me to carry you to shore, I feel I will save both our clothes and pride."

She hesitated only a moment before nodding.

He quickly scooped her up, attempting to ignore her scent of lavender or her warm breath on his neck. He put her down gingerly on the bank and she brushed herself off, all the while looking around to ascertain they had not been observed.

"I can assure you, Miss Elizabeth, your reputation is safe. No one was witness to either your fall or my—"

"Heroic act," she finished, casting her eyes downward before raising them to meet his. "It appears that I am not as capable as I believed," she said with a hint of mischief in her voice.

"We all slip on occasion. Not just on stones." He nodded kindly and held out his arm for her to take, certain he imagined the gentle squeeze from her fingers.

After a silence had elapsed and they were back in sight of their companions, Miss Elizabeth looked up at him and asked, "Mr. Darcy, please do not find me impertinent, but my youngest sister has found a great favorite in one of the officers. A Mr. Wickham?" He tensed at the name. "If I may be so bold to comment, I noticed you had a rather curious exchange with him at the assembly. Might you offer any intelligence as to the character of the man?"

His fists clenched at the very thought of his former friend and he could feel his blood boil. He walked onward for quite some time before appearing to gain his composure.

"If I might ask a question first, Miss Elizabeth? Has Mr. Wickham indicated to your sister that his interest is of some longevity?"

Miss Elizabeth lowered her chin and studied the stones on the path. "Sir, I presume you can imagine that my sister has a tendency to allow her own whims to color the world around her. She is but fifteen years old. She, therefore, is under the impression Mr. Wickham is planning on asking for her hand. My elder sister and I have made no such observation in the brief encounters we have had with him yesterday and earlier this morning."

Darcy sighed. *Will I never be rid of him?* "George Wickham was the son of my late father's steward. His father, the elder Mr. Wickham, was a man of good character— honest and forthright in all his business dealings. Upon his death, my own excellent father felt he owed a debt of gratitude to the memory of Wickham's father's service to our family and took the younger Wickham under his guidance."

"So, you grew up together?"

"Yes, practically like brothers." He leaned down to pick up a stone and toss it in the creek running by the path. "We were best friends." His eyes became distant and seemed lost in reverie. "We were inseparable until Father sent us to Cambridge. It was there I learned the true character of the man."

Miss Elizabeth waited for him to continue but he did not. "And might I ask what you discovered?"

He shook his head, picked up another stone and tossed it further than the last. "Miss Elizabeth, suffice to say, I would advise you to keep your sister far from my former playmate. He is not to be trusted in the company of young ladies. Too many have found ruination at the hands of George Wickham."

CHAPTER 6

S ir William, what a lovely party. I am so pleased to have been invited."

Charles Bingley looked from Sir William and Lady Lucas with his characteristic smile, while glancing over their shoulders at Miss Jane Bennet. Her blonde curls cascaded from a braided crown atop her head and her blue eyes danced at the conversation with her sister Elizabeth and Miss Charlotte Lucas.

"You have captured the perfection of a country gathering amidst your walls as no other."

"Yes, yes. Capital, capital," burbled the older man with more self-satisfaction than thanks. "At Lucas Lodge, we are delighted to present to you all good breeding and manners." He held out his arm and indicated the full expanse of the room. "Before you, sir, the finest families of our county."

"It is obvious, sir."

"Quite so, quite so."

"Pray excuse me. I believe I see Miss Bennet." With that, Bingley bowed to his hosts and made his way across the room.

"Superior society," snickered Caroline to her sister. "If he believes this is superior society, he has not seen the outside of his own home!"

"Caroline, hush, someone will hear you," Luisa Hurst said with a choked laugh.

"And if they do, I cannot imagine they would understand a word I said with their lack of education and refinement."

Both women clucked at the lack of culture surrounding them when a deep voice intruded upon their private joke. "I assure you, ladies, that not all of us have as little education as you believe. And if we did, the manner with which your message was conveyed would be enough to shine an understanding upon how you feel about the company."

Startled, both women looked up to find Mr. Hamilton and Mr. Darcy. Caroline sputtered an apology while Luisa covered her mouth with her hand.

"Mr. Hamilton. I am sure you misunderstood my meaning."

"No, madam, I think Mr. Darcy and I understood you perfectly." He nodded his head and both turned to stride across the room to take some refreshments.

"Oh, Luisa. What if that ruins my chances with Mr. Darcy?"

"Dear Caroline. I do not think your chances with him were ever very good. How can you forget he is to marry Miss de Bourgh? Do set your sights elsewhere." With no little guile, her older sister said, "If you want this, your third season, to be your last, you must put Mr. Darcy out of mind." Luisa seated herself on a nearby couch, frustrated with her sister but indifferent to mixing with Meryton's finest.

"Oh," Caroline whispered to herself. "I have always known I would never be the mistress of Pemberley. But I do not aspire to that

position. I only wish to be the mistress of one person in particular."
At that moment, Mr. Darcy glanced in her direction. She smiled at him
through lowered lashes, while he frowned and stiffly nodded as he had
done several minutes before. *This will work out the way I want it to in
the end.*

⁓

The clock struck eleven, as Mrs. Annesley said goodnight to her
young charges and retired for the night with a headache. Miss Darcy
was playing the last few bars of a sonata while Kitty Bennet lounged
in a chair nearby.

"I am so delighted you invited me to stay with you this evening to
keep you company. It has been so enjoyable pretending to be the grand
lady of an estate." Kitty stifled a giggle, attempting to be as well-
mannered as Miss Darcy and not reminiscent of Lydia.

"Someday, I am sure that will happen, Miss Katherine."

"No, Miss Darcy. I am not destined to greatness as you. I will
likely marry a parson or a barrister, which will suit me quite nicely."

"Oh, and what about a young, dashing officer?" Miss Darcy asked
with her eyes twinkling.

"No, I think my days of chasing regimentals is behind me. I do not
know if there is enough merit in all of England to make one good sort
of man in a red coat." Both girls giggled at the thought of their future
lives.

"And what is it that makes the little song birds twitter?" asked a
deep voice from the doorway. "I do hope, Miss Kitty, that your

thoughts on officers does not include all gentlemen serving in His Majesty's service."

Stunned, the girls turned to find George Wickham standing at the door. His arrogant grin made Kitty squirm.

"Mr. Wickham. What are you doing here? How did you get in without the butler's notice?"

Silence filled the room for but a moment. "Mr. Wickham? Georgiana, I have known you since your cradle, can you not call me George?"

"Why yes. George," she said, glancing at Kitty who was still attempting to collect herself. "You have come upon us unannounced and I am afraid we are preparing to retire for the evening. I shall ring for Fellows to see you out."

"Oh, what is the hurry?" He bowed solicitously to Kitty. "Miss Bennet. How do you do?"

"Very well, thank you, Mr. Wickham."

His eyes then swept around the room before resting back upon Miss Darcy. "Georgie, you sound so grown up. Not the child who followed Fitzwilliam and I through the woods of Pemberley on her little pony. You are a fine young lady now."

"That is true, sir. But what brings you to Netherfield and so late in the evening?" The tension in Miss Darcy's voice further added alarm in Kitty.

Mr. Wickham crossed over to the piano bench where she was sitting and sat down next to her. "Won't you play for me, Georgie? It would feel almost like we were back home at Pemberley before your father died." There was a catch in his voice and he looked away not meeting her eyes.

Miss Darcy visibly relaxed, reached over and tenderly took his hand in hers. "Of course, George. Forgive me. Would you like to hear Bach? I remember he was your favorite."

He smiled at her as she began to play Concerto Number 1 in D Minor.

Kitty knew not how to behave. Though Georgiana may not have noticed something in Mr. Wickham's eyes, as she played the piano, Kitty had. Stable boys looked at Lydia in much the same manner and her skin began to crawl.

At the end of the piece, both Kitty and Mr. Wickham clapped. Seizing the opportunity, Kitty stood. "Mr. Wickham, it has been a lovely surprise having you here this evening, but as Miss Darcy and I were about to retire, we must bid you goodnight. I shall ring for Fellows now."

"That won't be necessary, Miss Katherine." Wickham looked perturbed as he met her eyes, then glanced back at Georgiana. "I would love to seek a private audience with Georgiana if you feel the need to go to your room." She gasped as he looked hopefully at Miss Darcy.

"Oh, George, I do not think that would be proper," the young girl stammered becoming nervous. "Miss Katherine and I were…"

"Georgie, there is nothing improper about an older brother wanting to spend time with his sister who he hasn't seen in years. I only wanted to speak about your father and mother and the wonderful times at Pemberley. Miss Katherine has no connection to our memories and would therefore not be missing out on any of the conversation. You must know how I miss them both."

The look in her eyes softened, and she reached for his hand. "I miss Father as well. I loved the stories you would tell me about Mama. I would so enjoy hearing them again." Her eyes lowered. "Fitzwilliam so rarely speaks of them anymore. I believe he thinks me too young to manage my emotions…"

"He cannot recognize that you are a young lady, Georgiana, and not a child." He lowered his voice and whispered, "In more ways than one."

Miss Darcy gasped and raised her gaze as he bent over her hand and tenderly kissed it before speaking again.

"Unfortunately, I believe Miss Katherine may be correct. It is entirely too late to begin our conversation. However, would you promise me that we can meet again? I forgot how enchanting you are." His fetching smile was not entirely lost on the innocent girl, who blushed pink at the compliment.

Kitty had sat back and began to sew, feigning privacy. She had seen both Jane and Lizzy do the same many times in similar situations.

"Now, my dear. Let us not worry your brother about our meeting. He does not deem you old enough and would not understand our need to meet and think of the past as its remembrance gives us pleasure."

"Oh, I could never keep this from William. I think he would be so happy to know you were here. It has been such a long time." After a moment, Kitty peered back up at the two, catching Miss Darcy's eye and she cast a questioning look at Mr. Wickham. Cocking her head, Miss Darcy turned back to him. "George, I just realized you never stated your reason for arriving here so late. Unannounced."

An adoring countenance crossed his face. "I have joined the regiment and understood you to be in the neighborhood. I dropped everything to come, even at this late hour. I do not believe the rules of propriety dictate a family's affection, Georgie."

"No, no, I agree. But William will be so disappointed to have missed you. Are you sure I am to not tell him you are here?"

"He knows I am here, dear girl. It is I who only found out you were in town. No," he said, shaking his head. "Let's not bother him with the details of our meeting. I do not wish him to restrict my seeing you in his misguided attempt to spare your heart in remembering your parents. He will not object to me once we divulge our reunion in two weeks' time."

"Whatever do you mean? Two weeks' time?"

"Well, in that period, I doubt you will alter your affections or actions toward me. You can then give him proof you are old enough and mature enough to manage what he feels is too difficult for you."

"I wonder why he did not tell me you were here?"

"It must have slipped his mind."

"Yes, most likely." Miss Darcy quietly mulled the idea. "I do not like to deceive him, George. William is the best of brothers and takes prodigious care of me."

"Of course, he does, poppet. *But,* imagine how proud he will be of you when he realizes you were able to act in such a mature fashion with no guidance from him? He will be overjoyed!"

Miss Darcy looked over to Kitty who was cautiously watching the entire exchange. "Very well, George. I agree. I so want William to see me as a young lady and not as a child. This seems like a fine scheme. And with your guidance, I cannot go astray." She smiled happily at Kitty. "Now, Miss Katherine, you must promise to not divulge our secret. It will make me most unhappy if William finds out and the surprise is ruined."

"Of course, Miss Darcy. I would never go against your wishes." Kitty felt anxious and lowered her eyes as Mr. Wickham smiled and deeply bowed.

"Well, ladies. I will see myself out. Startling the butler would only lead to our secret being discovered and we don't want that now, do we?"

"No," said the girls in unison with variant degrees of pleasure.

Miss Darcy added, "Take care, George, that no highwaymen attack you."

"Georgiana, your concern does you credit." He bowed once again over her hand, allowing his kiss to linger a little longer than Kitty thought appropriate for a brother.

"And we are to make him welcome? This man who will one day remove us from our own home?" The sound of Mrs. Bennet's shrill voice echoed through the halls of Longbourn. "And he is to impose upon us for two weeks. Two weeks! What are we to do with this odious man?"

"Mama, perhaps he will not be as distasteful as you fear. Possibly his manners and breeding will surprise us." Mary leaned back in her chair and gave a placating smile. "It is our responsibility to offer Christian charity whether he will displace us from our home or not."

"Oh, who asked you girl? You have no compassion for my nerves!" Mrs. Bennet slumped down in the chair and appeared far beyond her forty-three years. The streaks of grey peeking through at her crown were not as evident as the small creases deepening at her eyes. Although past her prime, the beauty which had secured a country gentleman was still obvious, the most remarkable features appearing twenty years younger in her eldest daughter.

"Now Jane, we must make sure that you are not too friendly to this Mr. Collins. I do not want him imagining he can come in here and ruin the possibility of Mr. Bingley."

"Mama, what would give you that idea?"

Mrs. Bennet sniffed at Lizzy's question and curled her lip. "In your father's letter, he stated that with five lovely daughters and his impending guilt about the entail, he wished to do us a service."

"Mama that could mean anything. He might wish to attempt to establish dowries for us or offer us shelter if the worst should befall us before we are married."

"You believe that, Jane," said Mrs. Bennet wringing her hands, "but I know a thing or two about men, and once he sees you, he will have his mind set." Turning to Lizzy, she said, "There is no need for you to worry. Or you Mary. He would never be taken with someone as plain as you. I still wonder at Mr. Hamilton's attentions, but at least I will not have to worry about my eldest two. That will be a comfort."

Jane squeezed Lizzy's hand as Mrs. Bennet stood and straightened her dress. "No, I think Kitty will do."

"Me?" Kitty sputtered her hands freezing in the middle of a stitch. "Why me? We do not even know what this Mr. Collins is like! Although I am sure he is an amiable man, and a parson is an excellent profession, I am uncertain if I am ready to become a wife."

"And yet it does not matter," her mother retorted, sauntering to the doorway. "You will be the one who will save your mama from destitution and allow me to keep being the mistress of Longbourn until I die. I would rather it be Lydia," she said glancing at her youngest daughter affectionately, "but, she is not meant to be a parson's wife. She has too much of an adventurous spirit." Mrs. Bennet then exited the room calling for Hill.

"How am *I* to be forced into a marriage I do not aspire to; with a man I do not love?" Kitty cried frantically, looking from Jane to Lizzy. "How is this to be endured?" Her bravado left her as she slumped into the chair and buried her face in her hands, wracked with quiet sobs.

Lizzy looked at Jane and shook her head. "Kitty, darling, I understand your concern, but I think this is a rather premature. We are unaware of what the gentleman wants."

"Besides, Papa will not force you to marry anyone."

Tears were rolling down Kitty's face as she attempted to speak. "But Papa will not intervene if he is buried in a book in his study. Mama will have me on the continent on my wedding tour before our father even calls for his coffee, if she has her way."

"Well done, Kitty," Lizzy said, appreciating her sister's wit even during the unbearable situation. "Do not fear. Neither Jane nor I will allow our cousin to make off with you to the continent."

Kitty's hiccupping sobs had almost ceased as Lizzy reached over to wipe the tears from her eyes. "And if Papa does not leave his study to lend his support against Mama?"

"Then, dear Sister," Lizzy said, wrapping her arms around both Kitty and Jane, "we will convince Hill to allow us to hide in the cellar and eat strawberry jam and scones as we did when we were children."

"Yes!" Jane said, getting in the spirit of the moment. "And we will make ourselves sick and have to be taken to our beds for several days."

"By then," Kitty added, "maybe Mr. Collins will have tired of our absence and will seek his future bride elsewhere."

The girls giggled before resting back carelessly against the chair.

"Be not a witness against thy neighbor without cause and deceive not with thy lips," Mary quoted, raising her chin and exiting the room, leaving the sisters behind her.

"Oh, Mary." Lizzy sighed, resting her head against the back of the chair.

"No, she is right," said Jane. "We are not being fair to Mr. Collins. He may end up being everything a young man ought to be."

"Very true," Kitty said hesitantly. "But, I still am not ready to marry at seventeen."

"Do not worry, Sister. Mr. Collins will work himself out."

CHAPTER 7

L izzy looked out of the Bennet carriage and said a silent prayer that she and Sarah would make it to Ashby Park before the rain increased. Her day began with a quiet walk around Longbourn's gardens to watch the sun rise. Upon entering the house, Mrs. Bennet had also risen early to begin preparations for the arrival of Mr. Collins later that day.

"Lizzy, you are to dress at once. Mrs. Wallings requests your immediate assistance at Ashby Park."

"Mama, why would Mr. Hamilton's housekeeper send for me?"

"Her note said that Mr. Hamilton requested your opinion on fabrics in the parlor. This is a great honor to you, although you have done little to deserve it."

"It is an honor, Mama, but one which might be seen in the wrong light by our neighbors. No courtship has been announced. For me to be alone at Mr. Hamilton's house? I do not want to look at if I am forcing his suit. I cannot allow gossip. You must see that!"

"No, I do not see that!" The lines around Mrs. Bennet's eyes stretched as her frustration increased. "Girl, stop questioning and go allow Sarah to dress you this instant."

"Mama, I cannot go unaccompanied and my sisters all await the arrival of our cousin."

"Sarah will go with you then. I think we might do without her until this evening. It is only ten miles to Mr. Hamilton's estate and you should be back for supper. It is not quite nine o'clock yet. Hill shall prepare a basket for the carriage." With her orders set, she walked out of the room.

...And that is how my mother believes I will get a husband? I might as well put Lydia in charge of my courtship. Lizzy shook her head. *It is not a courtship. When he came yesterday to take his leave, he did not ask Father for a courtship. Although, I cannot say I am sorry—I am not sure I want one yet.*

Lizzy looked up to see the eyes of her traveling companion peering out the window. "Sarah, would you like another tart? You know Cook's are the best in all of Hertfordshire."

The young maid accepted the tart readily. "Thank you, Miss Elizabeth."

Lizzy's eyes roamed the countryside. It had been a rapid departure with her mother shouting for her to make haste before "...this opportunity slips through your fingers..." *And with Kitty chasing after the carriage because I forgot my reticule, too. Such an odd event.* She pushed the reticule and the troublesome thoughts of this excursion aside.

"This storm did sneak up on us, did it not? I am certain Mama would not have encouraged us to come if she had known it would be so severe today." *Well, she very well might have if she believed Mr.*

Hamilton to be in residence! She shook her head at her mother's machinations and sighed, grateful a good man such as James Hamilton resided in Hertfordshire—and did not see her mother, lack of dowry, or low connections as an impediment! *I only wish I was in love with him.*

"When do you believe we will arrive at Ashby Park, miss?"

"In about another quarter hour, Sarah. I am not expecting us to stay longer than an hour, and we will be on our way back home." *If the weather permits.*

✦

The china rattled as the table trembled with Lady Catherine's anger. "You are a charlatan. Leave my presence at once," she shrieked, hurling her cup across the room. She sat in the small sitting room of her London townhouse listening to the prognosis by the third physician she had seen in as many weeks.

"But, Your Ladyship. Miss de Bourgh is well. Her only malady is a weak constitution. With an equal amount of rest and light exercise and fresh air, she will live a long and happy life."

"Thurston," she said, ignoring the doctor and calling to her butler. "Remove this man from my home and bar his admittance again. He is slandering my daughter!"

"But, Lady Catherine," the confused man cried as he was forced from the room, "your daughter is hale. She must be allowed to—"

Thurston shut the door behind him as a smirk directed at his mistress quickly flashed across his countenance before returning to the room to await his next orders.

"Contact the papers and besmirch that man's name. I want him to understand that one does not disagree with the widow of Sir Lewis de Bourgh on the care of her daughter. Is that understood?"

"Yes, m'lady."

"Now, Thurston, remind Cook we must begin planning for the wedding breakfast. I want menus prepared with Darcy's favorites— lamb, fish, meat pies. *Everything* she has ever cooked that he has enjoyed."

"Yes, m'lady," he said as he retreated to the safety below stairs.

"I do hope they will not bring that upstart Caroline Bingley to the wedding. Her brother may be friends with Darcy but they are from trade. And she is hanging out for my nephew. Whilst he is engaged to my daughter!" she muttered to herself.

There was a rustle from the other side of the room, and Lady Catherine turned sharply to investigate the source of the noise.

"Anne? Anne! Girl. do not hide in the shadows. What are you doing there?"

"Mama, I have been sitting here for nigh on an hour. Do you not recall our conversation before the doctor arrived?" Her voice was quiet but firm, alluding to the strength of the young heiress. "I have been occupying my time reading while you finished your discussion with him. I must say, I believe the doctor made a good argument. I feel better now than I have in many months. Quite possibly, this illness has departed and I am healed. If that is the case—"

"Anne—" her mother slammed her wooden cane on the floor "—you cannot know what the doctor was saying. I am your mother. I know what is best for you. He was a charlatan and you are ill!"

"If that is the case," Anne continued, "maybe we should postpone the wedding. I believe Darcy is concerned about his estate. Let us allow him some time to prepare Pemberley for a mistress and not marry in such haste." The words died from her lips when she saw her mother's face.

"Such haste? Such haste? Anne, you are five and twenty!" The folds of skin across Lady Catherine's forehead and the corners of her eyes were full of menace as the vein in her temple pulsed. "Postpone the wedding? What nonsense! This marriage has been planned since your infancy. It is long expected by all of society, and it was the express wish of both your mothers. You will not disappoint me, girl." She rapped her cane again and glowered at her only child.

Anne raised her chin and took a fortifying breath. "But, mother, I do not love Fitzwilliam as a wife should love her husband. I never have nor will I ever."

"*Love?* Who said anything about *love*? Your life is not a novel. Darcy will do his duty. We do not marry for love. With this marriage, you will combine both our great families." She scoffed at the idea. "Love. Do you think I loved your father? You will marry Darcy and unify our estates, making us one of the most powerful families in the realm." She sniffed, standing to go upstairs and dress for the remainder of the day. "Love. You had better get that notion out of your head. Darcy will come again in a month's time to begin preparations for the wedding. I want no further mention of postponement, do you understand? We now have only a little over two months before the event, and I will not have it ruined by such drivel!"

Lady Catherine did not wait for a response, instead propelling her body out the door and up the stairs before her daughter could respond.

Anne's gaze wandered out the window to a small patch of blue sky. "Then I will be trapped in a loveless marriage to a man, who although I respect, I do not cherish. And he, who I do cherish, will never know." She sat there in quiet contemplation before Thurston announced Colonel Fitzwilliam.

"Richard." Anne beamed. "What brings you here, my dear cousin?" She extended her hands to him, and he walked forward and took them in his own, leaning forward to kiss her cheek.

"Hello, my sweet. I was given two weeks leave and decided to see my favorite cousin." The twinkle in his eye made her blush.

"You had better not repeat that in front of Georgiana. She will be devastated." They both chuckled and sat together on the sofa.

Colonel Richard Fitzwilliam was a second son, and though born into wealth and privilege, knew any happiness and advancements in life would be of his own doing. He had earned his rank, after his father purchased his lieutenant commission for him. Yet, he would still need to marry an heiress.

If only Richard would see how our temperaments suit, we would be the happiest of couples.

"Anne, how are you feeling? My mother said you were to have seen the doctor today. Yet look well."

"It depends on who you ask." At his questioning gaze, she continued. "Mother seems to believe the doctors do not properly diagnose me. This is the third one in the last month who has claimed

I am healthy and only need fresh air and exercise. But she is determined I am ill!" Anne shrugged her shoulders. "She does not believe I can become well, and therefore I cannot."

"That is most perplexing." He eased back in his seat before turning his steady mien on her. "She is most likely anxious because of your upcoming wedding to Darcy."

"Yes, possibly so. I told her this very morning that we should postpone the wedding if I am not in good health, but she objected." Had Anne not returned her attention out the window, she would have seen him start.

"And why is that, dear cousin? Do you not wish to marry Darcy?"

A catch in his tone made her heart skip a beat, as she looked at him with lowered lashes. He looked as if he wished to speak more when Thurston walked in the room.

"Lady Catherine wishes for you to join her in the Gold Room."

Business had kept Fitzwilliam Darcy in London an extra day but he had not expected the weather to further delay his travel back to Netherfield and he sent his carriage ahead, choosing to ride his newest mount, Ulysses.

"You with a wandering spirit," he said, stroking the stallion's mane, "do not go astray for twenty years."

He wanted to stretch his legs and escape the thought of the enchanting Miss Elizabeth Bennet. The best way should have been by visiting his betrothed, Anne, and his aunt Catherine—the aforementioned business. With that unpleasantness behind him, he had planned to leave early in the morning, but business with his attorney had delayed him until the afternoon, placing him in the path of a most violent rainstorm. "She had been in a rare mood, even for her," he said to Ulysses, "demanding I post the announcement in the paper and immediately prepare to remove myself from Netherfield to Darcy House. Lady Catherine forgets I am my own master and will not be led around through the nose."

And I might have done her bidding had Anne not seemed resistant to marry. He dropped his shoulder to allow the water which had pooled in a small pocket of his coat to run off. *I am sure I have ridden nearly two hours, but who can tell in this driving rain.* He lowered his head, knowing he would be chilled to the bone when he arrived at Netherfield.

I must be but a few miles from Ashby Park. Even if Hamilton is still in London, surely his servants will not turn me away.

"Mrs. Wallings, I am sure Mr. Hamilton will approve of either the wine-colored or the blue curtains. Both complement the new sofa and chairs nicely. The richness of the wood is shown to its greater advantage by both." Lizzy smiled hopefully, uncertain how the housekeeper's opinion of her, being there in the home of an unmarried man, could be any worse. "Mr. Hamilton should decide. It is his house."

"Yes, miss, but he insisted you come and make the final selection, so I must abide by my master's instructions."

Lizzy looked at this woman who had served Mr. Hamilton's aunt for years. She took a breath and picked up the swatch of fabric before holding it up to the wood work on the wall.

"If he insists, then let's go with the wine-colored. The fabric is of a much stronger material and therefore will last longer and not fade. That will be economical in the long run for him as well.

"Exactly right, miss," said Mrs. Wallings. "Tea will be served in the parlor if that is to your liking?"

"Oh, Mrs. Wallings, you do not need to trouble yourself. I would much prefer a basket with Cook's delightful tea cakes for the carriage." Lizzy looked up as the clock struck two. "It is much later than anticipated, and I must be home to welcome my cousin."

The housekeeper shook her head and pointed out the window to the rain still pelting the glass. "Miss Bennet, I think that unlikely. Mr. Hamilton instructed me to take prodigious care of you, and as the rain has not let up these four hours—nay, it has only increased, and I am afraid the roads will be treacherous. The master could never forgive me if you were to come to any harm."

"But…"

"Miss Elizabeth, you are most welcome here. Mr. Hamilton would insist. I've already shown Sarah to the servants' quarters, your room's fire is already lit, and your bag is unpacked—"

"My bag is unpacked? What bag?"

"Why the bag your man brought in shortly after you arrived. He said your mother sent it in case the weather turned and you were stuck here for a few days. Very clever of your mother, I say."

Mother!

"…you will find the accommodations much to your liking…"

"Of that, Mrs. Wallings, I can be sure. It is only that I am…I am…surprised at the foresight of my mother and hope it does not paint me in a peculiar light…"

"Miss Elizabeth, your mother has lived in this county for many years. And your character is above reproach." She grasped the keys swinging from her hip as she ascended the stairs. "I will show you to your room."

Lizzy followed her into what she understood to be the family wing. It was a beautiful house—not overly grand but she discerned the owner paid attention to all the finest money could afford him. And yet, there seemed a lack of *home* in the stiff, elegant furniture. There was of the pretense of formality, and she felt slightly ill at ease in the family wing.

Mrs. Wallings continued down the hall to one of the last remaining rooms. She opened the large mahogany door to reveal a lovely, feminine apartment. The walls were papered with a rose pattern, and a cream silk was draped atop the four-post bed. Fresh lavender permeated the air, while an impressive window, revealing a terrace over the back gardens and whose stormy view stretched to the surrounding woods.

"This will be your room, Miss Bennet. I am sure you will find everything to your liking. This is the last of the summer's lavender. The master instructed me to make sure it was in your room, as it's one of your favorites." The housekeeper walked into the room and across to the window, before turning to find Lizzy had not followed. "Miss Bennet, is something wrong?"

"Mrs. Wallings, I fear there has been some mistake. It appears you have brought me to the mistress's chambers, and as I am not the mistress, nor is there an understanding between Mr. Hamilton and myself, I feel most presumptuous. Please do not take offense but is there not another room in the guest wing?"

⌇

Twenty minutes later, as Miss Elizabeth was soaking in the hot bath, she was unaware of the conversation down in the kitchen between Mrs. Wallings and Mrs. Hines, the cook. "Eloise, I worked in this house forty years as a scullery maid, a lady's maid, and now the housekeeper, and I can say in all those years, I have never met a young woman less affected by the possibility of wealth. Mr. Hamilton has found himself a real treasure. What a genteel, well-bred young girl."

"You can say that after knowing who her mother is?"

"Yes, El, I can. She's a good and proper one, that Miss Elizabeth Bennet. I just hope the master is able to get his affairs in order before it is too late and another comes to take his place."

⌇

"Miss Bennet, dinner will be postponed for a quarter of an hour. There has been an unexpected guest due to the weather."

"Very well, Mrs. Wallings. But as I previously stated, a tray in my room would do just fine. I do not wish the household to go through all the trouble…"

"Yes, Miss Bennet, but Mr. Hamilton would insist you partake of Cook's talents. However, if you would prefer a tray, I can inform our new guest you wish to dine alone."

"No, I would not want to do that. I do hope all is well, and they did not come upon harm in this storm," she said upon reaching the last step of the majestic staircase.

"Might you prefer to wait in the music room, miss?"

"Thank you, I would. I understand Mr. Hamilton recently has a new instrument."

"Yes, a very fine Broadwood Grand. Please make yourself comfortable."

Lizzy walked into the music room. The blue and gold brocade chairs lined the walls. There was a very fine harp and two small couches in one corner but the centerpiece of the room was the new piano. *What a beautiful instrument.* She ran her hand along the rich wood. *I know he bought this for me, I heard him tell Mama as much before he left for London.*

She sat on the bench and began to finger the ivory keys. She leaned her head back and began to sing an old Irish folk song as her fingers rhythmically moved across the keys to the tune she knew by heart.

"The pale moon was rising above the green mountain,
The sun was declining beneath the blue sea;
When I strayed with my love to the pure crystal fountain,
That stands in the beautiful Vale of Tralee.
She was lovely and fair as the rose of the summer,
Yet 'twas not her beauty alone that won me;
Oh no, 'twas the truth in her eyes ever dawning,

That made me love her, the Rose of Tralee…"

Lizzy's clear voice echoed throughout the empty room, as she tenderly crooned the plight of the two young lovers. As she sang the last lines, a reverential hush hung over the room.

"Would that I too could find such a love." She sighed wistfully and rested her elbow on the instrument, grateful she was alone. "James is a good man, but can I be happy with him?"

She plunked a few notes upon the keys then continued her soliloquy. "I once believed only the deepest love would induce me into matrimony. Will I ever know? And if I do, will it be too late?"

She walked to the window and rested her palm on the glass against the cold outside. "I hope not," she said to the moon as the clouds sailed past, "for above all else, I long to be loved."

CHAPTER 8

F itzwilliam Darcy had not intended to intrude upon Elizabeth Bennet's private thoughts. He had been called by her siren's song, intoxicated by the sound of her voice. The maid had informed him that earlier in the day, the rain had stranded another visitor at Ashby Park, and the staff would hold dinner for Darcy while he made himself presentable. Now, he gazed into the music room at the one person he had thought best to avoid at all costs. To hear her angelic rendition of the song his mother had sung to him made his heart ache. He yearned for her but she could never be his. She was promised to someone else, as was he. Yet he had heard her confession—her lack of love for James Hamilton and her desire for a love of her own. *We suffer the same lot…but what is that to me? It can mean nothing! Because in less than three months, I will wed Anne. My own lack of love…*

And yet, there he stood, transfixed in a doorway, with the rain beating down on the panes, dreaming of a world with this woman, hoping he would not be discovered as she gazed into the night.

Oh, that I were free to love her. But she is now being courted by Hamilton. Not that he deserves her. He would tame her spirit like a horse! His frustration and guilt were great.

After a moment, he quietly removed himself from the doorway. He followed a footman toward the library; his thoughts were full of her. *She knows not how our conversation while walking at Netherfield affected me. Her observations confirmed that not only will I never be in love with Anne, but just how ill-equipped my cousin is to make a proper mistress of Pemberley.*

He ran his hand through his hair and slumped into the couch, staring at the ceiling. *How will this union allow Georgiana to advance in society? True, Anne will inherit Rosings Park when she marries, but what then? Soon Georgiana will need a proper lady to bring her out into society. And Anne will not do. She has not even been presented herself! And what of entertaining? She is more reserved than I. If only—*

He could not travel down that path and knew the danger of such musings. He tried not to think of what his world would become in a little over two months nor what it might have been. He leaned back and had only closed his eyes when he heard the door open and the soft step of a woman enter the room followed by the scent of lavender. In an instant, he knew his intruder. He inhaled deeply and opened his eyes to see her standing before him.

"Why Mr. Darcy, I have only learned you were the unfortunate traveler also marooned at Ashby Park. How do you do?"

"Miss Bennet," he said, quickly standing to bow. "I, too, was unaware of your presence until a moment ago. I would beg you forgive my appearance. I had thought to ride from London to Netherfield and was not anticipating dinner at Ashby."

"Think nothing of it." She smiled with a twinkle in her brown eyes. "I *should* feel guilty here in all this grandeur on my own little holiday away from home while my family welcomes the unknown cousin and heir to Longbourn. But I cannot."

Darcy offered her his arm as they followed a footman to the dining room.

"It is my duty you know, as the second daughter to help pave the way for family unity. Instead, I am two hours away on an accidental respite. At least—" she smiled, releasing his arm and taking a seat at her place at the table "—I am in the company of a friend and can expect a pleasant evening of conversation."

"I will endeavor to do my best, Miss Bennet." He sat down across from her. "And might I hope to hear you play this evening? I am sure nothing would bring me more pleasure." Noticing her hesitation, he said, "However, if you feel our situation alone might lead to speculation, I will gladly remain in my room all evening." He took a sip of his drink and silently prayed she *did not* feel that way.

Miss Elizabeth smiled as he signaled to the footman to begin serving. "Mr. Darcy, I see no call for that. My maid has accompanied me."

Conversation came easy speaking of books, music, and travel. Across the table, as candlelight danced across her animated face, Darcy could only imagine what an evening at Pemberley with her as his wife might be like.

"I have always longed to travel to Rome," Miss Elizabeth said after the final course.

Darcy stood by her chair waiting to escort her to the music room. "Rome? Why Rome? I believed all young ladies wished to travel to Paris to shop and be seen."

"But sir, have you yet to determine that I am not like all young ladies?" she asked with an impish grin. "My impertinence is legendary in Meryton." Darcy struggled to control his impulse to brush a loose tendril from the nape of her neck.

"Oh, but I have, Miss Elizabeth, and I would not call it impertinence as much as spirit." Elizabeth lowered her eyes, and he swallowed as she flushed with color from the rise of her bosom to her face. "Many of your sex speak only what they believe a man wishes to hear. But a man of character wants an equal, not solely in wealth and connections, but in intellect and sense. A powerful woman can lead a man to do great things."

Elizabeth sat down on the sofa and Mr. Darcy seemed to hesitate before taking the chair across from her in the music room. Soon after, Sarah entered the parlor and quickly took up her needle.

"We were speaking of my impertinence." She arched her brow in challenge.

"That conversation we will save for another day," he replied with a grin. "But why, Miss Bennet, would you wish to see Rome?"

"Oh, Rome. I have read books from Father's library about its rise and fall. I would dearly love to see the Coliseum and works from the masters. History and culture, sir, are two of my passions. I am not a simple country maid from Hertfordshire, you know."

"No, Miss Elizabeth. I would never imagine anything about you as simple." Her laugh tinkled around the room as his baritone joined hers. "I can attest to the beauty of Rome and its people. My father took me there once when I was just a boy. I was but ten and we were at a crowded market on the way back to our hotel. We became separated and I wandered for half an hour looking for him."

"Whatever did you do, sir?"

He sheepishly looked down tracing the pattern of the rug with the toe of his boot. "I did what any young boy in a foreign country would do. I sat down and began to cry. A little grandmother found me, swept me into her home and fed me. She sent her granddaughter to the post master who spoke some English and within five minutes, we were back at the hotel with my worried father standing out front talking to the local constable. That was the first time my father publicly embraced me," he whispered. He seemed to be affected by the memory as he lowered his head to study his boots. She found herself turning to look out the window in the following silence.

"I apologize if I made you uncomfortable, Miss Bennet, with such maudlin remembrances."

His nervous smile was met with her compassion. "Please, do not apologize to me. We—the weaker sex—welcome open demonstrations of paternal affection. However, not only the weaker sex needs affirmation from their parents."

Attempting to lighten the pervading somber mood, she asked, "Might I play for you?"

"I would like that very much."

She began to play the same Irish tune she had sung earlier. Instead of the tune reminding him of his mother, he thought how this woman was capturing his heart. He leaned back and rested his head against the chair allowing the music to transport and fill his mind with images of her. He imagined walking together throughout Pemberley with her small hand in his. He saw her with Georgiana, coaxing her out of her reticence. He imagined the sunlight peeking through the curtains of their bed chamber and casting a glow upon her cheek. He saw her with a little girl with chestnut ringlets and beautiful dark eyes like her mother and a young boy with dimples like his father climbing onto her lap to hear stories. Before him was the future he craved. *Blast that letter from my mother!*

As his thoughts changed to match his torment, Miss Elizabeth looked up. She stopped playing instantly. "Sir, I apologize if my playing disturbs you. I will leave you to your solitude. If you will excuse me."

Miss Elizabeth rose and curtsied before Darcy realized what was happening. The maid was as surprised and began to gather her things. Darcy stood and closed the distance, gently clasping her elbow.

"Miss Bennet, pray forgive me. Your playing was lovely. Just the balm I needed on such a rain-sodden day." His words stopped her. "I apologize if I have somehow offended you. My mind had wandered to an unpleasant obligation. Please do not end the evening. I had so looked forward to more music and conversation. That is," he said anxiously, "unless you are fatigued. If so, I will not importune you further." He released her elbow as his hand felt the loss of her touch.

She looked up at him before a smile played across her lips. "I suppose I might stay as long as my playing gives you pleasure."

"Unspeakable amounts, Miss Bennet." He gallantly bowed and extended his hand to hers. She lightly placed her fingers in his palm as he escorted her back to the piano. The young maid began her sewing again. He tried to ignore the warmth radiating up his arm from where her hand had been only moments before.

"May I turn the pages for you?"

"I thank you."

She sang for him for the next three quarters of an hour as he leaned over her to turn the sheet music. *She smells of lavender...lavender and sunshine.* These musing and stirrings in his chest distracted him from his task and he was grateful that she seemed to play from memory.

After another quarter hour, Darcy hesitantly laid his hand on her milky-smooth shoulder. "Miss Bennet, I fear the late hour and music has lulled your poor maid to sleep." She looked to the girl whose head rested back against the wall.

"Poor thing. We left so unexpectedly this morning, neither of us was well rested."

"How did you come to Ashby Park, Miss Bennet?"

Miss Elizabeth blushed. "I was only recently made aware of an appointment with Mr. Hamilton's housekeeper this morning. We came on a moment's notice."

"Yes, yes, of course." Clearing his throat and hating the words coming forth from his mouth, Darcy said, "Might I...wish you joy?"

"Sir, since our last conversation at Netherfield, my situation remains unchanged." The tone of her voice was tremulous.

"Pray, excuse me. It is only that Hamilton informed me of his intentions toward you and his plan on seeking a formal courtship before he departed for town. I had only assumed..." He looked at her with hesitation as her face did not bespeak happiness.

"Mr. Hamilton has not asked for a courtship, and there is no understanding between us. Though the expectation..."

Darcy tried to maintain the same manner of decorum as if he was sitting through tea. *Is James mad? Has he lost his senses! Assuming she will wait until he is ready to act.* Darcy's own emotions were bubbling to the surface but to what purpose? Elizabeth Bennet would never be his, whether she was Hamilton's or the blacksmith's. She was not his cousin Anne.

"—but I thank you for your words. I know they were kindly meant." She looked around the room awkwardly as Darcy sat down on the chair across from her still at the piano. "Were you able to see your betrothed in Town?"

"Anne? Oh, yes. I was able to spend the day with her and my aunt. Lady Catherine was my mother's sister."

"How lovely for you to still have your aunt."

"She is the eldest of the three Fitzwilliam children: my aunt Catherine, my uncle, Lord Matlock, and then my mother, Lady Anne."

"How wonderful for your mother to have had a sister. I know that I can always rely on my dear Jane."

"Yes, well, my mother and my aunt were very different." He rested his chin on his knuckled fist. "My mother was all that was good and kind. We were her everything, and she did all she could to ensure our happiness in the future." He paused before finishing his thought. "She died days after Georgiana's birth and there has been a hole at Pemberley ever since." He looked in Miss Elizabeth's face and saw patience and understanding. "I cannot explain why I keep sharing these melancholy tales with you."

"Mr. Darcy, a conversation between two friends is no imposition. I believe, if I may be so bold to conjecture" —he nodded— "we are very much alike in that manner. Only Jane knows my inner joys and turmoil, and even then, I share my heart with no one. Just me and the moonlight." Darcy looked away quickly lest she discover his guilt.

"Well, Miss Bennet, hopefully your confidant will see fit to show through these miserable clouds so that the roads are passable tomorrow."

Miss Elizabeth nodded. She woke her maid and took Darcy's arm. He gently held her hand before he bowed before her at the bottom of the staircase then slowly trailed behind her.

Upon reaching her door, she faced him and said, "I thank you, sir. Such a lovely and unexpected evening."

"It was my pleasure, Miss Elizabeth. Goodnight." He gently raised her hand to his lips. "Pleasant dreams," he quietly whispered.

"Good night, Mr. Darcy." Her voice faltered slightly as she turned to enter her room. He strode down the corridor to escape the maddening feelings welling up in his heart when he heard her jiggle the handle violently. "Mr. Darcy, I must impose upon you a little longer. It appears my door is locked."

"Locked?" He walked back the few steps before reaching for the handle and jiggling it himself. "How did that happen?" he asked looking at her and then at her maid.

"Sarah often locks our rooms from the inside while she is lighting the fire and preparing our night clothes." He raised his eyebrows. "Sir—" she laughed "—in a house with four other sisters, it is often when one's door is unlocked, our most prized bonnets and baubles go missing. Sarah will often lock our door when she is inside so she does not have to face the wrath of our youngest sister when she refuses to hand over our items."

A deep chuckle rumbled from his throat. "I will bow to your knowledge of thieving sisters, Miss Bennet. Georgiana has never attempted to steal any of my effects. But, if you would be so kind as to extract one of your hair pins, I will have this door open in less than a minute."

"Sir?"

"My cousin Richard Fitzwilliam and I used to play hide and seek at Pemberley when we were boys. Richard's favorite place to hide was the tack room in the stable. He would take the key and lock himself inside. I eventually figured out that if I had a pin, I could pry it open from the outside and find him. After that, it was more evenly matched."

"You would ask me to let my hair down, sir, solely for the use of a pin? Scandalous, Sarah, just scandalous." She winked at her shocked maid.

Darcy laughed. "I hope you know, madam, I would never do anything to damage your reputation nor your chances for future felicity."

Grinning, she carefully removed a pin. "One pin will not question my decency, sir. Two, however, might leave me to censure and ridicule."

He took the pin from her, bending it straight before inserting it in the lock.

"Oh!"

He turned at Miss Elizabeth's exclamation and did a quick intake of breath. Her silky, dark curls cascaded down around her shoulders.

"Pray, excuse me. It seems as if that hairpin was to be my undoing after all." She could barely meet his eyes while struggling with her remaining pins.

"Beautiful." He sighed looking into her eyes as her gaze tentatively met his. The surprise on her face could only mean he had shared his thought…aloud! He lowered his own eyes and silently chastised himself. "I beg your pardon."

A smile appeared before she answered him back. "Sir, you need never apologize for a compliment."

"But I…you—"

"Mr. Darcy, it is rare that a lady hears such praise while she is in disarray." She lowered her lashes and looked back up through them shyly. "I thank you for your sentiment. It is not often that I hear them."

"I cannot believe that, Miss Elizabeth. But, I thank you for your forgiveness."

"Shall Sarah get you a candle?"

"No, no," Darcy said, turning back to the door. "I only need to manipulate the pin around until I can feel the lock catch and release. Then I will have your door… there!" He turned the handle and flung open the door, bowing gallantly. The maid quickly slipped inside the door, leaving them alone in the hallway. His eyes caught hers as he stood to his full height. "And now, Miss Bennet," he said with all amiability, "I will return your hairpin to you with which you can tame your unruly mane."

"I thank you, Mr. Darcy for restoring me to my chambers. I will see you in the morning. Goodnight."

She walked past him and gently locked the door behind her, leaving him alone in the hallway with his thoughts and her lingering scent to carry him off to sleep.

CHAPTER 9

"Good morning, Mr. Darcy. How was your night?" she asked, picking up a plate and walking the length of the sideboard that displayed sausage, muffins, black pudding, and hard-boiled eggs but she decided on tea and toast.

"It would have been a dull night indeed without the adventure of breaking into the guest quarters at my old friend's estate." He smiled. "And you?"

"Well, thank you. But," she said, in practiced ennui, "I was slightly afraid of being harmed."

"Harmed, madam? By whom?" He set down his cup and leaned toward her.

"I was led to believe a confirmed manipulator of locks was in the house. I am grateful his intentions were honorable." She smiled behind her teacup.

Grinning, he leaned back in the chair. "Miss Elizabeth, I can guarantee your virtue was quite safe last night. One sound from your room, and I, as well as the butler and footmen, would have been there before you could have drawn your second breath. But luckily, this lock aficionado must have been kept at bay by the howling wind and exhaustion and, of course, a complete respect for you."

"Of that sir, I am obliged." She took a sip of tea and glanced to the window. "It appears the storm has passed and our sojourn at Ashby Park has come to an end."

"Yes, that it does." *Was that disappointment in his voice?* "I have already sent a footman out to determine if the roads are passable in your carriage and expect him soon. If they are, I will ride alongside to provide you escort…"

"Oh, Mr. Darcy. I believe the recent weather has encouraged all highwaymen and others with nefarious intent to go on holiday. Please do not feel obligated—"

"Miss Elizabeth, it is merely the action of a friend."

"Thank you, sir. Then I will accept. I will have Sarah pack my bag in preparation for our departure."

He took a sip of his coffee and laid the paper down on the table. "Your bag? You were prepared to stay at Ashby Park yesterday when you arrived?"

"With the weather as blustery as it was, my mother felt it prudent to send a change of clothes in case there was an unexpected happening. My mother may be many things, Mr. Darcy, but she is always prepared for any situation." *Or prepared to make a situation for her daughters!*

Darcy nodded. "A mother's attempt to provide for her children never seems to end."

"Too true, sir."

The butler walked through the door and said, "Young Jones has returned and is awaiting you in Mr. Hamilton's library."

"Excuse me, Miss Bennet. We will know shortly if we are to be off."

Taking a final sip of her tea, she too walked out of the room and up the stairs to her chambers.

⁓

"Mr. Darcy, what a lovely day. I thank you for making it your duty to see to my entertainment." Miss Elizabeth smiled as she clasped her hands behind her back and walked alongside him toward the house. Sarah followed behind.

"Well, Miss Bennet, since we are detained at Ashby Park for another day, I know how you enjoy roaming the countryside." He took her gloved hand and helped her over the stile then tucked it in his arm.

"That I do, sir. I cannot help but think how beautiful nature is and how lucky we are to be enjoying it." A light breeze lifted a loose curl at her neck and he wondered what it would feel like between his fingers. At that moment, a flock of geese rose from the pond behind them and flew overhead. "Breathtaking."

"I agree," he said before he could stop himself.

"I believe there is a primitiveness in nature which does not adhere to the dictates of society…which I find refreshing."

"Go on."

"I wonder what our lives would be like if society's expectations did not force us into roles we might not want to follow."

"Such as?"

"Such as daughters, wives, and mothers. What if I wished to be an actress, or write books, or even never marry? Yet, those are not things a woman can contemplate. For example, without a husband, women have nothing. We are at the mercy of the stronger sex."

"But marriage is an honorable institution. Even you can regard it as such."

"Yes," she said thoughtfully. "I can. I do. But it is unfortunate that women go from their father's home to that of another keeper. And hopefully to a home with affection."

"Yes, affection," he said moving his gaze from her to the meadows stretching before them. "It is unfortunate that in our society many marriages are made more for financial gain and connection than true affection."

"Yes, it is." She sighed. Seeming to want to rally their maudlin spirits, she said, "Isn't it fortunate that you will gain both society's expectations and personal affection from your own union?"

He walked with his hands behind his back and said almost too quickly, "Yes, yes, Miss Bennet. Fortuitous indeed."

He leaned his head back on the sofa in Hamilton's library as the clock chimed two in the morning. He could not rest upstairs knowing she was asleep but three doors away from his own room. Though there was nowhere he would rather have been, to be so close to her all day long, yet not have any chance to win her had been a sweet torture. *Elizabeth*. He swallowed the amber liquid and relished the burn down his throat. *She is the stuff dreams are made of.* Taking another drink, his thoughts continued to ramble. *Oh, Prospero. I have a Tempest in*

my soul, and must only wait out the storm until it passes and I can go on with my life.

He was in a certain state of undress having removed his cravat and jacket. He sighed, resting his face in his hands. "But why? Why Mother, what did you hope to accomplish?" He looked up at the ceiling while once again laying back against the sofa. "I could very well love this woman. A part of me already does. But there is Anne. Would that I could declare myself," he said, shaking his head. "She speaks of love. Of affection. I could give her that and so much more. But she will never know and nor will I. My dearest, loveliest Elizabeth!" He took the last swallow of his glass and rested it next to him, gathering up his coat and cravat as he stood. *I must be off to bed, for tomorrow this imaginary world will end and I will wake and accompany her home.* He blew out the candles, put the screen up in front of the fire, and attributed the fleeting shadow by the door to the dancing flames.

Lizzy had awoken from a restless sleep and unable to return to the Land of Nod, she determined it would do her well to retrieve a book from the library to calm her mind. Seeing Mr. Darcy alone and in partial dishabille, she turned to depart, not wishing to interrupt his solitude. However, she could not bring herself to leave. Having never seen a man's bare neck before, she was mesmerized—the rise and fall of his chest, his muscular form beneath the fine lawn shirt, the slow roll of his Adam's apple as he swallowed... By the time all lessons of propriety returned, it was too late.

Like a priest, she had heard his confession, yet was at a loss. *Can he be in earnest?*

As she darted up the stairs and down the hallway, she did not stop until she reached her own room. *Mr. Darcy admires me! How is that possible?* Her breath was rapid as she placed her hand on her chest in an attempt to calm her racing heart. *Fate is a fickle being. My heart is uncertain but I must hie to my bed and pray Mr. Darcy awakens without the dew from Puck upon his eyes.* "For if he looks with affection upon me," she whispered, "I would hardly know how to respond."

She held her breath as the steps stopped in front of her room for a moment, then continued on, ending only with the opening and closing of his door.

I must ease my thoughts. This will not do. If I wait for another quarter of an hour at least, Mr. Darcy will be asleep and I can peruse Mr. Hamilton's library.

She continued to walk about her room, stopping once to draw back the curtains and look outside at the moon peeking through the clouds. The beauty of nature made her pause once again and consider her earlier conversation with Mr. Darcy. *If I only had freedom, the true freedom to do as I wished.* She looked at the clock again, nodded to herself that enough time had passed, and deftly exited her room for the library.

Darcy did not call for the footman to act as valet when he finally made it to his room a little after two. As he readied himself for bed and added a log to the dwindling fire, his thoughts were full of a pair of fine eyes and a beautifully formed, impertinent mouth. *Anne. This is unfair to her. Elizabeth... Stop it, man! Miss Bennet is a wonderful woman who will make Hamilton a good wife. Though she has no dowry to speak of, her family's manners are atrocious, and she would never be accepted within society. And, there is Anne!* He thought again of his cousin and then his aunt Catherine. Darcy shuddered as the visage of his aunt came across his mind.

I will never forget the day my mother died. I died too, that day. Had Mother not had that letter drawn up for me to marry Anne, my life would be so much different now. I would be my own master, able to court Elizabeth Bennet if I so wished. But... He sighed. *I will not go against the dying wishes of my mother. I only wish she had spoken to me about it and not left it to Aunt Catherine. Or even allowed Father to know of the details.* He smiled at the memory of his father who had been gone these five years. Reaching for his father's watch, he realized he must have left it in the library. As the clock chimed three-quarters passed the hour, Darcy slipped back into his breeches and quietly left his room to retrieve his treasure.

Lizzy had almost decided on a book when she looked down and noticed a beautiful, gold watch resting on the table by a half empty glass. She picked it up and inspected the treasure. An ornate engraving of a majestic home facing a lake was on the front of the time piece. She opened the watch to find the inside engraved with the words:

To my beloved Darcy upon our engagement. I am forever yours,
Anne

She let out a soft gasp and quickly returned the watch to its original location—embarrassed to have discovered such an intimate gift. *Such words of devotion from his future bride. How can he not love her?* She began to question the enigma which was Fitzwilliam Darcy. *How can he profess his admiration for me when he already has the heart of another?* She shook her head, instantly thinking of Mr. Hamilton. *But, I guess we do not always love those who love us? Mr. Darcy is a good man. An honorable man. Who is promised to another.*

She sighed while deciding on a book of poems. Returning a heavy volume of "Beewick's Book of British Birds," she ignored the ladder, and stood on her tiptoes to place it flat on the shelf above her head. As she pushed it back with her fingertips, she felt a presence in the room and turned to see Mr. Darcy standing in the doorway observing her.

She started at the unexpected sight and inadvertently pushed the heavy volume off the shelf, crying in pain as the book hit her temple, knocking her to the floor.

He reached her with two quick strides. "Miss Bennet. Miss Bennet, are you well?"

"Yes, I believe so. I…" She reached up to touch her head and found her fingers covered in blood. "I…my head is spinning. Please forgive me," she said as she slumped against him and closed her eyes.

"Miss Bennet? Miss Bennet, can you hear me?" He lightly stroked her cheek.

"Yes, sir," she whispered. "It is only my head that throbs." She opened her eyes to find Mr. Darcy leaning over her as she lay on the couch in the library.

Grabbing the decanter and napkin from the sideboard, he splashed the cloth with brandy before pressing it tenderly against her wound.

"Are you comfortable?" Kneeling beside her, he said, "Shall I get you something to ease your pain? A glass of wine perhaps?"

"No, thank you."

She could not describe the warmth that spread through her as he retrieved the rug from the back of the couch and tucked it around her person. She attempted to ignore the intimacy of the act. He knelt beside her again and softly whispered, "Will that do?"

"Yes." The room was bathed in a warm glow from the fire which only added to the atmosphere. Her eyes, at first drawn to his open shirt, met his. She blushed at her own state of undress and drew the rug up to her chin.

He dabbed gently at her head again.

"It appears to have stopped bleeding."

"So it has," she answered, feeling his breath on her check as he spoke. She closed her eyes to block out the image he presented to her: a tender lover administering to his beloved. "I believe I should attempt to go to my chambers."

"Madam, you can barely sit up, let alone walk. Allow me to assist you, and then I will summon your maid."

"Sir, I am grateful for your aid… But what would be inferred to the household if you awaken my maid at three in the morning and I have a wound on my head and you in—" she looked at his state of undress "—a night shirt?"

"Very well. Shall we sit here for a moment longer, then?"

"Yes, I think that would do well."

They allowed the silence to envelop them. She was certain he could hear the beating of her heart. He noticed his watch resting on the table and quickly walked over to retrieve it.

"I saw your timepiece when I came in this evening. It is exquisite."

"It is. It is one of my favorite possessions." To Lizzy's surprise, he opened it and lovingly fingered the inscription. "This image on the front is of my home, Pemberley. It was a very thoughtful gift, was it not?"

"Yes, yes it was." A feeling she could only assume was jealousy began to rise and ignoring the pounding in her head, she forced herself to a sitting position.

"Sir. I believe I am ready to return to my chambers. No, no," she interjected as he cut the distance between them and attempted to grasp her arm. "I am grateful for your service but am able to manage well enough alone."

"Will you please allow me to help you?"

"No, Mr. Darcy. I appreciate your effort but have no wish to jeopardize our situations. Good night." She lifted her chin and as defiantly as one might with a splitting headache, began the trek to her room. She could feel his presence following her and heard his breathing as she made her way up the stairs but he allowed her to complete the task unassisted.

"Goodnight, Mr. Darcy," she said gruffly over her shoulder as she walked through her door and closed it behind her.

"Goodnight, Miss Bennet."

The next morning dawned just as the day before, beautiful with a crisp bite about the air. Lizzy had not slept well. Between her throbbing head and her rampant thoughts, she had welcomed the crow of the rooster like the plague. Her exhaustion after only a few hours of restless sleep only added to the confusion about the character of the man who had briefly secured her admiration.

No, it is not that I no longer admire him. He is a very handsome man with a sharp intellect. And I very much enjoy speaking with him. She gritted her teeth and ignored her headache as she allowed Sarah to help her dress to depart for Longbourn. *But to flatter me and then profess his love for a gift from his betrothed, shows an inconstancy of character, I think. Yes, we were thrown together these last two days in an unusual circumstance. But how could I have been so wrong to think this was more than a flirtation! And, as he is betrothed, he should not have been so attentive.*

Closing the door behind her she made her way down the hall toward the stairs which would lead her out the door and away from Ashby Park.

"I will inform the master of our discussion, Miss Bennet, and your preferences."

"Once again," Lizzy said with an awkward grin, "it is of little consequence what my opinion is, but if Mr. Hamilton feels it is of some import, then I thank you. And thank you for your prodigious care of both myself and my maid. I do hope we were not in any way a burden." She noticed Mr. Darcy in the doorway. Mrs. Wallings replied that she was pleased to have been of service to one of Hertfordshire's dearest ladies. She curtsied at the older woman and walked toward the door acknowledging Mr. Darcy with a quick nod, ignoring his questioning look.

As he took his great coat and top hat from the footman, he cast another befuddled look toward Miss Elizabeth. "Yes, thank you for your hospitality, Mrs. Wallings. I will be sure to apprise Mr. Hamilton of the excellent nature of his staff." He nodded quickly and strode out after Miss Elizabeth.

What the devil happened that she will not even look me in the eyes? Did I offend her by my proximity to her last evening? Brushing his hand through his hair before securing his top hat, he said, "Miss Bennet, according to my watch, with the roads as they are, it will take us at least four hours to arrive back in Meryton. Are you quite well enough to make the journey?"

"Sir—" she looked quickly at her maid then at him "—I am quite prepared to return home," she said with strained civility.

"At this early departure, we are sure to arrive back in Meryton, and then Longbourn before the noon hour, assuming the roads are as dry as Hamilton's groomsman stated they were."

"Yes," was her succinct reply.

"Miss Bennet," he said lowering his voice and looking around. "How have I offended you?"

After a brief pause, she said with a strained expression, "Sir, I merely have much to ruminate."

Two hours had passed as Lizzy lowered the curtain determined to get some much needed rest. She had tried to ignore the vision of Mr. Darcy on horseback outside her window for the trip thus far but found it more difficult as the miles passed.

Turning her attention to her traveling companion, she said, "Sarah, we are almost home. I hope the last two days have been pleasurable for you."

"Why yes, ma'am, they have. It's been nice attending to one lady instead of five." Her speech was interrupted by a quick sneeze and then another.

Reaching for a handkerchief in her reticule, Lizzy was surprised to find a letter inside. She remembered Kitty handing her the reticule and how she had thought no more of it. Sarah sneezed and she handed her the linen.

She broke the seal and recognized Kitty's handwriting at once.

Oh, Lizzy,

I am at a loss of what to do and need your counsel. I have assured a friend that I would not break a confidence but am concerned for her well-being. Miss Darcy has secretly been meeting with Mr. Wickham these last weeks. She has not sought out these meetings but he finds her no matter if she is riding her horse or sitting in the garden. She said he has also been very forthcoming with his admiration and affection, professing his love and honorable intentions.

However, I do not feel his intentions are honorable. He has spent many a day with Lydia walking out in the gardens and to Oakham Mount, and then finds his way to Netherfield to woo dear Georgie. Lydia has spoken with no little anticipation for an engagement, yet he tells Miss Darcy that he loves only her. I have attempted to speak with Lydia, but she will have none of it.

Miss Darcy confided in me yesterday that Mr. Wickham has asked her to run away with him to Gretna Greene tomorrow evening and how it will be a wonderful relief for Mr. Darcy, who with the stress of Pemberley and his own upcoming nuptials, will be overjoyed that his sister will be betrothed herself. She does not like the idea of disappointing her brother, but Mr. Wickham has convinced her that Mr. Darcy will welcome her marriage.

Lizzy, please return with haste and advise me. Do not dally at Ashby Park. I fear Mr. Wickham will only lead Miss Darcy and Lydia in ruination.

Kitty

She felt the blood drain from her face as she was reading the missive. Her worry increased as she realized the letter was written two days ago and the fateful elopement must have taken place the previous night. She looked out the window to Mr. Darcy but he had ridden ahead. Hopefully, they would be nearing a village soon and she would speak with him then.

Lizzy waited, tying and untying the ribbons of her reticule, earning curious looks from Sarah. When the carriage stopped, she threw open the door and stepped out, not waiting to be handed down.

"Miss Bennet!" Mr. Darcy exclaimed in surprise.

"Never mind, that sir. I must speak to you at once," she whispered softly, clutching her reticule with the offending letter within. "Might we take a turn around that courtyard, Mr. Darcy?"

"I am grateful for this opportunity to apologize to you but am uncertain as to the cause of my penance. However, guide my words and they shall be said." His smile was so unpracticed that for a moment, she almost forgot that she was both upset with him and about Kitty's letter.

"Please, sir. This is of the gravest importance. Upon entering the carriage at Ashby Park, I noticed my reticule had been forgotten in the confines of the vehicle for the last two days. When I opened the bag, I found this letter..." She looked about to make sure she was not observed. "It is a letter from my sister Kitty… It is in regards to Miss Darcy."

Before the words had finished spilling from her lips, Mr. Darcy had grabbed the letter and opened it.

"Good heavens!" he cried. "I must leave here at once and fly directly to Netherfield."

"At once! We must only pray you are not too late."

His breathing increased and he looked around in agitation. "Miss Bennet, I am grateful to you but I need not ask you to keep this in confidence."

"Of course."

"Please excuse me. I will instruct the driver to return you directly to Longbourn. I will call on you with Bingley when I find Georgiana."

With that he bowed deeply, walked to the driver without delay, and galloped away toward Meryton.

I only hope we are not too late, she thought as she watched him fade in the distance.

CHAPTER 10

"It was quite shocking to have Mr. Darcy come riding into our yard as if Napoleon himself was invading Meryton," Mrs. Bennet told her sister Phillips as Elizabeth made her way through the door an hour later.

"Where is Mr. Darcy?" Lizzy asked, removing her gloves and looking around the room expectantly.

"Oh, Lizzy. You are home. I was so concerned you would not be able to see Mr. Hamilton while you were at Ashby. Did the weather help your cause at all?" She picked up another biscuit and dipped it in her tea.

With much self-possession, Elizabeth refrained from rolling her eyes but instead took a deep breath and exhaled. "Mama, I had no cause in traveling to Ashby Park, other than to meet with Mrs. Wallings as you instructed me to do. And Mr. Hamilton did not arrive at his home."

"La, it is well enough that Mr. Hamilton wants to marry you anyway."

"Yes, Lizzy," agreed her aunt Phillips. "I was just talking to my maid about it. You shall be married before Michaelmas!"

"*Aunt!* I thank you both to refrain from discussing what you suppose to know about my private life." Stifling her anger, she turned back to Mrs. Bennet. "Now, Mama. What is this about Mr. Darcy?"

Mrs. Bennet yawned, rather bored. "He is gone. He and Miss Darcy returned to Netherfield only a quarter of an hour ago."

"Miss Darcy? Miss Darcy was here?"

Lizzy sat down on the closest chair, attempting to keep her jaw from going slack in astonishment while her mother relayed the events of the last forty-eight hours. "Well, that is a rather curious tale. Two days ago," she said to her sister, "Kitty came in to the parlor hurriedly and asked if she might invite Miss Darcy to stay with us as her particular friend. As Lydia was staying with you, Sister, and Jane has been engaged with Miss Bingley, and Lizzy was at Ashby…"

"And Mary?"

"Oh, she was doing whatever Mary does. Anyway, I determined it would be a good thing for Kitty to be occupied and make a good connection with such a distinguished family. She sent the invitation off to Netherfield and Miss Darcy arrived shortly thereafter.

"The girls were having such an agreeable time that they even sent their regrets down from Kitty's room when the handsome Mr. Wickham and Mr. Denney came to visit yesterday! I was quite disappointed that Kitty did not present herself to the officers, but Mr. Wickham has set his cap on Lydia, and who can blame him?"

Lizzy cringed at the thought. "And what of Mr. Darcy?"

"He came with much haste to collect his sister, and Miss Georgiana asked if Kitty could accompany them to Netherfield and stay for dinner. Of course, I could never tell Mr. Darcy no." She leaned in to Mrs. Phillips as she loudly exulted, "Especially since I believe he might have taken an interest in Kitty while he was here. He kept thanking her for escorting his sister and for joining them this evening. Mark my words, Sister. We shall have three weddings by Michaelmas!"

"Mama, he is betrothed to Miss…" *Oh never mind. There is no point when she has intrigues in her head!* Lizzy exhaled slowly, as all the fear which had possessed her since she had found the letter began to dissolve. *I am so grateful Kitty has befriended Miss Georgiana and her sense of propriety has grown so in her company. If not, I am uncertain what would have happened.* She ignored her mother's prattling and slid lower into the chair from both emotional fatigue and the long journey. When Mrs. Bennet mentioned Charlotte Lucas, Lizzy looked up.

"…and that odious man" —her mother wrinkled her nose in disgust while fanning herself— "who will throw us to the hedgerows when Mr. Bennet dies, chose her over one of my darling girls."

"Mama," Lizzy interjected, "what is this? Charlotte Lucas?"

Mrs. Phillips interrupted. "I know, Sister. How ill-bred! He should understand his obligation to the family!"

"Mama."

"Truth be told, I was frustrated with Kitty staying above stairs with Miss Darcy, and almost blamed her, but now that Mr. Darcy seems interested…"

"*Mama!*" Lizzy stood quickly, silencing her mother and Mrs. Phillips. "Tell me at once. What has occurred?"

"Your cousin, Mr. Collins, who you never met because you were off gallivanting at Ashby! Instead of making an offer of marriage to one of the daughters of the estate he is to inherit, he offered to Charlotte Lucas just this morning!"

"Charlotte Lucas? Well, that is wonderful! Charlotte deserves happiness, Mama."

"Maybe so, but she does not deserve to be the mistress of Longbourn when your father dies. And what will you say when we are all thrown out of our home? Such a plain looking creature."

"Mama, I must go to her at once." Looking down at her attire, she said, "I will go change and then be off."

"Suit yourself, child. But your father will wish to see you before you run off again."

Lizzy exited the room, but not soon enough to miss the derision in her mother's face. She could only imagine it was due to her continued friendship with the future mistress of Longbourn. Lizzy shook her head and walked toward her father's study. She smiled at the faint scent of tobacco wafting from under the door then knocked.

Hiding a smile, she pushed open the door and walked in to find her father exactly as he ever was.

"My, Lizzy. When did you arrive home?" he asked laying down his worn copy of Milton.

"Almost only this moment," she said, leaning in to give him a kiss on the cheek.

"And does Ashby Park still stand after your unexpected sojourn there? Were the servants shocked at the scheming of your mother?"

"No, Papa. Unfortunately, they were not." She grimaced. "But, they might not have had the chance to be, with an additional unexpected visitor." At his raised eyebrows, she continued. "Mr. Darcy was also importuned by the storm, and we were in each other's company for two days." As his eyebrows raised higher, she said, "Do not fear, Papa. We were accompanied by Sarah the entire visit."

"Lizzy, I would never think anything of it—he never looks at any woman but to see a blemish, but only wonder what your mother will now think? She is now quite set on him marrying Kitty, and with your interference, might have her plans dashed." He laughed and slapped his knee soundly. "Oh, this is turning out to be a great day, after all. First, Collins leaves to Lucas Lodge…"

"Did you not find him pleasing?"

"Pleasing? Yes, to me. He is not at all a sensible man and found him most diverting…" At Lizzy's confusion, he explained. "Even I can only delight in so much humor for one day, Lizzy. I needed respite from his constant chatter of his patroness and her fireplaces. My study was not even my own, as he would follow me in at all hours talking of Her Ladyship's buttresses. However, I believe he will be well received at Lucas Lodge. Yes, indeed."

Lizzy did not miss the twinkle in her father's eye, as she stopped at the door. "Papa, when Mr. Darcy arrived to collect his sister and Kitty, did he appear out of sorts?"

Mr. Bennet looked at his favorite daughter through the spectacles resting low on his nose and said, "I believe to the casual observer, the answer would be no. However, I thought he was effusive, a contrast to his severe countenance. Why do you ask?"

"No reason," she said, closing the door behind her. *How I wish I were at Netherfield.*

Once in her room, she set her pelisse and bonnet on the vanity before sitting at her window looking out at the early afternoon. Her thoughts were full of the last three days: being detained at Ashby Park;

Georgiana's near elopement; Lydia's behavior; Charlotte's engagement. *Has Charlotte found love? The type of love that one wishes for in life?* Mr. Darcy's image flitted before her eyes.

Mr. Darcy's feelings are confused. Yes, he may be attracted to me... But his half empty glass on the end table. Obviously, he was in his cups. Do not trust the drunken ramblings of a man. He is betrothed for heaven's sake!

She slowly traced circles upon the glass and allowed her thoughts to wander before reaching up to feel the small bump where his ministering touches from the night before could still be felt. *He was showing me kindness in his attentions, just as he would to anyone.* She ruefully smiled, remembering his contrite behavior that morning as they were preparing to leave. *He was so concerned he had offended me in the library. But, no, he had not. It was only my realization at the unenviable position I am in, which offended me. I believe I have found a man who, in disposition and talents, would most suit me, and yet, it is not meant to be.* She was not of a taciturn disposition and easily settled into a pleasant countenance as she rang for the maid to help her dress for her visit to Lucas Lodge.

Sarah entered after only a moment and smiled at her mistress.

"Miss Elizabeth, are you happy to be home?"

"Yes, Sarah, but I must be off again. I am to visit Miss Lucas to congratulate her on her betrothal. Would you please get my yellow dress and blue pelisse?"

"The dark or light blue one, miss?"

"The light one will do. And how are things downstairs? Did anything of import occur in your absence?" Lizzy asked as Sarah buttoned up the back of her dress.

"Oh, no, miss," the young girl said good-naturedly. "Everything is as it always was. There you are, miss. All ready."

As Lizzy grabbed her gloves, she said, "Before I go… What was the opinion of Mr. Collins from below stairs?"

Sarah suddenly became interested in a pattern on the rug and seemed to choose her words carefully. "Well, miss. The general feeling is that he is a…well…very…"

"Sarah, you make speak plainly."

"Very well, he is not sensible. He made demands on Mr. Hill who was acting as his valet that one would not expect…"

"Such as?"

"For one, he wanted a portion of each meal brought to him before the family sat in the dining room so that he could determine if it was up to his standards. Of course, Mrs. Bennet was *not* pleased when she learnt that."

"Oh my!"

"Nor was she happy when he requested Mrs. Hill instruct young Jerry count all the bricks on the chimneys. Some such to compare to his patroness's estate. Poor lad had a rope tied to his trousers and was getting ready to scale the wall before Mr. Bennet put a stop to it. And—"

"Thank you, Sarah. That will be all." The young maid nodded and left the room. *What has Charlotte done by accepting such a man?* "I must go at once and see him for myself."

Pacing back and forth, Darcy attempted to control his voice and not scare the two girls sitting on the chairs before him. "Dear Georgie. Please tell me what happened?" They were in his private sitting room in Netherfield, hoping to arouse as little attention as possible from the other inhabitants of the house. "I love you, and as long as no harm came upon you, I will remain calm."

Georgiana looked at Miss Katherine Bennet, who nodded gently at her before lowering her eyes and shaking her head. "Wills, I do not want you to think less of me. Please forgive me."

"Poppet, you have done nothing wrong," he said, praying his words were true. "You have remained constant to yourself and your family. Now, tell me the whole of it." He smiled and hoped he looked genial. Miss Katherine squeezed her hand and Georgiana began.

"The night of Sir William Lucas's party, Miss Katherine and I were here alone at Netherfield and were preparing to retire for bed, when Mr. Wickham walked in the room."

"Unannounced?" Darcy asked, his breath barely coming out evenly.

She nodded her head. "Yes."

"Where was Mrs. Annesley?"

"She had just retired with a headache. Miss Katherine and I had begged to stay up a few minutes more so that I could finish a sonata."

He nodded his head for her to continue and attempted to look impassive as his emotions roiled within him. "And what did Wickham say when he learned you were unchaperoned?"

"He said he did not dare bother the servants and it was going to be our secret so we might surprise you. I did not feel it was appropriate for him to be here so late but he reminded me that he was like a brother and loved me as one." She dropped her eyelashes to look at the floor, her cheeks turning pink. "He also told me I was more beautiful than he remembered and was a breathtaking woman."

"Which you are," Darcy said reaching for her hand. "But, a true gentleman who respects you will not sneak into the house when you are unchaperoned."

"Yes. That is what Miss Katherine said. Before he departed, he spoke of Mother and Father. I miss them so much, and I loved hearing them spoken of. He informed me he was going to be in Meryton for an extended period, and we would meet again. But, I was not to apprise you of our meeting. That you would not like it—"

"And I do not!"

"—because you still viewed me as a child and not a grown woman. I guess I proved him correct, did I not?"

"Georgiana, you are not a child, but you also have not been exposed to people such as George Wickham has become."

She began to cry and her quaking words cut him off. "Wills, he began to appear in the oddest places, whenever I was without Mrs. Annesley or you—in the garden, in the woods, walking to the stables. Yet, I believed I could trust him, I wanted to trust him…since he was like a brother to me. I would say, 'You just missed Wills,' and he would reply, 'Remember, it's our secret.' I became exhausted from holding the truth back from you."

"Tell him about three days ago," Miss Katherine interrupted.

"What happened three days ago?" Darcy asked, leaning forward.

"I found a letter in my room asking me to meet him by the pond in Netherfield Woods. I met him and he professed his undying love for me. Claimed he could not live without me. He asked me to run away with him to Gretna Green before you came home from London."

"And what did you tell him, poppet?"

"That I could not disappoint you. That I loved him too, but if he loved me as he said, he needed to speak to my brother."

"That was very wise of you, Georgie."

"I cannot claim credit for my words. Miss Katherine's counsel from the day before was still fresh in my mind." She clasped her friend's hand with both of hers and said, "I will be grateful to you forever."

"As will I," Darcy said, nodding at Miss Katherine, who began to color at the attention.

"I cannot claim that counsel myself. It is what I have often heard Jane and Lizzy repeating to each other. They are the best of sisters, and I have recently realized it is their example I should follow."

"Quite so," he said.

"But, that was not all that stopped my flight to Scotland," Georgiana exclaimed. "Miss Katherine also said her sister, Miss Lydia, spoke of Wickham's plans to take the inheritance from Pemberley, which was rightfully his, and anyway he could get it. When she asked how much his inheritance was valued, he replied with... he replied with..." Her voice cracked and she began to shake with quiet sobs. Darcy pulled her to his chest and stroked her hair until her tears were spent. "Please. Would you tell him?"

"As you wish." Miss Katherine took a deep breath before finishing his sister's account. "Lydia said that Mr. Wickham's inheritance was thirty thousand pounds—" Miss Katherine whispered the next "—and some scraps of young muslin." She took a deep breath and met

Darcy's eyes. "I knew for certain he was planning on hurting my dear friend." Miss Katherine reached out and clasped Georgiana's hand again while Darcy began to pace.

"Do you know what has become of him? I must find him at once."

"No, William," Georgiana cried, rushing to him. "No, you cannot call him out. It is too dangerous. Promise me. For my sake. I could not bear it if anything…" New sobs took over and he walked her back to her seat where she sank down and rested her head on Miss Katherine's shoulder.

After a few more minutes of hushed cries, she said, "Brother, can Miss Katherine stay this evening? I know it will be an imposition on our hostess but I would find comfort having a friend remain with me.…"

"Of course, my dearest. I will take care of our hostess. Miss Katherine, we will send a note to Longbourn. Is that satisfactory?"

"Yes, very much. But I would like to inform Lizzy that all is well. I am sure she is sick with worry."

Darcy started at the thought of Miss Elizabeth. He had all but forgotten her while concerned with Georgiana and her distress. *As it should be! You must forget Miss Elizabeth, and her smile, and her voice, and her eyes, and the way that one curl at the base of her neck always licks the curve of her shoulders…*

He shook his head with resolve. "Georgiana, we will leave in the morning."

"But Brother, why?" she asked, looking up with alarm. "You do not think Wickham will attempt to seek me out again, do you?"

"I am uncertain but am better able to protect you in London at Darcy House where the servants are loyal to us. I will take care of some business there, and then we will travel to Pemberley."

"…until the wedding?"

"Yes," he choked. "Until the wedding."

Georgiana lowered her eyes, as if in thought. "Brother, may I speak to you?" Darcy nodded and followed her to his bedchamber, leaving Miss Katherine alone by the fire.

"May I invite Miss Katherine as my particular friend to travel with me? She would be such good company in London. I also know Mrs. Annesley hopes to expose me to the company of gentle young ladies so I might prepare for my coming out. This would give her that opportunity." Her imploring eyes melted any thought he had of rejecting her, and he nodded his head in consent. "I will send a note to Mr. Bennet with your request this evening. If that be the case, however, you should ask Miss Katherine to make sure she is interested in your scheme."

He smiled, pleased with the young Miss Bennet's devotion to his sister. His smile deepened as he remembered the last few days at Ashby Park. After Miss Katherine had happily agreed to Georgiana's invitation, he excused himself to write the aforementioned note and ponder Miss Elizabeth's changeable temperament.

∽

"And the pin money she will have…" Mrs. Bennet exuded rapturously looking at the letter which had just come from Netherfield.

"Are you speaking of Charlotte?" Lizzy asked, walking into the room.

"Charlotte? Charlotte? Why should I care a straw of Charlotte Lucas marrying that odious little vicar? No, no. I speak of your sister. This letter just came from Netherfield." Her grin spread from ear to ear, and Lizzy looked expectantly at Jane.

"It seems Kitty has been invited to travel with Miss Darcy to London in the morning and then on to Pemberley with the family."

"It is not fair!" Lydia stomped. "I might not be Miss Darcy's particular friend, but I'm much more diverting than Kitty. I should be the one going to the theatre and concerts."

"Perhaps," Lizzy responded evenly, turning to look at her youngest sister, "Mr. Darcy desires a companion for his sister with more sense of decorum than you possess. This should be a lesson to you to behave properly and more opportunities for enjoyment might present themselves."

"La, I would not want to be with that old, stodgy Mr. Darcy anyway. My Wickham says..."

"Lydia, he is not *your* Wickham, and I would remind you to not repeat things he says about acquaintances. He has not been long enough in the country, and we only know what he has told us. There is no one to vouch for his claims. Mama," she said, turning to Mrs. Bennet, "you must see that. Tell Lydia she must not be alone with that man as we do not know his character."

"I will tell her no such thing, Lizzy. Mr. Wickham was raised a gentleman. He told us all about how he was forced into a life of service to the Crown because of Kitty's future husband. He is a good man who had a horrible wrong committed against him." She straightened her skirt and picked at imaginary thread at the seams. "I only allow Kitty to pursue Mr. Darcy so that when Charlotte Lucas turns me out, my future son will provide for us. I would never sacrifice Lydia to such a taciturn man. Lydia needs someone with more spirit. But, Mr. Darcy will do well enough for Kitty."

Lizzy's mouth fell open at the complete disregard for any semblance of modesty. Her mother had gone too far. "Mama! Mr. Darcy is engaged to be married to his cousin in less than three months. There has been an understanding since their infancy!"

"Yes, yes, I'm aware of that. *But*, it would not be the first time in history a pretty face has made a man forget himself. I am sure Miss de Bourgh would not have such a broken heart." Mrs. Bennet sniffed. "I understand she is a sickly girl with very little understanding of the world. She would find happiness elsewhere while our Kitty would secure our future."

"What nonsense you speak!" said Elizabeth.

"Mama, this is an invitation for a holiday, not for his hand in marriage," Jane gently murmured.

"Yes, but we must make it such. Lizzy, you will go with them to London…"

"But, I have not been invited."

"That is of little concern. No one cares a jot for those kinds of things. You will stay with my sister Gardiner in Cheapside and go to the warehouses to pick out fabrics for wedding clothes." She nodded to herself.

"Mama! I am not engaged nor is Kitty. Jane is the closest to that connection." Jane blushed. "If you want to scheme send her, not me."

In truth, Lizzy could not communicate why she was so averse to the plan. She enjoyed her aunt and uncle Gardiner and her dear, young cousins. She loved the theatre and museums. Admittedly, she even became giddy in delight while looking at bolts of fabrics and new patterns. But, the one thing she could not admit was how unnerved she might be traveling with Mr. Darcy in the confines of his carriage. Something occurred at Ashby Park between them that she would not acknowledge. And sitting in a carriage with him for hours would not help her cause at all!

"Yes, Mama. Send Jane to prepare for her upcoming wedding."

"Lizzy, you are more betrothed than I. Mr. Bingley has not declared himself."

"Nor has Mr. Hamilton," Lizzy said with exasperation. "Therefore, let's just send Kitty by herself as she was the one to receive the invitation." Lizzy dropped down in the chair and folded her arms.

"No, no, no. That puts me in mind... Mr. Hamilton is still in London. I will have your father pen him a letter that you are there staying with your aunt and would welcome a call from him."

"Mother! You will do no such thing! I will have some self-respect." She stood to her full height. "If you will excuse me. I have a headache and will retire to my room." Lizzy huffed down the hall, stopping to knock on her father's study.

"Come in, Lizzy."

"Papa, how did you know it was me?" she asked, closing the door behind her and crossing the room to sit in her chair.

He chuckled and lay his book down. "My dear. Just because I choose to sit in this room all day does not mean I am unaware what occurs outside these walls." He smirked and removed his glasses before steepling his hands in front of him. "Now you would like me to tell your loving Mama to allow you to stay home while Kitty travels to London to unwittingly secure our fortunes as the next Mrs. Darcy?"

"Yes. Well, no. Although, Mama's machinations are unorthodox, they are not my concern. I worry about Lydia."

"Lydia? What trouble has my youngest been brewing?"

Lizzy sighed at the mirth in his voice and attempted to help him see reason. "Papa, you must see that she is setting herself and our family on a path of ruin. Traipsing alone through the countryside with young men whose character may be in question."

Mr. Bennet clucked his tongue. "Oh, my Lizzy. I believe you are concerned with matters which have no merit. No intelligent man, which Mr. Wickham appears to be, would saddle himself with the silliest girl in all of Hertfordshire."

"But, Papa. You must understand…"

"No, my dear," he said replacing his glasses with a wry smile. "Your mother has insisted she knows what's best for our daughters in issues of matrimony. She wisely chose me so how can I argue with her logic?" A snicker came forth from his usually sardonic face. "Now, be off with you, my girl. You have packing to do."

"Miss Elizabeth, how fortunate we were leaving for London on the same day of your own departure."

"Yes, very fortunate," Lizzy replied, stifling a grimace as she wondered what Mr. Darcy must think of her. Her own thoughts were interrupted when she noticed he was looking upon her expectantly. "Pray, did you say something?"

"Only asked after your comfort. Are you well?"

"Yes."

Across from Lizzy, Kitty and Georgiana were whispering to each other, as Mrs. Annesley slept beside her. According to Kitty, although Georgiana was not as relaxed as she had been on previous occasions, Wickham's failed plan had not succeeded in unnerving the girl over much.

"Miss Darcy seems to be holding up well," Lizzy murmured softly to Mr. Darcy.

"I am so thankful for Miss Katherine's guidance to Georgiana and her wonderful example of all that is proper set by her elder sisters."

Lizzy felt her cheeks warm at the praise, then averted her eyes so he might not notice how much his compliment affected her.

"William," Georgiana interrupted. "Can you believe Kitty has never had a croissant? I believe Cook must make some along with her delicious scones while my friend is visiting."

"I agree, Georgie. Cook's delicacies are not to be missed."

The two girls fell back into conversation as Mr. Darcy leaned to Lizzy and whispered, "I am grateful that Georgie seems to have gotten over her most trying moments. Again, I am forever grateful to you. And Miss Katherine."

"Mr. Darcy, as your friend, it was nothing. I am certain you would have done the same had the situation been reversed."

"Undoubtedly."

"You have already proven yourself useful. Rescuing damsels in strange estates with only a hair pin. I am positive you would do so much more."

"I would do anything for a friend." He looked directly into her eyes, making her heart skip a beat, and she wondered what he meant by it.

The heat running up her neck caused her to look away but she was cooled in an instant as she noticed Mr. Darcy's thumb distractedly caress his watch.

CHAPTER 11

During previous generations, Cheapside might not have been the most fashionable of addresses. Over time, with the *nouveau riche* making names for themselves in trade and other business ventures, the neighborhood began a resurgence of prosperity. Elizabeth briskly walked toward her aunt and uncle's home after having spent a pleasant hour rambling through the park adjacent. Lizzy held the hand of her youngest cousin, Michael, and her maid followed.

"Come along, little one. I am supposed to be home shortly to accompany your mother on a visit to an old friend."

He looked up at her perplexed. "But, Lizzy, you are not very old. Why would you go visit old people?"

"No, silly." She laughed at his little face upturned in a question. "She is not old but has known your mother for a very long time. They grew up together at Lambton. We will, however, be visiting with her grandmother, as well." She squeezed his little hand and pulled him toward the house. *Aunt says Mrs. Worth's grandmother worked at Pemberley. It would be lovely to hear stories to tell Georgiana.* "Come Michael, we must hurry."

"But I'm tired from running after the ducks." His hand tugged her back and she modified her pace.

"And what purpose would there be in our dallying? Are you to finish your sums with the governess when we arrive home?"

His look belied her assumption and she laughed aloud. "Oh, Michael. I believe you and I are kindred spirits. Speak to me of history or literature and I will listen for hours. Recite sums or equations, and I will fall asleep," she whispered, wrinkling her nose.

"Yes, Lizzy. Please don't make me go back. Can't we go to the shop and buy some sweets? I will share." She looked at his entreating face and leaned down to tussle his hair.

"Unfortunately, Master Michael, we both have to play the part of a grown-up."

"But I don't want to be growed-up. I'm only five!"

Bending down to her young cousin as they reached the edge of the path, she said, "If you promise to not complain while doing your sums, I will ensure you have one of Cook's lemon cookies waiting for you."

"You will, Lizzy?"

"Yes, of course. Now," she said, picking up their pace, "let us return to your mother's home." *For I am anticipating an interesting day with Mrs. Worth's grandmother.*

Colonel Fitzwilliam looked around the sitting room and breathed a sigh of relief that his aunt Catherine was meeting with her solicitor.

His cousin Anne was pouring his tea and he could not catch her eye. "My dear Anne. We have spoken of your time in London, your visit to the theater, and all that has occurred since I was last here two weeks ago."

She smiled. "We have yet to speak on the lovely London weather. Do you believe the smoke and fog will hinder our entire stay in town?"

He chuckled. "If we are lucky, we may yet see more dark clouds on the horizon."

She let out a most unladylike snort and covered her mouth. "No, my mother is not expected back until after luncheon."

Richard let out a whoop and slapped his knee. "You are *filled* with impertinence. I forgot you had it in you, my Annie."

Her eyes locked onto his at the familiar name before she lowered her lashes. "You have not called me that since we were children."

He stood and walked over to sit on the sofa beside her. "No, I have not, and I should have...every day for the last fifteen years." She sat with her mouth agape, her eyes not leaving his. "Your mother interrupted our last conversation, Annie. You never answered my question."

"Question?" She breathed slowly, while her teacup seemed to rattle as she returned it to its saucer on her lap.

He took her empty hand in his. "Annie girl, do you want to marry Darcy?"

"I...I" Her words were stopped by the shattering of the tea cup as it slipped from her lap and onto the floor. She only hesitated a moment before summoning a maid.

After the maid departed, she faced Richard who was grinning boyishly. She cleared her throat and sat back down, before dropping her eyes. Her voice betrayed her anxiety. "Richard, I…"

"Mister and Miss Darcy," Thurston announced, opening the door and walking into the room.

"Blast!"

Anne immediately started and walked toward the fireplace before turning to face the door.

"Richard!" Georgiana squealed, rushing to him and throwing her arms around his neck. "Oh, pardon me." Seeming to remember herself, she stopped and her arms dropped quickly. "It is so lovely to see you. When did you arrive home?"

"Just this morning, poppet." He embraced his young cousin before clasping Darcy's hand. "I came as soon as I was able to get leave and will be here for a se'nnight." As the ladies quietly greeted each other, he said to Darcy in a low voice, "When can you apprise me of the situation you alluded to in your letter?"

"Tonight, after dinner, if you are available? Actually," he interjected, "I would rather not discuss it in Lady Catherine's home. It is of a sensitive nature." At his cousin's questioning look, Darcy continued. "Why do you not return to Darcy House with us? Your room has been ready since you left and Georgiana would welcome your lively disposition."

"Lively? Mother said that you have had two unmarried ladies staying with you these last few weeks. Is that not lively enough?"

"Two unmarried ladies at Darcy house indeed. Miss Katherine Bennet is a friend of Georgiana's and would have dined with us this evening if she had not taken ill earlier today." Darcy cleared his throat and flushed. "And Miss Elizabeth Bennet is her older sister. She is staying in Cheapside with her uncle and aunt and has visited a number of times. But no, she does not reside with us."

"Oh, how interesting." He smirked. "And how often is a number of times? Once? Twice? Maybe daily?"

Darcy cleared his throat again, before looking up at his betrothed. "She has mostly visited when I have been at the club or conducting business. Anne," Darcy said, interrupting his and Richard's conversation, "you are flushed. I believe you are standing too near the fire."

Richard looked at Darcy's awkward interaction before allowing a seed of hope to take root in his breast. *Curious. Who is this Miss Elizabeth Bennet?*

"It was unfortunate you missed Mr. Hamilton by only a few minutes," Mrs. Gardiner said to her niece.

"Yes," said little Ellen. "He waited for you for almost half an hour." Her large hazel eyes, blonde ringlets, and sweet countenance were so reminiscent of Jane!

"And what are you implying, Miss Gardiner?" Lizzy teased her young cousin.

"You have a beau, Lizzy." Ellen began to giggle, as did her little sister. They were quickly shooed out of the drawing room by their mother with an admonition to find their governess and continue their studies.

Lizzy excused herself and ran up to her room to change her clothes and grab her reticule. *Yes, it would be presumed I have a beau.* After the maid finished buttoning her dress and left the room, Lizzy said to her reflection, "I am sure he will make an offer at some point. Unfortunately, it will probably be after little Ellen is out of the schoolroom and Michael has returned from Cambridge." She laughed at her own cheek and tied the bow on her bonnet before hurrying down the stairs and out to the carriage with her aunt.

"…or the time we read the book about Edward Teach…"

"Blackbeard?" Lizzy interjected.

"Yes, Elizabeth, Blackbeard. Cassandra and I were fascinated by him," Mrs. Gardiner said before taking a sip of tea.

The three ladies were sitting in the parlor of Mrs. Worth's townhouse in Portman Square, reminiscing their past. The two older women had met by happenstance at a modiste the week before after having not seen each other for several years. The reunion was a happy one, one which they had decided to continue after discovering both of their husbands were in trade and had even partnered in a few ventures together.

"Yes, Miss Bennet, we were. Can you imagine? Two silly, English school girls passionate about a brigand. You see, my second eldest brother was in the Navy and would come home and tell us stories of pirates and treasure which would send our land-locked minds racing with adventure."

Madeline Gardiner laughed at her friend's response. "Cassie, remember when we walked all the way to the woods of Pemberley, certain the elder Mr. Darcy had buried a treasure there?"

"We were so determined to find it, we did not notice the light fade, the sun set, nor even when the moon was high in the sky?"

"We got our ears boxed for that one!"

"Yes, we did." Mrs. Worth chortled. "Please excuse me but my goodness, your aunt and I had some wonderful adventures together."

Lizzy set her cup down on the table. "How did you get home that night? The night you were digging in Pemberley's woods?"

"The elder Mr. Darcy was riding out in the woods returning from a tenant's home. At the sound of approaching horses, we stopped immediately and jumped in our freshly dug hole."

Mrs. Gardiner interpolated, "It was quite large, you see. We had been digging all day long with no intention of stopping."

"As they came nearer, Madeline began to sneeze, startling the horses and the elder Mr. Darcy."

"What happened?" Lizzy asked, astonished. "Did *he* box your ears?"

"Mr. Darcy?" Cassandra Worth asked. "Oh, no. Never Mr. Darcy. He was a kindly man. He did have us scared to death though. Made us get out of the hole and asked if we were poachers."

"Poachers?"

"He was teasing us, of course, but we did not know then. Can you imagine what we must have looked like? He recognized me immediately, as my grandmother was one of Mrs. Darcy's abigails."

She indicated the elderly woman staring out the window next to her in a chair.

"What did Mr. Darcy do?"

The two women chuckled. "He said he was going to call the magistrate. He was certain we were pirates hiding a treasure on his property," Aunt Gardiner replied.

"He alarmed us with that assertion. I was certain the King would lock us up in the Tower and my father would have to come to London."

"He then asked if we were the young girls the village was in an uproar over, and we both knew right then that anything Mr. Darcy threatened us with would be far better than the punishment we would receive when we arrived home."

"Yes, but in any event Mr. Darcy put us on Master Darcy's pony then brought us directly to Pemberley where we were turned over to my grandmother, who took us in the kitchen and *she* boxed our ears. He then ordered the carriage for us and gave my grandmother leave to see us home."

"You knew the younger Mr. Darcy?" Lizzy asked in surprise. "You have never mentioned it before, Aunt."

Madeline Gardiner snickered. "I would not say I knew him. He was several years my junior and we were of a much different sphere. However, Cassandra was in the family's company numerous times."

"I was." She turned to look at Lizzy. "They were the best of people. Mrs. Darcy was so beautiful. And she and Mr. Darcy were so in love. As you know, very often marriages in those circles are for financial gain only. I can attest that Mr. and Mrs. Darcy truly loved each other. His heart was broken when his wife died, and he never remarried."

Mrs. Gardiner nodded. "I remember that, Cassie. It was so sad."

"Yes. After Mrs. Darcy's death, my grandmother retired. Granny was so shaken by the loss of her mistress. That, and" —looking up at the elderly woman— "she had begun getting what the doctor called 'cobwebs' in her mind. My father felt it best she come and live with us in Lambton. Upon Father's death, and Mother moving to Kent to be nearer her sister, Mr. Worth was so good to allow her to move in with us here in London. It has been quite an adjustment, but we have managed. Is that not so, Gran?"

Mrs. Smith turned to her granddaughter and offered a distant smile, looking past them all. Her blue gown was styled from a bygone era. Her widow's cap fit loosely over her neatly arranged hair and her fingers tapped rhythmically on the arm rests of the chairs.

"We were just talking about Pemberley," she said raising her voice in her grandmother's direction. "And Lady Anne Darcy."

Cassandra Worth was met by a blank stare, and she gently smiled and reached over to pat the older woman on the hand. Turning to Lizzy and Madeline Gardiner, she said quietly, "We feel as if we have lost her already. There are moments when the cobwebs clear, but those are more and more infrequent."

After a moment, Madeline said, "My other niece, Katherine, has become particular friends with Miss Georgiana Darcy. She is actually staying at Darcy House, and she and Elizabeth will be accompanying the Darcys to the theatre tomorrow evening."

"How wonderful! Did you hear that, Grandmother? This young lady, Miss Elizabeth Bennet, knows young Master Darcy."

"Yes, Mrs. Smith," Lizzy said, turning to the little lady with wispy, white hair. "We have enjoyed the company of the Darcys for the last few weeks. They are a wonderful family. Might I give them your regards?"

The three women waited in silence for any response from the older woman, but when there was none, Lizzy smiled and turned back to Mrs. Worth. "My sister and I are quite delighted to accompany the Darcys tomorrow to the theatre, as we have never sat in a private box before."

"Won't there be speculation with Mr. Darcy accompanying you, Miss Bennet? Might we see your names in the Examiner soon?" She sighed dramatically. "Imagine, the future mistress of Pemberley drinking tea in my parlor."

"Pish-posh. Stir your tea, not your imagination, Cassie."

"But I think I will share a secret. It is not common knowledge but as you have a connection with the family, and it will be announced next week, I am sure I can tell you, Mrs. Worth."

"Only promise not to say a word, Cassie, until it is known to the public."

"Of course. As you recall, of the two of us, I am able to keep a secret."

Her friend smiled at the gentle barb as Lizzy continued. "Mr. Darcy is to be married to his cousin."

"His cousin? I was unaware Lord Matlock had a daughter. I believed there were only two sons: the Viscount and a son who had a commission in the army."

"No, not those cousins," Madeline Gardiner said. "What was the young lady's name, Lizzy?"

"She is Miss Anne de Bourgh, the daughter of Lady Catherine de Bourgh, his mother's sister. It had been the wish of both their mothers..."

The women recoiled at the cry from behind them. Turning, they saw Mrs. Smith standing in front of her chair, her eyes boring through her granddaughter's. "No, Cassie, no! Run to Pemberley at once and get Mrs. Darcy. Tell her he did not listen. We need to get the letter. I left it on the desk by the quill. Hurry, you must hurry. Get the letter."

Mrs. Worth spoke in a soothing voice and gently reached for the older woman. "Grandmother, what letter?"

The fragile woman collapsed back into her chair, put her face in her hands, and began to rock, sobbing like a child. "She said no. She said no, Cassie. I wrote it. I wrote it. Where did it go? She loved him and she told him no."

"Who, Grandmother? Who? You must calm yourself. Who?"

"Wills. She said, 'No.' He was her joy!" Tears poured from the aged woman's eyes and her sobs were uncontrollable. "It is on her desk. I put it on her desk. It is my fault. Get Mrs. Darcy, quickly. Or the master. Get Master Darcy at once. He will know what to do! And don't wake the baby!"

Without a moment's hesitation, Madeline Gardiner stood. "Cassandra, I think we will take our leave."

"Wait, Madeline. I will get the maid." At that moment, a young woman came rushing in. "Please take Grandmother to her room, and I will be up shortly to help give her medicine."

"Aye, ma'am."

Turning to her guests, Mrs. Worth said, "Madeline, Miss Bennet, I apologize. This has only happened once before, and that was in regards to a memory about my grandfather. I cannot understand how talk of the Darcys would cause such an outpouring of emotion."

"Nor could I," Madeline agreed. "Who is Wills?"

"I believe that is the name Mrs. Darcy called the young master before her death. But what letter can she be referring to?"

"Whatever it was meant very much to your grandmother. You know how some in their later life blend the past with the present or even confuse events." Madeline placed a comforting hand on her friend's arm. "Cassie, let us know if there is anything we can do."

"Promise you will come and visit again."

"Of course," both ladies said together.

"And Miss Bennet. I look forward to reading the society pages in two days' time of a certain Mr. D from the North and a lovely Miss fresh from Hertfordshire."

Lizzy smiled at her jest. "If we are, it will merely be to identify the paupers a benevolent Mr. D has taken to the theatre."

"Lizzy!" Mrs. Gardiner tutted at her niece. "Thank you again," she said as they made their way to the door. "We wish you a good day and your grandmother a restful night."

"Oh, thank you, Madeline. And I wish you, Miss Bennet," she said with a grin, "a lovely evening at the theater and the distinction of being identified with the most eligible bachelor in all of England."

Anne de Bourgh knew she was not a beautiful woman. Since the time she was in leading strings, she could only remember her mother, father, and even Nanny Flora remark how very plain she was. She looked down at herself as the carriage passed fashionable young ladies walking toward Hyde Park and grimaced.

Lady Catherine had returned to Rosings only that morning in response to an express from her gamekeeper. Soon after, Anne told the butler she was to meet Colonel Fitzwilliam at the new exhibit of ancient Egyptian artifacts and then dine with him before returning home. Despite the uncertainty in his eyes, he remained silent. *I sympathize for the poachers but hope their trial is of some duration.*

She leaned back in the carriage and glanced again at the women walking together, chattering away. How she wished she too had a confidant. Though she might confide in Georgiana, her cousin was much younger. *I am sure we would have nothing in common. She is so youthful and vibrant.*

Anne shook her head and whispered, "I have never felt young in my whole life." She looked across to Mrs. Jenkinson, her companion, who was already drifting off to sleep on this short carriage ride. *And how am I to feel young?* She smoothed her hands over her skirt. *I have the finest clothes, but they are for a woman more than twice my age. A London dowager would not be happy in these fine frocks. And my hair*—she reached up to touch the severe style her lady's maid had arranged that morning—*I might as well be wearing a widow's cap. How could I imagine that Richard would ever notice me?* "Enough!" she declared, startling Mrs. Jenkinson from her slumber. She grabbed the cane her mother kept in the coach and banged on the roof for the driver to stop.

When the footman alighted from the coach and opened the door, Anne ordered with all the authority as her mother's daughter, "To Madame Claudette's."

❧

Hours later, Anne strode up the stairs with Mrs. Jenkinson's harping beside her: "Hold onto the banister" and "Walk slowly, lest you trip." *I will not trip! Today is the rebirth of my existence. I have tasted freedom from my mother and will not fall back into the miserable world I have always known. This is how it feels to be my own mistress!*

She almost whistled while walking through the door and only stopped short at the sound of a raised voice from the sitting room. Her bravado left her, and she stood paralyzed before sinking into a chair in the hall.

"Has she returned?" Lady Catherine called at the servants laden down with packages alighting the stairs to their young mistress's room. "Where is she? Anne?"

With a rustle of silks and the clicking of shoes, in stormed her mother with a concerned Colonel Fitzwilliam behind her. "Where have you been, girl? Get up out of that chair! It is for the servants!"

Anne rose from the seat, attempting to maintain her dignity and air of assurance. "Mother, what are you doing here? I believed you to be at Rosings!"

"And is that why you were off gallivanting throughout London? Well, thank heavens the carriage wheel broke and we returned for the barouche. You might have been kidnapped and taken to Gretna Green! Then where would we be? Darcy would refuse to marry you…"

"Mother, there is no need for these hysterics," Anne replied with forcefulness. "I merely went out to shop."

"Unaccompanied?"

"Of course not! Mrs. Jenkinson was with me, and we went to Madame Claudette's. I must return in two days when the new fabric arrives from the drapers. I was quite safe."

"Why would Thurston say you were off to view the exhibit with Colonel Fitzwilliam, and yet he is here waiting for you with me?"

Anne looked from the retreating butler to the scattering maids before catching the eye of her cousin. "Why, I—"

"Yes, I was to meet Anne and her companion but was detained at White's. My dear cousin was only consoling herself with feminine pleasures upon my obvious lack of manners."

A grateful smile stole across Anne's countenance as Lady Catherine whipped around to the colonel.

"And you could not have informed me of this while I was waiting? While the house was in uproar?"

"I am truly sorry, Aunt. Allow me to make it up to both of you by accompanying you on a walk in the park?"

Lady Catherine sputtered. "A walk in the park? Have you no sense? A walk in the park will not do. Anne is more fatigued than is good for her. I will have to cancel my travel back to Rosings tomorrow to assure her health improves."

Panic was evident in Anne's voice. "Oh, Mama. You are all kindness, but I assure you that is unnecessary. Do not allow this misunderstanding to halt your responsibilities."

"It was fortuitous that I returned when I did."

Richard swallowed a chuckle before replying in a serious tone. "I can assure you I will do all in my power during your absence to guarantee Anne's safety."

"Including no delays at White's?" She made an inelegant snort before continuing on her tirade. "That is all well and good but I will contact Darcy without delay. He is her affianced and has the responsibility to ensure her protection. You" —she sniffed, waving a hand— "are merely her cousin."

This was not the first time Richard had been easily dismissed from his aunt's notice nor was it the first time Anne felt the sting for him, but he turned to her and gently smiled before responding to Lady Catherine. "As you say. However, I am certain Darcy has matters of business to attend to for the next few days while I am a man at leisure."

Lady Catherine harrumphed. "You had better be prudent, girl. But, with Richard here to look after you, I will continue with my plans and leave on the morrow."

Anne silently exhaled the breath she had been holding and allowed her mother to titter on about everything and nothing at all, as she followed both her cousin and matriarch into the drawing room.

CHAPTER 12

"What a lovely night to attend the theatre," Lizzy whispered under her breath stepping out of the carriage and taking Mr. Darcy's hand. "I only hope our country manners do not cause whispering, sir. Will not members of the *ton* believe you have been accosted by wild savages?" She laughed softly at his arched brow.

With careful consideration, he smiled, leaned down, and whispered in her ear, "My dear Miss Bennet, you *must* be unaware that I am bringing *you* amongst the savages."

She laughed at his wit, drawing attention to their little party. As all eyes bore down on her, she was grateful her aunt Madeline had loaned her a gown acceptable for a night in the private box of Fitzwilliam Darcy of Pemberley. The blue, crepe silk with ribbon embroidery was more sophisticated than was her custom, and the fine carriage and the elegant man escorting her gave Elizabeth courage, elevating her amongst the other theatre goers—above what she could ever have imagined.

It is true, Mr. Hamilton is a handsome man, but he does not have the presence which Mr. Darcy has. Nor even the inclination to escort me to events! Although I am allegedly marrying him.

She wrinkled her nose at the unwelcome thought. Only the day before her young cousin apprised her of the conversation she had overheard between Mr. Hamilton and her aunt.

The idea that he told Aunt I am too headstrong and must be taught to bend to others' wills? Insufferable! When did Mr. Hamilton become such a tyrant? I might be obstinate but I know my own mind. How can I be shackled to someone who believes me wanting in so many ways?

"Miss Bennet, what troubles you?"

"Pardon?"

"There appears to be something disturbing your thoughts."

He released her arm but she remained highly aware of his hand at the small of her back as he gently guided her away from the arriving crowds. Kitty and Miss Darcy followed.

"No, sir. I assure you, I am fine." Her voice remained calm, attempting to ignore her rising frustration as she realized her world would never be as she hoped. "Pray, lead us to your box."

"Miss Elizabeth." Her name on his lips was so soft she found she had to lean toward him to hear his words above the din of the crowd. Inhaling his scent, she heard him say, "I assure you, leaving the theatre would by no means suspend any pleasure of my own. As your host, I mean to ensure you are well taken care of. If you desire to leave, then we shall depart."

She observed her young companions standing a short distance away from them. Miss Darcy looked blithely at the smartly dressed crush but Kitty was in awe of her surroundings. She had never been to the theatre and certainly not with the possibility of sitting in a private box.

"No, sir. I thank you for your concern, but I can assure you there is nowhere else I would rather be."

He nodded and took her arm. "Then let us take our seats. The play will begin shortly."

She smiled at the picture she imagined the four of them presented: the Darcys and their mystery guests. Lizzy had heard whispers when Mr. Darcy handed her out of the carriage, and the whispers had only continued as the four walked into the theater and up to their seats. Mr. Darcy said so only she might hear, "I imagine the hens of the *ton* have already had much to speculate on." He winked as they made their way up the stairs to the find their box.

In a matter of minutes, the lights dimmed and the curtain rose but not before Lizzy made an amusing observation. *Mr. Darcy's ivory waistcoat with blue pinstripes harmonizes so well with my own blue dress with gold ribbon, one might think his valet and my maid coordinated our attire.*

Lizzy, having been so engrossed in the performance, did not discern until the final act a purring from the two girls seated in front of her. Resting back against the cushioned chair, she inclined her head toward Mr. Darcy and was immediately enveloped by his scent. *A blend of woody, spice, and citrus?* "It appears our sisters have been touched by Hypnos."

He raised a brow. "Georgie has wanted to see this for weeks. I am surprised she could not stay awake."

Elizabeth stifled a giggle. "You obviously have not been kept up sharing secrets with a sister until the wee hours of the morning, sir."

His boyish grin made her breath catch. "Blessedly."

She felt his whisper on her cheek and feared the audience might hear her heart beating wildly, even over the laughter. *Elizabeth Bennet, you must not allow your romantic heart to rule your mind. He is an engaged man!* They settled back into their seats but not before Elizabeth leaned over to her companion again. "I will, however, say I am surprised at their falling asleep during Shakespeare."

"He is one of your favorites?" Mr. Darcy asked, his breath causing the curls to brush up against her neck.

She rubbed her arms to hide the gooseflesh before replying softly. "Yes. But I am partial to his sonnets. I have considered poetry as the food of love."

Mr. Darcy nodded as the final scene reached its comedic climax before leaning toward her. "Of a fine, stout, healthy love it may. But if it be only a slight, thin sort of inclination, I am convinced that one good sonnet will starve it entirely away." He leaned back and crossed his leg at his knee, carelessly nudging her own knee. Then he tipped his head back to her and whispered, "Would not all women appreciate the words of the Bard if they were dedicated to them?"

She struggled to control the quiver in her voice. "I presume it would depend on the sonnet the man chose."

Darcy nodded a response. Moments later as she attempted to follow the production, he murmured, "My mistress's eyes are nothing like the sun; Coral is far more red than her lips' red."

A mischievous smile spread across her countenance as she whispered back. "If snow be white, then her breasts are dun; if hairs be wires, black wires grow on her head."

Much to her delight, Darcy continued the recitation. "I have seen roses damasked, red and white, but no such roses see I...in her cheeks." He softly cleared his throat before tugging at his cravat.

Her heart beat wildly. She felt Darcy's eyes intently on her as she whispered, "I love to hear her speak, but well I know, that music hath a far more pleasing sound."

"Miss Bennet." Slowly, Elizabeth turned her head to him. "I...grant I never saw a goddess go; my mistress when she walks...when she walks..." He looked down at his hands before looking back at her face. "She walks in beauty like the night, of cloudless climes and starry skies; and all that's best of dark and light, meet in the aspect of her eyes..."

They both started at a movement from the chairs in front of them. "Oh, Wills," Georgiana giggled, turning with Kitty to face them both. "You were both doing so well until you started quoting Lord Byron. Did you forget the rest of the sonnet? It is really one of Shakespeare's best."

Elizabeth could only feel her already inflamed cheeks burn at being discovered. Darcy only sat up straighter before admonishing his sister for her cheek.

Or will one good sonnet starve love entirely away?

⁓

"And what did you think of the evening's performance, Miss

Bennet?"

Lizzy and Mr. Darcy stood in the entrance hall as a maid removed her wrap and took her gloves.

"I enjoyed it very much. It is a new experience for me to delight such a luxury as a private box, but one I could get used to. There was no better seat in the house, unless I were to go down and play Kate to the Petruchio on stage." He laughed and guided her into the music room behind Georgiana and Kitty.

"Miss Bennet, I assure you, that although your lively spirit has been evident many times, you are no Kate."

"I feel there are others who would disagree with you, sir." She thought of her mother and then Mr. Hamilton, and a cloud passed over her countenance. As if reading her mind, Kitty spoke from across the room.

"It was a surprise to see Mr. Hamilton tonight, was it not, Lizzy?"

"Yes, it was. But not all surprises are meant to be unpleasant."

"What did he say to you when he drew you away from us? He looked very animated, indeed."

"He inquired after our parents and told of his communications with his housekeeper at Ashby Park. Nothing of consequence."

That seemed to pacify her younger sister, who turned back to Miss Darcy. Elizabeth looked out the window to the night sky, lost in thoughts. *Animated? He was trying to school his frustration with me. How I should have asked him to accompany us to the theatre or chosen to stay at home! Should he have not made the offer himself? We are not engaged nor are we courting. He has no right to make such presumptions. I am out in the company of friends. I am beginning to believe Mr. Hamilton is one of the last men I could ever be prevailed upon to...*

She shook her head and quickly allowed herself to be drawn back into the room.

"Shall we go in to dinner?" Mr. Darcy asked when a footman appeared at the door. "Cook has prepared a masterpiece for us this evening."

"I am famished, William, and do hope Cook made extra Shrewsbury cakes so I may sneak some to my room tonight." Miss Darcy giggled.

"So, we have a thief in our midst, do we?" He held out his arm to Lizzy as the two younger girls followed behind.

"We did it," Kitty blurted out before Miss Darcy could stop her. "We did it, and we took the strawberry preserves."

"Oh no!" Miss Darcy gasped, laughing at her friend. "It is only a game Wills and I play. Cook always makes extra cakes and keeps them in the larder for me to take at night, then reports to my brother that there is a thief."

Kitty's pink cheeks were indicative of her embarrassment, and she attempted to regain some ground by turning to Mr. Darcy and with no little grandeur asked, "And how did you enjoy the play, sir?"

It was all Mr. Darcy could do to contain his laughter to embarrass the girl further when the door opened and Colonel Fitzwilliam was announced.

"Richard!" Mr. Darcy beamed. "What brings you here?"

"I was at the theatre in Father's box and saw you leave. I wanted to come and see who your charming guests were but missed my opportunity in the crush. Knowing Cook had most likely prepared something divine, I hurried over to satisfy two desires: my hunger and my curiosity."

"Fitzwilliam, may I introduce Miss Elizabeth Bennet of Longbourn in Hertfordshire and her younger sister, Miss Katherine Bennet."

Colonel Fitzwilliam bowed to the ladies before following them into the dining room. "And who is that young woman with golden hair? She does look familiar, but much too grown up to be little Georgie."

"Oh, Richard." Miss Darcy harrumphed and rolled her eyes. "Will you ever cease your teasing?"

"Never, Georgie. When I cease to tease, you should be concerned." He flashed a toothy grin before taking his first sip of wine. "Now, Miss Katherine. How did you enjoy the theatre this evening?" he asked as the first course was brought in.

"I have never been to the theatre before nor seen such a lovely display of jewels."

"Ha! Yes, I will agree with you. The ladies were dripping tonight, were they not, Darcy?"

"I could not say I noticed," was his reply.

"Oh, I did," Miss Darcy said. "Everyone looked so elegant. It was as if the Season had begun early this year."

"Oh? And what do you know about the Season, little miss?" Lizzy grinned at Miss Darcy and unconsciously met the colonel's gaze. He continued. "What say you, Miss Bennet? Do you believe the women were over-trimmed this evening?"

She smiled thoughtfully before replying. "I believe ladies are resolved to act in a manner which will constitute their own happiness, without reference to anyone other than themselves. If attention can be drawn by a few cleverly displayed baubles, then so be it. However," she said, cocking her head to the side and arching her brow, "would a woman truly want a suitor who would merely notice her for her wealth?" She smiled again. "Yet, I do believe ladies enjoy things that are beautiful and distinctive. I confess, I fall into that category."

Her light laughter flitted about the room as Colonel Fitzwilliam nodded his accord. While Miss Darcy began to regale them with tales of her Italian tutor who had arrived earlier in the day, the colonel looked distracted.

"What say you, Fitzwilliam?" asked Miss Darcy.

"Pardon?"

"I asked if your parents are in good health."

"Yes. They are in perfect health and would have gone with me to the theatre tonight but Mama had a headache." He took another sip before continuing. "I had asked Anne but Aunt Catherine refused to allow her out of doors after her shopping excursion yesterday, fearing her health would take a turn before the great event."

"What great event is that?" Mr. Darcy asked at Colonel Fitzwilliam's raised brow.

"Only your wedding."

"Of course." Mr. Darcy took a long draught from his wine glass. "And is Anne in good health? She appeared well enough when we visited."

"She is fine."

When the white soup was finished, the veal consumed, and Cook's lemon tarts were gone, Mr. Darcy rose. "Let us go directly to the music room. Georgie, would you play for us?"

"Of course," she said linking her arm with Kitty's. "Miss Katherine and I have been practicing a duet we would love to play for you."

"Do you think it is ready? You are a much stronger player than I."

"Oh posh," her friend chastised. "Your playing has improved so much over this last month. I believe it almost rivals mine."

"Miss Darcy! What a falsehood." Kitty laughed.

"Then she is a true friend, Kitty." Elizabeth smiled. "To promote your ability above her own. And," she added in an exaggerated whisper, "to tell a falsehood to bring you comfort? You have met someone who values your heart and feelings as a true sister would."

"Miss Bennet," Colonel Fitzwilliam interrupted as Kitty and Miss Darcy moved to the pianoforte. "Am I to understand that you believe telling a falsehood is acceptable if it is for love?" He sat down in the chair next to her and leaned forward awaiting her answer.

"Now, Colonel. You would paint my character in a most unflattering light if you actually believed that. True love should not need lies, however an occasional falsehood to protect someone you love may be permissible. But remember, my statements are in theory only."

"Theory, Miss Bennet? Are you saying Cupid's arrow has never pierced your heart?"

She chuckled at his comment. "No, sir. I have not had the pleasure." Her eyes dropped, before glancing at the two girls giggling at the instrument.

"What say you, Darcy? Do you agree with Miss Bennet? Have you felt the arrow from Eros?"

Mr. Darcy had been caressing his watch and quickly snapped it shut when his cousin spoke to him. "What?"

"Do excuse me." Lizzy walked toward the girls. "I am so sorry," she said to the young musicians. "How can you play with no one to turn the pages?"

Fitzwilliam watched her go and from the corner of his eye, saw Darcy's eyes follow her retreating figure. *So, she is not mercenary and is quite indifferent to discussing money or wealth. She is not silly nor does she have any propensity to be such. It appears Darcy is not blind to this treasure of a woman. Blast that letter from his mother.* He swallowed the last contents from his glass when Darcy asked, "What trouble are you trying to stir up, Richard? Leave Miss Bennet alone. She does not need to be exposed to your base humor."

"Darce, I was merely attempting to sketch her character, nothing more. Besides, I am sure Cupid has been nowhere near the confines of your heart."

"What does that mean?" Darcy snapped, setting his glass down and glaring at his cousin. "If you are implying…" He ceased his tirade when he realized the music had stopped and all three ladies were staring at him. "Excuse me. Richard, might I speak to you in the study?"

"Ah, yes. Ladies," he said before bowing, "if you will excuse us."

When the clock struck half past the hour, Lizzy felt it was time for her to take her leave.

"Miss Darcy, might you call for the carriage? The hour is late and I do not wish to worry my aunt."

She stood to leave but Kitty cried, "Oh, Lizzy, will you not stay?"

"Oh, yes," Miss Darcy exclaimed. "Please stay, Miss Elizabeth. I shall have a room prepared near Miss Katherine's."

"We can stay up and tell stories, like you and Jane do. Oh, please?"

"I thank you for your offer but do not want to inconvenience your household at this hour."

"It would be no inconvenience. We shall send a footman to your aunt with a message and he can return with a bag. Tomorrow we can go to the shops."

"Please, Lizzy?"

As Lizzy began to make her excuses, she felt his presence behind her. "What is this you both are pressing Miss Elizabeth about?" Mr. Darcy asked with a smile in his voice. "Come Miss Elizabeth, I am sure you must agree to whatever their plan is; you will not get a moment's peace until you do."

"See, Lizzy? Even Mr. Darcy agrees with us."

"That I do." He leaned his head down close to her ear, and in a stage whisper asked, "And what am I agreeing with?"

"The girls—" she counted to five to steady the frisson in her voice that his breath on her neck caused "—the girls would like me to stay at Darcy House this evening. I assured them it was much too late and would be too much of an inconvenience."

"But it will not," Georgiana interrupted. "William said so himself. He agreed with us, did you not, Brother?"

"I...well..."

Then the colonel chimed energetically. "Oh yes. That is what I heard, poppet. Your brother invited Miss Bennet to stay. As it is late, I agree with your brother."

"I thank you, Miss Darcy, but Mrs. Annesley is not in residence. Did you not say she was helping with her grandson this evening? It would be highly inappropriate."

"Yes, that is true," Darcy replied clearing his throat. "It is unfortunate, but there you have it."

"But, your wonderful housekeeper is here. I am certain Mrs. Noyes' presence would stifle any gossip which could occur," Colonel Fitzwilliam said with a glint in his eye.

"Wonderful! She is to stay," Miss Darcy cheered. "I will have one of the maids make up your room at once."

"And let's not forget the extra Shrewsbury cakes out of the larder," said Kitty.

The two girls excused themselves and raced out of the room arm in arm, giggling the whole way.

"I too must depart," Colonel Fitzwilliam said, bowing to her and shaking his cousin's hand. "Pleasant dreams." To her mortification, she saw him wink at Mr. Darcy before he strolled out the door, leaving the two in silence.

After listening to the ticking of the grandfather clock, Darcy said, "And here we are again, Miss Bennet. Alone in a music room."

Lizzy looked up at him through her lashes as she sat on the couch. "Yes, sir. But this time there is no rain and no Sarah." She straightened her skirt and looked nervously about the room before resting her eyes back on his face. "If you will allow me to apologize, sir. Please forgive the girls for trapping you into their plan."

"Miss Bennet, I am not a man who easily falls prey to the manipulations of young ladies, even my own sister." He offered her a lazy smile that made her cheeks warm. "If I wanted to avoid the situation, it would not have happened. However, I did not like you departing so late. And so, you are our guest for this evening." They sat in silence for a while, before he asked, "Miss Elizabeth before you go partake in the mischief of young ladies, might you play the song you played at Ashby Park for me again? It is one of my favorites."

"Truly?"

"Yes. I...it reminds me of Pemberley."

"As you wish." She rose and walked to the piano where she sang the sweet Irish ballad again. In the third verse, she looked up and caught him studying her, his eyes penetrating hers, causing a shiver up her spine, before she turned back to the instrument and closed her eyes, singing the melody.

At the conclusion, Mr. Darcy's eyes were closed and he did not move. *I believe he is asleep. Poor man. He has had a long, arduous month.*

At the sound of the piano bench scraping backwards, Mr. Darcy opened his eyes, and quietly asked, "Were you going to sneak away without saying goodnight, Miss Bennet?"

"No, sir." She started at his voice. "I thought you asleep."

"I do not believe I could ever fall asleep in your presence."

"Sir, I—"

"I was merely remembering my mother. It was she that would sing that song when I was a child. I have not heard it since her death."

"I am sorry, sir."

He held his hand up. "It gives me nothing but joy to hear it again. My mother was a wonderful woman, as I believe I have told you before. That song connects me to her again when I feel I need her most. Please, stay."

She allowed herself to sit in the seat next to him and said, "That puts me in mind... I had the opportunity to meet a former maid from Pemberley. A Mrs. Smith?"

"Smith? Pemberley has always had a number of Smiths in our employ." Her brows furrowed but he continued. "And did this Mrs. Smith have positive things to say about my family?"

"Why, yes, Mr. Darcy, she did. Well, she was not quite...well she... It seems Mrs. Smith's granddaughter is my aunt's friend, and we visited them both yesterday at their house in Portman Square. Mrs. Worth, her granddaughter, has had the care of Mrs. Smith since she began to suffer." *How can I say this delicately?* "From what they refer to as cobwebs in the brain. She apparently served your mother as a lady's maid?"

"Mrs. Hazel Smith?"

"I believe so...well, she was with your mother when she passed."

"Yes, that would be her. Such a good woman. My mother truly cared for her."

The room was quiet but for the ticking clock.

"There was a strange occurrence when we visited."

"Oh?"

"When Mrs. Worth found that I was acquainted with you, she teased me about attending the play with you... and might she see our names linked in the paper?" A hint of smile appeared on Mr. Darcy's lips, and Lizzy could feel heat rise from her bosom to her ears but continued with her confession. "And so of course, I corrected her and explained you were intended for Miss de Bourgh. And then Mrs. Smith became exceedingly upset."

"How so?"

"She kept saying things, wild things. Finally, she had to be taken upstairs."

"What exactly did she say?" He leaned forward with his hands clasped and his arms resting on his knees.

Lizzy took a breath and blew it out before responding. "She was wholly upset and became quite insistent that we were to go to Pemberley and get your mother. That Mrs. Darcy had said no. That the letter was on her desk. That your mother loved you, and you were her joy."

Mr. Darcy was quietly still. "My mother always said that to me, that I was 'her joy.' I had almost forgotten about that. But what letter? What can she be speaking of? I only know of one letter during that sad time."

"I know not, sir."

"Miss Bennet, do you think Mrs. Worth would be averse to us paying her a call in the morning? I would like to speak with Mrs. Smith."

Darcy climbed the stairs balancing the tray of chocolate in his hands. The cook seemed surprised when he had come to the kitchen requesting to deliver the treats himself to his sister and her friends but said nothing.

As he approached Georgiana's door, he heard an uncommon amount of giggling from within. He smiled and was about to knock when he heard his sister's voice.

"Oh, please, Miss Elizabeth will you not play?"

"You must call me Elizabeth, but I do not know if I should play. 'Candor and Courage' does not sound like a game for an older woman preparing to embark on a future of respectability and structure."

"Oh, Lizzy," said Miss Katherine, "you are not so very old. Please play our game."

"Yes, Elizabeth," Georgiana said hesitantly. "A friend from a neighboring estate at Pemberley plays it all the time with her sisters, and it is so enjoyable. Though I have never actually played." The girls again fell into a fit of giggles. "And you must call me Georgiana."

Darcy knew better than to listen to the private conversations of ladies but was intrigued.

"Very well, Georgiana," Miss Elizabeth said. "I am at your disposal. What are the rules?"

"When it is your turn, you choose either 'candor' or 'courage.' If you choose the first, you must tell us the truth, no matter what question we ask. If you pick 'courage,' you must have the courage to do whatever we ask of you."

Darcy thought he heard trepidation in Miss Elizabeth's voice when she asked, "Anything?"

"Yes, anything," Georgiana answered giggling. "Within the realm of decency, of course."

"Of course," agreed her equally giggling companion.

"Well, then let us begin. Who is to go first?"

"I will," Miss Katherine exclaimed. "And I choose candor."

Georgiana asked if there was a gentleman who Miss Katherine admired. The girls cackled like chickens as the game continued. Darcy stood in the hallway listening, afraid to break this magical moment.

He shook his head determined to make his presence known, after hearing not only the examples of candor but also the courage of his sister hopping on one foot while singing "God Save the King."

As he was about to knock, Georgiana said, "All right, Elizabeth. Candor or courage?"

"Candor. I refuse to subject myself to hopping on one foot singing Heaven knows what!"

As their laughter dwindled, Georgiana said, "Very well. What do you think of—"

"Mr. Darcy," interjected Miss Katherine.

Darcy's hand froze in mid-air before he knocked. He held his breath, waiting for her reply.

"I am…I am uncertain of your meaning."

"Well," came Miss Katherine's voice. "What do you think of Mr. Darcy? Do you find him handsome?"

"Kitty, that is highly improper! You cannot ask me such a question!"

"But that's the game, Lizzy," she whimpered. "You would answer if Jane had asked you."

The question seemed to hang in the air before Elizabeth replied. "I agreed to play this game. However, Kitty, you must admit that in the past your ability to keep things of a sensitive nature *private* has not been reliable. You and Lydia delight in gossip."

"You are correct but I have changed. You have seen how I have changed. I promise I will not reveal this conversation to anyone."

"Nor will I," said Georgiana. "Now, Elizabeth, will you answer the question?" Darcy swallowed and felt the blood pounding even in his ears.

"Do you find Mr. Darcy handsome?" asked Miss Katherine.

Seconds ticked by. Darcy thought she was refusing the question and then, "I believe Mr. Darcy to be one of the most handsome men of my acquaintance."

"Are you in earnest?"

"That's the game, is it not?"

Darcy heard a tremor in Elizabeth's voice and he rested his hand upon the door.

"More so than Mr. Hamilton?" Miss Katherine asked.

More silence filled the air before Georgiana continued. "Remember, we will not breathe a word of this to anyone. The words spoken in this room will remain our secrets until we are dead."

Darcy smiled at his sister's dramatic tone.

"Yes. Even more than Mr. Hamilton."

"Would you say," Miss Katherine said, "that if Mr. Hamilton and Mr. Darcy both asked for your hand in marriage you would refuse Mr. Hamilton in favor of Mr. Darcy?"

"Kitty! That is much too impertinent of a question, even from you. Besides I answered your one question and will not answer another!"

"Oh, I wish you would," whispered the malingerer in the hallway, still holding the now cold chocolate.

"Oh, I wish you would," echoed Georgiana.

Darcy panicked for a moment, worried that his sister might have heard him.

"Georgiana, I..."

"No, Elizabeth. You mistake me. I love my cousin Anne and know that her marriage to my brother is a good match. However, I do not believe it was fair of my mother to dictate who my brother was to marry without giving concern for his feelings. What if there is a much better love match for him, but yet he has never had a chance to meet her? Or maybe he already has, but there is no hope?" Her voice trailed off and silence filled the room.

Darcy's throat constricted at Georgiana's words. *Have I been that transparent? Can even my young sister see my true feelings?*

"Georgiana, you must not think that—"

"I know, I know. My brother is to wed Anne, and you are soon to become betrothed to Mr. Hamilton. I am sure he is a good man, but please forgive me my fancy. I have never had a sister, and since our first meeting have not only been jealous of Kitty's fortune but dreamt of having it for my own as well."

Darcy could listen no more. His emotions were in turmoil recognizing his sister's true feelings and how they were so similar to his own. He was a man in love with a woman he could not have.

Regaining his composure, he lightly knocked on the door.

Light spilled from within Georgiana's room as she exclaimed, "Wills! What are you doing here? We thought you were the maid come with our chocolate!"

He ignored the slight quaver in her voice and the quick look to Miss Elizabeth as he entered the room to set down the service. "Good evening, ladies. I am at your disposal for your chocolate needs, however, I am afraid I was detained on a matter of business, and I regret it is now cold."

He finally brought himself to look at Miss Elizabeth whose face had turned a dark pink as he handed her a mug. "Cook also sent up some cakes, so you can attest for yourself what my younger sister was willing to begin a life of crime for."

Miss Elizabeth smiled nervously, and pulled her robe up closer to her neck, all the while peering at him.

"I thank you for your thoughtfulness, sir, but believe I am to bed now. I do not wish to consume such a delectable treat, and then have to deal with vapors of bad dreams. Even Chanticleer's true love knew the problems which food could cause."

"Are you too, a pilgrim, Miss Bennet? Off to find your salvation at Canterbury?"

She smiled at his reference and shook her head. "No, sir. My salvation cannot be so easily had, for I must do more than ride to a cathedral and rely upon others to give me strength. I must save myself." She waited a moment before standing and turned to her hostess. "Georgiana, my dear, I am to bed. Thank you for such an entertaining evening." She embraced his sister and Darcy heard her whisper, "Not a word." Georgiana grinned and nodded, while Miss Elizabeth embraced her own sister as well.

"Miss Elizabeth. I was hoping to retrieve the missive for Mrs. Smith's granddaughter. My man was going to deliver it in the morning. Is it ready?"

"Why yes, Mr. Darcy it is. Shall you wait here while I get it?"

He shook his head. "No, I am for bed as well. Would you mind very much if I wait in the hall?"

"Very well. Good night, girls." After Miss Elizabeth closed the door, a gale of laughter could be heard as they walked down the hallway to her room. She cleared her throat before she said, "I am down this way, sir, in the green room."

"The 'Woods' room," he said, more to himself than to her.

"Pardon?"

He chuckled. "It is a green room, but my mother called it the 'Woods' room when I was a child. She told me that there were fairies and nymphs that once came with us from Pemberley and escaped from the carriage only to find that room. They felt so at home, they refused to leave. But, have no fear, Miss Bennet. They are kind folk and will only sprinkle fairy dust in your eyes to help you sleep better. They will do you no harm."

"That is good to know."

"And the room your sister is in…"

"The yellow room."

"Yes, the yellow room. That was called the 'Sunshine' room. Mother said that only bright and joyous things could take place in there as the rays of the sun first touch that room in the morning and bring a warmth to it before any other room at Darcy House."

"What a fanciful character you are."

He grinned.

"Yes. I had never heard of a master of such a grand estate who believes in fairies, woods nymphs, or carries up chocolate to his sister. No, he is austere, drinks excessive amounts of brandy, and wastes his time at the gambling tables."

Darcy chuckled as they stopped in front of her door.

"I hope my jest did not offend, sir. My mother says that I am too impertinent for my own good. I will retrieve the letter."

Before he could respond, she darted into her room. When she returned with the note, her eyes seemed cautious to meet his. "Once again, I apologize for my poor jest. Good night."

"Miss Bennet," he interrupted before she could close the door. "I hope you do not believe all men are as you describe them, and I must apologize for my sex if that is the only example you have known."

"Well that is what the Bard would have me believe. And, as you say, I am no Kate waiting for Petruchio." She turned to close the door before stopping and quietly said, "And that is why I must save myself."

CHAPTER 13

"It is unfortunate that Mrs. Smith is unwell. According to Mrs. Worth's letter, she hopes her grandmother will be in good health soon."

Lizzy folded the letter and looked up at the gentleman sitting across from her.

Mr. Darcy's countenance fell at the news. He stood and walked over to stoke the fire on the chilly October day. They had both broken their fast and had waited in the drawing room for the reply from Portman Square regarding their visit. "I only wish I knew what she was referring to. I doubt it is the letter signed by my mother. I have read that letter and am aware of its contents."

"Perhaps there was another?" Lizzy suggested, laying the note down on the table next to her.

He nodded. "Yes, Miss Bennet. I am sure you are correct."

"Correct about what, Wills?" Georgiana asked while entering the room with Kitty.

"I have discovered Miss Bennet has met a mutual acquaintance of ours, a Mrs. Smith, who was Mother's lady's maid. She was *correct* that the elder woman had worked for us at Pemberley."

"How do you know her, Lizzy?" Georgiana asked expectantly. "I adore hearing stories about Mother."

Lizzy glanced at Mr. Darcy and gauged his countenance before subtly nodding. Remembering the events of two days past, she thought, *How am I to tell this young girl what she wants to hear?* Taking a deep breath, she began, "She is the grandmother of my aunt's childhood friend from Lambton. Mrs. Smith is of an advanced age and does not remember things as she once did. However, she did recall your mother was attentive to your brother, and also how she cared for you. It was an endearing picture she painted of the short time your mother had with you. Forgive me if I speak out of turn," she said, looking back to Mr. Darcy and raising her eyebrows in question.

"Not at all, Elizabeth," Georgiana replied for her sibling. "I very rarely learn things of my mother. I find it lovely. It is as if I am getting to know her even if through other's thoughts and experiences."

"And that you are, poppet." Darcy walked to Georgiana and kissed her on the forehead. "And now, if you will excuse me, I have some business to attend. Are you ladies still planning on spending the morning shopping before returning Miss Bennet to Gracechurch Street?"

"Yes, sir we are," Miss Elizabeth replied. "However, do not think you will be rid of me so easily, as Miss Darcy has accepted my aunt's invitation for dinner tonight, and you of course, were included in the request."

"Dinner?"

"Oh, Wills, I forgot to mention it to you. Do you have a previous engagement?"

"Not at all, Georgie. I would be delighted."

"Mr. Darcy, if it is too short of notice… We would not want you to appear at a disadvantage without preparation to exhibit yourself. I believe Georgiana said you sing?"

The sparkle in her eyes made his heart thump in his chest. *The minx!*

"Oh, look at the time," Miss Katherine cried at the gong on the half hour. "Your appointment at Madam Claudette's is in thirty minutes. We must leave."

"Miss Katherine." Darcy smiled. "My dear sister has become quite a loyal customer to Madame Claudette. I can assure you, you will not be turned away, no matter what time you arrive."

"And yet, we must depart, Wills." Georgiana pecked his cheek. Both Miss Elizabeth and Miss Katherine curtsied before they turned to walk from the room.

"And Miss Bennet?" he said, catching her attention as she prepared to leave. "You have been misinformed by my sister. I do not sing—"

"Sir."

With a straight face, he continued. "I play the bagpipes."

Miss Elizabeth's laughter was joined by his only to be interrupted by the butler. "Mr. James Hamilton of Ashby Park to see you, sir."

Miss Elizabeth gasped, then schooled her expression.

"Please, show him into the study."

The younger girls quickly looked at Miss Elizabeth only to be met by a hint of a smile from the older girl. "Let us leave Mr. Darcy to his business, girls."

"Do you not wish to greet Mr. Hamilton, Lizzy?"

"Of course, Kitty. But we must not be late for Georgiana's appointment. Besides, last night he stated he would be calling at my aunt Gardiner's soon." Turning her attention to Darcy, she said, "Good day, sir. We look forward to your arrival this evening."

"As do I, Miss Bennet. Good day."

After she exited the drawing room, Darcy heard the greeting in the hall between Miss Elizabeth and her almost betrothed. He waited until he heard the ladies depart, then counted to fifty before joining that gentleman in his study. "Good day, Hamilton. What brings you to Darcy House?" he asked, entering the room.

Standing to shake his hand, Hamilton replied, "I am come to ask about Ashby Park. If you have time, might I seek your advice?"

"Yes, of course. Might I also compliment you on your excellent staff from when I was caught there unprepared two weeks past? They are a credit to you, James. Now, can I offer you something to drink?"

"No, thank you. But I am grateful to hear my staff responded well to your unexpected arrival."

"Now, what can I help you with?" Motioning for Hamilton to take a chair, Darcy sat behind his large mahogany desk and asked, "Is there a crisis?"

"No, no crisis. Only a piece of business. With your expertise, I was hoping you could offer me proper guidance."

Darcy smiled. "How can I be of service, old friend?"

"Well, as you know, I am planning on offering for Miss Elizabeth Bennet shortly…"

"Yes," Darcy replied, digging his nails into the palm of his hand. "You informed me as much when we met in Hertfordshire. I cannot offer you any advice in that field, my friend. But I am surprised you have let it go this long."

Hamilton chuckled. "That I know. As I said then, I am hoping to tie this business up. A small piece of land abutting mine has become available, and I am inclined to purchase it."

Darcy nodded as the man continued. "There is a stream, forty acres of farmland, and a small working mill. I have not seen it myself, but my steward has recommended the transaction."

"Well, if your steward recommends it, you need to ask yourself if you trust your steward. If the answer is yes, then you must follow his counsel. Surely, he would not lead you astray."

Hamilton nodded. "You are right. I should—"

Both men turned as the door swung open and Colonel Fitzwilliam entered the room unannounced.

"Darcy, what a lovely sight I just beheld departing Darcy House. I see Miss Bennet took Georgiana up on her offer and remained last evening?"

Hamilton shot a look at Darcy and both men stood.

"Miss Bennet? My Miss Elizabeth Bennet?"

"Yes, of course. You saw her leave the house just now. She is a friend of Georgiana and the Bennet sisters were her guests last evening."

"Last evening, after I saw you with her at the theatre?"

"Yes."

"I imagined she had just met your sister for an early day of shopping." He stood and began pacing. "Do you know—" Hamilton snapped "—what it would do to her reputation if it were discovered she had slept at the home of an unmarried man?"

Darcy bristled at the insolence. "Sir, I have lived with the eyes of the *ton* on me since birth. I am well aware of the dangers of tittle-tattle amongst the *ton*. If I had any qualms…the Bennet sisters would not have been permitted to stay. I have my own sister's reputation to protect. Everything was done well within propriety."

Hamilton seemed to regard him warily, then nodded. "I thank you for your consideration. I would not want the lady I plan to marry to be regarded as anything less than respectable."

The men stood in silence for a few seconds with Hamilton glancing out the window before looking back to Darcy. At last, Darcy asked, "And when shall I finally be able to wish you joy?"

"Soon. With the acquisition of this other property, I can have a dowager house built for her mother and sisters should the need arise. My plan is almost at an end."

"Do you mean to say you will not offer for her until the home is complete?"

"Yes. What if the worst should occur before then? I cannot stomach the idea of residing under the same roof as her female relations, saving Miss Jane Bennet, of course. Can you blame me? You yourself have been exposed to them."

"But you had grown up with them. I would assume you could manage their oddities more than most."

"Just because I could does not mean I wish to."

His small smile was likely meant as a bridge between both men, but all Darcy saw was the censure of Miss Elizabeth in his eyes. "How can you dangle about? The albatross that is the mother cannot compare to your protection! You rent a home in London for Mrs. Bennet. Or you secure Longbourn from whoever is to inherit until the dowager house is complete. You should not risk losing the prize for these mere excuses."

"As you say. Well…" Hamilton extended his hand, interrupting Darcy's treatise. "I must be off, Darcy. Thank you for your time. And your counsel."

"Very well, then. Good luck on your endeavors."

After Hamilton exited the room, Richard poured himself a generous drink. Darcy raised his brow at his cousin.

"After what I just witnessed, I would imagine you could use something to calm your nerves as well."

"Calm my nerves…?"

"What was that about, Darcy?"

Darcy waved his hand dismissively. "Only some estate advice. He had a question about some land to purchase. That is all."

"Oh?" Richard took a drink and studied his cousin as he sat on an ottoman. "Well, if it is nothing, then let me continue on my vein of thought. How lovely to see Miss Bennet this morning!"

Darcy's eyebrows raised again, then he relaxed as a slight smile played at the corner of his lips.

Richard watched Darcy for a moment longer. "I have been ruminating on your future with Anne. Do you not think it would be appropriate for her to come by Darcy House more often to acclimate herself to her new home? She should begin to choose colors for the mistress's chamber and take up her role as the future lady of Darcy House."

Darcy then rose and walked to his bookshelf before choosing a tome. "You are right, Richard. There are only two months left before the marriage. Perhaps I need to concern my own efforts on preparing for my future."

"The banns have not been read, have they?" Richard swirled the liquid around in his crystal glass and eyed his cousin.

"No," Darcy said over his shoulder. "Aunt Catherine wants it to be done with special license so we can choose our date immediately with respect to Anne's health in the winter. I did not fight her decision."

"You never do."

"Pardon?" he asked turning to face his cousin before reclaiming his chair.

"I said, you never do. You never fight anyone's decision."

"Your point?"

"And why not?" Richard asked him, slamming his hand down on the arm of the chair next to him. "Why not?"

Darcy stared at his cousin, speechless.

Richard stood and set his glass on a small table. "Why? Why do you not fight for want you want? Why do you simply accept your duty?" Richard threw his hands up in the air. "Darcy, you are one of the most powerful men in England. You are a brilliant land owner. You have increased the capital of Pemberley and holdings in the five years since your father's death—more than in either your father's lifetime or that of your grandfather's.

"You are unwilling to accept less than perfection for your home, for Georgiana, from your staff…why would you not accept perfection for your own life?"

"Richard, I…"

"Do you love her?"

"Who?"

Colonel Fitzwilliam sat across from Darcy, leaned forward with his elbows on his knees, and sighed before looking up at his cousin. "Yes. *Anne*. Do you love her? Do you really love Anne?"

Fitzwilliam Darcy of Pemberley had been raised to hide his feelings. He was allowed the freedom to express his joy and fears as a child but with the loss of his father, duty and responsibility took the forefront of his life. He looked up at Richard and said nothing.

"My dear cousin," Richard said. "I am not the only one who knows your secret."

"Anne?" Darcy asked, darting to his feet. "Please tell me Anne has not perceived it."

Richard harrumphed. "How can she not? When you are in her presence, you hardly speak to her unless it is in regards to the weather or her health. You show little interest in her."

"Who would know her likes or dislikes other than her mother? And still, I can assure you that even Lady Catherine is unaware of Anne's favorites."

"Her favorite what?"

"Anything. Painter, author, color. Who would know those things? She would have to speak to learn any of these."

"Some might say learning such things are a necessity to a happy marriage."

Darcy shook his head. "Well... Honor and duty is all that is required of me to fulfill a lifetime of marriage."

"What would your mother say? Your father?"

Darcy threw up his hands and paced around the study. "It is my mother's wish so I assume she would agree."

After a moment, Richard cleared his throat. "Da Vinci."

"Pardon me?"

"Da Vinci. Anne's favorite artist is Da Vinci. Her favorite author is Shakespeare. She especially likes his comedies. But her favorite artist is Da Vinci."

"And how do you know this?" Darcy slowly walked to his desk and sat down, studying his cousin intently.

Richard met his scrutiny directly. "I asked her."

"You did?"

"Yes."

Darcy let out a deep breath. "And why Da Vinci?"

Richard waited a moment before answering. "Because he is not only an artist but an inventor, mathematician, and scientist. Anne found a book about Da Vinci's experiments and was enthralled by his discoveries. She has a very sharp mind."

Realization hit Darcy's as he wondered at his cousin's feelings for Anne.

They slipped back into silence.

"And where is this conversation to lead, Cousin? What has been going through your mind?"

Richard grinned and leaned forward in his chair. "Miss Elizabeth Bennet."

"Miss Elizabeth Bennet? I am not sure I understand your meaning."

"Do you not?"

"No, I do not." Darcy opened his ledgers and took up his quill. "Now, if you will excuse me, Richard, I have work I must attend."

"Work, eh? Very well, then, Darcy. If you want to hide away in your study and ignore what is happening in your world, that is your concern. But, you must realize you are affecting more than just yourself." Richard stood and walked to the door when Darcy cleared his throat.

"Richard. What would you have me do?" Richard turned to see his cousin resting with his elbows on his desk and head in his hands. "I cannot *not* marry Anne. You yourself know that is impossible. It is expected and common knowledge amongst the *ton.*"

"What does that signify? The ton? You are Fitzwilliam Darcy. The *ton* will cease their cackling with one word from you!"

"What about the scandal for Anne?"

"What scandal for Anne? She will claim her health has been poor, will return to Rosings, and all will be forgotten." Richard chuckled at the possibility. "What say you, Darcy? Do something for yourself, for once."

"For myself?" he mocked. "What have I ever done for myself since my father's death? I have responsibilities, Richard. There has never been a way out for me. This is my destiny. At any rate, it would be impossible for me to ask for Miss Elizabeth's hand. She is the daughter of a country squire with no connections, no dowry, and a vulgar mother. I... You must think me barbaric for my treatment of Anne."

"No, not barbaric. Just a man cornered who has accepted the fate others have condemned him to."

Darcy took a deep breath and set his jaw. "I must still marry her, Richard. It is my mother's wish. It is what is expected."

"Your sense of duty overpowers your sense of love?"

"Yes." He raised his chin. "Yes, above all things."

"Very well, then." Richard seemed to growl as he turned to the door. "I will see myself out and pray for your future felicity. And Anne's. I know she deserves it."

CHAPTER 14

T he sound of the bell as the door opened was overpowered by the lively chatter as the young ladies entered the modiste. Madame Claudette's was an exclusive establishment, one which Lizzy would never have dreamed to enter before she had made Georgiana's acquaintance. However, she was prepared to help her young friend select another lovely gown as a gift from her brother.

He takes such prodigious care of his sister, and although she has recovered with no noticeable scars from her almost elopement with Wickham, there are moments where I notice her withdraw in circumspection.

The girls were ushered in by a petite French woman. "Mademoiselle Darcy, how lovely to see you. We are so delighted to receive word from Monsieur Darcy to expect you and are so happy you have brought vos amis. You will be in the Lilac Room, where Madame Claudette will join you in a moment. Celine," she said, indicating the young girl following them, "will be at your service. If you need anything, let her know, s'il vous plaît."

"Perfect." Georgiana turned to Lizzy and Kitty. "Wait until you see. She thinks of everything." The three girls prattled as they were led down a long hallway and through a door into the largest modiste room Lizzy had ever seen. It was twice the size of her father's library at Longbourn and rivaled that of the small dining room at Darcy House. There were floor to ceiling mirrors on every wall and raised pedestals placed throughout the room. Lavender and buttercream draperies covered the windows. Fresh flowers rested inside crystal vases atop small marble-topped tables. The wall which their chairs faced had thick curtains cascading from the ceiling and pooling on the floor.

"This room is magnificent," Kitty whispered, sitting delicately on the edge of a chair and looking around in awe. "But, Georgie. Where are all the books?"

"Books?" Georgiana asked with a hint of a smile, sitting beside her friend. "What do you mean?"

"Why for all the patterns! How are you to choose dresses if you cannot see the pattern?" Lizzy asked.

At that moment, the curtains parted and out stepped a tall, elegant woman with striking features. "Mademoiselle Darcy," she said with a lilting, Gallic accent. "It is such a pleasure for us to see you today."

"Madame Claudette. May I present my friends? Miss Elizabeth Bennet. And Miss Katherine Bennet." The lady curtsied with practiced grace.

"What wonderful creations I have for you, I assure you, Miss Darcy. You will be delighted. Today, you will be the first in London to see my newest designs." With that, Madame Claudette clapped her hands and the drapery was pulled to the side and a young girl with Georgiana's height and coloring walked out in a pale pink, beaded gown.

"Oh, it is beautiful!"

"Georgiana." Lizzy turned to her young friend. "Is this how you select all of your dresses?"

"Yes. How else would I see her latest fashions?"

"That *is* wonderful." Kitty sighed. "Are there more?"

"Of course, mademoiselle," Madame Claudette said, clapping her hands again as the drapes drew aside to reveal another blonde young woman in a lovely lavender silk gown with pearl embellishments.

"Oh, Georgiana!" Kitty squealed. "That is the most heavenly dress I have ever seen! Look at the sleeves." The young lady walked closer to the girls and Kitty reached out and stroked the soft silk before resting her hands in her lap.

Georgiana, with a gleam in her eye, nodded at Madame Claudette to continue. Over the next hour, after having presented many gowns, the French woman smiled. "Miss Darcy, I must confess that I have one more dress." She glanced at Lizzy.

As Lizzy picked up her tea cup, the curtains opened again. "Oh." Her breath caught at the sight of the design before her.

The dark-haired young woman wore a deep burgundy silk with gold embroidered filigree patterns across the bodice and hem.

"It is exquisite," Lizzy said almost reverently. "Look at the beading on the sleeves. How they dangle so prettily against her skin."

Madame Claudette interrupted. "This dress is designed by my sister in Paris for a member of the royal family. This fabric was from an expedition to India. The Vicomtesse, however, felt it was un-French to wear a dress made from the fabric of a country supporting her enemy, and so her loss is our gain."

"Oh, Lizzy. You must try that on!" Kitty cried. "It would be so becoming on you."

Lizzy smiled at her sister's enthusiasm. "Kitty, this is not our appointment."

"Yes, let's try them on!" Georgiana cried. "I will try on the pink one. Kitty, you the lavender. And Elizabeth, this one is yours."

"Georgiana, surely Madame Claudette does not have time for us to try on dresses during your appointment—"

"Miss Bennet." The French woman smiled. "Miss Darcy can do as she likes. If she wishes for you to try on dresses, then that is my wish as well. Celine" —she beckoned to the young girl who had come in with them— "attend Miss Darcy and Miss Katherine. I will attend Miss Bennet."

Fitzwilliam Darcy was so grateful Miss Katherine Bennet had accepted his sister's invitation to Town. The reasons were numerous, but none more than seeing the girls happily off into the carriage for a day on Bond Street. He hated to shop. However, when he discovered his sister had unwittingly left her reticule behind, he was uncharacteristically predisposed to deliver it himself at Madame Claudette's.

Walking into the door, the smell of perfumes and the sound of female voices was everywhere. He had hoped to enter undetected, but his very presence caused a titter amongst the female patrons and most of the assistants as well. How often did the most sought after bachelor in all of London, nay England, appear in the most exclusive modiste without his sister?

"Monsieur Darcy, what a nice surprise. Might I escort you to Miss Darcy's private room?"

"Yes, thank you."

He was following the young woman, nodding quickly to acquaintances when he heard a soft but forceful, "William. What are you doing here?"

Startled, he looked into the face of his betrothed. "Anne? I was on my way to see you."

"At Madame Claudette's?"

"No, no." He stumbled over his words. "Georgiana forgot her reticule and I thought to deliver it on my way. How have you been?" He was surprised to see her in the blue silk and with such a glow in her cheeks. "You look lovely."

Anne smirked. "I am well, Cousin. And thank you. That is very kind. While mother has returned to Rosings, I have been shopping. You say Georgie is here?"

"Yes, with her friends. She is in a private salon." He shook his head in amazement and said, "I have never seen you so fashionably attired. It becomes you."

She gurgled at his surprise. "Thank you, Darcy, but please remember a woman needs to be flattered. Temper your disbelief."

He laughed heartily.

"*That* is why I could not speak with Madame Claudette. I was told she was with a very important client."

"Georgiana is here so frequently, I should offer to have a room built solely for my sister."

Anne chuckled at his jest. "What are your plans for the day? You have seen me now, so there is no reason to call at the house."

"I see. Ready to be rid of me so soon? Maybe I will take Georgie and her friends to lunch. Would you care to join us? Do you have a previous engagement?"

"No, I do not. I would like that very much. Thank you."

He extended his arm to her and they followed the young woman to the private salon.

"Tell me about Georgiana's friends. Richard was by earlier before he was to meet His Lordship at White's and said they are both charming. Very sweet and accomplished."

"They are true friends to Georgie, which she so rarely finds."

They were shown into the private room where two giggling girls stood, one clad in pink and the other in lavender. "Oh, Kitty, that gown is beautiful on you! Such a becoming color."

"Thank you, Georgiana. You look lovely as always." Miss Katherine was reverently fingering the pearled sleeves. "This dress is so…I have never worn anything so exquisite in my life."

"Well then Miss Katherine, the dress is yours." The girls turned in astonishment.

"Wills! Anne!"

"Madame Claudette. We will order all the gowns my sister likes as well as this one which Miss Katherine has fallen in love with," Darcy said, smiling at the proprietress.

Miss Katherine seemed stunned. "Mr. Darcy, thank you but I could never accept such a gift. It is too much."

"Nonsense," Georgiana said beaming. "It is the least we can do for my dearest friend. Anne, may I introduce Miss Katherine Bennet? Kitty, this is my cousin Anne de Bourgh."

"Miss Katherine, it is a pleasure to meet you."

At that moment, the curtains parted and a gasp escaped his lips. Standing before him was an ethereal beauty in burgundy silk.

"Lizzy, I have never seen you look so pretty in all my life!"

"Why, thank you, Kitty. I will try and see your words as the compliment they were intended," Miss Elizabeth said with a playful voice. "Mr. Darcy!" She colored prettily upon seeing him.

"Miss Bennet." He bowed, grateful for the moment to regain his composure.

"Elizabeth, you look lovely! Is that dress not the most becoming thing you have ever seen?" Georgiana squealed.

Darcy stiffly nodded his ascent before turning to Anne. "Anne, might I introduce Miss Elizabeth Bennet? Miss Bennet, my betrothed, Miss Anne de Bourgh."

"It is a pleasure to meet you," Anne said. She smiled serenely. "Miss Bennet, that dress is most becoming on you. I do not believe the queen herself could have looked so well in it."

"I understand it to be a castoff from Empress Josephine. Not French enough for her taste, I presume," she quipped.

"Oh, but you do look well in it."

"It is too bad we do not have an event for you to wear it to." Georgiana sighed.

"Oh, but we do," Anne said. "Aunt and Uncle Matlock are to throw a ball next week, and you are all invited."

"We are invited to a ball at the home of an earl?" Miss Katherine asked with wide eyes. "I can only imagine what Mama would say."

"Why is Aunt Ellen giving a ball?"

"It is our engagement ball, William," Anne said devoid of emotion.

"Of course."

"And you will undoubtedly garner the attention of many handsome beaus and jealous matrons, Elizabeth," Georgiana said playfully.

"Then it is a good thing I have no intention on buying this. I could not willingly take attention away from such a lovely couple at their ball!"

"Nonsense," Georgiana said. "I have never seen a more becoming dress in my life, and it will be my gift to you."

"Georgiana! That is too kind. But it is too much. I cannot accept."

"You cannot *not* accept a gift, Elizabeth. Can she, Brother?"

Darcy regained his wits and replied in the negative.

"Then it is settled. Madame Claudette, we will order all the dresses. Might these be ready in two days?"

"As you wish, Miss Darcy."

"Thank you. Now girls," she said turning her attention to the Bennet sisters. "Let us change for I believe if we use all powers of persuasion, we can convince my brother to take us for chocolate and cakes. Anne, will you join us?"

"Of course."

"It almost seems unpatriotic," Kitty said. "It is different when the cook at Darcy House prepares croissants but to be eating at a true French patisserie in the middle of London? I am worried Napoleon will come marching out of the back door and drag me to Paris!"

The delicacies were all the girls imagined they would be: croissants, petit fours, macaroons, éclairs, and cream puffs.

"I have never tasted cream like this! I wonder if Cook could replicate it."

Mr. Darcy chuckled. "The owner François uses only his grandmother's recipes and will not divulge them to anyone…not even for a fair price. Believe me, I have tried. Many a day have I purchased an éclair and a coffee to eat at White's. And Miss Katherine," Mr. Darcy said, smiling at the young girl. "François is an honorable man. Do not concern yourself that he is hiding foreign emperors in his kitchen."

"Not even the little emperor?" Lizzy smirked.

"His wife Marie would never allow it."

"Wills, would you escort us to the music shop? I would like to look over the new sheet music."

"Did I not just purchase you some last week?"

"Yes, but I would so like to purchase another duet."

"Very well," Mr. Darcy said rising. "Anne, Miss Bennet, would you care to join us or shall you wait here?"

Both women looked at each other before Lizzy said, "I believe I shall wait here, if Miss de Bourgh is not averse?"

"No, not at all. I am quite enjoying these macaroons."

"Very well. We will return for you." Mr. Darcy bowed to the ladies, not a little curious at the irony of the woman his heart yearned for and the woman he was to marry sitting in each other's company as he turned to walk out the door.

Once alone, a silence fell between the two women.

"And do you play, Miss Bennet?"

Anne de Bourgh was a puzzle. Lizzy had expected a woman full of condescension and haughty disdain for others—someone more like Caroline Bingley—someone who would parade her dominance as the future mistress of Darcy House. Yet, she did not.

"A little, and very ill indeed. I do not presume to delight as Georgiana. But, I do enjoy music. And you, Miss de Bourgh? Do you play?" As soon as the words were said, Lizzy remembered Mr. Darcy's confession of his intended's lack of accomplishments.

"Yes, I do. But, I prefer not to arouse anyone's anticipation in that area. Therefore, I am more apt to dissemble and say I am too unwell to play." The twinkle in her eyes caught Lizzy off guard. From all she had heard, Anne de Bourgh was sickly and spiritless. She had not expected such quick wit nor her dry sense of humor. Though she was a mousy thing, with very little presence, she had a quiet kindness which Lizzy sensed at once. *Maybe I could be friends with this woman? She obviously is intelligent and appreciates an intellectual humor.*

"Georgina has spoken very highly of your playing."

"Oh, she is all politeness," Lizzy replied.

"No, I am sure she is more than truthful." The corner of Miss de Bourgh's mouth turned up. "I do believe she might be showing a bit of partiality, but is that not why we adore youth so much? Their enthusiasm. Which as we grow older, we seem to lose?"

"You are quite an acute judge of character."

"I live a quiet life at Rosings. I prefer not to draw attention to myself. You have yet to meet my mother, correct?"

"I admit I have not had the pleasure."

Anne bit her bottom lip. "Well, some might say you are fortunate, Miss Bennet." Before Lizzy knew how to respond, Miss de Bourgh asked, "Now, what do you think of art?"

"And how is our Jane doing? Does her letter say if she and Mr. Bingley are still enjoying each other's company?"

Lizzy glanced up from the missive she had been reading and paused before she answered. "Yes. It seems she has not only dined at Netherfield Park several times since our departure but has also gone out riding." Lizzy furrowed her brow. "As well as a few shopping excursions to Meryton with Miss Bingley and Mrs. Hurst."

"Well, that is promising."

"Yes, it is. However," she said, setting down the note and rising to cross the room and look out the window, "there is something about Caroline Bingley I do not trust. Each time I was in company with her, I felt her condescension and censure. She feigns friendship to attain her end goal, of that I am sure. I have not yet determined what her interest is in Jane."

"Elizabeth, could it not be that Jane's sweet countenance has won over this woman? Is Jane to be punished because you and Miss Bingley do not have similar characters? Do not be so suspicious, my dear niece. Jane finds friends wherever she is because of her gentle nature. Those who would not do well with your spirit are quite comfortable with her tender heart. Do not begrudge her."

Lizzy shook her head. "You mistake my meaning, Aunt. I do not begrudge Jane, only... I believe that Miss Bingley's motives are not pure. But, no bother," she said, shrugging her shoulders, "as you say, I am much more suspicious than our dear Jane." She read more of the letter and said, "She also mentions her concern for Lydia's behavior. It has become so unpredictable that young Mariah Lucas is no longer allowed to be in her company." Lizzy bit the bottom of her lip. "It seems at the last assembly in Meryton, our youngest sister became more in her cups than ever and made quite a spectacle of herself with Mr. Wickham. If only Father and Mother could be prevailed upon to reign her in. She is ruining Jane's chances with Mr. Bingley."

"Is that what Jane has written?"

Lizzy turned from the window and sat on the couch. "Of course not. You know Jane. She is all sweetness and kindness. She claims Lydia has only grown more wild since Kitty left. She says that our youngest sister will soon see the error of her ways."

Aunt Madeline smirked. "And you know, my dear, your parents will never take pains to control her. She is too much as your mother once was, and Francis is remembering her own youth through Lydia."

"Of that we are all aware." *I must write to Father. With the incident with Miss Darcy not being made public, I am sure Father is unaware of the necessity of protecting our family from Mr. Wickham.* "I will write Father tonight to encourage him to check Lydia's behavior. If word is reaching London, I am sure it is elsewhere also."

At the sound of a carriage outside, Lizzy turned artlessly back toward the window. When the carriage continued past the house, she met her aunt's raised eyebrows with a tilt of her head. "I am only anxious to see Kitty and Georgiana. It has been several hours since I have been in their company. And I only wonder how they have occupied their day."

A knowing smile spread across Aunt Gardiner's countenance. "Of course. Anything else from home?"

"Mama writes of me securing Mr. Hamilton before I return, and if I scare him away, the regiment will be encamped for another month or two so I can find a young man there." Lizzy breathed deeply at the thought of the trial that was her mother. "I do not understand the union of my parents…"

"Remember, my dear. Often times in life, people do things they themselves cannot explain. Your mother was a beautiful woman who was quite enjoyable to be in company with, and your father enjoyed socializing decidedly more than he currently does. They complemented each other quite nicely."

"I can hardly imagine it."

"Yes." Madeline Gardiner crossed the room and sat by her niece. "However, there are often indications early in the acquaintance that people with different natures might not suit over time. There are signs of compatibility which should not be ignored."

"These signs you speak of…? Such as…if someone spoke of your obstinacy and had a desire to change you?"

Aunt Madeline took up her hand and held it between hers. "Yes, my dear it would. And, on that topic, your uncle has invited Mr. Hamilton to dine with us tonight as well."

Lizzy bit her lip while looking down at her hands. "I am not yet resigned to marry him. He has not asked me. But he is one of my oldest friends and he is a friend to Mr. Darcy. I will welcome Mr. Hamilton here tonight as a friend, and that is what he is. He has said nothing to me of his intentions."

"And my dear niece, would you accept the offer if it was made?"

Lizzy shrugged her shoulders before standing to complete final preparations for the evening. "Tonight will simply be dinner amongst friends."

∾

She could not look at Mr. Darcy. After the display by Mr. Hamilton at dinner, she was certain he was ignoring her as well to avoid another scene.

If only Mr. Hamilton had not acted so. But he had. James Hamilton had behaved like a possessive, green boy. *How difficult to remain civil to him when I was unable to converse with anyone else. And then to make a scene when he discovered he was not seated next to me!*

Lizzy blanched at the memory but was glad when her aunt sat beside her. In hushed tones, she said, "It has been quite an evening, has it not my dear?"

"Oh, Aunt. I know not how to make amends for Mr. Hamilton's slight on your excellent arrangements. I am mortified."

"It is not the most indecorous thing which has ever occurred to me. I only wish he would have had the sense to not show that side of his character in front of our guests. It does not paint him in a favorable light."

"Very ill indeed."

Sipping her coffee, her aunt continued. "I have noticed Mr. Darcy looks at you a great deal."

"I cannot think why. And he has not said more than five words to me the whole course of the evening."

"Elizabeth. A man does not have to speak to show his partiality. His eyes follow your movements and he is attentive when you speak. If he was not already engaged, I would suppose he was half in love already."

Lizzy swallowed her own drink, allowing the warm liquid to soothe her dry throat. "We are merely friends, Aunt. Nothing more. Mr. Darcy is an honorable gentleman who enjoys my friendship, and I his."

"I am sure that is all, dear girl, but please take care. More than one honorable man has been ruled by his passions and not his mind."

She thought back to his clandestine confession from Ashby Park and his watch with the beloved inscription. "And sometimes, dear aunt, men do know their own minds but must follow duty…no matter what choices they might wish to make. Either way, Mr. Darcy is as good as married, so it can be of little consequence to me."

Mrs. Gardiner nodded at the affectionate têt-à-têt between Kitty and Georgiana across the room, before whispering to her. "Mr. Hamilton had cause to be at your uncle's office this morning."

Lizzy narrowed her eyes uncertainly. "For what purpose?"

"He called upon your uncle to ask for permission to court you."

Taking a calm, steadying breath she continued. "What did my uncle say?"

"He asked Mr. Hamilton if he had spoken to you yet. He said that he had not yet but had known you all your life. Your uncle then deferred to you and your father for approval."

Lizzy's cheeks began to burn and her jaw tightened. Her fists clenched into balls in her lap, and she looked up at her aunt. "I am grateful to my uncle's forbearance in not assigning my fate, and assume I can only have you to thank for his intelligence on the subject. But, what am I to do when he speaks to me? I do not believe I wish to marry him."

Her aunt said nothing as she sipped her coffee.

"There was a time when the idea seemed pleasing but with regards to his recent opinions about my character, I will not marry a man who does not respect me or my person, no matter how secure I would be!" Her heart beat rapidly in a panic.

"I advise you, dear Lizzy, to have an open mind. Often men behave in ways they normally would not when jealousy intrudes. I am not counseling you to accept him," Mrs. Gardiner said, "merely suggesting you not make any rash decisions. He pays you a great compliment by singling you out. Make your decision carefully."

Then the parlor door opened and the gentlemen walked in to join the ladies. Mr. Gardiner smiled at his wife, Mr. Darcy leaned down to whisper something in Georgiana's ear, and Mr. Hamilton joined Lizzy, grinning with confidence. She welcomed him with a small smile.

"We did not expect to see you gentlemen so soon. Are the men not as stimulating conversationalists as we women are?"

"Not at all. I am thankful to return to the soft surroundings of your presence."

He smiled down at her and spoke to Mrs. Gardiner. "Might I compliment you on the delicious meal this evening? I have never had duck served quite like that before and if your cook would be so kind, I would love to attain the recipe for mine at Ashby Park."

"Of course, Mr. Hamilton. I will have it sent over to your townhome in the morning."

"Thank you." Looking intently at Lizzy, he said, "I want to make everything as comfortable as possible for the future. I do not wish to have anyone imagine I have not thought out all matters and small details."

Lizzy turned her head toward Georgiana and Kitty when her eyes momentarily met Mr. Darcy's. A shiver shot through her at the blackness in his eyes. Mr. Darcy walked to the window, clasping his hands behind his back and stared out in to the night.

After a few more minutes of genial conversation, Mr. Hamilton turned to Elizabeth. "Miss Bennet, will you not play for us this evening? I have heard little else that gives me such pleasure."

She bowed her head and gently demurred. "I thank you for the honor of the request, sir, but I am not inclined to play this evening."

James Hamilton's eyes widened at her rejection. "Come, Miss Elizabeth. Do not allow your false modesty to force me to ask again." His voice was teasing, but there was also an expectation in his eyes which made her uncomfortable.

"Pray, forgive me. I have a slight headache and regret my skills would be lacking this evening. Might we play cards instead?"

"I thank you, no. I believe the stakes would be too high for me."

Mr. Darcy had turned from the window to listen, while Kitty and Georgina had halted their conversation to hear the outcome. "Come,

Hamilton. She has already stated her reasons for not playing." Mr. Darcy said from the window. "Georgiana?" He nodded at his sister, who hesitantly stood.

"Mrs. Gardiner, Kitty and I have been practicing duets."

"Charming! Thank you."

James Hamilton's jaw tightened as he walked over to the sideboard where he took a drink from a footman. Mrs. Gardiner rested a reassuring hand on Lizzy's. *I should not have to perform for James Hamilton or any man! Had I wanted to play for him, I would have.* Her aunt's hand squeezed hers again and she realized she needed to regain her countenance.

Seething, she pasted a smile on her face and took a lesson from her aunt. *If she can sit here and be polite, surely I can bear his company for one evening!*

The following morning dawned sunny and warm. Lizzy was taking her exercise in the park across from the Gardiner's home when she rounded a corner hedge and nearly bumped into Colonel Fitzwilliam.

"Colonel! What brings you to Cheapside?"

"Miss Bennet! This is a pleasant surprise! I am here on business for my father and thought to stretch my legs. Might I accompany you?"

"Why certainly." Lizzy turned to her maid. "Hannah, you may return to the Gardiners. Colonel Fitzwilliam will see me back to Gracechurch Street."

As they strolled down the path, he said, "I have had the pleasure of being in company with your sister of late. She is quite a charming, young woman."

"Yes, Kitty has made it past the most trying time and seems to now settle into her role as a young lady. Georgiana has been quite a positive influence."

Colonel Fitzwilliam nodded. "I believe that my young cousin owes a great deal to Miss Katherine. And we are grateful for her goodwill."

Lizzy bent to smell the last of a late blooming rose. "I am grateful she chose to follow the correct principles which she had been taught and not allow a sense of silliness to guide her. I assure you, if my father saw Kitty now, he would not recognize her."

"You truly know not how your family has rescued the Darcys. My cousin will be forever in your debt."

"Mr. Darcy owes us nothing." Lizzy considered the small stream meandering through the park. "He is preparing for his marriage to Miss de Bourgh, is he not? I am sure that the gentleman has more pressing concerns than the family of a country squire."

"You believe that Miss Bennet?"

"Why, every new groom is always attentive to his new bride. And with the affection evident between the two... Surely after the wedding tour, Georgiana will reside with her new sister and brother and Kitty's companionship will not be as necessary."

He paused for a moment before responding. "I am in no doubt that my cousin has affection for Anne, however, as you know, marriages are not often formed from love. Surely, you must know theirs is not a love match."

"I apologize, Colonel, if I have spoken out of turn."

"No, no. I am just surprised my taciturn cousin has somehow allowed his affections to be so…forthcoming."

"Well, I have only seen them together once. Yesterday afternoon for chocolate and cakes. After a dress fitting. However, I know how much Mr. Darcy values her…gift. I have seen him looking at it fondly. In fact, he has actually told me how it is one of his favorite possessions. I think you have misjudged his affection for his cousin. Any man who would place so much value on an item must be in love."

"A gift, you say?"

"Yes, a gift. His watch. I only know of it because it was left in the library. At Ashby Park. When Mr. Darcy and I were confined there for several days. Because of the weather. And I happened to read the inscription. Attempting to discover the owner."

His eyebrows raised at this extraordinary speech. "Excuse me, Miss Bennet. Did you say when you were both confined at Ashby Park? Together?"

She felt herself blush at her uneasy explanation. "Yes. We were both trapped there in the storm. With my maid. And Mr. Hamilton's servants. I was unable to leave. And Mr. Darcy arrived in the downpour. Later I found my sister's note about Georgiana…"

"Yes, yes. Now that you mention it, I do recall Darcy informing me of *something* like that. But this gift?" Elizabeth turned her head and bit her lip but before she could respond, he said, "Would it be his gold watch? With Pemberley engraved on the front?"

"Yes. It is lovely. Since seeing it, I have wondered about the craftsmanship."

He clasped his hands behind his back. "It is lovely, Miss Bennet. You should ask my dear cousin."

"Ask your cousin?"

"Ask about the craftsmanship of the watch. At the engagement ball."

"Yes, yes, of course." She walked a few more steps before continuing. "And it was so kind of Miss de Bourgh to extend the invitation to my aunt and uncle. We are aware of the honor."

"Pish-posh. It was Darcy's wish that your family attend." As they approached the gates to the park, the colonel said, "I understand that Darcy received an express this morning from Bingley that Miss Bingley, Miss Jane Bennet, and he would arrive tomorrow."

"Jane is coming to London?" Lizzy asked brightening at the thought. "How marvelous. I did not know."

"I hope it was not meant as a surprise."

"I wonder if my aunt and uncle know. Oh, Colonel, you have brought much sunshine to my already sunny day."

He laughed at her exuberance and they walked on to the Gardiner's front steps. "It has been my pleasure, Miss Bennet. Until next time." He doffed his hat as she entered the house before he walked away, whistling.

CHAPTER 15

Darcy studied Miss Elizabeth's profile as her maid looked out the window of the coach. There was something very taking with the arch of her mouth and he wondered what it would feel like to run his finger along her cheek.

Miss Elizabeth turned her head and he felt himself blush being caught staring at her. Darcy cleared his throat while fidgeting with the edge of his hat. "I know, Mrs. Worth's letter stated she doubts her grandmother would reveal anything today, Miss Bennet, but I must see what she might know about a letter from my mother. If another letter might have actually existed."

"I do not want you to set your hopes too high, sir. I understand the cobwebs have not cleared her mind nor does the doctor expect better. It appears that her time is almost come."

"And yet, I cannot comprehend the reason for such an outburst as you described. And I would not forego the chance to meet with one so dear to my mother."

They continued on in silence as the carriage jostled over the cobblestone streets of London on the way to Mrs. Worth's house. Upon arrival, Darcy handed Miss Bennet out and escorted her up to the front door. They were shown into the sitting room by a butler while her maid was offered refreshment in the kitchen. Mrs. Worth put her needlework away and stood to curtsey.

"Good morning. Welcome."

"Thank you for having us, Mrs. Worth. Might I present Mr. Darcy of Pemberley?"

"How do you do, Mrs. Worth?"

"It is a pleasure to make your acquaintance and be in your company again after so many years."

"I thank you. I hope our visit is not too much trouble for you."

"Not at all, sir. I am honored to have you here. Some of my fondest memories from childhood involve Pemberley, the harvest ball, and your dear mother's kindness on more than one occasion."

"Your words are very kind."

Darcy sat on the sofa beside Miss Bennet across from Mrs. Worth and said, "Miss Bennet related the story of your pirate treasure in Pemberley's woods."

Mrs. Worth chuckled. "Yes, Mr. Darcy. Do you remember how your pony was requisitioned for Madeline and me to ride back to the great house?"

He shook his head. "I must confess, I do not. However, I do remember my father teasing about pirates getting lost in the woods and burying Edward Teach's treasure."

They both chuckled at the memory before Mrs. Worth continued. "I hope my grandmother can help you find what you seek today, sir."

"I do not know that I seek anything, Mrs. Worth. Possibly just a connection to my departed parents."

"Then, Mr. Darcy, if I may share a memory with you. Even if my grandmother is unable to replicate what she told Miss Bennet, in the very least you will be able to leave my home with a fond remembrance."

"I thank you."

Cassandra Worth grinned. "Your father was a wonderful man and your mother one of the most beautiful and compassionate women I have ever encountered in my life."

"That she was," he said softly.

"Her charity within the parish as well as your own tenants was well respected amongst the people of Lambton."

Darcy only nodded as she continued. "There was one day when I was but six years of age, I walked to Pemberley to deliver something to grandmother. I went in through the kitchen and Cook told me to wait while a maid went up to find her."

"Mrs. Baxter?"

"The very one! She made the most delicious candies and it was close to your father's birthday, and your mother had ordered some as a surprise."

"Yes, Father had quite a sweet tooth."

"Mrs. Baxter gave me a few and told me to sit in the corner, then promptly went back to work. Like all young children, I was restless and wanted to explore the vast hallways and rooms of Pemberley. My grandmother spoke so much of the house that I must have felt as if I was intimately connected with all its occupants.

"Waiting until Mrs. Baxter moved to the pantry, I crept up the servant's stairs and ended in the music room where your mother was playing the loveliest song, 'The Rose of Tralee.' I was mesmerized by her voice. I had never heard anything so beautiful in my young life. I sat down in the corner and listened to her play song after song and eventually fell asleep. Your dear mother found me. She spoke kindly while delivering me to my grandmother. I remember she smelled of lavender and roses."

"Yes, she did." Darcy leaned forward in earnest and said, "Thank you for sharing that story. I cherish such remembrances of my parents. I must also thank you for the opportunity to speak to your grandmother. When Miss Bennet informed me that Mrs. Smith mentioned another letter, I could not rest until I could ask what she meant."

"I have to tell you, Mr. Darcy, after Miss Bennet left, Grandmother was quite restless. She was distressed to learn of your impending marriage."

"Will she join us shortly? I am anxious to reestablish the connection."

"Yes, sir. The maid is helping her and she will join us momentarily. But, I must warn you, she may not remember any of the information divulged here last, nor you, nor anything of consequence for that matter. Recently her decline has been…"

He nodded his comprehension. "I understand, madam. And if at any point you wish us to cease our conversations or questions, we will do so and depart."

"I am uncertain how she will respond but hope you will be met with success."

"As do I."

All three looked up as they heard movement in the hallway and the door opened with Mrs. Smith entering the room.

"Grandmother," Mrs. Worth said, standing to take her hand and assist her to the chair across from where Mr. Darcy stood to greet her. "You remember meeting Miss Bennet last week?"

Mrs. Smith's eyes were a mask of unrecognition. She glanced straight ahead and sat gently down in the proffered chair.

"And this, Grandmother, is Mr. Darcy of Pemberley. He has come most specially to meet you."

Hazel Smith did not stir but continued to stare out the window at the garden.

"Good morning, Mrs. Smith. It is a pleasure to meet you," Mr. Darcy said. "My mother often spoke well of you in my youth, and I often remember your generosity of sweets when you had returned from Lambton." He smiled warmly but it had no effect on the older woman's memory or recognition.

He regulated the frustration in his tone as inquiry after inquiry went unanswered. Finally, after ten minutes of polite one-sided conversation, Darcy stood.

"Mrs. Worth, I am grateful for the opportunity, but I fear I may be tiring your grandmother. I apologize for taking up so much of your time. We should depart."

"I apologize. If there is any moment of clarity, I will ask her about a letter and contact you immediately with her response."

"I thank you. I am grateful for your willingness to have us visit. Good day."

Miss Elizabeth rose and curtsied to Mrs. Worth. "Thank you again for having us."

"Please give Madeline my best and tell her I look forward to our tea Monday next."

"I will." A maid handed Miss Elizabeth her wrap and gloves in the hallway.

"Good day, Miss Bennet. Good day, Mr. Darcy."

An unfamiliar voice from across the room halted them in their steps. "Mr. Darcy? Is the master here all the way from Pemberley?"

"Grandmother?" Mrs. Worth stepped cautiously back into the room. "Did you ask a question?"

"Of course, I did, girl. I thought I heard you say the master was here. But why would he come all the way from Pemberley to London to see me?"

At that question, Darcy walked back in the room and quickly made his way to the seat across from the older woman.

"Mrs. Smith, it is I."

"Mr. Darcy! It is you, sir," she smiled brightly. "What brings you to London? Where is my lady?" She looked over her shoulder and upon seeing Miss Elizabeth, scowled.

"This young lady is Miss Elizabeth Bennet, a dear friend to Georgiana."

"Oh, sir. Now I know you are joking me. Miss Georgiana—or young Master Henry—has not been born yet."

Darcy gasped but after a moment continued. "Yes, you are correct. This young woman is our future governess for young Fitzwilliam."

"That dear boy. What a precious child he is. 'He is my joy,' Lady Anne always says, and she is right. He is a treasure."

Darcy fought to control his emotion while listening to the ramblings of his mother's maid. "And how was Lady Anne when last you saw her?"

"Glowing, sir. She cannot wait for the babe to be born. I know that she hopes to give you another son, but…" Mrs. Smith leaned in and whispered loudly to him, "I know in her heart she'd love a daughter as she states the young master is practically perfect. My lady says she can't expect to have two perfect sons."

Darcy had no idea how to continue. The memories of his mother were so tangible he could feel them swirling around him. But, he pressed on. "Mrs. Worth, has your mistress asked you to post any letters recently?"

"Only one, sir."

"Only one? Do you remember to whom?"

"Why, yes, sir. To her sister, Lady Catherine."

"To Lady Catherine? Might I ask if you remember the contents of the letter?"

"Of course, sir. Lady Anne requested Lady Catherine visit after the babe is born—not before—she wants time with you and the young master."

"When was this letter posted?"

"Just yesterday, sir. With the babe set to arrive by the end of the month, she wanted to make sure the letter could get to Rosings without ruining Her Ladyship's travel plans."

"And there was nothing in this letter about Fitzwilliam and Anne de Bourgh's betrothal?"

"Oh, sir. Now I'm certain you're funning me." Mrs. Smith laughed uproariously and grabbed her sides. "Mrs. Darcy has no desire for that 'great event' to occur. She wants the young master to choose his own bride." She leaned in and whispered, "I believe that is one of the reasons she does not want her sister to come. She worries she cannot protect the young master during her confinement." She sat straight up and nodded at him as if making a silent pronouncement. The old woman reached over and took a drink of water from the glass sitting on the table next to her. She stared out the window and began to hum.

Darcy was shocked at the old woman's declaration and after collecting his thoughts, he began to probe more. "Mrs. Smith, were there no other letters my moth…my wife had you post?" He waited for a response. "Mrs. Smith?"

"Yes?" at the old lady turned back to him. "Who might you be?" She glanced from Miss Elizabeth to Darcy as her eyes glossed over.

"Mrs. Smith? Mrs. Smith?" Her face was impassive and her soft humming filled the room.

"I am sorry, Mr. Darcy. You see how it is," Mrs. Worth said, standing. "I must get her upstairs before she begins to become agitated. I hope you feel your trip was not in vain?"

"No, of course not. The connection to my parents was a blessing."

"If I might say so, you do greatly resemble your father—not only in appearance, but also in essentials."

He bowed his head to her. "I thank you, Mrs. Worth. My father was the most excellent of men, and I can only hope to emulate his character."

"And sir, if you would like to visit again and speak with my grandmother, you are welcome anytime. I will inform the servants that even if we are unavailable, you will have admittance."

"I thank you, madam. Good day." He bowed and took Miss Elizabeth's arm as they met the Gardiner's young maid at the carriage.

"I am sorry you did not receive the news you wished. But maybe, if you keep looking it will be discovered."

"Yes. It is true that I did not come away with what I hoped" —he lowered his voice and leaned across to Miss Elizabeth— "but today I received a message from the grave."

~

"What do you mean we need to postpone the ball? It is tomorrow night. My mother is not going to like that." Richard stirred his coffee as Darcy paced his study. "Lady Catherine will never allow it. Are you not ready to have a mistress of Pemberley? One as lovely and charming as our dear cousin?"

"There is something I might have discovered. I need to see that letter from my mother. There is something niggling at me that I cannot quite grasp."

"And what is the significance of this *niggling*?" Richard asked. "Are you saying you are hoping to release Anne from your engagement?"

"Richard…"

"What is *niggling* at you?"

"A letter from my mother."

"A letter from your mother or a lovely lass from Hertfordshire?"

"Cousin, you speak out of turn. Leave Miss Elizabeth out of this discussion."

"But, it is evident you know to whom I referred."

Darcy could not deny his cousin's accusation and thought it best to hold his tongue but his cousin persisted. "I do not believe—"

"Richard! Anne is my betrothed. There can be no one else."

"Don't be coy, Darcy." Richard straightened his shoulders and pointed his finger at his cousin. "I know you!"

"And I know you, Richard and you are upset about something. Is it a woman?"

"A woman, Darcy? Are you going to give me advice on women?"

Darcy turned back suddenly at the bitterness in Richard's voice.

The room was heavy with silence before Darcy could speak. "You love her. You love Anne." He sat down as his eyes sought his cousins. "I have suspected, but…"

Richard met his gaze again and after he set aside his coffee, he nodded his acquiescence. "For almost as long as I can remember."

Shaking his head in disbelief, Darcy said, "Then why did you not make your feelings known?"

"To whom?" Richard threw his head back and laughed sardonically. "To you, my cousin with the strongest sense of duty and honor? To my aunt, who has salivated like a hound at a hunt with the prospect of her daughter marrying into the wealth of Pemberley?"

"Blast, Richard! How was I to know?"

"No one was to know. But what can be done? Are you ready now to step aside out of sense of duty? For love? Has anything changed by your knowing?"

"You know it is impossible. This has been expected since our infancy. Anne expects it."

"Anne?" Richard barked. "Anne? You think that if you must. You have no idea what she desires. Have we not already established that? She does not love you!"

"Are you saying she loves you?"

Richard shrugged. "But how does any of this matter? You have been searching for a letter from my aunt Anne which may or may not exist. Which may or not refute Lady Catherine's claim to you."

Darcy deflated. "Richard, I am sorry, but I fear it is an impossible quest. And what of my duty to Anne? It is the expectation of our family."

"Expectations be hanged!" Richard cried, standing abruptly. "Why must we do as our families dictate? Why must you marry Anne? Why must I someday marry an heiress I hardly know who my mother will choose only because she has a fortune? We are men from wealth and power, of the Upper Ten Thousand, and yet we are not free to choose the course of our own lives! Darcy, you are master of your own destiny. Would that I was born the son of a blacksmith." Richard's bravado began to fail him, and he sank back down in his chair.

If only there were a way.

～

"Your dress for the ball is exquisite!"

"It is," Lizzy said, fingering the silk. "It is much finer than anything I have ever owned—or may ever own again. But not you, dear Jane. Now that you are to be a married woman, this gown will pale in comparison in your wardrobe as Mrs. Charles Bingley."

"No, Lizzy. I cannot imagine wearing the dresses which Caroline favors. Charles is very generous and has spoken of setting appointment with the drapers for the Season already, but our wedding is not for two months."

"Yes," Lizzy said, holding her new gown to herself in front of the mirror. "And before the Season, we could have a little Charles on the way."

"*Lizzy!*" Jane replied, flushing red.

"Oh, darling, I am so happy for you. Mama must be in raptures." Lizzy embraced her sister and taking pity on Jane's discomfiture, returned to the conversation of her gown. "I should not have accepted it but Georgiana was insistent."

"Yes, as was Mr. Darcy, I hear," Jane said slyly, looking at the dress. "Aunt Madeline said he has become quite a fixture at Gracechurch Street." When she received no response from her sister, she continued. "Aunt also said Mr. Hamilton has been a frequent visitor as well."

"Jane, Mr. Darcy is to be married to Miss de Bourgh. Their engagement ball is tomorrow night, remember? He has no interest in me, other than that of a friend to his sister."

"Then what of Mr. Hamilton?"

Lizzy allowed the question to hang in the air before sighing. "I so want to marry for love. I know that love comes in many different forms, but I had hoped, dear Jane, for the type of love that you and Mr. Bingley have found."

Jane lowered her eyes and blushed at Lizzy's words. "Is it so obvious?"

"Oh darling!" Lizzy laughed. "When you are near, he lights up like the fireworks at Vauxhall Gardens." She leaned over and squeezed her sister's hand. "I am so happy for you. Your goodness has been rewarded by a pure love which will last throughout time.

Generations from now, your grandchildren and great-grandchildren will look back on your marriage as one to emulate."

Jane blushed a deeper pink and giggled. "Stop!"

"Very well then, sweet sister. Generations from now, your descendants will speak of you in legends and wonder at your patience and your happy marriage despite Caroline Bingley living under your roof for all those years."

Jane only snickered at her uncharitable quip. "It is true Caroline can be rather tiresome, but I find she has improved upon further acquaintance."

Lizzy looked at her sister doubtfully. "There, there, dear Jane. I will ask you no more, as there must be some level of pain to appreciate the perfection which is your Charles Bingley."

"Charles is not perfect, Lizzy. He has faults just like any other man. But, we have spoken of our own feelings. Have you considered this with mister… with Mr. Hamilton?"

She esteemed James Hamilton for the friend he once was, and the kind person he showed himself to be. *Am I too headstrong? I must accept Fitzwilliam Darcy will never be mine.* She sighed and looked up to see Jane studying her intently. *Had I never met him, I might had been quite content with Mr. Hamilton… James is a good man who has always been kind to my family.* Just as she was about to say she was only resolved to do what was in her best interest, the maid announced she had a visitor.

She and James Hamilton had made their third circle around the small park across from her aunt's home with Jane following dutifully behind them. They had exhausted numerous topics—family, friends, London. His anxiety was evident by his stuttering speech but not half as anxious as Lizzy as she anticipated his true intentions.

"Miss Elizabeth…Lizzy," he said, stopping to take one of her hands in his. "We have known each other for many years, and although you might have believed there were times I was indifferent to you, that is not so. You are so much better than I deserve, but I have had a strong attachment to you which over time has grown. I am hoping you will agree to a courtship."

Lizzy sighed in relief. A courtship was not as binding as an engagement. She felt dizzy and wondered if the adult *Elizabeth and James* would be as happy as the childhood friends *Lizzy and Jimmy*.

"If it is agreeable to you, I will depart for Longbourn in the morning and speak to your father."

Lizzy looked at the people milling about the park. The governesses wielding their young charges; little boys sailing boats in the pond; young girls reading to their dolls.

She started when he cleared his throat. "Elizabeth? What say you? Shall I ride to Longbourn in the morning?"

"Mr. Hamilton—"

"James. Please, call me James as you used to."

"We have been friends for many years, and I used to think you knew me better than anyone outside of my family, save Charlotte Lucas. But I must ask why you told my aunt I was an obstinate, headstrong girl?"

This was not the reaction he expected and he colored. "I did not know your aunt was to be so little trusted."

Lizzy shook her head. "Please do not blame my aunt. My young cousin told me first. Then my aunt attempted to defend you."

He kicked at a small stone with his toe as he did when they were children. "I am sorry, Miss Elizabeth. I confess I am mostly frustrated because you have been much in the company of Darcy. I said things I did not mean nor should have said. I fear I have been jealous." He lowered his eyes again, before looking back at her. "Miss Elizabeth, please do not allow the last few weeks to alter our future. Will you not accept my request?"

Lizzy turned away from him and looked across the park contemplating her future. *He is a good man who will treat me well. The love I seek can never be had because it is promised to another.*

"I would be very happy to accept a courtship with you, James." He took her hand and kissed it tenderly. She made herself smile but could not enjoy the sensation. *Should I not feel something akin to my heart racing?* He tucked her hand in his arm as they walked back to Jane and shared the good news.

CHAPTER 16

"**D**o you think it is appropriate, Jane? This neckline is so much lower than I remembered." Lizzy bit her lip and gazed at her reflection in the mirror. Their aunt's abigail had just completed pinning fresh flowers through her curls.

"You look lovely, Lizzy. And that gown fits you to perfection."

"If you are sure…" she said, turning slightly to see the back of the gown. The gold brocade pattern trailed down her back and wove around the hem. "Hannah, did a lovely job with my hair, but I wish I had something more than flowers. They seem so mundane for such a regal gown."

"Maybe some feathers?" Jane suggested innocently.

"I believe your Mr. Bingley's sister will be wearing enough feathers for a complete hen house."

"Now, Lizzy. She is a thoughtful woman, who is very attentive to her brother's needs. She is, I will grant you, a little opinionated."

"A little? Oh, Jane, your kindness is a blessing." She turned back to her reflection. "I do look well, yes?"

"Yes, Lizzy. It is unfortunate that Mr. Hamilton will not be in attendance. But he had to travel to Longbourn to visit Papa, then …?"

"Then to Ashby Park in preparation for a possible bride. But do you not find it odd that at the beginning of our courtship he has abandoned me for his estate?"

"Lizzy…"

"It is fortunate that we have known each other since our youth—"

"Might I say something which you may find impertinent?"

"Impertinent? You?" Lizzy chuckled. "Jane, you could not be impertinent if you tried."

"I am concerned. I thought to see more sparkle…"

Lizzy shook her head rapidly. "No, no, Jane. Mr. Hamilton is a good man and a wonderful match. I am just anxious about the ball." Attempting to change the subject, she said, "Oh, I almost feel as if I am playing dress up in Mama's sitting room as we did when we were children."

"You are an elegant lady. You have yet to truly see yourself, my dear. Now the carriage should be here shortly. Shall we go down?"

As they gathered their wraps from the bed, a maid entered. "If you please, Miss Elizabeth. This just came for you."

Lizzy looked from the young maid to Jane before taking the package. "Thank you. That will be all." The girl bobbed a curtsy and left the room while Lizzy unwrapped the brown paper from the small box. She looked quizzically at Jane on seeing the name of the establishment embossed on the lid. As she opened the box, she gasped. Two diamond encrusted gold combs lay delicately wrapped in velvet.

"Oh, Lizzy. They are beautiful! Who are they from?"

"There is no card."

"I am sure they are from Mr. Hamilton."

"Yes. They must be. But what a surprise! He was to be off early this morning." She traced the fine edges of the combs and sighed.

"I will help you to not displace any of your curls." Jane pinned them up effortlessly. "Perfect."

And they were. Lizzy could not deny how the stones set off the strands of dark honey-gold in her brown hair. "But, Jane. Surely, these combs are more than Longbourn brings in at quarter day. How can I flaunt such wealth?"

"You can, my dear sister, because tonight you are not Elizabeth Bennet of Longbourn. You are Elizabeth Bennet, future mistress of Ashby Park."

Hundreds of candles reflected off the mirrors throughout the hallway of Matlock House. Conversation hummed all around leading to the ballroom. Greenery and flowers dripped from bannisters, chandeliers, and candelabras while footmen moved fluidly throughout the crowds with crystal flutes filled with champagne.

"Is this not the most elegant place you have ever been?" Jane asked, leaning into Lizzy while walking through the crush.

"It is, Jane. I am in awe that we are here."

Miss Bingley sniffed at her comment and rolled her eyes before smiling ingratiatingly at an acquaintance.

Mr. Bingley cleared his throat and said, "Miss Elizabeth, allow me to say how very fine you look this evening."

She smiled sweetly at his sister before thanking Mr. Bingley.

"I understand, Miss Elizabeth that Darcy and his sister have been often in your company. How do you find Miss de Bourgh?"

"I have only met her once, Mr. Bingley, but in that short amount of time found her company quite pleasant."

"Of course, it would be," Caroline Bingley snapped. "She is the heir to Rosings Park and the future mistress of Pemberley. Could you imagine her as anything less?" Lizzy swallowed her retort and ignored this implacable enmity.

Upon entering the ballroom, Bingley was met by several acquaintances and he introduced his intended with much animation. Lizzy recognized few faces but was pleased for her sister's triumph. After a moment of realizing she was not the center of attention, Miss Bingley excused herself to join a party of ladies

Oh, my dear Jane. Pray Miss Bingley finds a husband soon or even your patience will be tested while she resides with you.

Caroline Bingley paid little attention to the prattling of the freckle-faced gentleman and his sister next to her while Lord Matlock called for the first dance. Mr. Darcy led Miss de Bourgh to the top of the set. She was not about to be sitting on the side while Jane Bennet danced with her brother, Eliza Bennet danced with Colonel Fitzwilliam, and Mr. Darcy danced with that dowdy cousin of his!

"Yes, Mr. Knight," she said, realizing too late he was two inches too short. "I would be honored to have this dance."

After twenty minutes of less than stimulating conversation, she learned that Mr. Knight's estate was a short distance from Pemberley, that he and Mr. Darcy had known each other as boys and later at Cambridge—and her scheme was hatched.

"I say" —Charles Bingley smiled over his glass while leaning over to Colonel Fitzwilliam— "my sister seems to be quite taken with Knight."

"Bertram Knight?" The colonel sputtered into his cup. "That cannot be possible." The two men looked across the ballroom to see Caroline Bingley casting a coquettish glance to their old school chum. "Do you think she has accepted that Darcy is no longer an option? Has she broadened her choices?"

Bingley shook his head in wonder. "As of this afternoon, I would have said no. But maybe this ball has made her reconcile her hopes are all for naught."

"If that is the case, she is not the only one here tonight with disappointed hopes."

Bingley wondered at the slight edge in his voice but laughed instead at all the broken hearts their friend was leaving behind. "I tell you, Colonel, if Knight approaches me with any interest in my sister, I will not hesitate. He would work well for my future plans."

"Ah, yes, Bingley. Allow me to congratulate you on your betrothal to Miss Bennet. She is all that is lovely."

"That she is, my friend. Both she and her sister do not begrudge Miss de Bourgh's fortunate alliance. They have their own to celebrate."

"Her sister? Miss Katherine?"

"No, Miss Elizabeth Bennet."

Colonel Fitzwilliam choked on his wine while Bingley smacked him on the back. "Miss Elizabeth?"

"Yes. She accepted a courtship with James Hamilton only yesterday. He has ridden to Longbourn this morning to seek her father's approval, and then on to Ashby Park for estate business."

The colonel scanned the room, attempting to locate the aforementioned woman. He found Miss Elizabeth standing with her sister Miss Bennet, who was in conversation with another young woman. Miss Elizabeth seemed to be paying more attention to the conversation behind her than her own sister's and by the alarm on her face was none too pleased with what she was hearing. As Colonel Richard Fitzwilliam glanced from Elizabeth Bennet to the retreating woman, he pondered two things: Why did Miss Elizabeth agree to marry Hamilton, and what had Caroline Bingley said that upset her so?

Fitzwilliam Darcy had a headache. He felt as if he had been dancing for hours, a skill he excelled in greatly but abhorred. He was not truly a snob, but dancing forced him to be amongst many he did not enjoy. However, this was his engagement ball, and although he had no choice in the matter, he was grateful his aunt Ellen had moved forward with the event even with Lady Catherine still at Rosings and constricted by assize judges regarding the poaching incident. *At least I do not have to deal with her overbearing presence!* After catching his aunt Ellen's eye, he indicated the hallway toward the library and escaped for a moment to refresh his spirits. He excused himself from Anne, waiting not a moment longer, lest another guest approach him.

His footsteps echoed on the marble tile and he was grateful for the dim light which did not aggravate his headache. Entering the library, he breathed in the scent of generations of thought and study. Darcy was a man of few words but relished the craftsmanship of Keats, Wordsworth, and Shakespeare. He was most comfortable in a room where his pronouncements were the least important. He poured himself a drink before selecting a tome which he felt befitted his mood. "Dante's Inferno," he said aloud to the empty room. "I am in my own personal Hell, but not one of my making. Which ring would this be?"

He sat down heavily on the couch and propped his feet up on the ottoman prepared to relax for a quarter of an hour before returning to his family duties. As he looked up at the clock, he heard the latch of the door click. "Richard?" he asked, expecting to see his cousin. Instead he was stunned to find Caroline Bingley.

Lizzy's mind and heart were racing. Not five minutes before she had watched as Mr. Darcy quietly slipped out the door leading to what she was assuming was the private family wing of the house, only to be followed shortly thereafter by Caroline Bingley. Lizzy would not have concerned herself with these activities had she not overheard Miss Bingley's boast.

She wasted no time in finding Colonel Fitzwilliam. He was in the midst of a discussion with a fellow officer.

"Colonel?"

"Miss Elizabeth. Might I present you to my good friend, Alastair Thompson? Colonel Thompson, this is Miss Elizabeth Bennet, one of the loveliest exports from the county of Hertfordshire."

"How do you do, Miss Bennet?"

"I am well, Colonel Thompson, thank you. I hope you do not think me impertinent to steal Colonel Fitzwilliam from you? And your mother?" The colonel looked at her curiously and excused himself to find his mother. "Thank you, Colonel. I will await you by the door to the hallway. Colonel Thompson, it was very nice making your acquaintance."

"And I you, Miss Bennet. And if you have a dance available, might I claim it?"

"You may, sir."

She curtsied and walked briskly to the door, waiting for the colonel and Lady Matlock. When she saw him across the room stop to speak with his mother, she became restless.

Finally, Elizabeth apprised her hosts of what she had overheard earlier and they briskly walked toward the library. The colonel held up his hand as they approached the door. "Mother. Miss Elizabeth. Allow me to determine if there is a need for your presence." The colonel stepped forward and pressed his ear to the partially opened door. Lady Matlock hissed. "Richard! This is my house. This is my nephew. Get in there and get that scheming woman away from him."

～

"Miss Bingley. What are you doing here?" Darcy asked, immediately standing. "Are you lost? Might I help direct you back to the ballroom?" She answered him with a cloying smile.

"No, Mr. Darcy. I have found what I am looking for."

The gooseflesh began to creep up Darcy's arms as he realized her intent. "Miss Bingley, I suggest you make your way back to the ballroom before your absence is noticed."

A throaty laugh escaped her lips. "Oh, Fitzwilliam. Do not be coy with me. I know what you need. Do you think I would allow you to strap yourself to that sickly woman and lock away all your passion? I realize you cannot marry me. I will marry Mr. Knight, then we can have it all."

"Bertram?" Darcy asked, shaking his head. "You are to marry Bertram Knight?"

"Yes," Miss Bingley said, slowly making her way toward him. Darcy took a step back. "There can be no suspicion if I already reside nearby. We can continue our relationship with no one being the wiser."

"Nonsense. We have no relationship nor will we ever. You will stand on that side of the room while I call for a maid, and we will not mention this to anyone."

Her laugh echoed throughout the silent room. "Oh, Fitzwilliam. Do not force me to run out into the ballroom and tell everyone I have just been compromised by Mr. Darcy."

His whole life had been an avoidance of circumstances such as this. He had never been placed in a situation where he could be ensnared by mercenary daughters—or mothers for that matter—until today. His face remained set and his eyes steely while he listened to her continue with her demands.

"Knowing that I cannot be the true mistress of Pemberley, I will accept your carte blanche."

"Madam," he interrupted, his jaw tightening harder, "you know little of my character to imagine that I would ever keep a mistress. When I take a wife, she will be the only woman I share any part of myself with. I suggest you cease this ridiculous conversation and remove yourself immediately from my presence before you regret your actions."

"Oh, Fitzwilliam…" She smirked. "You will do as I say, or *you* will regret *your* actions."

He stepped toward her and said, "Miss Bingley, I have never laid my hands forcefully upon a female before…"

"But I have." Standing in the doorway was his cousin Richard. Lady Matlock and Elizabeth Bennet peering around his shoulder.

"Colonel!" Miss Bingley started but gathered her wits quickly. "I am so grateful you are here. Mr. Darcy tried to…" She crumpled onto the nearest chair, whimpering. "What shall I do? How shall members of the *ton* think of me when they learn…?"

Before he could retort, he heard his aunt hiss through clenched teeth. "Miss Bingley, how unfortunate that you became lost while looking for the cloak room. I had heard about your early departure."

"Oh, I am not leaving," Miss Bingley said confidently, wiping away her feigned tears.

"Oh, but you are, my dear. Because, Miss Bingley, if it became known that you were propositioning Fitzwilliam Darcy of Pemberley at his engagement ball, in my home, I can assure you, your future in London would be bleak."

"But that is not…"

"Is that not what you heard, Richard? Miss Elizabeth? Let me tell you something, Miss Bingley. The stench of trade still emanates all about you. That could never be overlooked if you so much as *hinted* a scandal involving my nephew. You would be fortunate to marry a blacksmith because I would make sure that no one in polite society acknowledged your existence."

Miss Bingley blanched.

"And I would recommend that you treat yourself to a long holiday… somewhere far away. Because, you will not find a welcome from anyone in London until I have recovered from this insult to my person."

"Yes, Your Ladyship."

"Good. Now," she said with practiced ennui, "allow me to escort you to the door."

"Yes, Your Ladyship."

Lady Matlock linked arms with Miss Bingley and walked briskly out of the room. "Oscar" —she called to the footman— "Miss Bingley is feeling ill. Please have her brother's carriage called for immediately."

"Of course, my lady."

Darcy took a deep breath and collapsed on the settee. Massaging his temples, he said, "Richard, I thank you for your timely entrance." He reached out and extended his hand to his cousin, who stepped forward to take it.

Richard said, "Think nothing of it. You would have done the same."

"I would."

"But, the real thanks should go to Miss Bennet." He turned to Miss Elizabeth who blushed slightly at the praise. "She discovered Miss Bingley's plan and alerted me."

Standing immediately, he said, "Miss Elizabeth. How can I thank you? You have rescued me again. You have just witnessed the basest of characters and behavior. I apologize that your delicate sensibilities might have been affected." His heart raced as he gently clasped her hand. "It would seem without you I would have entered into the worst type of prison imaginable. I am now indebted to you for the freedom of both my sister and myself. How can I ever repay you?"

Miss Elizabeth raised her eyes to meet his, and softly whispered, "I am only grateful I could help a friend in need."

He observed her comely face and could not help but raise her hand to his lips reverently. "Your friendship means more to me than you know."

"You shall always have it, sir," she said quietly.

Richard coughed, breaking the moment. "We must allow Miss Elizabeth return to the ballroom."

"Yes, yes. Of course." Darcy released her hand and felt the loss instantly.

As Miss Elizabeth stepped toward the door, Richard said, "Darcy, before she goes, you might wish Miss Elizabeth joy."

Darcy quickly snapped to attention and cocked his head. "Is this true, Miss Elizabeth? Has Mr. Hamilton made you an offer?"

Pausing in the doorway, she nodded. "He has asked for a courtship, sir, and I...I have accepted."

He felt his heart squeeze and his stomach roil but he managed to say, "Then, I wish you joy. He is a fortunate man to have won your heart."

"Yes…well…I thank you." She stepped out of the library but not before Richard called out. "Miss Bennet, you should save a dance for Darcy so he can tell you a story."

Darcy's eyes flashed to his cousin but Richard only smirked.

"A story?" she asked, stepping back inside the library and seemed to quiz them both with one arched brow.

He had no notion of Richard's intent but he could not deny himself this opportunity. "Miss Bennet, will you do me the honor of the supper set?"

She nodded her acquiescence but looked at Richard expectantly. "Oh, Miss Bennet. Darcy must tell you about his favorite gift. You know, Darce," he said turning to his cousin and grinning widely, "your watch."

She did not have long to wait before the colonel and Mr. Darcy returned to the ballroom. He sought her out with his eyes, just as he had done the first time she saw him at the Meryton assembly a little over a month before. And just as at the assembly, they ceased their search when they found her. Her breath caught at the intensity of his gaze. She held his look for minutes, hours, seconds—she knew not but was startled from her reverie when she heard Jane's companion say, "My brother Bertram is quite taken with Miss Bingley. I have not seen much of her since school, but by her actions tonight, I am expecting to see her often hereafter."

"Your brother appears to be quite an amiable young man," said Jane.

"He is. He only needs someone with a little fire to liven him up."

Caroline has that in spades! Elizabeth grimaced at the deception Caroline had played on this gentleman and his family and all she could think to say was, "I had heard Miss Bingley was planning a trip abroad…"

As the orchestra began to play the supper set, Elizabeth looked up to find Colonel Thompson walking toward her.

"Miss Elizabeth, if you are not already spoken for, might I have this dance?"

"Sir, I…"

"I hope you were not planning to give my dance away to the colonel," a voice behind her said.

"No, I…" She felt her face flush and turned to look up at Mr. Darcy.

Without removing his attention from Lizzy, he said, "Thompson, I apologize, but you will have to wait until the next set. Miss Elizabeth promised this dance to me." He then took her hand and walked her to the dance floor, not once allowing his regard to falter.

"Good evening, Mr. Darcy." Her tremulous voice almost betrayed her thoughts. *How perfectly shaped his lips are…*

"Miss Elizabeth. You are looking well this evening. That gown is most becoming on you."

Her breath caught at the compliment. "Thank you, sir." As the music began, they were separated by the dance, but when the steps returned him to her side, he said, "What lovely combs you are wearing. They complement your dress so well."

"Thank you. They were a gift. But they were delivered anonymously."

The dance once again separated them, but upon his return he replied, "Anonymously, you say? Perhaps I can solve the mystery. You see, my sister adores you and wants nothing more than to make those she loves happy. She had them delivered anonymously so you could not return them."

"Mr. Darcy, they are much too fine a gift. I must return them."

"You must not, as I promised her I would faithfully convince you to keep them. Please, Miss Elizabeth. Do not disappoint our Georgie."

Our Georgie. At that moment, he was charm itself and she would have agreed to almost anything he proposed.

They were separated again by the dance but when brought back together, he whispered, "Miss Elizabeth. As loath as I am to speak of it, I am sure you understand I could never convey enough of my thanks for your actions this evening."

"There is no need. I am only grateful my inquisitive habit was of use. I would be devastated for you, and Miss de Bourgh, if you were forced into a situation you did not wish to find yourself in."

"Yes, yes, well…"

"Yes. It would have been unfair for you to be yoked to that woman, as my father would say, when you truly loved another."

At that point the partners changed, and Lizzy found herself clasping hands with Colonel Fitzwilliam, and Anne de Bourgh was partnered with Mr. Darcy.

"And what are you and my cousin discussing, which has him so curiously animated?"

"We are merely talking about the grandeur of the ball and the number of couples," Lizzy replied with an arch smile, glancing from the colonel to Mr. Darcy and Miss de Bourgh.

As the final bars of the song ended, the colonel said, "Darcy, have you the time? I need to check in with Mother at half past the hour."

"Of course," he said, removing his watch from his pocket. "You have ten minutes."

"Thank you. You should tell Miss Elizabeth about your watch." He winked before whisking Miss de Bourgh across the ballroom.

"Miss Elizabeth, would you care for some refreshment?"

"No, I thank you. But I do need some air. I am feeling a little warm in the ballroom."

"Let us refresh ourselves on the veranda." He placed her hand on his arm and escorted out the doors into the cool night air.

"Mr. Darcy, I would not wish you to feel duty bound to ignore your betrothed in order to give me comfort. Please, do not trouble yourself. I will be fine."

"Miss Elizabeth," his deep baritone voice murmured, cutting through her and making her heart race with an expectation of she knew not what. "I am quite content in your company. I only wish I knew why Richard wants me to tell you about my watch."

Feeling all the embarrassment of the moment, she said, "The colonel and I met earlier this week by chance and I mentioned what a beautiful watch you had received."

"My watch?"

She looked out across the darkness hearing the music wafting from the ballroom. "When we were at Ashby Park. I went to the library to retrieve a book, and it was on the end table. I picked it up to examine. I was immediately taken by the beautiful estate on the front."

"Yes, thank you. And might I say, I am grateful you do not have a scar from when that book hit you?"

She smiled at the memory and her finger went to her temple. "As am I."

"Miss Elizabeth, might I ask what you thought of the engraving of Pemberley?"

"If the artist's rendering was faithful, it is a home without equal."

He smiled gently, as he pulled the watch from his pocket to look at it. "It is, and indeed it has no equal. Pemberley is a part of me."

Lizzy looked out into the night sky at the stars and drummed her fingers across the bannister. "There is something about a man who respects his obligations, no matter the obstacles that lay in his path. You are the best of men, Mr. Darcy. Once again, I am relieved of the happy outcome this evening. I do not wish to imagine what would have become of your dear sister or estate if that woman had succeeded."

"I cannot agree more." The air became thick with emotion as they gazed out over the gardens lit by torches and the moonlight. Lizzy worried he might hear her heartbeat when he said, "Would you care to hear the story of my watch?"

"If you would like to tell me," she whispered. She felt dizzy trying to control her whirling sentiments.

"It is true this watch is my favorite possession. I love it more than any gift I have ever received."

She smiled wanly. "I understand."

"How so?"

"Well, sir, it is obvious you love your home."

"Yes."

"And you must also love the giver exceedingly, and they you."

"True."

They fell into silence again.

Lizzy blurted out the next words unexpectedly. "You are truly fortunate. Not everyone is as blessed to achieve such a love match and have one's partner understands them so precisely."

Mr. Darcy sputtered. "Excuse me?"

"Your betrothed. Miss de Bourgh. The watch proves you and she are equals in all things."

Mr. Darcy shook his head. The chill air made his breath come out in puffs. "I do not understand. I am fond of my cousin, yes. We are friends from childhood but I am uncertain how my watch proves a love match." He rubbed his thumb across the engraving of the estate.

"I beg your forgiveness. I did not mean to overstep myself." She turned to go back inside before Mr. Darcy reached out to her.

"Miss Elizabeth, please stay. I want to understand your meaning."

She felt flustered. Her cheeks were beginning to burn from embarrassment as she faced him. *How could I have presumed such a conversation with him?* "It is nothing, Mr. Darcy. Just a misunderstanding on my part. I meant no offense."

"And none is taken," he said, gently guiding her to a bench but they did not sit. "I only wish to know…"

She looked up at his dark eyes and slowly reached for the watch in his hand, unintentionally resting her fingers on his and sending a shiver down her spine. "The inscription, sir," she whispered. "Only someone with the deepest love could convey so much emotion in so few words." With that she popped open the watch and read the inscription aloud, her voice catching on the words. "'To my beloved Darcy upon our engagement. I am forever yours, Anne.' Those are words of intimacy. Tenderness." Her fingers traced the script before sliding down the chain and returning the keepsake to him. "I am grateful that such a friend has found true happiness."

He moved toward her and breathed out her name. "Miss Elizabeth. It is true that I loved the person who inscribed this watch, and they me."

Lizzy felt her heart squeeze and sputter while she turned away to hide the tears welling up.

"But, I am not the first Darcy to own this watch and I pray I am not the last. You see, my mother, Lady *Anne* Fitzwilliam gifted this to my father, *George* Darcy, upon their engagement, and it became mine upon his death. I am not the Darcy in the inscription and my cousin is my mother's namesake."

"Oh," was all her lips could form. Through unshed tears, she looked up at him. "This watch was not a gift from your intended?"

"No, it was my father's."

"Oh," she said again, uncertain where to look. A weight she did not know she carried lifted from her heart. *It is not from Anne*, she almost exalted at the thought, and bit her lip to keep her joy within. She heard voices approach, and after a glancing look at him, turned back out to the garden and wiped her eyes.

"Darcy, Miss Elizabeth. There you are. Jane and I were looking for you. Shall we move into supper?"

"Bingley, Miss Bennet. Yes, let us," Mr. Darcy said extending his arm to her. "Miss Elizabeth was a little warm, so we decided to get some air."

They walked back inside the house as Elizabeth fought down several different emotions, the last of which was resignation.

"Yes, the ball is quite a success." Upon entering the dining room, Mr. Bingley scanned the crowd. "Lady Matlock informed me Caroline had taken ill and left, but I want to speak with Bertram Knight before the evening closes."

"Bertram?"

Mr. Bingley nodded while escorting Jane to a seat. "His sister said he wished to speak to me." He leaned back and lowered his voice before responding to Mr. Darcy, "I can only hope this means Caroline will soon be off my hands."

Mr. Darcy cleared his throat.

"That is what is so curious," Mr. Bingley replied to the unasked question as he pulled out the chair for Jane. "Caroline seems besotted with him. Besides, Bertram is a grown man. If he is not interested in Caroline, he can say so himself."

Mr. Darcy remained silent as he gestured to a chair for Lizzy. She cocked her head at him, curious how he could ever explain to his friend what had occurred in the library. She sighed. *And even more so, how to explain to myself what occurred on the veranda.*

CHAPTER 17

T he muted sound of the rain tapping against the windows on a wet November day was all but lost to both Lizzy and Jane Bennet of Longbourn. They were reclining lazily on the deep, blue cushions of their aunt's very comfortable furnishings in the sitting room on Gracechurch Street. With a trousseau to purchase for one and the possibility of a trousseau for the other, letters were exchanged with rapid pace between the young ladies and the mistress of Longbourn.

Thus, they were engaged in this ordinary manner when a sharp rap was heard at the front door. Neither expected visitors—Mr. Bingley was in meetings, Mr. Hamilton still remained at Ashby Park, and Kitty and Georgiana were to arrive later from Darcy House. Lizzy tucked a novel and her mother's missives aside. The door to the sitting room opened and Mrs. Gardiner's housekeeper entered with a message in her hand.

"If you please, Miss Bennet. This came express."

Lizzy stepped forward to take it, handing the woman coins for the rider. "Thank you, Mrs. Williams."

The housekeeper closed the door as Lizzy tore open the letter. A second note fluttered to the floor and Jane bent to retrieve it. Lizzy read the first line and gasped. "It is from Mama. She says we are ruined!"

"Is it Father?" Tears pooled in Jane's eyes as she collapsed on the couch. "Is he unwell?"

She shook her head. "I am uncertain." Lizzy read aloud.

"My dear girls,

We are ruined! There is nothing we can do but pray Mr. Bingley and Mr. Hamilton will take pity on us and continue forward with the weddings. If they will not, we will be tossed in the hedgerows by that odious vicar and Charlotte Lucas. What will become of you all? If Lydia had not..."

Lizzy paused. The next lines were smudged.

"Lizzy, what does it say?"

"I cannot make out the rest! What does that note say? Anything at all? All we know is that something has occurred with Lydia!"

Jane unfolded the second note. "It is from Mary. Things are not as dire as our mother paints them, but my father, mother, and sisters will arrive tomorrow in London to stay with my aunt and uncle. Mother wished to come shop for my trousseau and Father relented."

Lizzy sat next to Jane and read over her shoulder:

Sisters,

I do not have much time to write before Mama sends her letter express. We will all arrive on the morrow, so please inform my aunt and uncle. Late this afternoon, I decided to walk out into the garden to feel the strength of God in nature when I was immediately stopped by a noise—to be truthful, there were people arguing in the copse behind the hermitage. As I approached, I determined the voices were Lydia and an officer I could not name. I was about to make my presence known when their words arrested my movement. Lydia was angry and accused the man (who I had then recognized as Mr. Wickham) of lying to her. She had learned he was to marry Mary King. She said she had expected to elope to Gretna Green with Mr. Wickham herself! I will not dignify his response, only suffice to say, the blood from his nose after Lydia hit him blended well with his regimentals.

Luckily, no one outside of myself, Lydia, Mr. Wickham, our parents, and Hill know the particulars. I am certain Mr. Wickham will not acknowledge he was bested by a young woman who blessedly refused to forsake her virtue for a cad such as him.

Mother is in quite a state and blames Lydia. Not for what you would assume, but something else entirely, which I do not have time to divulge. I am quite disappointed with her maternal sensibilities and only hope her heart will be touched to see the error of her ways.

Father had granted Mother leave to come to London to help Jane shop for wedding clothes and has now determined we will all go to remove ourselves from the militia for a time.

I must close as I hear the rider outside but shall see you on the morrow.

God Bless,

Mary

Both girls leaned back into the couch and said not a word. Lizzy squeezed her sister's hand before she stood to find her aunt.

〜

"And to imagine we are to Pemberley tomorrow," Kitty said breathlessly, sipping her tea, and reveling in the jealousy of her younger sister. "For two weeks, we shall drink in the wonders of Derbyshire."

"Not all of us," Lydia replied glumly, looking at her bandaged hand.

"And Kitty, I understand your enthusiasm for the trip but realize it may not be pleasure bent. The fire at Pemberley could be rather extensive. Mr. and Miss Darcy are quite concerned about their home."

"Yes, that is true," she replied, thoughtfully tapping her tea cup. "Although Georgiana said the letter from their steward told them not to worry. She said Mr. Darcy would have left immediately had he not had to meet with his solicitor this morning for the marriage settlement."

"Take every opportunity to enjoy yourself, Kitty," Jane said. "You deserve this treat. I have been so proud of you and your behavior."

"As have I," said Lizzy.

Lydia snorted. "It seems one Bennet is not as ladylike as the others."

"That is correct, young lady!" Mrs. Bennet affirmed, walking into the parlor of the Gardiner's townhouse and standing by the fireplace.

"As your father said, you must comport yourself befitting a gentleman's daughter."

"Mama, she was defending her virtue from that vile man!"

"Hold your tongue, Miss Lizzy! You know not of what you speak. She should not have put herself in that position. She could have forced his hand!" It had been a week since the Matlock's ball, and the ladies of Longbourn had descended upon Gracechurch Street only two days previously. "Lydia, if you had only allowed Mr. Wickham a few liberties, you might now be a married woman."

"Mama! You would encourage our sister to put herself under the power of a disreputable man to secure a husband?" Jane cried out while Lizzy asked, "A husband with no morals who would most likely retreat at the first sign of discord?"

"The loss of a woman's virtue—"

"Hold your tongue, Mary. And you, missy," Mrs. Bennet tutted, turning to Lizzy, "are too high in the instep if you ask me. You are lucky Mr. Hamilton has finally asked for a courtship—although, I do not know why. It is strange that he has stayed busy at Ashby Park since his request of your father. Mind you stop expressing your independent ideas! Men do not like women who think. They want someone who is sweet, and…"

"Madam, that is quite enough!" Mr. Bennet snapped. The ladies startled at his unexpected presence and found him with their aunt Gardiner at the door. The vein at their father's temple throbbed. "Jane, you must allow your mother time to refresh herself and prepare for your outing to the drapers today. It would appear she is fatigued and is not behaving as the ideal example of womanhood. She will meet you and your aunt Gardiner later today after she takes something for her nerves."

"Mr. Bennet, I am quite healthy, and do not need my salts. My nerves are fine!"

Ignoring his wife's outburst, he turned to his youngest daughter, save one. "Kitty, I have been pleasantly surprised at the fine, young lady you have become these last months. Such progress. And what a good friend, your Miss Darcy! You seem to have found a true confidant who values you."

"Thank you, Papa. And I her."

Turning to his middle child, he continued. "Mary, had we heeded your wise council, we might not have found ourselves in the current situation."

"Yes, as in Proverbs 22:6. 'Train up a child—'"

"And you as well, Elizabeth. I should not dismiss my girls' opinions in the future. Also, we know that Mr. Hamilton is an enterprising, young man which will not always allow him at your beck and call."

She nodded.

"Do not allow his absence to make you believe him indifferent to your charms."

"I will not."

Finally, he addressed his youngest. "It may shock us all, Lydia, but I am prodigiously proud of you, even though it has caused you this injury. It shows much fortitude and spirit—despite your, let us say, *silly conduct* leading up to the...*unfortunate* encounter." Lydia snickered but was silenced with a look. "I am humbled to say that all of my three youngest daughters have shown more sense than I have given credit."

Unused to praise from this parent, she scrambled to his side and kissed his cheek. "Thank you, Papa."

He inhaled deeply. "And now. Mrs. Bennet. Your maid has prepared a tonic for you." Holding his hand up to her objections. "I will brook no opposition."

Mrs. Bennet raised her chin as she strode out of the room in a flurry of huffs and complaints.

Mr. Bennet watched her go, and then turned back to the girls. "Kitty, when do you return to Darcy House?"

"I will be leaving in a quarter of an hour."

"Safe journey, my dear."

"Thank you, Papa." He then kissed her cheek and said, "I will be in your uncle's study if anybody needs me. Not to be disturbed."

"Jane, I must check on the children in the nursery. Shall we leave at half past?"

"Of course, Aunt. I will be ready when you are."

When the sisters were left alone, Lydia declared, "Lord, our mother... When did she become such a doddy? She has more bottom than sense."

Lizzy fought to keep her mouth from gaping at this unexpected revelation.

"Well, she is! I used to believe her encouragement was good fun. But, why she should be angry at me for protecting the very thing which would make me desirable to a husband, I don't know!"

"Lydia!"

"La! Mr. Wickham might have had good reason to suspect I would be a willing party to his desires, but I was not. He had told me all along that we would marry. That he did not care I had no fortune. Now I see it was all a lie. And Mama's actions show me what I fool I have been."

Jane put her arm around her sister's shoulders and said, "We are very proud of you, dearest."

"Yes, it would have been easy to succumb to the flattery of Mr. Wickham," Kitty interjected, "or any man if you believed he truly loved you."

"'Who can find a virtuous woman? For her price is above rubies,' Proverbs 31:10." Looking over her spectacles, Mary continued. "You might have disappointed your earthly parent, but your Heavenly Father is pleased with you."

"I appreciate that. But do not expect I want you reading 'Fordyce's' out to me after dinner."

With uncharacteristic, impish verve, Mary quickly countered. "At least I know when I have read it to you and Kitty while you sleep, it has made an impression."

※

"Elizabeth? Lizzy, are you awake?"

She rolled over and roused herself as the clock struck two chimes. "I am now."

"May I come in?" Lydia opened the door, not waiting for the answer. She quickly snuggled under the blanket next to Lizzy.

"What is it? Do not wake Jane," she whispered, indicating her eldest sister asleep in the bed across the room. "Can this not wait until morning?"

"No," she said, tossing her plait over her shoulder. "I need to confess something to you."

"Is it something to do with Mr. Wickham?" She bit her lip fearful of the answer.

"Yes, it is. I lied to you and my sisters."

"You can tell me anything, dear."

It was as if her words released a dam. "I did allow Mr. Wickham liberties. I did allow him to kiss me, more than once. His kisses left me so weak, I could barely walk home."

"Dearest, I am not your priest. You do not need to confess these sins to me…"

Lydia continued headlong into her confession. "To be honest, I was so foolish I might have allowed him more liberties had he not…"

"Mentioned Mary King?"

"No, no. He never cared three straws for Mary King. She is such a nasty, little freckled thing…"

"Lydia! That is uncharitable!"

"She is. Wickham always said so. He is only after her ten thousand pounds, I am sure."

"Then I am sorry to hear it. What caused you to quarrel, dear?"

Tracing the pattern of the counterpane with her fingers, Lydia whispered, "He said I was cheap. And a real man would not see fit to waste his time on a girl like me."

Tears flowed freely as she gathered Lydia in her arms and let her cry it out.

Father always said Lydia would never be easy till she exposed herself in some manner. How terrible to be humbled by such a man. Alas, there is hope for her yet.

~

And here I am again. Lizzy had been staring at the same page in her novel for she knew not how long as the Darcy carriage rolled through the small village. *How is it that I, a nearly engaged woman, am sitting across from a man who is not my betrothed, but is instead the man who... the man who... the man who occupies all my dreams?* Her cheeks burned from the visions she knew she should push from her mind. *What has caused the Fates to conspire against me? Am I Prometheus, forever bound to misery, only to repeat myself until I have found some relief?*

Lizzy shook the errant thought from her consciousness and returned to her book. Both Kitty and Georgiana were sleeping soundly across from one another: Kitty's head against the rich panels of the box and Georgiana leaning against her brother. Lizzy peeked over her book at her companion to study his excellent features as he stared out the window to the bustling town. His shoulders looked strong, exuding confidence and respectability. His fingers drumming a tattoo along his long leg, drawing her eyes to his athletic build that was shown to great advantage by the cut of his traveling clothes.

"Miss Elizabeth, are you unwell? You look flushed."

Covered in mortification at her own imaginings, she managed to say, "I must be warm."

Mr. Darcy coughed, and she further felt herself blush upon seeing his breath in the crisp air. "I hope my sister's insistence you travel with us was not an imposition. With the unexpected illness of Mrs. Annesley's son, her continued presence in London was necessary and we welcome your gracious company."

"I am honored to visit your Pemberley. When Georgie accompanies you on your wedding tour, I will be separated from my young friend, and we will miss her so." He cleared his throat and she looked at him expectantly. When he did not respond, she continued. "I must own that I have been curious to see your home. I have heard such lovely accounts. I am eager to view it for myself."

"I hope it meets with your approval."

"I am certain, sir, it shall." Closing her book, she looked out the window to the country side speeding past. "I did not realize Pemberley was such a great distance from London."

He grinned. "That is one excuse I give for not attending many events during the season. 'Estate business' can be quite cumbersome."

She gurgled at his unguarded statement. "Now, I can never trust a man again who claims 'estate business' as motivation to miss an event."

His rich, baritone laugh startled Georgiana, who woke briefly then resettled herself against the carriage squabs. He leaned forward and whispered, "I assure you, Miss Elizabeth. I would never use that reasoning to excess."

His playful grin and candor made her cover her mouth with both hands to stifle her amusement. After a moment and peace restored, she said, "Although your manner seems untroubled, I know you must be concerned for what we will find when we arrive."

The turn in conversation did sober him, and he nodded weakly. "In this instant, I cannot take the word of my steward over my own eyes."

"Do you truly believe the fire to be extensive?"

"No," he said, shaking his head. "I trust my man implicitly, but Pemberley is the air I breathe, just as Longbourn is to you. My father gave me stewardship for future generations of Darcys. Until I see Pemberley still stands, I cannot rest easy." He flexed his hands, then clasped them together.

"And how much longer until we arrive?"

"Once we reach the crest of the summit, we will enter Pemberley Woods. Roughly one half hour."

"And your steward said the main house was not damaged?"

"He wrote there was minimal damage to the main house. I am aware we lost a stable and a hot house."

"I wish the Grecian Temple burned to the ground." They both startled at Georgiana's voice.

"Georgiana," he said with an affected warning as Lizzy exclaimed, "A Grecian temple? That sounds exotic, sir."

He smirked. "A month after my mother's death, my aunt Catherine sent builders to erect a monument to my mother's memory."

"Not a welcome gesture?" Lizzy asked evenly.

"Although Father appreciated the gesture, it has always seemed like a monstrosity that had been dropped on our grounds to remind us of Mother's death."

"Georgie. Do not speak so."

"But it is true, Wills. Father even said so. Mother would not have liked such a large, out-of-place *thing*."

"Georgiana." His tone ceased her conversation and she closed her eyes to feign sleep. Mr. Darcy looked across to Lizzy and he rolled his eyes at his sister's girlish pluck. She could not help but bite her lip at his boyish response.

"Have we almost arrived?" Kitty asked, arching her back. "How long was I asleep?"

"Not too long, dear. And Mr. Darcy said we should be there within the hour."

"Yes, but we shall see the house much sooner than that," Georgiana replied. "Brother, may we stop at the crest of the hill?"

"Of course, Georgie. But do not be frightened for what we may see."

"All will be well, Brother."

They gradually ascended through the wood and found themselves at the top of a considerable eminence. Mr. Darcy signaled the driver to stop. The footman opened the door and the unmistakable scent of burnt wood greeted them. Mr. Darcy stepped out first, turning to hand down the ladies. Georgiana and Kitty ran ahead of them and disappeared through a copse.

He grasped Lizzy's hand and they ran to meet Georgiana. Upon reaching the clearing, they gasped. There, with the glint of the sun reflecting off the lake, stood Pemberley, proud and erect as it had stood for generations.

Tears welled in Georgiana's eyes, as she reached her brother and buried her face in his chest. "I did not realize how afraid I was until I saw that our home still stood. Forgive me."

He wrapped his arms around her and lowered his head to kiss her tenderly. "Now, now, poppet. There is no need for tears. Our home is safe." He continued to soothe her, and her crying turned to gasping hiccups.

"Pray…forgive me," Georgiana said, addressing the Bennet sisters while wiping her eyes. "You must…think me…such a watering pot."

Lizzy placed a hand upon her shoulder. "My dear, it must have been so frightening for you to come all this way and not know for certain. I would have reacted the same way…"

"As would I," agreed Kitty, stepping up to embrace her friend.

"Only neither Kitty nor I have a brother to comfort us."

Georgiana took a deep breath and seemed to have recovered some of her composure. "Of that, Lizzy, I cannot envy you there. I would not trade my dear brother for all the sisters in the world and only wish you could experience it for yourself. There is no greater feeling of comfort and safety than in William's arms."

A glaring silence followed, and Lizzy could only mumble, "I am certain you are correct, Georgiana, but I… I…"

Georgiana herself blushed an indeterminate hue. "Lizzy, you misunderstand me. That is… I do not mean to say… I did not wish… for you to feel my brother's … I…"

Kitty seemed to be attempting to swallow her rising mirth and even Mr. Darcy's own countenance glowed. "But the Miss Bennets are to gain a brother very soon. Charles." He cleared his throat but before he could offer another statement, Lizzy salvaged the moment.

"I know what you meant, Georgie. Never you mind. Now," she said, calling over her shoulder as she walked toward the carriage and hoping to hide the tremor in her voice, "let us hie to Pemberley. I cannot fathom waiting a second longer when our destination is so desirable."

CHAPTER 18

E lizabeth rolled over and burrowed deeper under the feathered quilt, closing her eyes again to the morning sun. After their arrival the previous week, she had been quite in awe of Mr. Darcy and his home. She was not mercenary, mind you, but was enthralled watching him as master of his estate. He interacted amiably with his servants and the few tenants who came to meet with him. He knew everyone by name, and although he was decidedly the master, his level of concern touched her. *He is a much different master than my father. These people are a part of him because they are a part of Pemberley.*

She peeked out from under the quilts, hearing the sound of the birds outside calling to her. She heard a maid in her dressing room and another had brought in a small breakfast tray. *I must be very late indeed.* She stretched one last time and threw her legs over the side of the bed, dangling her toes until they touched the rug.

They had a wonderful time at Lord Donnelley's dinner party the previous evening and she expected a lively discourse with Kitty and Georgiana as to the events which had raised such splendid expectations. Kitty's charms had captured the attentions of Lord

Donnelley's second son and she had shown great pleasure in his company. *Would that not be astounding were Kitty to make a match with the son of a lord? Mama would faint!* Lizzy smiled at the notion as she sipped her chocolate and allowed the maid to dress her. After her hair was managed into an acceptable bandeau, she grabbed a scone from the tray and headed down the stairs, anticipating another enjoyable day.

Fitzwilliam Darcy never ceased to be in awe that she was in his home—she who had haunted his dreams and captivated his almost every thought. To hear her laugh with his sister, hear her kindness to the servants, hear her proclaim with pure delight the wonder and beauty of his library—it was all he could ask for. *Not quite all.* He closed his ledgers and leaned back in his large wing back chair. His breath caught as he saw her in his mind's eye standing at Ashby Park with her hair cascading in ringlets down her back. *Her skin so soft, her lips so full.* He let out a small groan and shook his head to clear the image. Opening the ledger again, he began to scribble notes to discuss with his steward.

Drumming his fingers in thought, he stopped mid-motion when he heard her. That laugh which toyed with him in even in his most alone hours was just beyond his study in the library. He fought the urge to see her by continuing his notes.

That lasted all of two more minutes before the urge was too great. Standing abruptly, he grabbed a book from his shelf, opened the adjoining door to the library but halted where he stood when he found her alone.

Her fingers traced the spines as she walked along his collection and she spoke to select tomes as she passed. "Well, Beowulf, son of Edgetho. As intriguing as your adventures may be, they will not do today for a quiet visit in the garden. I am searching for something less *daring*—more fanciful. And you, Lord Byron" —she giggled touching a collection of poems— "you I most assuredly will not take with me to the garden *alone.*"

Darcy silently watched her from the doorway. Her teasing tone and curious banter was enchanting, and he wanted nothing more than to sit in the nearest easy chair and partake of this world she was creating. However, with her next sentence, he almost lost control of his senses.

"And you, my sweet William, you undo me whenever you are near." She seemed to purr, caressing a worn copy of Shakespeare's sonnets. "No, it is best that I stay far away from you while I am at Pemberley, because your words seem to control me at times, and I am so unlike myself, I hardly know what to do."

His mouth went dry and he clamped it closed, waiting to hear what would fall next from her sweet lips.

"And yet still another William to woo my affections," she said with a smile in her voice as she picked up another small copy of poems. "You, Mr. Wordsworth, might possibly be the winner. You will be the William who will join me on my ramble through the woods today. You see," she said lowering her voice with a conspiratorial tone, "Mr. Shakespeare causes me great consternation with the outcomes for many of his heroes, and Mr. Blake" —she continued tapping another book on the table— "is too fanciful speaking of lambs and tigers, but then too morose with young chimney sweeps. Yes, sir, it is you." She picked up the book and walked to the window, staring out at the November day. "You are the William I choose. For there is no other William…save one, who I wish to sit with by the lake and share my thoughts." She spoke so softly he might have imagined it all.

She walked out of the library and a few minutes later, he watched her through the window skip along the well-worn path. His heart soared at the thought she held him in such esteem. Yet, he knew his dreams were hollow. *No matter where our futures lead us, I will always think on her as nonpareil. The most amiable but also the handsomest woman of my acquaintance. There can be nothing more.*

The day passed with the same serenity which seemed to consume all her days at Pemberley. Hours after leaving the library with her book, her hunger for the written word satiated, she now sought her friends to continue her pleasure.

Approaching the house, she was a surprised to see a carriage pull up to the entry. She was aware that travelers often requested tours of Pemberley during the spring and summer months but infrequently during autumn and winter. However, it was none of her concern and she walked up the stairs to the veranda and into the music room where Georgiana was attempting to master a difficult movement and Kitty was embroidering a cushion.

"Lizzy, how was the lake today? It looked entirely too cold for my liking, but I knew you would still enjoy the sunshine."

"You are right, Kitty. Wordsworth and I had a lovely time," she said, handing her cloak and gloves to a footman. "I came in hungry for your companionship and am rewarded also with my favorites." She smiled as she sat next to her sister, set her book aside, and reached for a lemon biscuit from the tray.

The three girls were chatting amiably when the door opened and the butler came in the room. "Pardon me, Miss Darcy, but the master wishes for you and the Miss Bennets to join him in his study."

With no little curiosity, they followed the butler. When they entered the study, Mr. Darcy stood and they were greeted by three guests.

"Why, Mrs. Worth, what a pleasure to see you again!" Lizzy took the woman's outstretched hands in her own.

"Thank you, Miss Elizabeth. The pleasure is ours. Might I introduce my husband to you?" she asked, nodding to a tall man about her uncle Gardiner's age with a kindly mien. When all the introductions were made, Lizzy approached the old woman seated by the chair at the window. "And Mrs. Smith. How lovely to see you! I hope your trip was pleasant?" When there was no response from the old woman, Lizzy asked Mrs. Worth, "What brings you to Pemberley?"

Mr. Darcy interpolated, "Doctor's orders."

"Yes. We have been encouraged to take her to locations which gave her pleasure, where she spent most of her years. Lambton and Pemberley were our first thoughts. We arrived yesterday morning and after going through the village, we decided to appeal to Mrs. Reynolds for a tour in hopes of stimulating any repressed memories."

Mr. Darcy said, "Might I suggest a general tour? And also the family suites? She would have spent many hours with my mother in that wing."

"Truly, sir?"

"Yes. And may I suggest we first attempt my mother's room." He stood and called to a footman. "Please have Mrs. Reynolds remove the holland covers in the mistress's apartment and prepare the room as it would have been in my mother's day."

"Yes, Mr. Darcy."

"Also, please inform Cook we will take some refreshment in the front parlor. If I remember correctly, Mrs. Smith loved strawberry tarts."

"And still does," Mrs. Worth replied gratefully.

"If everyone would join me in the parlor while the rooms are prepared." The guests followed a footman out of the study, and Mr. Darcy said quietly, "Georgie, I would also like you and the Miss Bennets to join us. You might be disquieted by Mrs. Smith's maladies, but I believe if she does remember anything of our mother, you would welcome the opportunity to hear her."

After half an hour of pleasantries, Mrs. Reynolds informed Mr. Darcy the apartment was ready. Everyone made their way above stairs to enter a room which very few had entered in years.

Lizzy's eyes roamed around the most intimate, tangible representation of the woman Fitzwilliam Darcy loved above all others, save his sister: the lavender walls, the plum canopy on the large mahogany bed, the paintings of Pemberley's woods and gardens, and a portrait of a small boy with precocious eyes, a dimple in his chubby cheek, and brown curls with that tell-tale lock across his forehead. She could not help but smile at the child who would grow into the man who stood mere feet from her.

As she was studying the picture a low voice behind her spoke, "Do not let that starched collar and velvet coat fool you, Miss Bennet. That little boy waited only moments when he was dismissed from the artist to tear off his formal attire and go down to the pond to dig for worms with his older cousin Richard."

"I do not know if I can believe you, sir. The future master of Pemberley was born with a propensity to do only what is expected of him. I do not believe that he would disobey his nanny, could he?"

Smiling, he said, "It was not disobedience if his mother encouraged it."

"Mother allowed you to dig for worms?" Georgiana asked, laughing at the idea and sitting on the edge of the great bed. "Lady Catherine has always left me with the impression that you were very proper as a child—that mother made sure you were always buttoned up and polished."

"Buttoned up and polished?" A strange voice laughed. "Master Fitzwilliam? Oh, no. He's a regular goer as soon as he was in short pants, miss." Everyone turned to Mrs. Smith who was standing by the desk straightening the flowers Mrs. Reynolds had seen fit to place in a vase. "Such a precious child. He's your joy, isn't he, my lady?" she asked, staring intently at Georgiana. "But, you...you are not Lady Anne, yet you look so much like her."

"No," Georgiana said with a quaking voice. "Lady Anne was my mother. I am Georgiana Darcy. The youngest child of George and Lady Anne Darcy."

Mrs. Smith gaped at Georgiana, then turned to look at Mr. Darcy. "Then you are…"

"I am Fitzwilliam Darcy, Mrs. Smith. The young scamp who used to hide behind your skirts from my nanny and would accept your sweets as a secret between two friends."

She looked back and forth between the siblings, then at her own granddaughter. "Cassie, I'm so confused."

Mrs. Worth held the older woman's hands. "We have come to Pemberley on holiday, Grandmother, and have called on Mr. Darcy and Miss Georgiana. After tea, we will join Mrs. Reynolds in the servants' hall so you can visit if you like. Does that please you?"

"Yes, yes, of course…I just…everything seems so strange." She looked down at her hands. "Why are my hands so wrinkled? Am I that old?" Her face spoke fear and uncertainty as she and her granddaughter walked slowly around the room and examined her surroundings. "Everything is as I remember, except for the rattle. I placed it on the end table." She paused, tracing her finger along the dust-free wood. "My dear mistress has been gone for quite some time?" She exhaled at her granddaughter's nod of confirmation.

Taking a moment to digest her lucid thoughts, Mrs. Smith turned to Georgiana. "You are so like your mother. I thought for a moment you were her." The old woman's eyes glossed over with tears as she continued. "What a beautiful person. And the kindest, gentlest soul. She could have asked me to leave her employ as I grew old, but she didn't—always loyal to those who loved her."

She lowered her voice. "I am sure you wonder about her, miss. You must know she was so full of life. Her laugh was like fairy bells and she always smelled of lavender. She loved Shakespeare and long walks through the woods. And playing the piano. And spending time with the master—theirs was a love match, there was no doubt." Mrs. Smith took Georgiana's hands and sat on the bed next to her. "And child…how she loved you. She might only have been on this Earth with you for a short time, but I have never in my life seen a woman more devoted to her children." Mrs. Smith patted Georgiana's hand. "And she is here, child. Her presence is in Pemberley, and it is in you. You have been given the gift of both her and your father's love to guide you. They were great people who only wanted you to be happy."

This strange speech made Lizzy feel as if George and Lady Anne Darcy's love swirled forth about the room, embracing their children in long forgotten memories. Mrs. Smith held Georgie's hand and Darcy leaned over and gave his sister a handkerchief before drawing up a chair next to his mother's old servant.

"And you, sir…the master of Pemberley. What a fine gentleman you have become. Your mother would be so proud of you. I don't know if you remember her last days…"

"Yes, I do."

"She was so proud of you for how you cared for your baby sister— told me later one of her regrets was that she wouldn't be here to play with *your* children."

Mr. Darcy could only respond with pale smile.

"You are a credit to them both." She reached over and gently patted his cheek. "And raising your sister on your own? It is evident you have taken admirable care." She smiled and lowered her hand into her lap and began glancing around.

Mr. Darcy cleared his throat. "Mrs. Smith, I thank you for the kind words. It is rare for me, even more so for Georgiana, to hear such sentiments about our parents."

"I am happy to be of service."

"Could I trouble you to reflect back upon my mother's last days?"

"Of course."

"On that morning Lady Catherine arrived... I have been told my mother had you write a letter to me. Do you remember that?"

"I most certainly do. I stood right over there and wrote it at her desk. She was too weak by then to do it herself, you see. She told me what to say, and I wrote it word for word."

"Very well. Do you remember what exactly was in the letter?"

"Hmmm... well, I can't rightly say I remember everything. I do remember she spoke of her love for you and the babe," she said smiling at Georgiana. "She wanted you to remember to be a good boy and that she always wanted you to be happy."

"Did she say anything about my cousin Anne?"

Mrs. Smith sat there for a moment, seemingly trying to remember that day so many years before. Slowly, she said, "That she did, sir. I remember her saying she wanted you to be happy." She looked up at Lizzy and continued. "That Anne de Bourgh was a lovely girl. And that she wanted you to be happy...yes, she wants you to be happy. You are her joy." She smiled at Lizzy. "Yes, quite lovely. She will make you quite happy...happy."

Realizing Mrs. Smith's mistake, Lizzy's embarrassment was great and she did not know where to look.

"This is Miss Bennet. She is not my betrothed…"

"Yes, she wanted you to be happy…yes, yes she wants you to be happy. You are her joy."

Mr. Darcy glanced at Mrs. Worth, confusion written on his face.

"Happiness. She will be so happy for your happiness."

In a hushed voice, Mrs. Worth said, "It is the cobwebs, sir."

Before Mr. Darcy could respond, Mrs. Smith smiled and asked, "Will there be anything else, Mr. Darcy? Lady Anne has asked me to repair her cream silk before you are to depart for London tomorrow."

Mr. Darcy sighed and shook his head. "No, Mrs. Smith. I thank you. That will be all. However, if you will show our guests down to the blue sitting room for refreshments?"

Hazel Smith eyes glazed over, looking straight ahead at nothing, and sat with a look of contentment on her face.

No one moved and Mrs. Worth said, "Mr. Darcy. Once again, I apologize."

"No, I thank you, ma'am. I received the information I was seeking about my mother's final days. I can be at peace, and I know the moments of your grandmother's lucidity gave comfort to my sister as well."

Georgiana nodded, once again wiping the tears away. "I feel as if my mother spoke to me from the beyond. I thank you."

"Please join us downstairs for refreshment," Mr. Darcy said. Mr. Worth gently guided his wife's grandmother down the stairs behind them.

"We thank you but must decline," Mrs. Worth said. "My grandmother should rest. With your permission, however, we will be in the village for a few days before we are on to visit relatives further north. Might we trespass upon your kindness once again and visit the servants then?"

"Of course. I will let Mrs. Reynolds know to expect you."

"Thank you, sir, for your hospitality."

"Thank you, ma'am. And if you can delay your departure for a few moments," he said, "I will see to it that Cook prepares a basket with Mrs. Smith's favorite strawberry tarts."

"You are too kind, Mr. Darcy."

"Think nothing of it."

When the visitors were on their way back to Lambton, Mr. Darcy excused himself and locked himself in his study claiming "estate business" which he had neglected until that moment.

Lizzy sighed, remembering their conversation in the carriage and knowing exactly what he meant.

CHAPTER 19

T he stillness of the day spoke to Lizzy as she picked one of the final blooms of autumn and continued to walk through the worn path she had come to favor over her weeks in Derbyshire. *This will probably be my last ramble as the weather is changing. I would not be surprised if we woke up on the morrow to find a heavy dusting of snow.*

It had been a wonderful visit: sunny but brisk strolls by the lake, carriage rides into Lambton, devouring numerous books from Pemberley's library. *And in three days it will cease, and I will return to London, and then to Longbourn...and then finally to Ashby Park.* There was no hint of anger or sadness, just resignation. She knew what her future held, and although it was not... No! Lizzy was not by nature melancholy and accepted that her life would be one of contentment with James.

I am to be mistress of Ashby Park, married to a man who I will learn to love as my husband. This—she looked back toward the great house—*and all it entails is so far above me; I am ridiculous to even have dreamt it for a moment.* The spires peaked above the tree tops and swirls of smoke from the chimneys floated to the clouds. *Even had Mrs. Smith not visited and sparked hope in my heart... He is Fitzwilliam Darcy of Pemberley—nephew to the Earl of Matlock, son of Lady Anne Darcy and George Darcy, one of the most illustrious families in all of England.* "And I...I am Elizabeth Bennet," she said aloud for the trees to hear. "Niece to a country attorney and a London tradesman. Daughter of an insignificant country gentleman and his silly but good-intentioned wife." With a heavy sigh, Lizzy turned and continued in the opposite direction, deciding to follow the path to the end, uncertain where it would take her.

❧

Kitty stood nervously at the window of the music room, watching the unexpected snowflakes fall. She was only partially listening as Georgiana played through another of Beethoven's sonatas. "Does it usually snow so much at this time of year?" she asked, turning a worried gaze back at her friend.

"Pardon? I was not attending, Kitty."

"I asked if it usually snows so much at the end of November." She waved her hand at the window. "I was sure Derbyshire had snow in December but I believed we would miss it on this trip."

Georgiana laughed and continued to play. "That is one thing my brother often says. 'You cannot predict a Derbyshire winter.' As you can see, he tells the truth." After a moment, she finished her piece and rested her hands on her lap while her face became animated. "Oh, Kitty. We will have such a jolly time tomorrow making snowmen, having a snow ball fight, and doing all the things *ladies* might find childish." She waited for a response, but after receiving none, asked, "Why, Kitty. Whatever is the matter?"

Kitty turned away from the window. "I am only distressed about Lizzy."

"Lizzy?"

"Yes, she has not returned since leaving for her walk this morning…"

"Elizabeth has not returned?" Georgiana asked with sudden alarm on her face. She stood instantly and walked out into the hall toward her brother's study. "Oh!" She stopped abruptly and looked with wide eyes at her friend. "Wills is not here. He is at Lord Donnelly's helping with some tenant dispute. Quickly, we must get Mrs. Reynolds."

Kitty hurried after her friend, noting the snow beyond the long windows of the great hall falling at a tempest's pace.

❧

Once we leave this great estate, I will write to Mr. Hamilton and express more affection than I feel. Ours might not be a true love match, but I will make our union a happy one. "He is a good man," she said to a small woodland creature scrambling up a tree. "He is respectable and kind to me. He is…just…what…a young man ought to be." She had difficulty professing the last words as the vision of a tall man with brown eyes and errant curl falling across his brow stole through her thoughts. No amount of blinking or shaking her head could dislodge the image of Mr. Darcy from her mind—opening her eyes to find him leaning over her at Ashby Park, his hair disheveled, his nightshirt unbuttoned exposing his neck and collarbones.

She began to breathe a little faster, due in no part to her long walk, and excused her final thought of his dimpled smile in the carriage. *Oh, Georgiana! How your words have tortured me these last weeks at night, knowing I will never find equal comfort or safety in anyone's arms... save William's.*

She stopped in the middle of the path in the conifer woods and began to berate herself. "Elizabeth Anne Bennet, that is enough! You will make James a good wife, and he will make you a good husband. Many marriages begin with less and succeed."

She continued to walk, kicking a pebble, when she came out of the shelter of the woods and into a clearing. "Oh!" She was stunned by the blanket of snow before her. Realizing her error in having roamed so far and for so long, her heart raced in panic. *They will not know where to look for me! I do not even know where to look for me!* The wind had picked up and an icy chill shot through her as she looked down at her pelisse and gloves. *I must move forward. I must find shelter. Somewhere. Maybe through the meadow. Behind that grove of trees.*

A distance which would should have taken her a few minutes stretched out as she traversed the exposed field. Her vision was obscured by snow and wind, and her pelisse became heavy with wet snow. At the edge of the trees, she could spy a rustic structure. Her heart leapt at the sight of what must be a hunting lodge, and she increased her pace. She was grateful the door gave way and she quickly closed the wind and snow behind her.

The room was musty from disuse but still well kept. Finding a stack of wood by the hearth, she smiled at the thought of making a fire for the first time. She found a row of simple rooms that must be the servants' quarters, walked back into the small hallway and made her way down to handsomely appointed bedrooms with hunting scenes adorning the walls. *I must find dry clothes. I am certain this is a man's domain but am hopeful for any forgotten clothing to keep me warm.* The two smaller ones were still larger than her own room at Longbourn but the master's suite had a large bed. She pulled back the holland covers of the armoire and opening the drawers, she found a man's night shirt, a fine lawn shirt, breeches and a tartan scarf along with a worn book of poetry. "Wordsworth," she said aloud. "My old friend."

She set the book atop the dresser, hastily removed her clothing and let everything puddle in a pile next to her wet half-boots. The blush on her cheeks warmed her as no fire could at the thought of the man who invaded her dreams. She pulled his own night shirt over her head, donned a pair of huge woolen socks, and attempted to ignore his lingering scent which clung to the fabric.

The length of the garment dragged behind her, attesting to the height of its owner, while she made her way back into the main room. Kneeling down, she grabbed the wood and put it on the hearth as she had seen the maids do in the early mornings. She found the tinderbox, and after several failed attempts, set about warming what would be her home for at least the night.

❧

Fitzwilliam Darcy was wet and cold. He had left Donnelly Hall before the snow fell, believing he could outrun the storm. He realized now he was sorely mistaken. With the collar of his great coat pulled high around his ears, and his hat pressed low across his brow, even without the storm howling around him, his visibility was limited. Propitiously, he knew the grounds of his estate as he knew each room in his home. *I am still at least an hour from the house. I should not have left Donnelly!* He stopped his horse amongst the cover of trees and patted his withers. "Do not worry, old boy." Remembering the old hunting lodge, he turned the stallion down another trail in the woods and dug his heels into Ulysses' flanks.

～

Georgiana was right. Mrs. Reynolds knew exactly what to do. She had immediately summoned the butler who summoned the game keeper who gathered the men. They combed the grounds as best they could in the raging storm until they finally had to give up. Mrs. Reynolds had attempted to send a rider to Donnelly Hall to alert the master but to no avail. He returned saying he could not see the road ahead of him once he left the main gates of the estate.

The two young girls held each other in fear on the couch watching the darkness descend rapidly outside. Georgiana whispered words of comfort, just as Kitty had done for her the night she almost eloped with George Wickham.

They took a tray in the music room but lacked any appetite. About half past, they heard a commotion in the hall. Running to the great hall, they stopped at the sight.

"Where is my nephew?"

The fire had been roaring for nearly an hour and Elizabeth had completely thawed out. Her only concern now was for Kitty and Georgiana knowing they would fear for her safety and would have certainly sent out a search party. *Pity there is no way to get word that I am safe and warm.* So warm that Elizabeth had unwrapped herself from the blanket on the couch, kicked off the woolen socks, wiggled her toes, and stretched her legs, luxuriating in the warmth of the fire. Earlier she had found candles, a tin with some stale biscuits, had unpinned her hair, and was curled up reading Wordsworth when she drifted off to sleep. Not knowing how long she had slept, she woke to hear the door rattling. Grabbing a blanket, she threw it around her shoulders and dashed to the door, expecting someone from the house had come to her rescue.

His cousin Richard had told him once that when one travels through the desert, the mind returns again and again to water, to satiate the thirst welling up uncontrollably inside. Fitzwilliam Darcy, nearly frozen, stood there at the door, with the snow blowing into the room, drinking in his fill. *I must be dreaming. I must have succumbed to the elements, fallen off my horse in the woods, and am dreaming.* But the warmth of the room, contrasting with the cold behind him, testified this was no dream.

"Miss Bennet? Pray do not be alarmed," he said, while continuing to stare at her, her ankles exposed.

"Mr. Darcy! Quickly, come inside before you catch your death of cold."

Standing there in her night gown—*my night shirt*—he realized, swallowing a ragged breath, she closed the door behind him, shutting out the outside world and the reality of their lives.

Regaining his composure, he shook his head. "Miss Bennet. What are you doing here? How did you come to be in my grandfather's hunting lodge?"

She smiled anxiously. "No, sir. There is time to tell that tale, as I fear this storm will rage all night long. Come," she said, grabbing a candle from the table and leading his stiff limbs toward his room. "You must go and change. You are wet through. I have a fire here and will make you a cup of tea."

"I fear I will need something stronger than tea," he said in a low voice, following her down the dark hallway as if this was her home and he was her guest.

She stopped outside his room, moved her free hand up to his shoulders, and began to remove his soaking outerwear. "Let me take your coat to dry it by the fire. We must have you out of these clothes and warm, Mr. Darcy," she said, all the while pulling his sleeves down his arms until his great coat was off.

Heaven help me! I cannot stand here like a eunuch while she is undressing me only wearing my nightshirt! Give me strength!

As if reading his thoughts, Elizabeth stopped when her warm hand rested upon his chest, her eyes growing large. No doubt feeling his heart pounding through his clothes, she looked down at her hand and up at him before pulling it away as if on fire.

"Mr. Darcy, forgive me. I was only… I was…not attending."

"Miss Bennet," he replied, attempting to control his strained voice as the tension enveloped them. His heart raced as his eyes searched her face for…he knew not what. "I know you meant…"

"Yes…" She fiddled with the candle stick and finally pointed through the doorway into his room. "I believe you will find more clothes in …well, yes, of course, you know …if you leave your wet things …" She gasped.

His gaze followed her eyes and recognizing her own forgotten clothes and undergarments on the floor, he swiftly turned to face the opposite wall, while she quickly picked them up.

"Pray excuse me, Mr. Darcy," she murmured. She left him the candle and rushed from the room.

He closed the door behind her, realizing he had not spoken more than four sentences since his arrival and walked to the large chair next to the empty fireplace and slumped down onto the holland cover, feeling an emotional exhaustion he had never felt before. *Trapped. Trapped and alone with her. With no servants and a raging storm outside. This is a dream. And a nightmare.*

After a moment, he peeled his wet clothes from his body and stepped to the dresser, opening the top drawer where he knew there were spare clothes, then stopped. *How am I to survive the night with her in this house wearing nothing but my nightshirt?* He grasped both edges of the cold wood and took a fortifying breath without raising his head. *I will conquer this! I must!* Shrugging his shoulders, he pulled out buckskins, a shirt, and a waist coat. With no cravat or jacket, his shirt fell open at the neck. *This is the best you can do, Darce.* He walked back over to the hearth, took some of the wood, and quickly built a fire to warm the room, laying out his clothes to dry. After several more minutes, he stood and took another breath. "You cannot hide in here forever, old man. Go see what you can do to make her more comfortable." And with that, he released his breath and walked out to face the greatest challenge of his life.

"Miss Bennet?" Darcy whispered as he came back into the room. She was wrapped in the blanket on the couch in front of the fire, reading his book of poems. She looked up at him, and a slight rosiness spread over her cheeks. *I should retire immediately if I am to remain in my senses.*

"Pray, sir. Forgive me for making myself at home here."

"Of course not," he interrupted. "Pay it no consequence. You have already taken the lay of the land. I should count myself fortunate that you have everything prepared for my unexpected arrival." He was about to sit on a wooden chair but noticed her pelisse draped across it.

"Oh, I can move that into the kitchen. I had planned on it," she said, scrambling to get up.

"Miss Bennet, please do not trouble yourself. However, if you would like to place your …garments in my room, there is a roaring fire going and…well, everything…might dry more quickly. From my own experience," he said, "this kitchen does not get hot enough to dry clothes, unless the undercook is here making bread. You had much better follow my suggestion so you would have clothes to wear on the morrow." She blushed, and he was certain his cheeks burned the same.

"If you are sure?"

"Of course."

"I thank you. I will remove them this evening before you sleep and place them out here."

"Miss Bennet, I will not allow you to sleep out here in the sitting room."

"No, Mr. Darcy, I will sleep in one of the guest quarters."

"Of that, I cannot allow either. You will take my room, and I will sleep out here."

He swallowed the lump in his throat in order to speak but she continued. "Sir, that is not possible. I cannot take your room. Either of the other rooms will be quite sufficient. They are larger than my room at Longbourn—"

"And unbeknownst to you, Miss Bennet, they are extremely uncomfortable. Even Bingley can attest that the couch is more comfortable than those beds. I daresay, it's the couch or the stables for me."

"You cannot very well sleep in the stables!" She tilted her head to the side and a few tendrils spilled down her shoulders, joining the rest of her tresses. He thought her pluck quite charming in the firelight. "Uncomfortable? I find it difficult to comprehend that anything on the grounds of Pemberley would be uncomfortable for a guest."

He laughed at her response and sat beside her on the couch. "When I was young, probably seven or eight years old, my uncles, Sir Lewis de Bourgh and Lord Matlock, came for a hunt with Father. Father had only returned from a business trip from France, and Mother and I missed him terribly, but there was nothing to be done. This hunt had been planned and my uncles were already arrived."

He shifted to face her while resting his elbow against the back of the couch and his fist against his cheek. "What was supposed to be a two-day hunting trip, turned into a week."

"Was your mother not upset?"

"Exceedingly." He smiled.

"I was surprised to discover a fine hunting lodge such as this on the grounds. Whyever did your father have it if your mother did not like him away?"

"It was built in my grandfather's day. My grandfather enjoyed the convenience of his private retreat. And as *you* know, the grounds are ten miles around." Darcy chuckled.

"Whatever happened?"

"Apparently Sir Lewis was having a splendid time without my aunt, and my uncle Matlock was having a splendid time without his mother-in-law who was visiting Matlock House. As my father was the host, he could not leave."

"Was she able to convince your father to shorten his trip?" Miss Elizabeth leaned forward with curiosity. The firelight glimmered in her loose curls, making Darcy wonder again how it would feel to pull her to him and… He swallowed and looked away.

"Yes. One day, Father's valet came back to the house for a change of clothes, Mother inquired when the men went out shooting in the morning and when they returned. She then sent servants to the attics for two very old and lumpy mattresses and instructed them to exchange the mattresses at the lodge."

Miss Elizabeth clapped her hands and squealed with unguarded laughter. "And what occurred? Please tell me her plan worked."

He smiled at her enthusiasm. "It did, almost instantly. The next morning the men awoke and told their servants to pack up, that they had enough and were going back to the house, that they had never slept so poorly in all their years. Father returned that afternoon, and after they recuperated for a few nights at Pemberley, my uncles departed."

"Ha! And I suppose she never had the mattresses replaced? Oh, how I believe I would have enjoyed your mother's company. She sounds like a kindred spirit." Miss Elizabeth laughed even harder and leaned back into the couch, allowing the blanket to slip off her shoulders. Darcy swallowed again at the sight of her bare shoulder aglow in the firelight.

He made no comment for a moment but then, "Yes. I do believe she would have adored you." Restless, he stood to find a stronger drink in the kitchen then thought better of it. "So you see, El...Miss Bennet," he said, making his way to the pot of tea, "I insist you take up my bed in the master's chambers."

"But... That is *your* bed. I cannot..."

She blushed from her bosom to her ears and Darcy could hardly look away despite his embarrassment for yet another incriminating, unintentional innuendo. He quickly interjected, "I am not being forced to do anything I would not do for a friend."

"You would do the same for Mr. Bingley? For Colonel Fitzwilliam?"

"No, no. Bingley prefers the couch, and Fitzwilliam can sleep on anything after having chased Napoleon's armies all over Europe." He laughed at her jest. "No, Miss Bennet. You have caught me out. I would only make this offer to you."

At that moment, she glanced up at him through her lashes; the fire making her eyes sparkle, almost took his breath away. "Then I accept, sir," she said quietly.

Darcy nodded and walked to the cabinet. *I do believe I will need that drink after all.*

~

The ruckus caused by the late arrivals had finally calmed after Lady Catherine retired early, insisting Anne follow her within the hour. Colonel Fitzwilliam sat comfortably next to his cousin Georgiana and Miss Katherine in the parlor while Anne remained on the chair nearer the fire.

"Cousin, I am still confused," Georgiana asked, "how you came to be at Pemberley? In this storm?"

"As are we, Sprout," he said ruefully, smiling at Anne. "We are all aware of the persuasive tactics which our aunt uses to achieve her goals. I am afraid we were coerced into visiting Pemberley. Apparently, she received a letter of some importance from Darcy and she claimed she must speak to him in person."

"Why did you not stay in an inn when the weather turned?" Miss Katherine asked, glancing at the swirling snow outside.

"Because my mother did not wish to stay in an inn when the pleasures of Pemberley were a short five miles away."

He snorted at Anne's reply. "A short five miles away. I think the driver and footmen were icicles stuck to the carriage. Those poor devils! But who am I to question my aunt when a more important concern is before us." Turning to Miss Katherine, he continued. "I am certain your sister is well. She is a bright, strong woman who has impressed me with her resourcefulness, and I am certain in her tramp through the countryside, she came upon a tenant's cottage and now sits amongst their family, playing with their children, and helping put them to bed."

"Do you think so, Colonel?"

"I do, Miss Katherine. And I look forward to being here when the joyful reunion takes place."

~

"I see you are engrossed in Wordsworth. Is he a favorite of yours?"

It was quite late, and the storm had not relented outside, only adding to the isolating atmosphere. Mr. Darcy was reclining in the chair, more at ease than Lizzy had ever seen him before, his glass dangling over the arm rest in his fingertips, his shirt collar open, his hair disheveled, and his leg crossed over his knee. Her attempts to not stare were in vain. She was grateful, however, her open admiration and curiosity seemed to go unnoticed.

They had spoken of numerous topics, exhausting the obvious, and now they seemed to have settled into a comfortable silence, each having taken up a book—Mr. Darcy choosing "The History of British Warfare" and Elizabeth with the poetry book by William Wordsworth she had discovered earlier.

Smiling at the inscription, *For my dear Fitzwilliam. You are my Joy. Forever yours, Mother*, she closed the book and said, "I do enjoy Wordsworth but must say that tonight I am more in the mood for a gothic novel. Does it not seem as if our situation would be ideal for

Miss Radcliffe to compose a new tale? A low fire burning, the wind howling outside. Our circumstances are perfect, are they not?"

He smiled, the twinkle in his eye evident. "Yes, but I would not welcome visits from ghosts or tyrannical adversaries in an effort to keep you safe. I am much more content viewing our situation while sitting by the fire in a warm lodge with my only concern that we shall have enough firewood to get through all of tomorrow if necessary. Besides, Miss Bennet, I am not the romantic hero type—I am sure Miss Radcliffe would discount me from her list of possible protagonists immediately."

"And why is that, Mr. Darcy?" She laughed, resting the book on her lap. "Do you not have heroic qualities?"

He rolled his eyes. "Well, I suppose I have been described as brooding."

"Yes, that is true, but that is not the only aspect of heroes in novels." She tapped her finger on a crooked smile. "He must also attempt to protect the virtuous maid while being gallant, honorable, and handsome."

"Am I to understand you find me handsome, Miss Bennet?"

Lizzy felt her cheeks glow. "No… I mean to say…yes. That is… that is not what I meant, Mr. Darcy."

He enjoyed watching her fluster. *Her skin turns the most lovely shade of rose.* He took a drink, feeling more than the burn from the spirits warm him to his toes.

"What I meant was your *gallantry* has been evident in many of our dealings and I am grateful that Miss Radcliffe's heroes have some basis in men that I am familiar with in real life."

"Then, I thank you for the compliment." Changing the subject to spare her further embarrassment, he said, "The book you are reading is a gift from my mother. She gave it to me on my tenth birthday and promised that if I read it faithfully, I would discover the secrets of life."

"What a lovely sentiment. And have you found them?"

"I am afraid not." He leaned forward, cradling the glass of spirits in his hand and began to rub the edge with his thumb. "In my youth, I mistakenly believed that all answers were easily laid out before those who sought them. As I came into my majority, I realized that life had many secrets, some were easily discovered while others were unwilling to divulge the smallest piece of information about themselves. No," he said, taking another sip, "I have not discovered life's secrets."

Miss Elizabeth pursed her lips. "I believe that often we expect others to fulfill our hopes for us, when in fact, we must look to ourselves for understanding and direction. I pray you find the answers you seek."

He gazed up at her and held her eyes. "I thank you, Miss Bennet. And when I find the answers, I pray they will be mine to take."

He could not look away, feeling all the tension between all that was said and unsaid. "Are you warm enough? Shall I add another log?"

"No, thank you," she said, stumbling over her words before regaining ease in speech. Her playful voice charmed him. "I am quite warm and only require another one of those delicious tea cakes. You are quite the wizard, sir, for procuring these delightful treats."

He grinned at her compliment and again at their volley, hoping to avoid the true topic. "I am no wizard, madam. Lord Donnelley's cook was the undercook at Pemberley when I was a child. She knows these are my favorites and sent me home with a tin to share with Georgiana."

"Then I am sorry there will not be any left for her. Maybe we should save one?" Miss Elizabeth asked, pulling her hand back.

"No, do not trouble yourself. As soon as his cook discovers I ate them all while trapped in the hunting lodge, she will send some post haste to Pemberley. Lord Donnelley stated there are times he only invites me to dine because he is guaranteed his cook will make them."

They both chuckled before Miss Elizabeth voiced one of the topics which was on both of their minds. "And what, sir, do you propose we do about our situation? I understand how some would view this evening and...well...knowing their suspicions are unfounded, I am at a loss."

"I am aware of the implications, and my sole purpose will be to preserve your reputation." He raised his glass and took a sip of his drink while staring into the fire. "We will say nothing because no one must ever discover we were in this predicament or you would be ruined."

Miss Elizabeth gasped. "But, Mr. Darcy. Do you think under the circumstances it would be understood there was nothing we could do?"

"Other women have been ruined for far less. This is unpardonable in the eyes of the world, and although my reputation would be intact, yours would be in tatters. I will not allow that."

He could see the moment the comprehension was made. "What are we to do? You cannot very well sleep in the stables." Her voice had become small, losing all its bravado from a moment before.

He cleared his throat. "We will do the only thing we can do. You will sleep in my room, and I will sleep here on the couch. When the weather clears, you will begin walking to Pemberley, and I will follow ten minutes later. Then when asked, we can truthfully say I came across you on the path."

"And what of where I slept?"

"You can truthfully say you slept in an uninhabited building on the estate grounds." He looked back down at his hands, rubbing his knuckles with his fingers. "Miss Bennet, disguise of every sort is my abhorrence, but in this case, I feel it imperative that an alteration in the facts will be beneficial to your future. I will not put you in jeopardy!"

The vehemence with which he spoke surprised them both and a quiet settled over the room, only interrupted by the crackling of the fire and howling wind. "I thank you, Mr. Darcy. On that note, I believe it is time for me to retire. Goodnight," she said, gathering up her damp clothes to allow them to drive in the bedroom.

Darcy stood as well. "Goodnight, Miss Bennet. You will find the fire should still be hot, as I put in some large logs which will continue to burn all night. If you are in need of assistance, I will remain here so you can find me." He gave her a teasing grin as she turned to walk out of the room, wrapped in her blanket with her naked feet and ankles peeking from the bottom. He waited until he heard the door close, then sighed, and sunk down onto his makeshift bed for the evening. Reaching for the decanter to pour another drink, he glumly allowed the words of the Bard to filter through his mind with slight alteration: *Tonight is the winter of "my" discontent.*

Elizabeth woke with a start as a bolt of lightning cracked outside her window. It took her a moment to remember where she was. She did not need to look outside to know the storm raged on, and she was preparing to burrow back under the warm covers when she felt drawn to check if Mr. Darcy had indeed remained in the lodge.

Rising, she wrapped a blanket around her shoulders and proceeded down the hallway to the sitting room. There he was, in slumber on the couch, his deep, even breathing attesting to his exhaustion.

The poor man must be cold as the fire has almost died down. Seeing his blanket had fallen to the floor, she picked up the errant cover and proceeded to place it over his form. *Such a handsome man.* As she started back to bed, she heard him.

"Elizabeth," he mumbled.

She stopped her forward motion and turned to him, shocked by the familiar address. However, he was still asleep, apparently lost in a dream, and she smiled knowing she was occupying his slumber as he often did in hers.

"Stay."

Although she knew she should not, she returned to the couch and knelt down to watch him sleep. His face was relaxed and vulnerable, not the usual expression of the serious master of a great estate. She was entranced by the rise and fall of his chest through his open shirt, and once again could not look away as her own breathing increased. *Imagine waking every morning to that face, those lips, those arms...* She unconsciously reached to smooth the all too familiar errant curl on his brow, then caught herself. *This man has made me lose my senses.*

She was startled by the sudden movement as Mr. Darcy rolled over onto his side directly facing her. Lizzy held her breath for fear he would wake and discover her in such close proximity. After a moment, he settled and seemingly fell back to sleep. She decided to stop tempting fate and began to rise and return to her chambers.

"I love you." She stopped. "Marry me." A soft snore attested to Mr. Darcy's nocturnal state, and she released the breath she was holding.

Leaning perilously close to the sleeping gentleman, she softly whispered to his dream-self, "Yes, William, I will marry you."

A large smile spread across Mr. Darcy's face as he reached up and wrapped her in his arms. "My Elizabeth," he whispered, pulling her to him and kissing her with such a tenderness that bolts of lightening charged through her.

Her body stiffened in astonishment until the gentle cadence of his lips caressing hers compelled her to relax into his embrace.

She ignored the voice in her mind admonishing her, demanding her to stand and wake Mr. Darcy. She was reveling in the love of this man—the man that she loved in return, but who would never be hers. For this one glorious moment her world was perfect.

His passion increased and she matched him with equal affection. "Elizabeth," his ragged voice murmured between breaths. "My love," he said in a hush, his fingers running through her curls until quite suddenly, his eyes opened and he stopped.

"Elizabeth?" He pushed her away and stood, retreating across the room, looking around wildly before realizing his surroundings. "Good heavens, what have I done? Forgive me." He rapidly ran his hands through his hair and stuttered in agitation. "How could I...? What are you doing in here?"

Lizzy had never been so mortified in her entire life. She covered her mouth with her fingers. "There was lightning and...and...and...I came to check on you and your blanket had fallen, and...and...I was going back to my room, and you called my name..."

"I called your name?"

"Yes," she said, fidgeting with her hands as tears were fighting to spill forth.

"Did I say anything else?

"I leaned in to hear you and...well...you smiled and..." Here, her voice faltered.

"Pray, do not continue." He took a deep breath and lowered his head in shame. "I took advantage of you."

"No, sir. It was... You would not have acted so if you were awake." She clenched her jaw to fight back the tears. "I, too, have had dreams. Please, no one knows but us. You are engaged to be married, and I am... well, I am to be... It meant nothing. I *know* it meant nothing. Goodnight."

She walked toward the hallway, attempting to control the sobs welling within her. *I cannot cry. This was never meant to happen. I should not have allowed myself to get carried away with hope.* She wiped the tears trickling down her cheeks.

"Miss Bennet, please..." he called after her, but she could not stop. *Ten more steps and I will be in my room.* His room. She straightened her back and kept walking.

"Elizabeth…" His gentle plea stopped her but she did not face him. "I beg you to listen to me."

"There is nothing you can say that will change our circumstances," she replied, lowering her head, her voice catching. "Goodnight, Mr. Darcy," she said as she closed the door behind her, crawled into the massive bed and wept silently into the pillow.

CHAPTER 20

E lizabeth woke to a fairyland of frosted woods when the moon still hung high in the heavens of a clear cloudless sky. In actuality, she had not awoken at all because she had never slept. Her mind could not cease its ramblings through the events of only hours before, and her lips still burned from the sensation of his kiss. *What will he think of me? How will he behave with me when he awakes? I could not stand to see his derision or sympathy.*

She looked at her watch on the bed stand. *Four o'clock.* It had been only a few hours since the events since he had kissed her. Sitting up in bed, Lizzy made a decision. She hastily dressed, grabbed the tartan wool she had discovered, and slipped out the back door hoping to arrive at Pemberley before Mr. Darcy woke.

Colonel Richard Fitzwilliam rose before the sun, grateful the howling wind had ceased its lamentations. He quickly dressed himself, having no need or use for a valet, and made his way down the stairs to the breakfast room. Knowing Darcy's staff would have some type of offering ready to fit the early risings of their fastidious master, he grabbed a roll and a cup of coffee and continued to the stables. Today, within the next few hours, he would find Miss Elizabeth Bennet, even if he had to wake up every tenant on the estate to help. He would not allow more time to go by when that helpless woman would be out on her own. *I will protect that which my cousin holds dear.*

He surprised the stable hands and instructed them to saddle the horses to begin the search again. He prepared for battle the only way he knew how—giving orders to ordinary men who would complete extraordinary tasks when asked.

⸎

Darcy woke later than he anticipated. He was normally an early riser but due to the amount of drink he consumed after Miss Elizabeth went back to bed, his body would not assent. His watch said the time was six in the morning, and his head believed it. He berated himself for his blunder the night before. *How could I have lost control so easily? How could I, who worked so hard to protect her, have violated her innocence?* He dropped his head into his hands and ran his fingers through his hair, all the while worried she would walk into the room at any moment.

But she did not. After a length of time, Darcy made his way to one of the guest rooms to prepare for the day. He paused outside his own room and hearing nothing, continued on, trying desperately to concentrate on how he was going to make the situation comfortable for the both of them.

Completing his toilette, he went back to the sitting room, picked up his book from the night before, and settled in to await the appearance of Miss Elizabeth.

～

Richard and the stable hands had been riding for hours. They had ridden up to the northern edge of the estate first, then over to the west. He was beginning to worry, when he decided to check the south-east portion where the woods were dense. *I am looking for Don Quixote's needle in a haystack. There are over six thousand acres of land to cover with more tenants than my mother has gowns. How shall I find her? And where is Darcy?*

They continued to ride, pausing frequently to call her name and listen for a response. When he checked his watch at nine o'clock, he determined it was time to turn back and see if there had been any word at the house. *Maybe she did stay with a tenant family last night, and they bundled her up in their cart and brought her home first thing this morning. She might now be sitting in the music room listening to my aunt criticize her for scampering about the countryside in a snowstorm!*

Chuckling, he raised a hand and pulled on the reins of his horse to give instructions to the men riding up behind him when from the corner of his eye, a splash of color caught his attention. He immediately dismounted and ran toward it: a tartan wool scarf at the top of an embankment.

It was seven o'clock when the sun was reflecting off the snow outside the lodge, blinding him before he once again retreated to his book. *I know that Miss Elizabeth is an early riser. She must be avoiding me.* Darcy turned at what he thought was a noise, but there was nothing in the hallway. *I will give her another quarter of an hour, then must wake her if we are to return to Pemberley in good time. There will be questions, but I will silence anyone who comes too close to the truth.*

He stood and paced the length of the room, attempting to formulate what he would say when he knocked on her door. *Will she be loath to see me? She is to marry Hamilton. Although I know her affections for him were not completely engaged at Ashby Park, maybe…*

At length, he checked his watch again before realizing the time had come. Striding down the hall, he took a fortifying breath before gently knocking on the door.

"Miss Elizabeth? Miss Elizabeth, I apologize to bother you, but it is time for us to prepare to leave. We must hasten to Pemberley while the weather remains friendly as another storm could move in at any moment."

He waited patiently, not hearing a sound from the other side of the door. "Miss Bennet? Miss Bennet, are you awake?" He knocked again, with a bit more energy before he decided to enter the room. "Miss Bennet, are you well?"

He turned the handle and entered the all too familiar master's chambers. He looked straight at the fireplace, unable to look at the bed on his right. "Miss Bennet," he said louder. "I apologize for entering your room but…"

In less than five minutes, his great coat had been thrown on, he had saddled Ulysses and was galloping down the pathway following a pair of footprints toward his home.

～

Richard had sent one of the stable boys ahead to have Mrs. Reynolds send for the doctor from Lambton and prepare a hot bath. The other youth rode behind him, prepared to do anything the good colonel asked.

Miss Elizabeth was still unconscious, a small gash on her head, but she was breathing. *She is breathing!* She was curled against him under his great coat, her body still limp. It took all his strength to hold her and the reins of his horse while riding to Pemberley, but he would not fail!

As he came around the side of the house, he saw Mrs. Reynolds and the butler open the door. He stopped short in front of them and opened his coat, sliding Miss Elizabeth down into the waiting hands of two footmen. He immediately dismounted, scooped her from their arms, and carried her rapidly up the stairs to her chambers, ignoring cries from Georgiana, Anne, and Miss Katherine—and the screeches from his aunt.

It was eleven o'clock when Darcy finally saw Pemberley in the distance. He had lost her tracks about an hour before, but there were obvious hoof prints leading to the house, and Ulysses pace increased at his master's insistence. He rode directly up to the door, slid from his mount, and threw the reins at a waiting footman before running up the stairs.

"Darcy, welcome back. Please come into your study so we can have a word."

"Not now, Richard," Darcy snapped, walking toward the stairs.

"She is here," he whispered, making Darcy stop in his tracks.

His body tensed at the news.

Richard held his hand out to the side and he followed his cousin, closing the door behind them.

Darcy walked over to the couch and dropped down, his body almost collapsing from fatigue and concern. He leaned forward, resting his head in his hands before once again running them through his hair in nervous agitation. "When did she arrive?"

"Cousin, I think you need to tell me what happened."

"Richard, I think you need to tell me when she arrived." Richard did not miss the ferocity in Darcy's voice and complied.

"We found her about two hours ago at the bottom of an embankment. She hit her head and was unconscious but was still breathing. Her lips were almost blue, Darce. She had only a light coat and gloves, and the doctor said she likely survived at all because of this wool scarf," he said holding up the tartan, "and sheer luck."

Darcy stood and began pacing, his stoic gaze unreadable. *I almost killed her. She who I love more than my own life... My actions scared her to the point of running out into the night and attempting to walk several miles after a snow storm!*

"Darcy? Darcy? Did you hear what I said? How did you know she was missing? We were unable to send word to Donnelley Hall yesterday. Did you cross paths with a tenant this morning who may have heard from one of the estate hands yesterday?"

He waved away Richard's question. "It is of little consequence how I made the discovery. Is she awake yet?"

"Yes. Mrs. Reynolds informed me a few minutes before your arrival that Miss Bennet opened her eyes."

"Thank heavens!" A great breath was expelled from his lungs and he kept his eyes averted from his cousin.

"Darcy, do tell me how you learned of Miss Bennet. Also, where did you stay last night? You appear worse for the wear. Lord Donnelley's man would have never allowed you to leave looking like this. You have not even been shaved!"

Darcy raised his chin before coolly replying, "How I learned of Miss Bennet is immaterial. And as for where I stayed last evening, I took up residence in grandfather's old hunting lodge at the far end of the property." He nodded and strode to the door. "Now if you will excuse me, I must go and attend to my guest."

This bit of information seemed to have no effect on his cousin who picked up the scarf. "I suggest you wait."

"It is of little consequence to me what you suggest. I must go and see to my guest."

Richard said, "Is this your scarf, Darce?"

He stopped abruptly and turned with exasperation. "What?"

"This scarf. Do you recognize it?" He asked holding up the bright red and green tartan. "We found it in the snow with Miss Bennet."

"Then it is most likely hers, Richard. Now if you will excuse me."

"No, it is not, Darcy." He interrupted his cousin's retreat.

"Then who does it belong to? I imagine there is something to this story you are not divulging to me."

Richard smiled—a sad, slow smile. "There is, Darce. You see, this scarf belongs to me."

"Belongs to you? I would like to remind you it would be highly improper to have imposed upon her with a gift."

Richard smiled at the irony of Darcy's words. "You are correct, Cousin. That would indeed be highly improper and could damage her reputation irretrievably. However, I did not give this to her. She took it."

Darcy visibly started and took two steps toward his cousin. "You cannot be serious. Are you accusing Miss Bennet of stealing your personal belongings?"

"In a manner of speaking, yes."

"And when, Richard? When would she have had an opportunity to travel to Matlock House and go through your possessions to procure said scarf? This is absurd! Enough with your tales. I must see to Miss Bennet! If you will excuse me!" He turned for the second time in as many minutes toward the door. He only made it a few steps however, when Richard's words halted him.

"It was not at Matlock House, Darcy. I left this particular scarf with my mother's tartan, the scarf my mother's brother, the Duke of

Lennox, gave to me—I left this scarf at your grandfather's hunting lodge in August when I came to hunt grouse."

Darcy's voice was small. "The hunting lodge?"

"Yes."

"And you are certain?" His shoulders sagged with the weight of his cousin's words.

"Yes. I believe, Cousin, we have need for more conversation."

~

Anne sat quietly with Georgiana and Miss Katherine in Miss Elizabeth's room as the shadows of the day stretched, finally disappearing as the maids lit the candles. Anne knew each had their own reasons for keeping vigil and she admitted to herself that Elizabeth Bennet was her only chance to convince her cousin to marry for love so she might do the same.

"It appears almost time to dress for dinner. I will let Mrs. Reynolds know I will take a tray here…" said Georgiana with little energy.

"As will I," said Miss Katherine.

"And I," echoed Anne.

Each woman looked at the other and smiled when there came a knock at the door.

"Come," Georgiana said and her brother entered the room.

Georgiana rushed to him as her tears began to fall. "Oh, Wills. Did you here what happened? Do you believe Elizabeth will be well?"

"There, there, Sprout," he said, smoothing Georgiana's hair. "Richard said the doctor expects a full recovery. And that she was not unconscious from her fall, but likely from exhaustion and the cold."

He stared at the sleeping figure and his eyes darted away when he saw Anne studying him.

"Yes," Anne said, placing her hand on Miss Katherine's shoulder as she had begun to weep. "She will be fine and needs only time to rest."

Darcy released Georgiana and turned to her. "Anne, I apologize for not being here to receive you properly."

"Thank you, William. Do not concern yourself for us, as my mother made herself quite at home upon our arrival. Georgiana, why not take Miss Katherine for a turn about the gallery? It would do you well to leave the sick room for a bit."

"Yes, Sprout. That is a marvelous idea." Darcy kissed his sister's blonde head and nudged her toward the door. "Anne and I will keep watch over the patient. If there is any change in your sister, Miss Katherine, we will send for you."

"Very well, Wills. Come along, Kitty."

"Yes, and I must write to Mama and Father. I should have done so immediately but was so distraught, I did not even think of it."

"Maybe you will have happier tidings to include before you post it. Once your letter is written, please give it to Mrs. Reynolds. I will add my own letter and send it express."

Miss Katherine kissed her sister's cheek and took Georgiana's arm before closing the door behind them.

"Do you think we need a proper chaperone to have the door closed?" she quipped.

Darcy rolled his eyes at her and quietly said, "You are quite safe with me."

Noting her cousin's tired eyes, her curiosity was as strong as her concern. "I am so grateful to have you returned safely. How did you avoid the storm last night?"

He cleared his throat. "I was able to seek shelter in my grandfather's hunting lodge on the edge of the estate."

"Oh, wonderful. So, you were in relative comfort."

"Yes."

"And knowing you, you enjoyed the solitude only a true Derbyshire snowstorm can produce."

He did not respond but only nodded.

"Cousin?" She did not know when she might have another private moment with him so she blurted, "I believe it is time we speak on a matter that my mother would not have us discuss."

He looked up at her curiously, seeming to see her for the first time in the last few minutes. "What would you wish to discuss, Anne?" He walked over to the window and stared out into the darkness, his hands clasped behind his back. *Good heavens! Has Anne discovered the truth of last night as well?*

"Our future."

"Our future? That has already been decided."

"Yes, but not by us. I would like to hear your thoughts on the matter."

"I…I would be happy to speak to you about this subject or any other." He turned and looked at her, the weight of the last sixteen years not pressing him down as greatly as only moments before.

Before Anne could go on, she was interrupted by her mother's voice in the hallway.

"Where is my nephew?" The door was thrown open and Lady Catherine seemed to fill the room. For a moment, he was taken back to the bedside of his dying mother all those years ago. "There you are!"

Miss Elizabeth's comfortable sleep was broken and she sat up in a daze, crying out before falling back against the pillows.

Anne rushed to her and stroked her hair. "Miss Elizabeth, it is Anne de Bourgh. You are safe now. You are at Pemberley. My cousin Richard found you this morning and Darcy is here now. You are safe."

As she said his name, Miss Elizabeth seemed to startle, but upon recognizing her surroundings and Anne, she retreated back into the comfort of the blankets.

However, at this outburst, Lady Catherine pronounced Miss Elizabeth's manners to be very bad indeed. "I shall never forget her appearance this morning. She really looked almost wild when the colonel carried her in. I could hardly keep my countenance. Very nonsensical to be scampering about the estate in this weather. It seems to me to show an abominable sort of conceited independence, a most country-town indifference to decorum. If I were to..."

But Darcy could not hear the rest. A fury erupted through his perfectly exemplified *master under good regulation* persona. "Decorum? Woman, you will not speak thus in my home. *You* will leave this room at once, retrieve the letter I asked you to bring, and wait in your quarters until you are summoned to my study. Do I make myself clear?"

The vein in his forehead and the clenching of his jaw indicated he would brook no opposition. Lady Catherine was taken aback and looked to counter but only for a moment. Her eyes narrowed and she steadily replied, "I hope that you have not been taken in by this country chit's arts and allurements. Let me remind you, you are engaged to be married to *my* daughter in less than a month's time."

Lady Catherine's words were met with no response but his steely gaze.

"I have never been thus treated in my entire life!" She blustered and slammed the door behind her, causing Miss Elizabeth to flinch.

"William, you should leave as well. I will see to Miss Bennet. Go find her sister."

"Very well." He had all but forgotten their conversation from only moments before. Darcy told a footman to find the girls and bring them to Anne. He then walked to the family wing and his own chambers, practicing all restraint not to slam his own door.

"And this woman, this former lady's maid…"

"Mrs. Smith is her name."

"Yes," Lady Catherine said evenly. "This Mrs. Smith has come to Pemberley to claim that this letter from your mother, with your mother's signature, is not what she wrote?"

"Yes, Lady Catherine," Darcy said. He stared out into the night sky with his back to her, his words clipped. "And I believe her."

Lady Catherine walked to his side and stared out the window. "And why would you not wish to believe her? You have never wanted to marry Anne."

"That is not entirely true, madam. I would ask you to top giving credence to ideas which are not mine."

"Now, now. Watch that tone with me, young whelp. I am almost your closest living relative and am doing what is best for you." Darcy did not respond and she seemed to soften her tone. "Well, then. Believe what you will, but I know you! No young man wants to have someone dictate his future for him. You are a man in his majority. The master of one of the most powerful estates in England."

Darcy slowly turned to her, surprised by her response.

"You and Anne are formed for each other. You are descended from the same noble line. And your fortunes are splendid. You are destined for each other by the voice of your dear departed mother and my own in her stead. There are women of your acquaintance with much more beauty. Much more knowledge of the world. But, we had the foresight to plan this alliance to protect the family."

"But Mrs. Smith said…"

"Mrs. Smith is a doddering, old woman who does not remember one day from the next. She would have no true memory of what your mother asked her to write. But, she does not have to remember because this letter, right here, I wrote, as you know. Your mother and I corresponded for weeks as to our hopes. And then, she became ill, and I had to rush to Pemberley with my only copy. She barely had the strength to sign.

"Here. Read it for yourself again. Read it and see how much your mother loved you. And wanted to protect you, Georgiana, and Pemberley for future generations. It is all right here."

She handed him the letter he had seen only twice before: the first, at Rosings when he was fifteen years old and his father had sent him for Easter with his cousin Richard; and the second, shortly after his father's death five years ago, as if to remind him of his loyalties. But this letter appeared often in his dreams: the black ink forming thin, precise letters, his mother's broken seal. He would dream of the letter on a desk, or consigned to a field as he rode his horse, or the most recent yet disturbing, in the hands of Miss Elizabeth Bennet as she sat in his library, smiling at him over the pages.

Darcy took the letter, walked to the window.

My son,

You are aware of the illness that is taking over my body. I regret I will not last to see you grow up into a man. Know that I love you, that you are most important to me, as is Georgiana.

You will inherit Pemberley, and all its holdings, however, I have instructed my sister to ensure my Matlock inheritance go to Georgiana. I fear your father is not in support of this, and I beg of you not to discuss it with your him as our wishes do not align.

My sister and I believe the best course of action to ensure the felicity of your future is to marry your cousin, my namesake, Anne. She is a dear girl who will make you a wonderful wife. This is my dying wish, that the houses of de Bourgh and Darcy be united long into the future through you. Nothing would give me greater pleasure than looking down on our family and knowing that not only was it secure, but also that you loved me enough to honor my final wish.

All my love,

Your mama,

Lady Anne Darcy

"It seems such a formal way to end such a letter." He raised his head to meet Lady Catherine's gaze. "Something just seems amiss…something that I cannot see clearly."

"Darcy, I presume I have not been the most affectionate aunt, but you are the son of my only sister—my baby sister. Allow that I understood her wishes for you more than a servant. Do not dishonor me so."

"But I still—"

"Yes, yes I suppose the letter is a bit formal. However, she feared it would be contested and therefore made it as such. She loved you and wanted you and our dear Anne to not worry about your future. Can you not see?"

Darcy knew that he could not, no matter what his heart wanted, reject the dying wish of his mother.

"Yes, Lady Catherine. Now, if you will excuse me, I have estate matters to attend." He bowed briskly and strode out the door, resigned to his fate.

It had been four days before the doctor allowed Miss Elizabeth to venture out of bed. The roads had cleared and Lady Catherine and Anne had returned to Rosings to prepare for the wedding ceremony. Darcy had not spoken to Anne alone since his conversation with Lady Catherine, and Anne reluctantly acceded her attempts to dissuade him were fruitless.

The snow had begun to fall again in Derbyshire, not stinging snow which had trapped them in the unthinkable situation five days previous, but soft powder which cast a fairy-like wonder around the whole estate. Miss Elizabeth was sitting in the library staring out the window wrapped in a large down blanket when Darcy walked into the room. He had not expected to see her and stopped short.

"Miss Bennet…I did not know you were in here, or I would not have presumed to interrupt your solitary repose."

"Think nothing of it, sir. This is your house, your library. I am merely an invalid who Mrs. Reynolds does not trust to travel up or down the stairs alone."

He smiled at her feisty remark, a sure sign of her return to health. He had instructed Mrs. Reynolds to keep him abreast of the lady's condition and had met with the doctor after every examination, questioning the progress of his guest. "You are looking in quite well." He enjoyed seeing the color bloom in her cheeks.

"The doctor says I should be ready to travel in two days' time. I have instructed my maid to begin packing, and Kitty and I will leave for Longbourn."

"So soon?"

"Yes. We must leave as you will be departing shortly thereafter for Kent to prepare for the wedding." The last words were spoken with conviction, not hesitantly or with any sign of sadness.

"Yes, yes, I must leave, but that does not signify that you must depart if you are still unwell."

"No, sir. That will not do as I received a letter only two days ago that I must hasten to Longbourn. My mother requires my assistance on matters significant to my own future."

"Yes…yes…and might I wish you joy as well?"

"I thank you, Mr. Darcy."

The room fell silent, engulfed by the ticking of the clock and the battle of unspoken words.

"Good day, Miss Bennet." He bowed quickly before turning to leave the room and attempted to convince himself he did not hear her soft reply.

"Good day, William."

CHAPTER 21

L ooking back out the library window, she wondered how she could leave him. Yet, she knew she must. Even to dwell on such thoughts were sure to undo all the work she had done to forget his kiss; his arms around her; his love drunk words of affection. Those brief, tender moments she would never forget, *could* never forget.

Blessedly, Georgiana and Kitty assisted her to the music room, where they regaled her with silly duets they had been practicing to lighten her spirits. By the time they were supposed to begin to dress for dinner, her mood had lightened and she was prepared in temperament to sit across the table from him. However, as Kitty helped her climb the stairs to her room, she heard a voice she could never mistake and both girls recoiled. Lizzy held onto the bannister with both hands at the shock.

"Where is my Lizzy? How is my dearest girl?"

Kitty squeezed her sister's hand in sisterly solidarity and both Bennet girls descended the stairs to greet their mother. They were not surprised to see their father one of the party but Lizzy gasped at the sight of their companion.

"Mr. Hamilton! Why, what are you doing here?"

"That is a fine greeting, Elizabeth," he chided, amiably. "I have come to retrieve you, my dearest." He then bent over her hand for a lingering kiss, as Mr. Darcy and the colonel walked in.

Mrs. Bennet beamed, and Mr. Bennet raised his eyebrows at the gallantry of the man who was not quite his daughter's fiancé. She was vexed at her father's smirk, knowing he was enjoying the idiosyncrasies and charades that were sure to come.

"Welcome, Hamilton. Mr. Bennet. Mrs. Bennet. This is a pleasant surprise."

Mr. Hamilton extended his hand to his old friend. "Darcy, please forgive our intrusion but when the Bennets received your express, we determined to leave post haste to retrieve the girls ourselves."

"Might I present my cousin, Colonel Fitzwilliam? Mr. and Mrs. Bennet of Longbourn."

Had her mother found Lizzy in any present danger, she knew Mrs. Bennet would have been miserable, but being she found her nearly recovered, she said, "If not for such good friends, I do not know what would become of her. What business she has about always going here and there, with no consideration for my poor nerves. And leaving me all the worry that she is being properly cared for."

"Mama!" Lizzy cried shamefully. "Mr. Darcy and his staff have been nothing but obliging, seeing to my every comfort. The doctor has been here every day, and Mrs. Reynolds has offered me every possible attention to ensure I would have a quick recovery."

"Yes, yes, I am sure they did. I am not questioning your hospitality, sir. I only speak as a mother concerned for her dearest child." With a calculating eye that could only make her daughter cringe, she continued. "I do hope you will offer us a tour of your grand home."

"Of course, ma'am." Mr. Darcy stiffly nodded. "We were just going up to dress for dinner. Might I suggest you follow Mrs. Reynolds to the guest wing and prepare for dinner yourself, and I will show you the house afterwards." His tone was very controlled, and Lizzy was sure he was regretting the association.

Her mother quickly followed the housekeeper, leaving her father and intended to trail behind. Mr. Hamilton squeezed her hand and Mr. Bennet winked at her before leaving the room. When the door closed behind the group, there was a collective sigh from Kitty and Lizzy.

"Sir. Please allow me to apologize for my mother."

Kitty nodded her acquiescence but kept her own eyes cast downward.

A polite smile graced Mr. Darcy's lips. "Miss Bennet, neither you nor Miss Katherine owe me an apology. I merely saw a mother who was concerned about the well-being of her daughter. There is nothing to forgive. Now if you will excuse me, Fitzwilliam and I have some business in my study." He bowed before walking through the doorway and leaving them to go up and prepare for dinner.

The party had retired after dinner to the drawing room, having separated only long enough for the men to pour themselves a brandy.

"What a lovely meal, Mr. Darcy."

"Was the venison to your liking?"

"Oh, yes, sir," Mrs. Bennet said. "But, I am guessing with your income, you would make every accommodation for guests to feel at ease and receive the best treatment."

"I do the best I can, ma'am." He refrained from rolling his eyes and instead he asked, "Georgiana, might you play something for us this evening?"

"Kitty and I have been practicing a new piece. Might we play that for you?"

"Of course, poppet." He took her hand and led her to the piano bench before walking to the window to observe the full moon.

Hamilton joined him at the window and said, "Darcy, I wanted to thank you for being so hospitable toward the Bennets and myself."

"There is no need to mention it. Consider it recompense for your staff's hospitality when I was waylaid at Ashby by weather."

"Yes, I know, but I know that my future mother can be quite a handful, and I am grateful you did not throw us out on our ear at some of her remarks."

"Hamilton, I would never think to do that to a friend's mother."

"Yes, yes, but she is not my mother—not yet, at least."

"Yes, well, I was referring to Miss Bennet."

Hamilton seemed to weigh his words before asking, "Darcy, what occurred with Elizabeth? How did she come to be discovered alone in Pemberley's woods?"

Darcy's jaw clenched. "I was at a neighboring estate. When I discovered Miss Bennet was lost in the storm, I did all in my power to find her. Luckily, my cousin was quicker than I, and because of his speed, her life was preserved." Darcy took a sip from his glass and turned at the opening bars of the duet. "If you will excuse me." He walked over and stood next to his cousin where he could see the piano better.

When the girls were done and polite applause had subsided, Richard entreated Miss Elizabeth to play.

"Miss Bennet, if you are up for the challenge, might you enchant us with a song as well?"

"Richard," Darcy said. "This is her first day down from her room."

"I thank you, Mr. Darcy, but I am feeling quite recovered and would love to play once again on this fine instrument before we depart tomorrow."

"Is that quite fixed then?" he asked, turning to Mr. Bennet.

Mrs. Bennet interjected before Mr. Bennet could respond. "Yes, sir, it is. We must get Lizzy home to finish preparations for dear Jane's wedding and of course, begin hers to Mr. Hamilton. Although it's not official, I am sure the young man will not mind me saying so amongst such dear friends?"

Elizabeth pushed on the keys, sending up an awful noise. "Pray, excuse me." She turned her attention back to the piano, bit her bottom lip, and flexed her fingers.

"Would you like me to turn the pages for you, Elizabeth?"

"No thank you, Mr. Hamilton. I will play from memory."

When she began the song, Darcy knew it was meant for him. *This is her farewell to the life we could never have together.*

"The pale moon was rising above the green mountain,
The sun was declining beneath the blue sea;
When I strayed with my love to the pure crystal fountain,
That stands in the beautiful Vale of Tralee…"

～

"Would you care to join me for some fresh air. I would like to check on my horses and that all is right for tomorrow's travel?" Hamilton asked Mr. Bennet as the ladies had gone up to bed. He looked at Darcy and Fitzwilliam and shrugged. "It's a habit of mine. I like to check on my own."

Mr. Bennet nodded, then said, "I think I would prefer to get these old bones to bed. Gentleman." He bowed to the men and left for his bed.

Hamilton bowed as well and accepted his coat from a footman. Entering the great barn, he noticed a young man around his age organizing the tack and realized if it had not been for the kindness and condescension of his great aunt, that might had been his lot. As he checked his own horses, he was roused back to the present by a conversation of the two men mucking out a stall.

"No, he's a good man, our Mr. Darcy. I'll never say a word against him."

"Aye, nor will I. They are a-talkin', though, ain't they? Lord Donnelley would have their hide and send them out with no wages if he heard what they were saying in his stables."

"Aye. He's an honorable man, Lord Donnelley. But…you do have to admit it is curious. Mr. Darcy left in the snowstorm and told our people he stayed in his grandfather's old hunting lodge…"

"I was a lad when his grandfather was the master. I remember him coming into town and giving all us children candy for Christmas and a farthing for the new year."

"He was a good man, and his grandson is just the same. But that young lady who was lost in the woods… Missing since early the morning before. She'd be dead if she'd been out in that ditch all night—would froze solid through!"

"Now, Joe. We don't rightly know the facts of the matter. That's all just gossip from the scullery maids. Watch what you're saying," the older man sputtered. "You're accusing Mr. Darcy of taking advantage of a lady, then leaving her out in the woods? No, I don't believe it, and you'd better hold your tongue 'afore someone hears you!"

"That's not what I was saying at all. I was just saying it was right curious how she wasn't dead, then the master come flying in on his horse like he was being chased by the devil, ran right up them steps, and was stopped at the stairs by the colonel."

"Well, I think the ways of the rich are things we don't understand. Mr. Darcy is an honorable man, and I don't care what you are thinking in that pea brain of yours. I tell ya', he'd never do anything to harm a fly. Now, if I were you, I'd not bring this up again. That young girl is going home to be married, and according to what I heard, Mr. Darcy is leaving to go get married too, and you and I…? Well, we'll still be mucking stalls when they have children and grandchildren. So, it's none of our concern."

Hamilton had not moved from where he stood. The men walked to the other end of the stables, never realizing the damage their simple conversation wrought upon the life of an unsuspecting woman and her betrothed.

"I thought I would find you here." Fitzwilliam had walked into the billiard room and discovered Darcy in the middle of a game. "Playing yourself again, Cousin? Your own nemesis, I see."

In billiards or all things pertaining to my life? Darcy scowled and sent the cue ball flying into the pocket.

"A scratch, Darce? I am unaccustomed to you not winning. Let us play a new game, shall we?"

"I am not in the mood, Richard."

"You have yet to hear what I am proposing."

"There is no need, as I can see the glint in your eye. She is leaving on the morrow, and I am following to Rosings to prepare for my wedding with Anne." He looked at his cousin's forlorn face. "I know that pains you, and I am sorry, but take solace in knowing Anne will be provided for and taken care of…"

"And loved? Do you promise to love her? Or will she be just another business acquisition to you?" His voice was harsh but a moment later, he said, "Forgive me, I spoke out of turn."

"No. No, you did not. I am the one who should apologize, yet I cannot." He set his cue stick down and walked the length of the room before turning around. "I saw my mother's letter."

"The one Mrs. Smith wrote?"

"No. I am afraid that one most likely does not exist. The one Aunt Catherine has been holding me hostage with for the last thirteen years." He lowered his head. "Every time I see it I cannot believe that my mother signed it. But it was signed by her own hand."

"And you truly believe *that* is what she would want of you? To be married to a woman who although you love as a cousin, you could not love as a wife? Darce, I remember my aunt. She loved you and only wanted your happiness. This has forever reeked of our Aunt Catherine's machinations."

Darcy sniffed at the veiled hope in his cousin's voice but understood how he was destroying Richard's hopes as well. As Richard picked up the other cue stick and racked the balls, Darcy knew they were in a losing battle.

~

Her final day at Pemberley arrived without fanfare. It was a clear day with brilliant blue skies reflecting off the light dusting of snow. The maid had packed her things the previous night and the footmen taken her trunks down to await the carriage. She was alone in the room which had come to feel like home.

Standing at the same window where she had stood many times before to admire the great estate she had come to love, she savored the view even more knowing this would be her last day, her last hour on his lands.

She did not want to leave. Could not bear to break the hold this place had on her but knew she must. This was her fate and she was resigned, accepting that her marriage to James was better than many women would ever achieve.

She picked up her pelisse on the way out the door and was met at the top of the stairs by the butler.

"Mr. Reynolds, I thank you for your hospitality during my stay."

"It was my pleasure, Miss Bennet. Your family awaits you in the drawing room. Mr. Darcy ordered light refreshments before you depart, and Cook prepared a basket with some of your favorites including the blueberry scones."

"Do thank her for me." She walked down the stairs and into the drawing room only to be met by her mother's loud pronouncement that she was her slowest daughter of all five, and that she was lucky Mr. Hamilton did not mind waiting like the rest of the world did.

Lizzy cast an apologetic smile toward her Mr. Hamilton, but his lips remained set in a tight line and he did not look her way. *Oh, Mama. You have pushed even James too far.*

Colonel Fitzwilliam took her hand and led her over to the chair next to his. "Miss Bennet, if we are to lose your company within the hour, I will monopolize it while it still remains. You do not mind, Hamilton?"

"Colonel, I do not believe I ever properly thanked you for saving me. Without you, surely I would have perished."

"Yes, Colonel," Hamilton pronounced tightly, "thank you for seeing to the safety of my beloved Elizabeth. It is a miracle that her life was preserved for a full night lying in an embankment in the woods during a raging snowstorm."

Mr. Darcy swiftly sent Hamilton a look, but it was the colonel who was quickest to reply. "I only did what I know *any* man would have done to help a lady, sir. It is not my place to question Providence. Had Miss Bennet been anywhere else, she might not have been rescued in a timely manner."

Lizzy felt her heart race at her deception.

"You are right, Colonel. However, we are grateful whatever occurred, *did occur*, for everything was made right. Elizabeth is safe and returning home to Longbourn with her family. You will head to the continent. And Darcy will leave on the morrow to marry his intended." He took a sip of his tea. "Yes, everything is as it should be."

Mr. Bennet set his cup on the side table and stood. "Yes, well, we had better be off. Thank you for your hospitality toward my girls. If you or Miss Darcy are ever near Hertfordshire, know that you are welcome to Longbourn."

"Thank you, Mr. Bennet," Mr. Darcy said. "I am certain my sister and Miss Katherine will ensure a visit happens not too long in the future."

"For certain," Kitty said squeezing Georgiana's hand, both girls trying to hold back tears.

"Yes, Mr. Darcy. I am sure they will."

"It is a shame you will not be able to attend Jane and Bingley's wedding," Mrs. Bennet said. "But, I presume with your own so close, you must go to Rosings to prepare for it. However, I promise you, you will miss a wedding breakfast like no other!"

"Of this, I can attest," Mr. Bennet affirmed with a roll of his eyes. "Our cook has been working tirelessly since word reached Longbourn of this monumental event. Well, let's be off." He extended his hand to the colonel and then to Mr. Darcy. "Once again, thank you both. Colonel, until you have a child, you will never understand the gratitude I feel for you."

"Miss Bennet is a treasure that the world could not do without."

Kitty approached Mr. Darcy and the colonel and curtseyed. "Thank you, Mr. Darcy. Words cannot express how much my stay here has meant. So many lovely memories."

"You are always welcome to Pemberley and Darcy House."

Mr. Hamilton shook Mr. Darcy's hand, and Lizzy could feel her heart pounding as she knew she must say the words. Her last words to him.

"Mr. Darcy," she said, maintaining an even tone despite the emotions roiling beneath the surface. She raised her eyes to his blank expression. "Thank you," was all she could mutter before he nodded.

"I wish you happy, Miss Elizabeth. Hamilton."

Mr. Hamilton bowed succinctly before ushering Lizzy out the door and down Pemberley's steps. He handed her into the carriage before offering his hand to Kitty and then climbed in to sit beside Mr. and Mrs. Bennet.

Lizzy could not avoid James Hamilton's gaze while watching the estate she had grown to love, and a lone figure standing in the window like a sentinel at her departure, fade in the distance.

CHAPTER 22

December 17th, 1810
Hertfordshire

T he morning frost had settled on the dead branches in the
orchards and the only sound challenging the babbling of the
stream was Lizzy's footsteps crunching through the grass. It had been
almost two weeks since her return to Longbourn, and she was just as
confused as when she had left Pemberley. Her feelings were as they
had always been, but she had pushed the yearnings of her heart aside
to concentrate on her sister's wedding and the inevitable proposal of
Mr. Hamilton.

She had not seen him since his carriage had deposited them in
London before they returned to Longbourn. He had spoken to no one,
save her father, on the journey home. He had excused himself at the
coaching inns, and even Mrs. Bennet, with her minimal powers of
observation, asked why Mr. Hamilton was avoiding her. She had been
lost in her own misery and had not paid much heed to his inattentions.

He was expected today for the wedding, and her mother would not
be pleased if she was out wandering through the woods and not

preparing for his arrival. *I am sure there has been another woman in history who has not looked with joy upon her own proposal. Like... Poor Charlotte... In reading her letters, I have realized she has married a man who she cannot respect but has accepted instead of the consequences of spinsterhood. Could I do that? Would I rather be the old, maiden aunt?*

She knew the answer to that, but it was a ridiculous notion, because this was James. *No, Jimmy Hamilton!* Who she grew up with and played with as a child. He knew her and valued her, and she valued him as well...

He does not make me feel as William does. "Stop this!" She berated herself throwing her hands down at her side and increased her pace. *It is Mr. Darcy, the brother of your dear friend, who is preparing for his nuptials to Miss de Bourgh as we speak. You cannot think of him in any other way.* She thought of the way his curl would fall over his forehead. His dimple that appeared from nowhere when he smiled. *The way he held me when we danced at the Matlock ball...* She sat down on a log and closed her eyes, resting her face in her palms. *The way he kissed me in the hunting lodge and said my name as if he was drunk with love.*

She allowed the emotions to course through her, she vowed again, for one last time, unable to resist if she had tried. Her shoulders sagged for a moment before she took a deep breath, straightened them and rose to return to Longbourn. *You are not going to the guillotine, Elizabeth Bennet! You will survive this.*

Darcy pulled Ulysses up at the edge of the valley in Rosings. He had been riding hard for hours, and his dependable steed needed a respite. It had been a difficult week with Lady Catherine demanding more of his time and adulation than he was willing to give. His wounds were still too raw from both watching Miss Elizabeth's carriage drive out of his life and into Hamilton's, and the letter he had received from Bingley two days previous:

'...The only regret on my wedding day is that you will not be there to share it with us, my friend. However, you may hear the effusions of my future mother as I have it on good authority that Mr. Hamilton will petition for Miss Elizabeth's hand shortly after the wedding breakfast. Jane's felicity will know no bounds as my new sister is eager to accept him...'

But it could be of no consequence to him. He was less than a week away from marrying Anne. She had proven to be quite pleasant, but he could almost attribute that to the presence of Fitzwilliam. *I know how difficult this must be for him, but he is doing what he must for our family. I could not be at Ashby Park and prepare to watch Elizabeth wed Hamilton...maybe Fitzwilliam does not love Anne as I love Elizabeth?*

Darcy bit the inside of his mouth and deigned to give his cousin the decency he deserved by forcing that thought from his mind. The sound of hoof beats behind him drew his attention, and the man in question was riding up to meet him.

"Darce, I have been looking for you for half an hour at least."

"Yes, well, you have found me. I have been riding the estate grounds making notes of repairs. What troubles you, Fitzwilliam?"

He tightened his reins and maneuvered his horse alongside Darcy's. "Nothing troubles me, but our aunt has summoned you to finalize wedding preparations."

Darcy huffed with indignation. "How many plans does one need to marry? There must be a license, a wedding contract, and a parson. What more is required of me?"

Fitzwilliam stared out over the valley below. "There are others who would willingly take your place, Darcy, if you would like it to be so."

The solemnity of the moment caused him to ask a question he promised himself never to voice. "Do you believe she loves you?"

Richard was still for a moment before stammering a response. "I am uncertain as to Anne's true feelings for me. However, I know I could woo her since my only rival has made no attempt." He watched as Darcy lowered his head at the hit, and then raised it again, facing the accusation ringing with truth. "I had hoped to secure her affection before a grave mistake was made."

"Richard, I am sorry, but it is impossible. You must see that. I cannot disappoint the memory of my mother, no matter what feelings I may or may not have. Over time, surely my feelings will increase. But, until then…"

"Until then—" Fitzwilliam pulled his reins tighter and attempted to control his anger "—until then, I advise you to prepare for a life of misery. Not for you, Cousin. No, you will acclimate to whatever you choose and accept it as necessary to keep your beloved estate moving forward. But more importantly, a life of misery for Anne."

Darcy sat taller in his saddle. "I thank you, Fitzwilliam, for your wishes of felicity and hope to see you at the happy event."

Without another word, the colonel turned and rode off, leaving Darcy to stew in their conversation.

The idea that Anne does not love me—that she would not want to marry me! It is what is expected. *Of course she would want to marry me.* "Does she not?" He turned his horse in the opposite direction of Rosings and allowed him to walk freely amongst the meadow grasses while he pondered his cousin's words. *True, she wished to address our future at Pemberley, but she too must see we have responsibilities to our family. Regardless of our own feelings, I must continue down the path my mother prepared for me.* His mind was resolute as he kicked Ulysses in the flanks and thundered across the meadow.

The sound of laughter and music filled the air of Longbourn that afternoon, as revelers drank to the health of the new bride and groom. Jane was resplendent in her new gown, the soft pink rosebuds sewn along the hem and bodice of the cream silk only added to her natural, joyful glow. The ceremony had been beautiful: the Reverend Smart—having baptized Jane as an infant—presided, the sun had shown brightly after fears of rain, and Miss Bingley had been silent the entire time. A small miracle.

The ladies of Longbourn had done their best to ensure preparation for an unforgettable ceremony, one which could have no rival for years to come. And as Jane and Bingley's carriage left the gates of

Longbourn toward Netherfield, Lizzy's arm was entwined with that of Charlotte Lucas, who had been given leave by her husband to attend the event.

"Oh, Elizabeth. What a splendid wedding breakfast. Your mother has outdone herself."

"Yes, she has. Poor Cook and Mrs. Hill have not slept this entire week attempting to pacify the demands of my mother. Father has been holed up in his study, and we girls have done all in our power to make it as easy as possible for Jane, who was overly concerned for mother's nerves."

Charlotte let out a little laugh and smiled. "This is not to be your mother's only wedding, however. Do you not expect the same magnificent preparations for yours?"

Lizzy rolled her eyes at the idea before replying. "Now, Charlotte. As my dearest friend, you know the answer to that. Mother's least favorite daughter will be lucky to receive a new dress for the grand event."

"Elizabeth Bennet!"

"No, I am not serious. Mama has already ordered a haunch of pork from the butcher in preparation, but you are aware of my tastes. I do not wish an elaborate affair. Small and intimate suits me fine."

After donning their cloaks, the two friends walked out to the garden, arms still linked together and paused to sit on a bench where the roses would bloom in the spring.

"And do you have a notion when that event will occur?"

"No, I do not. Mr. Hamilton has not spoken to me since my return from Pemberley. And as you saw, and as *everyone* in attendance today saw, he has not deigned to be in my presence for more than a minute's time."

"Did you quarrel?"

Her laugh reverberated through the garden. "How can we quarrel when he only glares at me? I know not what I have done but expect he will move beyond his mood. Remember as children? He does not stay angry for long. I just wish I knew what troubles him."

"And you love him? You always said you would only marry for love..."

Lizzy knew the answer but was uncertain if she should voice it so openly. "James is a good man who cares for me and will provide for me. I esteem him and value his friendship."

"But do you love him?" Charlotte asked quietly. "I know you, Lizzy. Can you be happy in a marriage of convenience?"

"But, there will be things which will make me happy—helping with his tenants, running my own house. There will, I am sure, be children. I will pour my love into them." *It is interesting that a topic which made be blush when thinking of Mr. Darcy merely seems a task to be completed with Mr. Hamilton.*

Charlotte was silent and reached over to clasp her friend's hand while looking out beyond the garden. "Eliza, I am not romantic and only have wanted a comfortable home. Let me not have the grief of seeing you unable to love and respect the partner you have chosen— for love is necessary for your happiness."

The silence settled around them while the two friends observed the goings on of the wedding guests through the windows.

"It is true, Charlotte, that I do not love him the way I had imagined loving a husband, but he is a good man. I know he respects me, and he is able to accept impropriety of my mother. Granted," she said, turning her head to the side in thought, "he does believe I am too obstinate at times, which I am, but he cannot alter me."

"But, will he try?"

Lizzy looked at Charlotte with an odd expression. "I should hope not, but we shall see." After a moment, she laughed and patted Charlotte's hand. "Enough worry of me. We have had little time to discuss your new role as the mother of a parish. Tell me more about your home. Mr. Collins. Rosings Park." At the last, Lizzy's voice faltered.

"Mr. Collins is, as I suppose, as he always was. He is very dedicated to his patroness and amasses all his time and attention to the upcoming wedding of Miss de Bourgh and Mr. Darcy. Pray, forgive me, Lizzy. But I am to understand from Kitty that you spent a great deal of time in that man's company."

"Yes, I did. We became good friends."

"From what Kitty tells me, you would often find yourself discussing books or politics at dinner."

"Oh, Kitty." Lizzy smiled at the memories. "Yes, he is a very knowledgeable man who has very admirable qualities. Have you been in company with him much since his coming to Rosings?"

"No. Not at all, as Lady Catherine does not extend invitations to dinner to the parsonage when she has company. And with the wedding preparations, she is besieged with tasks which must be resolved."

"Yes. It is difficult being the mother of the bride, I am sure. As I have had daily proof."

The girls laughed before standing to return to the house. "Lizzy, if I may be so bold…"

"Of course, dear Charlotte. What is it?"

She took a deep breath and sighed. "As a woman who married for comfort, I encourage you to act in a manner which will only constitute your own happiness without reference to any person so wholly unconnected to you."

"I will. Fear not, Charlotte. My melancholy mood as of late is due to the impending separation I will suffer with Jane's departing as a married woman. My future is bright, of that I am sure."

"As it should be, Lizzy."

～

As a child, Darcy's trips to Rosings had been one of miserable anticipation. He did not enjoy the trips to see his aunt, uncle, or cousin Anne. Lady Catherine was not the kind of aunt who would sneak one sweets when his mother was not looking, buy him gifts which his father had said he was too young for, or allow him to slide across the newly polished wood floor in his stockings. No, Rosings meant formal meals, criticism, and awkward, probing questions that a child, especially one so reticent in company, dreaded.

Not much had changed since he aged: the meals remained uncomfortable and rigid, the criticism was now disguised as suggestions, and the probing questions were not questions at all, but dictates from one who believed she had the right to impose her will upon another.

Lady Catherine's private sitting room was Darcy's least favorite room in the house. As a child, he had been summoned there numerous times for his aunt to go over his deficiencies of character and other complaints about himself, his father, and even his mother. He found that he did not have to attend to the conversation but need only occasionally nod to appease his aunt. After a quarter of an hour, she was ordinarily finished and would dismiss him to return to the others.

As he walked into the room, he realized nothing had changed in all those years, including his aunt. The blue velvet couch still sat in the same place, the pictures of de Bourgh family members adorned the walls alongside water colors painted by Sir Lewis's mother and grandmother. Time seemed to stand still. This was evident not only by the decorations of the room but also by the conversation of his aunt.

"Where have you been? I sent Richard out two hours ago to find you. Why did you not come immediately?"

He took a breath before responding. "Richard found me merely thirty minutes ago. I finished my tour of the park and came straight away to see to your concerns. What can I do for you, Aunt?"

She grimaced before replying. "You can be more punctual next time. I am not a woman to be trifled with."

"I came when I completed my tasks for *your* estate, madam. As you now see, I am here."

"Very, well. I have a matter I wish to discuss with you."

He walked to the sideboard and poured himself a glass of brandy attempting to stifle his frustrations.

"I need you to sign this."

"Sign what?" he asked, setting down his drink to look at the document she indicated on the table. "What is this?" He walked over and attempted to pick it up before it was ripped from his hands.

"Only an amendment to the marriage contract. There was a small part which your solicitor was remiss in including. Take the pen and sign it."

"I will not sign it unless I can read it first."

"I have told you what changes have been made. Do you not trust me?"

"Lady Catherine. I am a man who has been my own master for the last five years, and I profitably run an estate that rivals any in the whole country. I do not take orders from anyone including you. Let me see this at once!" He grabbed it from her with a force she was not expecting and retreated to the other side of the room, reading it as he went.

"Darcy, it is one insignificant clause. Sign it and be on your way. You have more important things to concern yourself with than..."

"What is this?" His voice thundered, looking up at her and glaring from across the room. "What does this say? An allotment of twenty percent of Pemberley's yearly income will be used for the upkeep and renovation of Rosings. If Anne dies in childbirth or before her own mother's demise, you are to receive the sum of Anne's pin money and marriage settlement until the end of your own lifetime. *You* will maintain residence at Rosings and have access to the Dowager House at Pemberley and will take the place of the mistress in all major decisions, even if *and* after I remarry. Is *this* the insignificant clause you speak of?" He stormed across the room, tearing the parchment in two and throwing it in the fire.

"Darcy, you are being unreasonable. Listen to me..."

"No, you listen to me, Aunt," he said to her with a slow, controlled voice which made her visibly shrink back. "My life will not become yours to order around and dictate because I am marrying Anne. You will have *no* access to Pemberley unless Anne or I invite you. You will have *no* control over your daughter once she is married, and you will have *no* claim to *any* of the Darcy money. Never." He strode out of the room, closing the door forcefully behind him.

~

"And he is gone?" Kitty asked Lizzy that evening while laying across the bed. "And he did not make you an offer?"

Lizzy pulled out the last of her pins before picking up the brush and running it through her tangle of curls. "Yes, Mr. Hamilton is gone back to Ashby Park, and no, he did not make me an offer." She shrugged her shoulders and began to plait her hair.

"But, Lizzy. Were you not expecting an offer today? We have not seen him in almost two weeks. Whyever is he waiting?"

Lizzy laughed. "Kitty, if I were able to answer that question, I could solve all the mysteries of life. Why does a man do anything or nothing at all? He has business concerns, estate concerns, concerns I as a woman know nothing about. I am sure, however," she said, tying a ribbon around the bottom of her braid and walking over to sit on the bed, "that it will not be much longer. He spoke with Father this afternoon…"

"Yes, I know. Maria Lucas and I saw him knock on the study door. But why must he wait? Jane's wedding was such a jolly affair. I am anticipating the same amount of felicity from yours."

"Oh, I see that your motivation is self-serving, dear sister." She threw a bonnet at Kitty who dodged it, laughing.

"No, I am merely anticipating what I will write to Georgiana. She is to write me when Mr. Darcy weds Miss de Bourgh, and I am to reply back with your proposal and all the details. You *will* tell me all the details, will you not, Lizzy?"

Lizzy felt her blithe mood began to falter. "Of course, dearest. Now, let us bid each other good night. I woke earlier than usual and cannot wait for the Land of Nod to claim me. Go on then…out with you." She picked up a pillow and playfully swatted Kitty with it.

"Very well, then. Goodnight, Lizzy."

"Goodnight."

"And Lizzy? I agree that Mr. Hamilton is not as handsome as Mr. Darcy, but he will make you a good husband, will he not?"

She smiled at the innocent question of her young sister who was more oblivious to the intricacies of marriage than her. "Yes, Kitty. I am sure he will."

CHAPTER 23

December 20, 1810
Rosings

L ife at Rosings had remained constant in the three days since Lady Catherine had presented him with the amendments to the wedding contract. Although Darcy's anger had subsided, his aunt's had not. Instead of being met with criticisms and suggestions, he was ignored. *No bother. This censure serves my purpose well as it saves me the need to speak at dinner.*

Estate business had ruled his days and the library his nights. When he should have been doing more to secure his future happiness with his cousin, he had buried himself in the mundane running of Rosings, meeting with every tenant and the local magistrate.

He had determined to go through and recalculate the whole of the estate's ledgers for the last ten years, when there was a knock at the door. "Sir, Mrs. Collins, the parson's wife, has asked to speak with you."

"With me and not Lady Catherine?"

"Yes, sir."

"Very well. Give me a moment, then show her in." Darcy stood and slipped his coat on.

The door opened again revealing the same footman and a very plain woman.

"Mrs. Collins," he said bowing to her. "Please do be seated."

"Thank you for seeing me."

"How might I be of service to you today?" The lady sat in the soft leather chair opposite him and he had a niggling feeling he had seen her before. Although he had been in company with her husband more times than he cared to remember in the last three weeks, she had been away visiting family.

"I apologize for interrupting your day, sir. But I have just come from visiting my parents in Hertfordshire and a mutual friend asked me to pass a correspondence on to you." She looked over her shoulder to confirm the door was closed before slipping the letter out of her reticule and passing it over the desk to him.

Darcy did not recognize the female script, but as he turned the letter over to inspect the seal, her delicate scent wafted up from the paper. For a moment, he felt his heart seize and then swallowed the lump in his throat. "Is this from Miss Elizabeth Bennet?"

"She was concerned others would misconstrue the meaning of a letter between two friends, so I told her I would deliver it. Apparently, she received a note from London and felt there was information she needed to pass on to you."

He coolly accepted Mrs. Collins' explanation, unable to remember anything she said, but knowing he could not open this letter in front of anyone. Standing, he bowed and set the letter down on the edge of his desk. "I thank you, Mrs. Collins. If I find there is need for a response, may I utilize your discretion?"

"Of course."

"Until then, if you correspond with Miss Bennet, please convey my wishes for her health and happiness."

"It would be my pleasure. Might I also convey my best wishes to you, sir?"

"I thank you, madam. Wilson will show you out."

He waited until the door was closed behind her before breaking the wax seal.

Sir,

I hope this missive finds you well. I wanted to inform you I received word from my aunt this morning that Mrs. Worth's grandmother, Mrs. Smith, had passed away while visiting relatives in Scotland. She was not lucid at the end, and her final moments of clarity had been indeed at Pemberley in Lady Anne's room. I pray that her words brought you comfort and that you are joyfully preparing for your marriage with Miss de Bourgh.

I send you my deepest wishes for felicity and pray that God keeps you safe. I leave you with this quote from Wordsworth. "That though the radiance which was once so bright be now forever taken from my sight. Though nothing can bring back the hour of splendor in the grass, glory in the flower. We will grieve not, rather find strength in what remains behind."

Adieu

EB

He dropped the letter on his desk, leaned back in his chair, untied his cravat, and stared up at the ceiling, brooding about what would never be.

⁓

With Jane's departure for her wedding tour, and Charlotte's return to Hunsford, Elizabeth could find little that interested her. She had walked through the grounds of Longbourn, made numerous errands into the village to visit her aunt Phillips, buy ribbons, and go to the book seller. She had even contemplated taking up a new hobby such as riding.

One would know how truly distracted I am to consider such an extreme sport, she chuckled to herself and kicked a stone out of the road. On this morning, her exercise had brought her to a prettyish kind of little wilderness leading to Oakham Mount. She rested on a bench underneath a large oak tree and pulled out her book of Wordsworth when she heard a footstep behind her. Turning, she was surprised at the presence of Mr. Hamilton.

"James. What are you doing at Longbourn again so soon? I believed you to be at Ashby Park through Christmas."

"Yes, well, as it is only a few days away, and I had finished all matters of business, Elizabeth. I need to speak to you." He clasped his hands behind his back and cleared his throat.

"To speak to me? Since Pemberley, I believed you had lost the ability." The teasing lilt in her voice could not be missed nor could the biting tone.

"Yes. Let us discuss Pemberley."

"Very well. What do you wish to speak of?"

He sat beside her for a few moments, and then getting up, paced before her. Lizzy was surprised but said not a word. After a silence of several minutes, he came toward her in an agitated manner, and thus began.

"Elizabeth, it has been brought to my attention that, please forgive me, you…have participated in some behavior that if discovered would lead to your ruin."

The cold fingers of a memory from the hunting lodge began to crawl up her back and neck while she attempted a level of control.

"When your parents and I were at Pemberley, I was made aware of the possibility that you and Darcy inhabited the same cabin the night you were lost in the storm. Do you deny this?"

She was fearful to respond.

"Elizabeth, answer me. Is this true?"

"If I might ask, where did this information come from?"

He looked down and began to fiddle with his hands. "Two stable hands…"

"And sir," she cried, standing to face him, "did you not roar them down?"

"No, I did not. I… but Elizabeth, you have not answered me. Did you stay alone in the same lodgings as Darcy?"

"It was not what you think."

He sank into the bench. "Then you did! Then, you were not faithful to me. He defiled you!"

"James Hamilton. *If* you truly believe that it was my intent…"

He sprang to his feet. "He forced himself upon you? Is that what happened? I will call him out."

"No," she said putting her hand on his arm to calm him. "He did not force himself on me. Mr. Darcy was a complete gentleman. I was trapped in the storm. He also needed shelter. We could not get back to Pemberley in the storm. There has been a misunderstanding…"

He swallowed and cleared his throat. "Elizabeth, please respect me enough to answer this question… Did you kiss him?"

Her eyes lowering, she quietly whispered, "Yes."

He snorted and gave a guttural laugh. "Of course, you did," he said raising his head to the clouds. "Of course, she did. Who can refuse the master of Pemberley over the master of Ashby Park?"

"James. It was not like that. Do not make this nothing into something."

"Nothing?" he cried looking at her. "You are mine, Elizabeth. The future mistress of *my* home. The future mother of *my* children… That kiss was mine." She blushed at this pronouncement, but he continued. "And now I see that I have been cheated. The woman I believed to be whole and pure has given her favors to another!"

She was dumbstruck. Her eyes wide, and her mouth agape with no sound coming forth.

"And now, I have to decide if I will marry you and save you from yourself and your shame…unless…unless he has made you an offer?"

"To what are you referring? He is to marry Anne de Bourgh."

James snorted with disgust. "There are other offers to be made, Elizabeth. Darcy is a wealthy and powerful man. He can set you up in a house nicely concealed on his grounds. Maybe your small lodge? Yes, that would do well for your trysts."

Mute with shock, she slapped him across the face. His eyes flashed in anger as he put his hand to his cheek.

His jaw clenched as he attempted to control his breathing. "However, owing to our long acquaintance, I cannot allow you to cheapen yourself any more than you already have. I will still marry you, Lizzy, as it is what is expected. But you will obey me. You will cut all contact with Georgiana Darcy and not acknowledge the Darcys when we meet in London." He waited for her response but when none came, continued. "I never thought it would come to this, Elizabeth. I never did. I expected this of Lydia, never of you."

Waiting for a response and receiving none, he looked back at her only to be met with a steely gaze. Finally, words burst forward. "I have never been so insulted in all my life. You have widely mistaken my character if you think I can be worked on by such persuasions as these. Forgive me, Mr. Hamilton, for… my transgressions against you. But I must return to the house."

"You will not marry me?" he sputtered.

"How can I marry you? You do not trust me. We are no longer the same Jimmy and Lizzy who played in the glen and raced to Oakham Mount. I do not see how we can get past this." She felt resolved in her actions. "I admit I have wronged you but not as you have imagined. I can only wish you happiness."

"Elizabeth, be sensible. You might never get another offer of marriage, especially if this were to be made public. You should reconsider your position and that of your unmarried sisters."

"Mr. Hamilton, as miserable as the prospect is which you have placed before me, I would rather live a life of solitude than with a husband who could not trust or respect me. Good day."

CHAPTER 24

December 27, 1810
Rosings Park

W ith only two days until his wedding, Darcy had become numb to his prospects. He had not had a civil conservation with his aunt since the day he tore up her attempt at stealing his fortune, and she kept mostly to her private study. Colonel Fitzwilliam had left unexpectedly earlier in the day after receiving an express from his commanding officer but was expected back in the evening, and his betrothed remained mostly in her rooms. *I have nowhere to escape. Even though I am alone in this great house, I feel suffocated by my surroundings.*

He buried his head in the estate books, working hard to make the transition from one estate to two as seamless as possible. *With Georgiana arriving tomorrow, I must complete all my tasks to protect her from Lady Catherine's biting comments. I am grateful she will be joining us on our wedding tour.*

Lady Catherine sent word that she was dining with Lord and Lady Strathern at their estate. He asked a footman to have a tray sent into the study so he could continue working. A quarter of an hour later, here was a knock at the door.

Anne entered, followed by a servant with a tray. "Anne." He stood quickly and struggled to tie his cravat. "I was not expecting you."

Waving her hand, she said, "It is of no consequence. I have seen you much worse. Do you not recall the pigsty when I was nine?"

Darcy's laughter echoed throughout the room. "My dear Anne. I forgot all about that. How angry your mother was at me for not protecting you!"

"For not protecting me? How could you when I pushed you in, then slipped myself?" Her laughter joined his, then silence settled around them as the servant departed. She waited for the door to close before shakily starting. "William, there is something I must tell you."

"I believe I know what you are going to say, but I must tell you, you are wrong. We will have a good marriage. I will be kind —"

"Darcy, stop." She hesitated a heartbeat. "Today, after my mother left, I went into the safe to choose my jewels for our wedding. I found tucked in the back of the safe, a letter." She reached into her pocket but Darcy stopped her with a wave of his hand.

"Yes, Anne. I have always known about this letter your mother wrote and my mother signed. Lady Catherine showed it to me when I was just fifteen and again three weeks ago at Pemberley." He took it from her and looked at his mother's words again. "Yes, our marriage was my mother's greatest wish."

"No, William. I do not believe it was."

His head snapped up quickly from the paper. "What do you mean?"

"Read the letter again. I realized something today that you have missed. What does the letter say in regards to my young cousin?"

Darcy found the appropriate spot in the letter:

...Know that I love you, that you are most important to me, as is Georgiana...You will inherit Pemberley, and all its holdings, however, I have instructed my sister to ensure my Matlock inheritance go to Georgiana. I fear your father is not in support of this...

Darcy looked up at Anne. "I do not understand? What does this..." He shot to his feet. "Lady Catherine has always told me she wrote this letter weeks before her arrival. That she had no time to rewrite it and that her solicitor approved it...but the date from the solicitor is after my mother's death!"

"And?"

"And," he said, deflating back into the chair. "How did she know the babe would be a girl? If she wrote this weeks before Georgie's birth, she could not know." He dropped his face into his hands. "She lied to me. All these years, she lied to me."

Anne was silent for a moment, and then replied quietly, "She lied to us, William, and I cannot conceive why."

"I can, and I will confront her for it."

"But there is more." She reached back in her pocket and pulled out another letter. "I also found this. It is from Lady Anne addressed to you."

His heart racing, Darcy saw the wax seal of his mother on the opened letter.

"I was not the one who opened it, as it is written to you, Cousin."

He held the letter in his fingers and stared at it before looking back up at her. "Anne, as you said, we are not to blame for the actions of your mother. Whatever this letter contains may or may not change the course of our lives. But I would beg you, allow me a moment to read it alone."

"Of course." She stood and retreated to her rooms, while Darcy, for the second time that week, waited for a lady to leave the room so he could read a letter from a woman he loved.

My Dearest Fitzwilliam,

My heart breaks knowing that when you read this letter, I will no longer be with you. You are my joy, my sweet son, the pride of your mother's heart. You are everything I have ever wanted in a child— honest, dependable, generous, kind. There are so many things I wish to say but the most important is this: follow your heart. Do not allow others to dictate your life. My sister, your aunt, has decided you shall marry Anne. As dear as Anne is to me, I wish you to find a wife for yourself. Do not allow family obligations and honor to impede your judgment. If Anne is your choice, then I wish you happy. If she is not, choose a woman who I would be friends with, who will challenge you, and bring pleasure to your heart.

Speak of me to Georgiana, the mother who loved her. Protect her. Surround her with women of confidence and affection, who will bring her happiness and be examples to her.

Listen to your father. He is the best of men, and ours was a love match, forged in the heavens. Know that I am always with you.

I love you, sweet son.

You are my Joy,

Your dearest Mama

He did not recognize the script but the signature was hers. *This must be the lost letter Mrs. Smith wrote!* He had read it for the third time when the footman knocked and entered the room. "Colonel Fitzwilliam to see you, sir."

The colonel brushed past the footman and planted himself directly in the chair Anne had abandoned moments before.

"Richard."

"Darce, I…"

He held up his hand to forestall his cousin's speech. "Richard, I owe you an apology. I was thoughtless and unfeeling. But something has recently come to my attention that affects us all."

Darcy handed his mother's letter to Richard, then leaned back in his chair with his fingers steepled in front of him. When Richard was finished reading, he looked across at his cousin.

"What does this mean…"

"You love her, Richard. Go to her. Take her to Gretna Greene or to London and ensconce her in Darcy House. I will send a note with you for the servants to not allow entrance to none but you, if you wish. Get a special license and marry the woman you love. Waste no time. Aunt Catherine is dining out. Take my carriage. I will follow tomorrow." Darcy pushed back from the desk and stood. "I have lived the last five years to please others, and I am now going to please myself. You must do the same!"

Richard waited mere seconds for the revelation to register before standing and pulling his cousin to him. Emerging from an impulsive embrace, he slapped Darcy's back. "Yes, well. I must be off. Do you think my Anne will enjoy haggis and bagpipes?"

"There is only one way to find out, Cousin. Godspeed. I expect to see you at Pemberley when the dust settles."

Richard turned and was about to exit the room, when he stopped and looked back at Darcy. "Are you for Hertfordshire?"

"I fear I may be too late."

Richard clicked his tongue and shook his head. "It is never too late when a woman looks at you the way Miss Bennet looks at you. Stop licking your wounds and go to her. You deserve happiness."

"We shall see, Richard. But first must take care of matters here. Would you please stop by my room and ask Briggs to see to my bags?"

"Of course," he said, walking briskly through the door.

Now, just to wait for the prey to return.

The sound of the approaching carriage made Darcy sit up and put on his coat. His cravat was rumpled, but he did not care.

Over the last few hours, his emotions had gone from anger to hatred to disgust. The only consolation was that Richard and Anne had left the hour before for who knows where but even that did not matter.

He waited until he heard the click of his aunt's shoes across the marble floor in the hallway before opening the door and asking her to join him.

"Whatever you have to say, we will discuss in the morning. It is late."

"No. We will discuss this now." Lady Catherine turned cautiously toward him.

"You will not speak to me as such. I demand respect."

"And I demand an explanation."

"Yes, yes. I made an error in judgment attempting to have you support Rosings. Now, I am for my rooms." She was halfway through the door when his next sentence stopped her.

"I read the letter."

"Yes, I know. I showed it to you."

"No, not that letter. *This* letter." He pulled out the crisp paper from his pocket and held it up.

She paused for a moment. Upon recognizing the document, Lady Catherine charged forward, attempting to grab it from his hand. He easily evaded her and with an even voice stated, "I will not marry Anne."

"Where did you get that? That is not your property!"

"It *is* my property. It has my name on it and is from my mother."

"You will marry Anne!"

Darcy folded the letter and slipped it back in his pocket. "That is both improbable and impossible."

"My daughter will do anything I tell her to do."

"As you say."

"What do you mean? Where is she?"

He pulled out his watch and smiled. "I expect on the way to Gretna Greene."

Lady Catherine paled and collapsed in a chair. "And who is the fool willingly marrying my daughter? No, let me guess. Richard."

Darcy stilled.

"What a foolish, stupid girl. She could have had the master of Pemberley, vast estates in not only England but Ireland and Scotland as well, but yet she chose to marry a second son who can give her nothing."

Darcy allowed his aunt to simmer in her anger for a time. "And that is why you contrived this farce all those years ago? You wished to have Pemberley and Rosings as well, believing I would roll over and do your bidding for you? It would never have happened."

The venom in her voice was evident. "You are just like your father. He was a brilliant man until he met my younger sister. Then, everything he did, he did for her, almost allowing Pemberley to fall to ruins."

"My father ran the estate well!"

"Yes, until *she* came along."

"You were jealous of her. Why?" Recognizing her vehemence as jealousy, clarity came over Darcy in a moment. "You loved him? You loved my father and he did not return your affections."

"Oh, he returned my affections," Lady Catherine hissed, "until your mother arrived home from school. Then, I was cast aside. Your father continued to call, and Anne was sent with us as an escort on our walks, but he did not talk to me—it was always her. The morning after her coming out ball, he petitioned my father for *her* hand. I was humiliated! Humiliated and grateful that Sir Lewis was hanging out for a rich wife to save Rosings. My dowry did nicely and my humiliation was short-lived.

"But then, I had to listen to how happy my sister was with such a perfect child as you and how excellent a husband your father was. I prayed that there would be some calamity that befell their happiness, and because God is merciful, it did. I knew I would enact my revenge through you…"

Darcy was dumbstruck for a moment, then found his voice. "I thank you for the thoroughness of your confession as it spared me the concern which I might have felt in forgiving you had you behaved in a more penitent like manner." He walked from the room, planning to never return.

CHAPTER 25

December 27, 1810
Longbourn

Mrs. Bennet moved seamlessly from planning her eldest daughter's wedding to planning another for her second daughter. Though it had not been announced and Lizzy had not even requested assistance, one could never be too prepared for an opportunity to showcase both her talents as a hostess and the fortunate circumstances of another of her daughters marrying a wealthy landowner. Lizzy wondered how long until her mother realized Mr. Hamilton had not been seen by the inhabitants of Longbourn since Jane's wedding save one, nor had any letters arrived for her in the post.

It was on a lovely, late December day that said mother raised her head at the breakfast table to make a request of her least favorite child.

"Lizzy, today we must go into Meryton, as Mrs. Coles has received the lace I ordered for your veil. We will decide which bonnet looks best on you, then we will return home to finish planning the wedding breakfast. Although a wedding in January would not be my first choice," she said, waving her hand dismissively. "However, if it is necessary, so be it."

Mrs. Bennet returned to her lists and Mr. Bennet raised his brows at Lizzy.

That look reminded her of their conversation one-week prior indicating she must tell her mother the courtship was no longer honored by either party…

"And may I ask, Lizzy, when this change of heart occurred?"

"Change of heart?" she had asked, attempting to avoid her father's gaze.

"Yes. It has always been evident that you cared for Mr. Hamilton, and I am at a loss for when that ceased."

"Papa, I can honestly say I am uncertain I ever loved him. I did always esteem his person and character but do not know if I would call it love."

"I did not ask about love. I asked when you stopped caring for Mr. Hamilton."

"Well, I have always cared for Mr. Hamilton and still do."

"Then why are you unwilling to marry him?" Her father had sat calmly waiting for her reply.

"I have always felt I would only marry for love. Being in a larger expanse of society while staying with the Darcy's helped me to see that I do not need to solely accept what I am used to. That there are other honorable men who could love me and I could love them in return. Not only would a marriage be achieved but a union of like minds and respect. Mr. Hamilton does not respect me, Papa. He told

my aunt Gardiner that he wishes to change me. That I am too headstrong and opinionated."

"You are."

"Father!"

"You are, my girl. That is how I raised you, which is not what polite society expects. But I know you could be neither happy nor respectable, unless you truly esteemed your husband, unless you looked up to him as a superior. Your lively talents would place you in the greatest danger in an unequal marriage. You could hardly escape discredit and misery. My child, let me not have the grief of seeing you unable to respect your partner in life. You know what you are about..."

However, Lizzy had preferred to avoid her mother's wrath and allowed the deception to continue. Mr. Bennet cleared his throat and looked pointedly at his daughter. "Yes, Lizzy. I think it is time you and your mother discuss wedding details. What say you?"

"I thank you, Father, but I do not believe now will be the best time. Maybe later in the day?"

"My dear girl, I am certain Mrs. Coles would appreciate your honest discourse as no proprietor wishes to lose income on unpurchased items."

"Unpurchased items?" Mrs. Bennet guffawed, splashing her coffee in the saucer. "You have given me leave to spend as much as Jane's wedding on Lizzy, and I mean to do it, Mr. Bennet. Someday my younger daughters will marry, Lydia and Kitty for certain, and Mary might find a suitable vicar. I will purchase the remaining yardage for decorations for them. Mrs. Coles will not be losing any finances, you can be sure."

The clanking of Kitty's fork on the plate caused everyone to glance her way before Mrs. Bennet once again found her target. "We must also choose ribbons for your sisters and new gloves for Lydia. She is growing so quickly, and it is likely Mr. Hamilton and Mr. Bingley will have eligible gentleman to throw in the way of my girls."

Mr. Bennet cleared his throat again and nodded at his second child over his newspaper. Lizzy was not afraid of many things, least of all her family, but she dreaded how she would live under the same roof with her mother after she learned the truth.

"Yes, well, Mama, I regret to inform you that Mr. Hamilton will not be frequenting Longbourn any time soon."

"Of course not, child. Men have no need to plan weddings. They merely arrive before the vows are spoken, then retreat with their wives back to their estate. No," she said clucking her tongue, "we do not expect Mr. Hamilton here until the date itself. By the way, child, when is the exact date? We need to tell the vicar."

Lizzy met her mother's gaze and was grateful for the sympathetic looks from her sisters as her father's were all amusement.

"There is no date, Mama.

"Then we need to pick one. I cannot wait on you forever, girl!" She harrumphed and took a bite of her muffin. "January 28 will do well enough. Such a good, solid number. Never fear, Lizzy, your Mama will make it all right in the end."

A silence came over the breakfast room, before Lizzy spoke. "I thank you for the favor, Mama, but I do not particularly…need your help at the moment. Maybe another time?"

The words hung in the air for only a moment before Mrs. Bennet replied, "How you vex me! What could she mean by this?" she asked, turning to address Mr. Bennet.

"Only she knows the answer to the question." Mr. Bennet hid his mirth behind the paper.

Lizzy took a deep breath and squared her shoulders, awaiting the attack she was sure would come. "It means, Mama, that Mr. Hamilton and I no longer have an understanding."

The shocked silence of Mrs. Bennet lasted for only a moment. "What, what?"

"Mr. Hamilton and I no longer have an understanding, Mama." She picked up her fork and continued her breakfast with vigor.

"Elizabeth Anne Bennet. Is this a joke? Are you trying my nerves for sport?"

"No, Mama, I am entirely serious."

"What was the matter? What occurred? What did you do?" She slapped her hands on the table. "Now, Lizzy, you had better explain yourself with an outcome more to my liking."

Lizzy finished her tea and cleared her throat. "I am sorry to upset you, Mama, but that is not possible. Mr. Hamilton and I have agreed that we no longer suit. He has withdrawn his offer of courtship, and I thoroughly agree with him."

The stunned silence was enough for Lizzy to encourage her to stand and excuse herself from the table. However, Mrs. Bennet was too quick. "You will remain where you are, Lizzy! You will immediately send a note to Mr. Hamilton, requesting an audience with him here at Longbourn. You will then make him come to realize you were holy mistaken in your judgment of the situation. All will be well."

"I will not."

"You will go to your room and will not come down until the letter is written to my satisfaction. Or I will never speak to you again."

"Mama, I…" She looked to her father for help but saw only the top of his head behind the newspaper.

"Go, now!" Mrs. Bennet's feelings seemed more tranquil on the occasion to her frustration and Lizzy huffed, then marched up the stairs.

⌒⌒

December 28, 1810

She had been awake for hours, only forgoing her morning walk for fear her mother would be informed by the servants she was out. *I am not yet ready to face her unsound hopes.* She had finished dressing herself and pinning her hair up in a simple twist, when she heard the creak of the floorboards outside her door.

"Lizzy? Lizzy, are you awake?"

"Yes, Papa, I am awake. It is well past sun up. You know I am awake." She opened the door and allowed him entrance, before closing it behind him. "What brings you to the tower to see the prisoner?"

He chuckled before sitting on the edge of her bed. "You are not a prisoner, my girl. Since you did not come down last night for supper, I have come to check the progress of your letter to Mr. Hamilton."

"It is as you see," she said pointing to the blank paper on her writing desk. "I am not writing the letter, Papa. I will not be coerced into marrying someone I do not love."

"You have sense and I expect you to use it." Mr. Bennet grunted, nodding his head. "Well if this is the case, my love, you should know, I have settled it all with your mother. This gives you a sort of distinction. It is a comfort to think, whatever may befall you, you have an affectionate mother who will always make the most of it."

⌒

Wasting no time upon his sister's arrival at Rosings the next day, Darcy immediately turned the carriage around and they returned to London. Georgiana was overjoyed at the revelations for his cousins and hopeful for her brother's prospects.

"Wills, you must leave me with Mrs. Annesley and rush to Hertfordshire. Elizabeth will not refuse you!"

He only grinned at her youthful exuberance and hit the roof with his cane for the carriage to stop. "I will ride alongside the rest of the way. I am afraid my legs need to stretch."

Upon reaching London that afternoon, Darcy's man was readying for him to travel to Hertfordshire, when his butler entered with a note.

"Sir, Colonel Fitzwilliam charged me to put this directly in your hands immediately upon your arrival."

Nodding, Darcy dismissed him and tore open the missive.

Darce,

I regret this letter more than any I have ever penned. In preparation for our departure to Scotland, Anne and I came upon James Hamilton. I assume he has secured the hand of Miss Elizabeth as he stated he would convey our best wishes to her as he was sending a letter to Longbourn that day. My shame is great as I now live in a world of joy and you do not.

My regards,

Richard

CHAPTER 26

December 30, 1810
Darcy House

H e had survived the previous two days by removing the knocker from the door and finding solace in a bottle of French brandy. However, that morning as he pulled off his counterpane, he realized the pain would never go away and neither would his responsibilities as Fitzwilliam Darcy, the first of which was his sister. In the breakfast room he found her going through her post. "Good morning, Georgie."

"William."

She said nothing more, pursing her lips together and taking a knife to spread lemon curd over her beloved scones.

"And what have I done to deserve such a response so early in the morning?"

"You have disappointed me, Brother!"

He was taken aback at her fervor. "I have disappointed you? How so?"

"William, you are free to do as you please, and yet here you sit doing business, planning a trip to Pemberley, going through your correspondence..."

"Georgiana!"

"Why do you not go to her, William? Go to Hertfordshire! Elizabeth loves you. I know it. You love her! What reason do you have for not charging to Longbourn?"

"Georgiana, you know not of what you speak!" Her imploring countenance showed her confusion, and Darcy's jaw tightened. "She is engaged, Georgie."

"That is impossible!"

"It is not and has been confirmed by her new brother. I had it in a letter from Bingley while at Rosings. He wrote of how Hamilton spoke to Mr. Bennet the week leading up to Bingley's wedding, and how even Mrs. Bingley was certain Miss Elizabeth was eager to accept. And upon our return, I received a letter from Richard." He paused, regulating his tone. "He and Anne saw Hamilton in London. He intimated that Miss Elizabeth had accepted his proposal. You see, Georgie?" He picked up his toast then took a sip of his coffee. "Things do not always transpire as they do in your romance novels, dear girl."

Eager to end the conversation, he rose to leave. "I will be meeting with my solicitor then dining at White's this evening."

Georgie shuffled through her letters, not listening to her brother. As he made to leave the room, she exclaimed, "Wait! She is not engaged!" She waved a letter at him. "Kitty says Elizabeth refused Mr. Hamilton!"

"What? When?" Darcy spun on his heels and took a step toward her. "What did you say?"

"She refused him. More than a week ago. She said she could not marry a man she did not love nor one who did not respect her. She said that—"

"She is not engaged?"

"No, Wills, she is not. And according to her sister, she will not become engaged unless the man she loves asks her!"

"Turner, Turner! Tell the groom to saddle Ulysses immediately and Briggs to pack a bag. I will be leaving at once, Georgie..." he called over his shoulder.

"Go, Wills. Do not concern yourself with me! Go and bring me home a sister!"

⁓

Finally, having appeased her mother by her penitent withdrawal from her room, Lizzy was met by her father with a letter in his hand, while coming down the stairs.

"There you are. I was coming to find you. Come into my room." She followed him thither and her curiosity piqued. "I have received a letter from Mr. Hamilton. His man delivered it this morning with some haste, and as it principally concerns yourself, you ought to know its contents. It seems he would care to remain on friendly terms with our family despite the inadequacy of the match...but listen to this, *'I still look with shame on my proposal and ask her forgiveness. Although my words were truthful, they were not the words of a gentleman and were spoken in anger at what I had discovered. I will not insult you by repeating them in a letter but ask your daughter to erase them from her mind. No lady of her integrity should ever have those accusations cast in her direction.'"*

Mr. Bennet paused and looked at her. "What did he say to you, Lizzy? What could he have accused you of?"

She shrugged her shoulders and watched an unseen object outside the window. "Nothing of consequence, Papa, I assure you."

Her father looked down his nose over her spectacles and said, "Well he does say he would be grateful to remain on friendly terms. *'It is with true charity that I wish Elizabeth joy in her life, and no ill will for her future.'* And, he also added a post script. *'I also pass on the best wishes of the former Miss Anne de Bourgh. I was able to see her and her husband in London before their wedding trip to Scotland and Ireland. I felt it best to not air our private lives to our acquaintances as of yet, and therefore said I would pass on her best.'"*

Her father looked up quickly at Lizzy's sharp intake of breath and said, "You look as if you did not enjoy it. You are not going to be missish, I hope."

"No, no. All is well. I am happy Mr. Hamilton holds no ill will."

"I wonder how long it will be until your mother decides that Kitty or Lydia would do for him? He does have three or four thousand a year, you know."

"Yes, yes. Pray excuse me, Papa," Lizzy said as she walked out to escape the prison which had spread to every room in the house.

It was almost dusk. The sun had been creeping down behind the woods but Lizzy was loath to return to the house, fearing what she would face in regards to her mother's silliness or her father's indifference.

She had been sitting on the grass under one of her favorite oak trees wrapped in a cloak and the woolen tartan which had somehow found its way into her bag from Pemberley. Wishing the duties of her life involved more than finding a man who made three thousand a year, she lamented her position but not her decision. *I have made the choice, and I do not regret rejecting James, even if I am to live my whole life alone as the maiden aunt.* Her thoughts had wandered from moving to London to find employment to moving to Italy to become a Catholic nun.

Alas, I am not Catholic, so that would be very difficult. She snickered at her jokes and reflected back on James' letter for the hundredth time. Or rather, she reflected back on only one part of his letter. *I am glad that marriage agrees with Anne. She is a kind woman and deserves happiness.* "Not that I am not a kind woman. I too deserve happiness and am sure someday there will be someone for me..."

But her words were hollow. She knew she was lying to herself, and it was better to face her mother than to sit out under this tree and catch her death of cold, wallowing in self-pity. And yet, she could not make herself move. She understood that whatever the future held for her would not contain *him*—the man whom she still dreamt of. *Will I be married, with children of my own and still have him walking through my dreams?* She sighed heavily. *Most likely so, as the Fates are sometimes cruel.*

Shivering, Lizzy watched as the shadows grew longer and realized there was no prolonging her present fate, knowing she could no longer avoid the complaints of her mother. Gazing up at the moon, she thought maybe she should write her aunt Gardiner to beg for an invitation.

~

Although Darcy had ridden hard, it was dusk when he arrived at the Kingsmill Arms in Meryton. Knowing full well it would be too late to call that evening at Longbourn, but unable to resist seeing her home with the knowledge she was inside, maybe thinking of him, he continued on toward his destiny. He cantered evenly down the road, pausing outside the gates of Longbourn and realizing what a scene it would cause if he did knock on the front door. He imagined Mrs. Bennet's shrieking and the one sister with the glasses, *Mary,* solemnizing about propriety and decorum. *No one would question my manners,* he chuckled softly, *as I asked Mrs. Bennet for her daughter's hand. She would most likely sit down in shock.*

He turned as he heard a horse behind him slowly coming down the road. Looking at the rider, he was surprised to see Mr. Bennet.

"Ah, Mr. Darcy. The rumors are true then. I was just in Meryton at my brother Phillips' house on business and his maid had told him you were seen at the Kingsmill. Welcome back to the neighborhood, sir."

"I thank you, Mr. Bennet."

"Might I ask what brings you to Longbourn this evening? We were to understand from a correspondence today that you were on your wedding tour in Scotland with the former Miss de Bourgh."

"No, sir. There has been a misunderstanding. You must mean my cousin, Colonel Fitzwilliam. I am yet unmarried."

"Truly?"

"Yes, truly."

A smirk appeared at the corners of the older man's mouth. "Well, then I am sure there are at least two people in my home who will be eager to see you. Come, let's not stand on ceremony. Besides" —the older man chuckled— "it will put my wife in a fine fettle, and that is something I attempt to do at least twice a week."

The two men road amiably up to the house speaking genially of the weather and their respective estates before they were met by the stable boy who took both horses.

"Now, Mr. Darcy. Prepare yourself for a most ebullient welcome. Mrs. Bennet will look on you quite as the Odysseus lost to us for twenty years."

Both men entered the house and could hear the wails of Mrs. Bennet coming from the drawing room.

"Oh, that girl. Who will ever take her off our hands? What man could want such an obstinate, headstrong thing? We were so blessed, Mary, that Mr. Hamilton was blinded by their childhood together. And then, she has gone and ruined it. Oh, Kitty…what are we to do? I pray that you or Lydia will make a good match to support Lizzy when your father is dead and I am thrown into the hedgerows."

"Let us hope, my dear, that that calamity will be many years in the making. Might I present to you our good friend Mr. Darcy?"

"Mr. Darcy!" Mrs. Bennet shrieked, standing at once and knocking a small plate of biscuits off her lap. "How good of you to call, sir. Will you not sit down?"

"Why yes, I thank you. I must beg forgiveness, ma'am, at the hour. I was riding by and Mr. Bennet encouraged me to come and see the family." His eyes darted across the room at the ladies before him. "How lovely it is to see all your daughters…save two?"

"Yes, as you know, our Mrs. Bingley is on her wedding tour, and Lizzy… Why, Mr. Darcy, are you not in Scotland? We received a letter that an acquaintance spoke to your wife, and you were for Scotland."

He shook his head, waiting for the reaction he guessed Mr. Bennet was so looking forward to. "No, ma'am. You speak of my cousin Anne, I presume. She married my esteemed cousin Colonel Fitzwilliam. I remain unmarried."

Mrs. Bennet's chin inched higher and her eyebrows rose. "Unmarried, you say? Well, that is good news, indeed. Kitty, ring for tea."

"No, I thank you, ma'am. I do not wish to trouble you." Darcy moved as if to stand, wondering where *she* might be.

"It is no trouble. Kitty, do as you are told. Or, better yet" —she stopped mid-sentence— "I have a better idea. Why not show Mr. Darcy the garden? It is lovely in the moonlight."

"Mama …"

"Kitty, do as your mother tells you," Mr. Bennet said with a twinkle in his eye. "And while you are taking a turn about the grounds in the dark," he said, raising his eyebrows at Mr. Darcy, "advise Elizabeth it is too late for her to be out alone."

Mr. Darcy stood immediately and extended his arm to Miss Katherine. "I would be pleased to accompany you outside. I am sure Longbourn has some flowers which have not frozen over as of yet."

Miss Katherine excused herself to get her wrap. As he donned his own outerwear in the front hall, he could not help but overhear Mrs. Bennet's excited whisper. "Oh, Mr. Bennet. We will have another wedding yet, mark my words. Kitty will make a lovely mistress of Pemberley. Mr. Darcy has attempted to pursue her for months and is now free to follow his heart."

"You believe that, Mrs. Bennet. If it gives you comfort."

Ten minutes had passed while he and Miss Katherine wandered the grounds of Longbourn. "Oh, let us try the edge of the grounds. I am sure she went to Oakham Mount but she never stays out this late. I am certain we will find her—" and then if by magic, she was there. Not quite thirty yards from where they stood, Miss Elizabeth, with her back toward them, was staring up at the moon. "If you will excuse me, sir. I remembered that I must speak to my mother." And with that, Miss Katherine turned and walked briskly toward the house, leaving him alone in the dark with the woman he loved.

He took careful steps not to startle her, but she did not turn around. As he came within ten feet of her, he heard her talking aloud.

"Dear moon, you are back to tease me tonight, I see. You and your brilliance shining in the sky. Yet, you still cannot give me what I want. Who I want." She sighed and shook her head. "No, I am destined to be the eccentric spinster aunt who will teach my beautiful nieces and handsome nephews passable Latin and to play their instruments very ill indeed. Oh, I am resigned to my fate," she said, holding up her hand and wagging her finger at the moon. "Do not try and change my mind, as I now comprehend that he was exactly the man who in disposition and talents would most suit me—there will never be another." She sighed and lowered her chin to her chest, and after a moment, let out a soft chuckle. "I know you are there, Kitty. You now know the truth which you have long suspected of the secrets of my heart."

He waited before he answered, expecting her to turn around. She did not. "I hope I am not disappointing you when I say that I am not Miss Katherine."

Miss Elizabeth spun around to face him with her mouth agape and her eyes wide. "Willia…Mr. Darcy. You are here?"

"As you see," he said with a mischievous grin.

"And not in Scotland with Miss de Bourgh…I mean Mrs. Darcy."

"No, I am not in Scotland."

"Is she unwell?" She spoke rapidly, rubbing her thumbs over her clasped hands. "Such an odd time of night to be out, but we can return to the house for some refreshment."

"I just came from the house, I thank you."

"Is Mrs. Darcy inside? We must not leave her unattended with my…unfamiliar… family for an extended length of time."

"I came alone." He allowed the statement to hang in the air. "There is no one inside, but your family." He looked her directly in the eyes and continued. "Miss Elizabeth, I have a confession to make."

"You do?"

"Yes." He took off his hat and rubbed his hand through his hair. "This is not the first time I have stood in the shadows and listened as you professed your thoughts to the moon."

"It is not?"

"No. However, this is the first time I meant to be discovered."

"Oh. Well, I beg your pardon. My words…were not meant the way they sounded."

"I hope they were." He took two steps toward her and continued. "You see, I have another confession to make. I am not an impulsive man."

"Yes, I am aware of that."

"A report of a most alarming nature reached me just this morning and although I am now sure it is not a falsehood, I instantly resolved to set off for Longbourn to make my sentiments known to you."

"And what report was that, sir?"

"That you are not to marry Mr. Hamilton."

She averted her eyes, looking back at the moon. "Yes."

His heart racing, he took another step forward. "And might I ask why?"

She did not look at him until after she replied. "He asked and I refused."

"But why did you refuse?"

Shrugging her shoulders, she began to ramble. "I realized we did not suit. He is a kind man but does not understand my temperament. I would not make him a good wife."

He took another step closer and raised his hand, tracing her jaw with the back of his fingers. "Elizabeth," he said, his voice husky with emotion, as she closed her eyes. "Why did you refuse?"

She began to lean into his touch then stopped, straightening her back and opening her eyes. "It does not signify now, sir. I think we must return to the house."

The moonlight captured a lone tear that had escaped and was streaming down her cheek. "Please tell me," he whispered, as he rubbed the wet trail with his thumb, cradling her face with his hand.

She wavered a minute longer before almost breathing out her answer, while raising her eyes to meet his. "Because it was not you." His heart beat so loudly, he wondered if she could hear it.

It took him only a moment before he ran his thumb across her lower lip. "Elizabeth, my love," he breathed, slowly leaning in and gently kissing her. She did not resist and his kiss deepened.

All at once, her hands came up to his chest and pushed him away. "Mr. Darcy," she said, wiping her lips with the back of her hand. "You are a married man! I am not Miss Bingley who would steal another's husband. If you will excuse me." She briskly walked toward the house.

"Elizabeth, wait. You must listen to me!" Her pace only increased as he ran to catch up with her. "You must hear me out."

"No, sir. I cannot. Your words would be like water to a parched soul. Do not ask this of me."

Her steps did not slow, but he quickly overtook her. He reached for her arm and stopped her. "Elizabeth, listen to me." She continued to struggle out of his hold. "I am not married to Anne."

She stilled.

"I am a free man."

"How? How is that possible?" she asked, spinning to face him.

"Anne found the letter from my mother which Mrs. Smith wrote. It exists! Lady Catherine had hidden it at Rosings and was forcing the marriage for the sole purpose of having control of Pemberley. I did not marry Anne."

"You did not marry Anne?"

"No." He smiled, tracing her arms with his hands and slowly clasping her fingers. "I cannot marry a woman who is in love with another."

"Colonel Fitzwilliam?"

"Yes." He raised her hands to his lips and kissed her fingers. "She loves Richard, and he her."

"So, you are not married?"

"I am not married."

"Truly?"

"Truly." He nodded.

"You are not married," she murmured. Breathing deeply, she released his hands, reached up and seized his jaw, pulling his mouth down to hers. Matching her passion, he wrapped his arms around her waist and clutched her to him, unwilling to end what he had wanted for so long.

Darcy finally broke the kiss. "Elizabeth." His breath as ragged as hers, he whispered, "I must speak to your father."

"For what purpose?" she asked, biting her lip as she traced her fingers up and down the front of his coat.

Siren! He exhaled sharply and drew from all of his lessons on self-control before answering. "Because I cannot trust myself to stop again if you kiss me like that." *Or if you continue to run your fingers up and down my chest!*

"So, are you to tell my father of our meeting in the garden or is there something else?" she asked archly.

"Minx! Why, I will ask him for your hand, of course."

"Before you have even asked me?"

He took her hand and brought it to his lips. "I presume that should be the first order of business." Kissing it gently, he said, "Elizabeth, I am not a man who makes speeches, but I promise I will show you for the rest of our lives how much you have blessed my world. Marry me?"

With her free hand, she reached up and traced his cheek. "Yes, William. I will."

EPILOGUE

I t was with great joy that another of Mrs. Bennet's daughters married a fine gentleman with an abundant estate—or dare we say estates, as Mr. Darcy's holdings were not limited to Pemberley. Elizabeth Bennet became Elizabeth Darcy in a beautiful burgundy dress originally worn for her husband's ill-fated engagement ball and her curls were secured with the gold combs from her newest sister. Their engagement had been short, and the wedding breakfast shorter, as the happy couple rode in his finest carriage to London the day of their wedding before traveling directly to Italy, as Elizabeth had confessed her desire to him those weeks ago in Ashby Park.

And what of those who traveled this path with our dear couple? Had their lives been filled with the same felicity?

Jane and Bingley resided happily in Netherfield for a full year after their wedding until an estate by Pemberley became available, and the two sisters were united within an easy distance of less than 20 miles of good road. Their children grew up together riding their horses between Pemberley and Vickland Hall.

Anne and Richard returned from their wedding tour more in love than when they departed. Nine months later they were blessed with twins, a boy and a girl, who also grew up to enjoy the haunts of Rosings and Pemberley as their parents had before them.

Mrs. Bennet, in all her joy of her daughter's fortunate alliances, was ill-prepared when her most unappealing daughter, Mary, caught the eye of the future earl of Bristlewhite at Georgiana's coming-out ball the following season. Apparently, the plain young man had a propensity for the church but was doomed to the earldom as the firstborn son. Mrs. Bennet collapsed from a case of nerves and never awoke, forcing Mary to wait three months for her own wedding.

Mary and her earl shunned London society, and six months into their marriage he renounced his succession to his younger brother, and Mary and her husband lived out their days in a parsonage in Hunsford, where he was the rector for one Anne Fitzwilliam of Rosings.

Mr. Bennet grieved the loss of his wife for several months before marrying a woman fifteen years his junior, who immediately produced a son, thus breaking the entail to Mr. Collins.

Mr. Collins, who the reader has still never met, became so distraught over the loss of Lady Catherine's patronage at Rosings and his future stewardship over Longbourn from the birth of the Bennet heir, boarded a ship for the New World, hoping to bring salvation to people seeking his wisdom and guidance. After a year, Charlotte returned alone, Mr. Collins having suffered the fate of attempting to convince a tribe of Iroquois that he was the mouthpiece of God. All that remained was a locket with his hair and a rosy-cheek child, who grew in friendship with young Christopher Bennet.

Kitty and Georgiana had a joint "coming-out" ball; both later made excellent matches, Georgiana to the nephew of the future Duke of Wellington, and Kitty to a humbled, young man who had a small estate named Ashby Park. Yes, *that* Ashby Park!

Lydia grew in wisdom, learning much from her father and new mother. She never married, choosing instead to help raise her brother, the words of Wickham having seared deeply into her soul.

What about our villains? Lady Catherine was sentenced to the dowager house upon her daughter's return from her wedding tour. Although Anne had extended an olive branch by naming her daughter Moira Catherine, Lady Catherine's pursuit to legally remove her granddaughter's first name was the final stroke which severed their relationship.

Wickham's life ended in debtor's prison, as the father of a girl he ruined purchased most of his debts from London proprietors, both reputable and not. Wickham was buried at Potter's Field outside of London.

Miss Bingley had little choice in her future after her counsel from Lady Matlock to take an extended holiday. Further, her public flirtation toward Bertram Knight the evening of Darcy and Anne's ball sealed her fate. Bertram was more than happy to inherit a fiery woman whom he kept at his parent's Irish estate, as he sold the property closest to Pemberley to raise funds to cover his father's mismanagement. Once Caroline was removed from the pandering of the *ton*, she began to enjoy the life of a woman both challenged and adored by her husband. She produced eight children in nine years and lived a long and healthy life, only returning to London society twice in her lifetime for the weddings of her brother's children.

And once again, one might wonder, would a courtship wrought with such consternation allow the Darcys of Pemberley to be truly happy? If anyone found it odd that the once fastidious master would choose a young woman with no dowry or connections who would rather wander the grounds of his ancestral estate than participate in a London season, it was never mentioned. Or maybe it was, yet the happy couple paid it no mind. They were much too busy enjoying the succession of snowstorms which afforded them the solitude they desired while ensconced in *their* hunting lodge each year upon the anniversary of their marriage, nibbling on lemon biscuits and devouring the words of Wordsworth. When the embers in the hearth had died, and no wood was to be had, they created a warmth of their own to rival a Guy Fawkes celebration. There was no longer a need for guarded feelings or unspoken avowals; their marriage was one founded on love, whose story and example would endure for generations to come.

And what, might you ask, became of the two objects which caused our dear couple such consternation in their lifetime? Both the watch and the letter from Darcy's mother were framed and displayed on the mantle. He had a new watch now to keep the time—an etching of Pemberley on the front and an amended inscription inside:

To my beloved, William, on our wedding. I am forever yours, Elizabeth

Made in the USA
Middletown, DE
11 May 2017

GARDEN CITIES
THEORY & PRACTICE OF
AGRARIAN URBANISM

ISBN 978-1-906384-05-0

GARDEN CITIES
THEORY & PRACTICE OF
AGRARIAN URBANISM

Agriculture is our wisest pursuit, because it will in the end contribute most to real wealth, good morals and happiness.

- Thomas Jefferson to George Washington, 1787

I am delighted to be able to introduce the fifth in a series of small volumes by the Senior Fellows of my Foundation For Building Community. Each volume provides an important entry into a global conversation about the creation of whole places that improve the lives of people, and yet are not apart from Nature. Senior Fellow, Andrés Duany, is a man whose insights and skills I have valued for many years. His book on Agrarian Urbanism is particularly close to my heart, as it brings together two of the subjects that I have returned to again and again throughout my life: the importance of genuinely sustainable agriculture and good food and the vital role of our built environment in improving people's health, well-being and happiness.

Throughout the years, I have tried in my own way to contribute to the growing global movement for organic sustainable farming, Slow Food and local food, through my Home Farm at Highgrove. At the same time, I have tried to demonstrate that places which embody the best and most timeless qualities of historic cities and towns can be built today and be profitable. This approach can be seen in Newquay, where the Duchy of Cornwall has developed not only a sustainable urban extension to the town, but also a local supply chain and a local food strategy. In the Southern Test Valley, my Foundation is working with The Ashfield Estate to meet both the demand for new housing and employment alongside implementing a local food and farming strategy.

With all these projects, the goal is not just to increase the supply of local food, but also to reconnect residents with a culture of food-growing as well as reconnecting the town with its rural hinterland. In the end, I think it is this reconnection that is most important – between people and their communities, between farmers and the people who consume their food, between town and city dwellers and the rhythms of Nature.

It is gratifying that an awareness of the importance of designing with food in mind now seems, at last, to be dawning, both in the United Kingdom and the United States. Putting food production back in the hands of communities can help to reinforce the importance of local, seasonal varieties of produce, as well as supporting smallholdings and family farms.

This useful and lovely book provides a practical framework for much that is dear to me and of vital importance for our children's and grandchildren's future.

It is time to cut out what we do not need so we can live more simply and happily. Good food, comfortable clothes, serviceable housing, and true culture—those are the things that matter.

-John Seymour

PREFACE – A FORMER SKEPTIC

I was among the most skeptical: Agriculture as a lifestyle choice? You cannot be serious!

I belong to the Seaside-Pienza Institute, an organization dedicated to local agriculture in Italy. Part of the research involves studying at great rural restaurants and we have enjoyed many wonderful meals lasting several hours. It became my habit to leave the table between courses and walk out into the piazza where I would sometimes come across the people who grew what we were eating. They were physically strong, of course, but they were also rough, with coarse skin and stiff limbs. Men and women both looked years beyond their age. Growing food was obviously very hard work. My somewhat disruptive theme at the Institute became that tourism was a blessing to such country people, because any farmer, given the choice, would gladly trade for another occupation. The lifestyle of the chambermaid and the waiter was much better than that of a farmer. I thought it was absurd of my colleagues at the Institute to think otherwise.

Cultivation on a small scale was only for enthusiasts such as the Prince of Wales. This skepticism persisted despite my knowledge of Prince Charles' long involvement with agriculture at the Home Farm at Highgrove. I had followed his rural initiatives virtually from their beginnings, but only because they were integral to a holistic conception that included the urbanism of Poundbury, which is my métier. Seeing a photograph of the Prince in his Wellingtons standing in the mud examining a filthy little lamb just confirmed my belief that agriculture was *hard*.

As further evidence of my skepticism I disclose that for years I had on my bookshelves no less than three unread copies of Michael Pollan's *The Omnivore's Dilemma*. They were gifts from friends who proposed a connection between what I do as a town planner and Pollan's description of growing food. But they remained on the shelf until one of these friends absolutely insisted that I get down to reading it.

Pollan's compelling book forced a first opening of the mind. Although I was interested, I could not yet see a connection with the practice of New Urbanism. I remembered those Italian farmers and insisted that tending food was just not credible as a real estate amenity.

Sometime thereafter, the Vancouver developer Sean Hodgins retained my urban planning firm to design an "agricultural community." When we began the process, in a barn on the farmland site, I was my usual pragmatic self and still skeptical. But gradually, under the tutelage of experts, including the master farmer Michael Ableman,[1] I became truly involved in developing an agricultural urbanism. That was in 2008. Since then, my colleagues at DPZ have continued refining what became the plan for Southlands, which has evolved into what I now understand to be "Agrarian Urbanism"—a concept that involves food not as a means of making a living, but as a basis for making a life.

Hence the change in terminology: rather than "agricultural," which is concerned with the technical aspects of growing food, the term "agrarian" emphasizes the *society* involved with all aspects of food.

Agrarian Urbanism is not for everyone—but it is one of the more beneficial methods to develop and dwell on the land. The thesis of this book is that if the food-growing machine which is the traditional village were reorganized to minimize

[1] Also consulting at the charrette were Doug Farr, Michael Von Hausen, Janine de la Salle, Mark Holland and Kent Mullinix.

those hardships that I observed in Italy, it could be viable again; and that because of its mitigating effect on climate change, a neo-agrarian way of life should be made available to as many as possible, for ethical reasons no less than practical ones.

As Michael Pollan argues, our food production must change; and as Leon Krier argues, so must our sprawling communities. Agrarian Urbanism addresses these two great concerns simultaneously. We cannot overcome the machine-enabled efficiency of agribusiness unless we enable more hands to tend food. This will happen only if we introduce the agrarian community as a model within modern development practice. To make a difference at the scale required to mitigate climate change will require engagement with conventional real estate operations—which is the way most places get built. And so this book is directed primarily to 21st-century developers, with apologies to those who will doubtless shudder at its periodic commercial excursions.

I was able to keep this treatise short by off-loading the techniques of tending crops, animal husbandry and soil care that are integral to agrarian urbanism. That expertise is mature, with many superb publications already available. One more is not necessary. There is, however, a dearth of literature about urban design dedicated to the production of food under modern social circumstances. Therefore, to the readily available technical knowledge on growing food, this book overlays techniques for the design, implementation, marketing, and management of settlements so dedicated.

This book is illustrated exclusively by projects from Duany Plater-Zyberk & Company, with research by Christina Miller. Most of the magnificent drawings were by Chris Ritter and Eusebio Azcue. Graphic editing was by Judith I. Bell. Editing was by Nancy Bruning and Shannon Tracy.

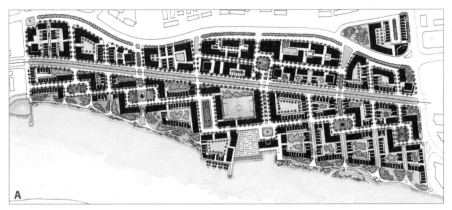

A

B

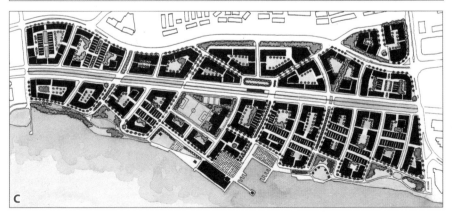

C

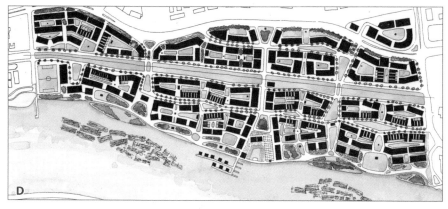

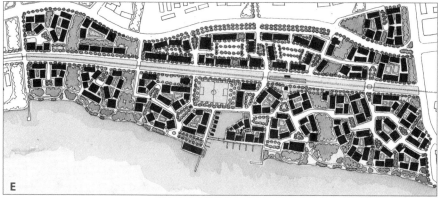

*Urban design is not tightly deterministic. There is always a range of possibilities to be studied, not just as a matter of aesthetics, but as an exploration of performance. Variables may affect phasing, transportation, the environment, social issues, and the suitability for growing food. Such alternatives were considered for this large brownfield site. Alternative **A** was determined primarily by social issues. **B** and **C** were responses to orientation. **D** had agricultural potential. **E** had an enhanced (Light Imprint) hydrology.*

• *East Fraserlands, Vancouver, Canada 2005*

Food shapes our lives, for better or worse. The way we grow, store, and eat our food creates cultural, ecological, and economic patterns that form how we as individuals and societies live and relate. The transformative power of food is absolute.

- Janine De la Salle and Mark Holland

CHAPTER 1 – FOUR RELATED MODELS

At the Congress for the New Urbanism, one of the organization's missions has been to establish a vocabulary shared across the many disciplines that participate in creating the human habitat. Without a lexicon,[1] it would be impossible to work efficiently. Thus, we begin by making distinctions.

1. AGRICULTURAL RETENTION refers to an array of techniques deployed to save existing farmland. This is of first importance. It is also exceedingly difficult, as Agricultural Retention operates at the regional and the macroeconomic scale, where planners have historically had little effect. In the United States too few farmland trusts are currently in existence, although there are stellar ones such as those in Louisville, Kentucky, and Lancaster County, Pennsylvania. In Great Britain the "greenbelts" are very much in evidence, having successfully been used to retain farmland for more than a century. European Union policy may yet undermine this achievement, just as the American Free Trade Agreements have weakened the economic argument for Agricultural Retention.

2. URBAN AGRICULTURE refers to cultivation within existing cities and suburbs, sometimes using space that is underutilized as a consequence of depopulation. Urban Agriculture is usually a secondary activity for people who are concerned primarily with other economic pursuits. The format includes community gardens and even small farms overlaid onto vacant blocks. Where there is no surplus land, gardens may be installed in private yards or on rooftops. (New York City is calculated to have 14,000 acres of unused rooftops!) The food produced is supported by distribution and processing systems such as farmers' markets, community kitchens, food cooperatives and

[1] Lexicon of the New Urbanism by Andrés Duany

contracted restaurants. While Urban Agriculture initiatives have recently become associated with distressed communities like New Orleans and Detroit, even the most economically successful cities foster allotment gardens as a public good irrespective of land value, as in Boston and San Francisco.

3. AGRICULTURAL URBANISM refers to settlements equipped with a working farm. The agriculture is economically associated with the communities' residents and businesses, but it is not physically or socially integrated. Anyone may visit, volunteer, and learn from the farm, but few of the residents participate in the productive activities. There are several modern developments that have implemented this model: the ancestor is Village Homes in Davis, then came Prairie Crossing outside of Chicago, and, more recently, Serenbe near Atlanta, New Town St. Charles near St. Louis, and Hampstead near Montgomery. Their management protocol is a version of Community Supported Agriculture (C.S.A.).

The theoretical basis for Agricultural Urbanism was proposed a century ago by Ebenezer Howard in the stolid *Garden Cities of To-Morrow*. Letchworth, in Hertfordshire, is an applied example of Howard's theory, complete with a surrounding greenbelt sized to feed the community. Some food in Letchworth may well derive from the surrounding farms, but the town's urban pattern is indistinguishable from that of a well-designed suburb attached to a transit-oriented town center. It does not support engagement in agriculture beyond conventional purchases at the markets. This precludes what is here defined as Agrarian Urbanism.

4. AGRARIAN URBANISM refers to settlements where the society is involved with food in all its aspects: organizing, growing, processing, distributing, cooking and eating it. A distinction of Agricultural Urbanism is that the physical pattern of the settlement supports the workings of an intentional agrarian society. Rather than the simpleminded prophylaxis of urban boundaries that perversely assure an economically and socially sterile hinterland, Agrarian Urbanism is a complex pattern that trans-

forms lawn-mowing, food-importing suburbanites into settlers whose hands, minds, surplus time and discretionary entertainment budgets are available for food production and its local consumption.

The ethos closest to that of Agrarian Urbanism was conceptualized in the 1920s and 1930s by Leberecht Migge, a personality even less humorous than Ebenezer Howard, if that is humanly possible.[2] Partly because Migge and Howard are no longer around to help, Agrarian Urbanists may now be capable of persuading a significant proportion of the population to productively inhabit the countryside. Instead of agribusiness, with its centralized machine operations, many willing hands would become available to work in all kinds of productive formats, from the tractor farm to the window box. To be sure, the many downsides of rural life must be mitigated by appropriate planning and organization.

Agrarian Urbanism ·assimilates successful precedents, but it is not a restoration of tradition for its own sake. It is a typically pragmatic New Urbanist construct—a combination of that which works best in the long run. It proposes an evolution of the village—one that is agriculturally productive even if largely inhabited by part-timers overqualified or underqualified (depending on point of view) to farm. It is a village bred to certain practices of modern development, including professionalized management and marketing, which cannot be counted among its many failures. In fact there is much to be learned from aspects of all kinds of places, the Garden City and the German social garden of course, but also the contemporary golf-course community, the 1960s commune, the Mormon Stake, and certainly the kibbutz. While all these models have failed to some extent, the experience they provide remains to be studied in a more complete and rigorous treatise.[3] To make a difference in the campaign against climate change, Agrarian Urbanism must succeed in being profitable, popular and reproducible—with no downsides if possible.

[2] *When Modern Was Green* by David Haney
[3] *Agrarian Urbanism* by Duany, Khoury and Miller, in preparation

9

The first set of illustrations, on pages 11 to 29, show projects that explore the four models just described. They are the work of Duany Plater-Zyberk & Co. from 1994-2010. Note: some of the images show only a small portion of the project, and they do not necessarily represent the final plan. For more complete presentation of this work see the archive at dpz.com.

The second set of illustrations, on pages 41 to 43, explains the Transect and its relationship to food production.

The third set of illustrations, on pages 48 to 59, is from one project. It takes images from an earlier and a later version of the design for Southlands.

The illustration on page 75 is a theoretical diagram in support of a general theory.

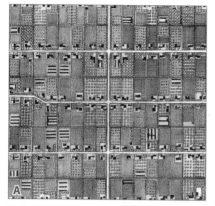

Agricultural Retention operates at the scale of the region. The ideal is to keep farmland in use as such, but this is not always possible. The catalyst for this county-wide study was the Central American Free Trade Agreement, which undermined the commercial viability of produce, while urban growth had simultaneously raised the value of the land for development. This state-initiated study analyzed the economic implications of several scenarios.

• *Agricultural Retention Plan, Dade Co. Fla. 1997*

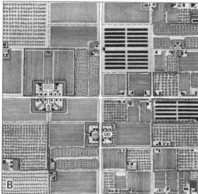

A. In the existing condition, land can legally be subdivided into five-acre parcels. These are large enough for some farming.

B. Clustering of development into hamlets allows a greater diversity of agriculture.

C. Villages deliver the expected development value while retaining the majority of the land as larger farms. This requires the transfer of development rights organized by a land trust.

D. All three scenarios perform better with the provision of cooperative facilities (Market Squares) providing rental equipment, management, slaughtering, processing and distribution.

AGRICULTURAL RETENTION

Land trusts are dedicated to retaining open space and agricultural land. Their strategy involves the purchase or donation of the development rights of a parcel to a trust that will keep it as is. This is a difficult mission to sustain, as the market pressure for development is simply decanted to the next farm, which then must be purchased.

There are two possible strategies. The first is based on the realization that the farmers generally do not

expect the windfall associated with full development of their farms. In fact, they usually expect to subdivide lots only along their frontage roads, connecting to the utilities that run alongside. A farm-wide subdivision requires costly infrastructure—a large debt that cannot be serviced by what is typically a slow rural real estate market. Thus only the frontage of the farms need be purchased by the land trust, with the rest remaining in agriculture as

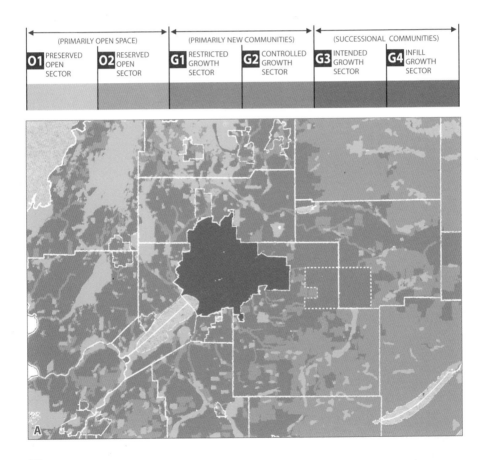

a condition. This would occur only within the O2 and G1 Sectors as mapped below.

The second strategy is to have the trust purchase land at rural crossroads, planning proper villages and offering the lots at less than market value—to absorb the market need. This would undermine the haphazard farm subdivisions or catalyze the frontage sales to the land trust at lower value.

• *Regional Plan for* Onondaga *Co. N.Y. 1999*

A. *The county, mapped into sectors on the basis of G.I.S. information.*

B. *Rural crossroads to be laid out as villages by the land trusts.*

C. *A village plan, dense within the first quarter-mile and sparse along the road frontages beyond. This incorporates both strategies described above.*

D. *A crossroads village in the early stages of development.*

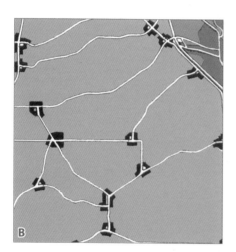

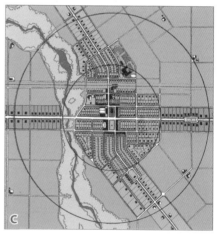

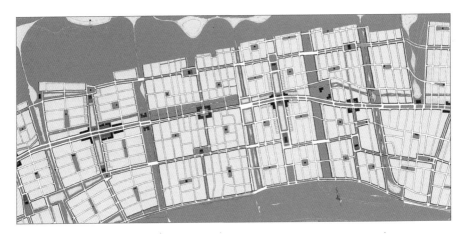

Urban Agriculture is often applied to cities that have lost population and choose to reduce their footprints. The residual land must be allocated to some use if it is not to revert to wilderness. The most common strategy has been to assign the land to allotment gardens. St. Bernard Parish (above) was the area most devastated by Hurricane Katrina. Its recovery plan dealt with the projected loss of population, first by a categorical withdrawal from the northern lowlands, assigning these to farmsteads. To the south, the remaining houses would be co-alesced, conjoined, or condensed into Urban Villages clustered around new squares. The pair of images below shows the existing and intended conditions.

• Plan for St. Bernard Parish, La. 2006

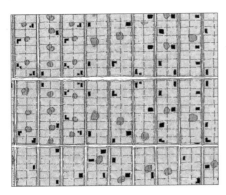

A. Surviving housing

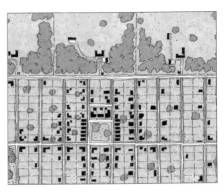

B. Housing coalesced

The following are three techniques by which partially abandoned urban blocks may be modified to Urban Agriculture:

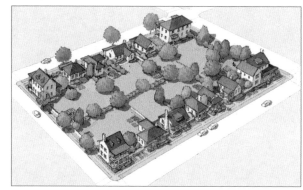

A. COALESCING *the buildings brought from elsewhere. The resulting open land elsewhere is also coalesced into large homestead farms.*

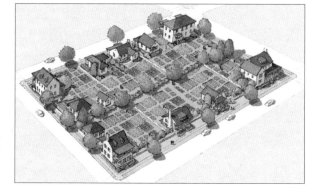

B. CONJOINING *the remaining buildings and adjacent open lots for larger and more useful private gardens.*

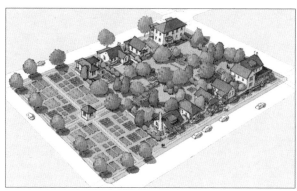

C. CONDENSING *the remaining buildings locally to enable community gardens.*

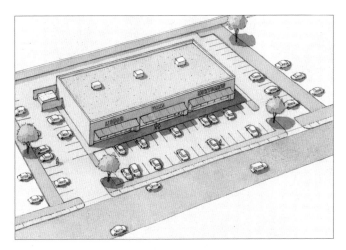

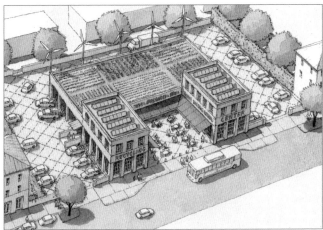

Not all Urban Agriculture emerges from the urban fabric of decaying cities. There are other urbanisms in crisis. In fact, urbanism in the 21st century will primarily involve the succession of dying suburban sprawl. Conventional strip centers, for example, have the potential to become market squares—the equivalent of those shown for Agricultural Retention (p. 11) and for Agrarian Urbanism (p. 57). These perform the support functions of organization, processing, leasing equipment, distribution, consumption and recycling that add commercial and social value to urban agriculture.

• *Sprawl Repair Manual, Galina Tachieva*

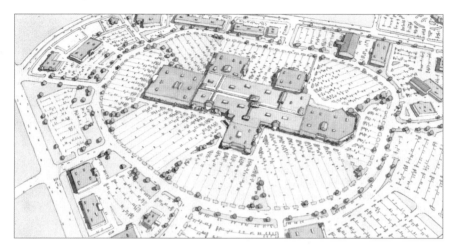

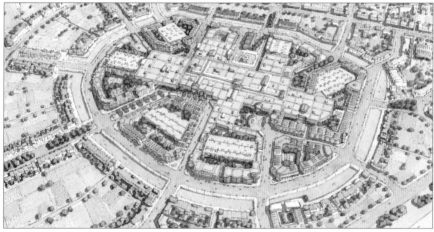

Each place-type of suburban sprawl has potential for re-urbanization, some by retrofit with agricultural patterns. The most promising candidates are the shopping malls, as they are well-located for public transportation and their parking lots represent immediately available buildable land. The carcass of the mall itself is retained for commerce, perhaps with a vegetative roof. The parking lots within the ring road are urbanized to rebalance the residential deficiency. Outside of the ring road, the outparcels are scraped and reverted to farming. A comprehensive hydrological system appears as a canal/swale along the ring road. This offers the possibility of creating a defensible community—as some of the resiliency scenarios for the 21st century must envision periods of social instability.

• *Sprawl Repair Manual, Galina Tachieva*

17

Agricultural Urbanism involves a large farm that is economically associated with a settlement, but independent of work by the residents, who
commit only to purchasing the produce on a model similar to Community
Supported Agriculture. The private gardens may be ornamental or cultivated for private consumption. The island community of Schooner Bay
has a farm for crops and livestock, preserved woodland for foraging, and
a harbor for fishing boats. These operations create jobs for the population
of a small island. This is a type of community that may appeal to the
survivalist market segment (p. 67).

• Schooner Bay, Bahamas 2006

Ladyfield is designed to be one of the coming British Ecovillages. The urbanized areas are split by the existing waterflows, which are taken seamlessly to the agricultural land downhill and the excess thence to the riparian wetlands and the river beyond.

• *Dumfries, Scotland 2010*

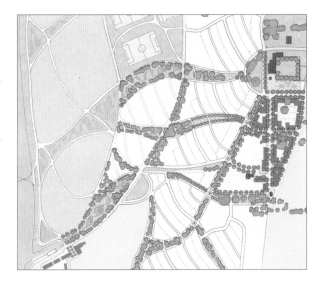

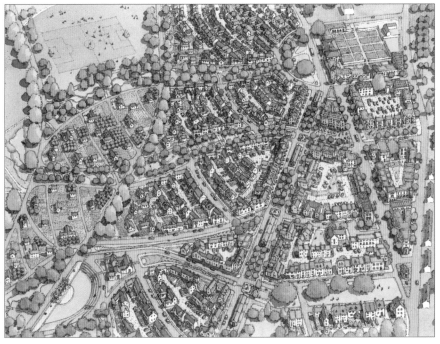

AGRARIAN URBANISM

Woodmont Commons may be considered a hybrid of Agricultural Retention and Agrarian Urbanism. It is a model applicable only where crops are easily compatible with housing. In this case an apple orchard had been undermined by imports. The grids of trees determine the precise parcel layout, such that the least number would need to be removed as houses were inserted.

The residents are required to keep at least those that form a hedgerow at the edges of the lots. The apple grower is thus able to retire while the crop continues with the part-time tending of the new residents. The existing processing facility is retained as part of a Market Square (beyond the bottom edge of this drawing).

• *Woodmont Commons, Londonderry, N.H. 2010.*

Farmsteads traditionally provide a process of subdivision that can be applied to modern real estate development. Sky also sells farmsteads of four acres instead of individual lots. Each is granted a subsidiary development potential of eight dwellings. Drainage is provided in the center by a pond (that may be stocked). The master developer provides only the pond, a well, and electrical power. Sewage is to be composted on site. The homesteaders are then allowed to conceive, design, and sell compounds for creating their own society. The original developer has a minimal investment—downstreaming even the responsibility of recruiting the buyers for the progressively subdivided farmsteads. With the cash flow of the homestead sales, the village center can be developed, to perform the usual social and commercial functions of the Market Square. The "Sky Method" was developed by Steve Mouzon.

A. The farmstead with the inaugural dwelling.

B. Seven additional dwellings of diverse types.

C. The village center and the farmsteads.

• Sky, Calhoun County, Fla. 2006

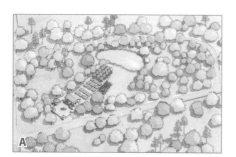

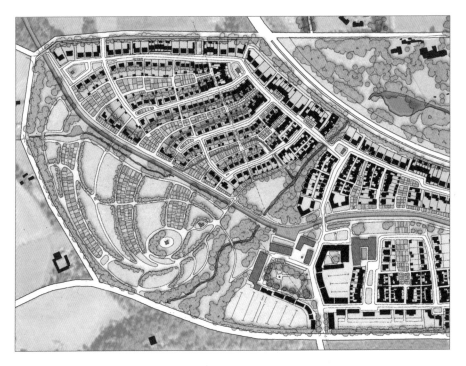

The Calyx is the unique instance of the new National Garden for Scotland. Rather than being dedicated to exotic species as would have been the traditional botanical garden, the mission of the Calyx is the technical development and teaching of ecologically and socially sound garden practice. The plan is a hybrid, with the Agricultural Urbanism of the Calyx as well as a community of Agrarian Urbanism. The technology developed at the Calyx (at the lower-left quadrant of the drawing) is to be decanted to the community across the canal. The town center (in red) is shared by both the community and the visitors. Instruction would include activities in the agrarian community.

• *The Calyx, Edinburgh, Scotland 2010*

In 2008 Hertfordshire County, northeast of London, was assigned a growth target of 83,000 dwelling units by the year 2021. Four potential allocation strategies were studied: 1. Following existing trends (doing nothing); 2. Using brownfield sites only; 3. Extending towns on their edges (bolt-ons); and 4. Placing the entire allocation in a new town. These were independently assessed for their social, economic, environmental, and political implications. Only the latter two scenarios proved to have sufficient capacity for all the dwellings. Of these, the most evident, but also the most unpopular, was the town extension. Those living at the urban edge would not condone having their rural views blocked. A fifth scenario was then generated: the creation of independent villages out just far enough to not block views. These greenfield settlements could be environmentally justified only if they were dedicated to the original purpose of a village: to grow food. The plan of this model is not quite that of a traditional English village. It is structured on a clear Transect. Each of the arms that extend into the countryside is virtually identical to the diagrams on pages 42 and 43.

• Hertfordshire Guide to Growth 2009

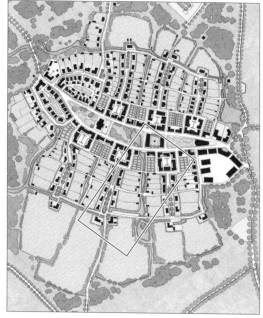

Varying degrees of association between the residents of a community and its agricultural operations can result in hybrids that straddle Agricultural and Agrarian Urbanism. Cloudrock, on a mesa in Utah, and Sandy Point, on a bay in North Carolina, are examples. Both have a clearly delineated urban sector with conventional yards, and an outlying sector where the Agrarian

• Sandy Point, Albemarle Sound, N.C. 2003

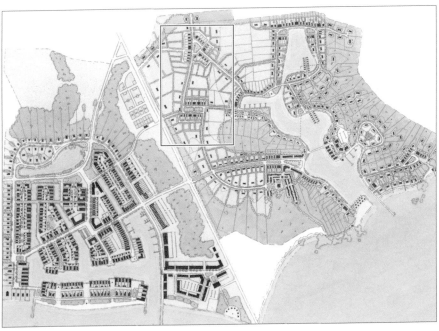

Urbanists undertake to grow food for the community as a whole. At Sandy Point, there are harbors for fishing boats to provide a source of protein. Cloudrock has a golf course, which is an unfortunate drag on the agricultural mission in terms of labor and water resources.

• *Cloudrock, Moab, Utah 2005*

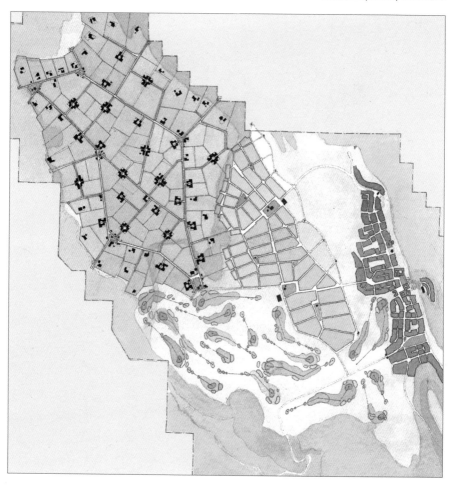

AGRARIAN URBANISM

Agrarian Urbanism may develop complex layouts, as residents may desire supplementary agricultural land for certain seasons, and at other times choose to subcontract the work of their land to neighbors. The design for Santa Gloria studied five patterns (upper half of the pages) of extendable gardens to provide flexibility to satisfy this uncertainty in the desires and capabilities of the residents. Elsewhere, in **A**, an existing watering hole is turned into a pond for pole fishing. The two Transect Zones catalyze patio-house urbanism in **B** and rural crossroad hamlets in **C**.

• *Santa Gloria, San Miguel, Mexico 2010*

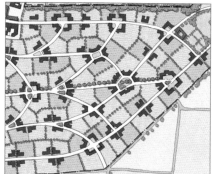

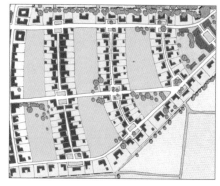

27

Agriculture in Goodbee is enabled by a complex checkerboard of squares dedicated to community gardens. The overlapping urban blocks have turned lots at their ends—a layout which allows every dwelling to enfront a square while maintaining a density three times that of a simple checkerboard. The land is very flat so the inwardly sloping squares provide water retention at their bottom. This can then be used for irrigation or released by pipes into the adjacent bayou.

• *Goodbee Square, St. Tammany Parish, La. 2008*

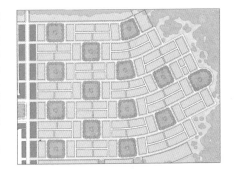

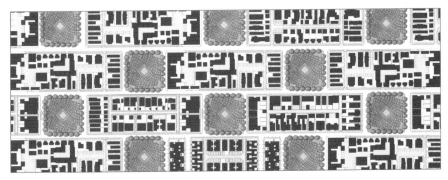

Even within Agrarian Urbanism, perhaps not all residents participate in growing food. For those who may choose to pay their share instead, there are patterns that integrate agricultural activities within the urban area. One involves a rural weave of farming through an urban network. With this hybrid, the urban apartments share the presence of agriculture, while only the willing "rural" population works on growing it. Everyone enjoys the benefits of consuming the food, having "looked over" the crops.

• Lakeside, Flower Mound, Tex. 1994

Neither agrarians nor New Urbanists are opposed to progress, but each insists that progress occurs in conversation with the past. Not surprisingly, both groups are routinely accused of nostalgia. This, however, is not a sensible objection, for why should it count against the reasonableness of a practice that it has a long history?

-Benjamin Northrup and Benjamin Lipscomb

CHAPTER 2 – TRUNK: NEW URBANISM

Agrarian Urbanism works best when grafted onto the mature trunk of the New Urbanism, and so this set of principles requires a brief recapitulation. Fortunately, The Prince's Foundation's *urban village* is the exact equivalent to the New Urbanist *neighborhood*. They are both conceived as alternatives to suburban sprawl, sharing the following fundamental attributes.

ATTRIBUTES:

• The neighborhood is the standard urban increment which, when clustered with others, becomes a town and, when standing free in the landscape, becomes a village. The specific density varies according to the natural and social circumstances.

• The neighborhood is limited in size, so that a majority of the population is within a five-minute walk of its center. The basic needs of daily life are available within this pedestrian shed, whose center should supply a transit stop, work places, shops and community facilities.

• There is a network of thoroughfares providing alternate routes to most destinations. This multiplicity allows them to be small, with slower traffic and the provision of parking, trees, sidewalks, and buildings close to their edges. They are equitable for vehicles, bicycles and pedestrians.

• The thoroughfares are spatially defined by buildings that front the sidewalk in a disciplined manner, uninterrupted by the gaps of parking lots.

- The buildings are diverse in function, but nevertheless harmonious because they are compatible in size and in their disposition on the lot. They are houses, terraces, flats, shops, offices, and warehouses.

- Open space is deliberately provided in the specific form of squares, greens, parks and, parkways—not as residual space left over after planning.

- Civic buildings (schools, meeting halls, theaters, churches, clubs, museums, etc.) and other important structures are placed on squares or at the termination of axial vistas.

- Ancillary buildings are available in backyards. These foster home businesses and provide affordable housing interspersed with regular housing.

ADVANTAGES:

- By bringing most ordinary daily activities within walking distance, those who do not drive (usually the young, the old, the poor, and the principled) gain independence. This satisfies the basic right to get around one's neighborhood and city even without being forced to own an automobile.

- The young, below the legal driving age, are no longer dependent on adults for their social needs. Nor must they be bused to schools or isolated at home.

- Seniors may continue to live independently, rather than being consigned to specialized retirement communities.

- By providing appropriate building concentrations at easy walking distance, public transit becomes a viable alternative to the automobile.

- By reducing the number and length of necessary automobile trips, traffic congestion is minimized, the public expense of infrastructure is limited, and air pollution is reduced.

- The possibility of not owning an automobile provides a virtual subsidy that can be applied to housing costs. There is no more organic way to increase affordability.

- By interspersing a range of housing types and work places, local employment is facilitated and daylong urban vitality is assured.

- By providing ancillary housing, any parcel can provide an income supplement or be a cross-generational compound.

- By providing suitable civic buildings and spaces, self-governance by the community is encouraged. Placed at important locations, such buildings serve as landmarks for orientation.

Agrarianism is a way of thought based on land ... Agrarianism, furthermore, is a culture at the same time that it is an economy. Industrialism is an economy before it is a culture.

-Wendell Berry

CHAPTER 3 – GRAFT: AGRARIAN URBANISM

If Neighborhoods and Urban Villages have environmental, economic, and social advantages, it follows that they should become the basis of Agrarian Urbanism. There are, however, flaws that have become apparent with the stresses confronting the 21st century. These can be addressed through Agrarian Urbanism.

A major problem is the assumption that social interaction would be based around shopping as leisure occupation. This is so pervasive that it has never been seriously questioned.[1] Planners continued to rely on retail as a magnet, even if located in the less relentlessly commercial environments of a Main Street and Town Square. But, as the primacy of shopping necessarily wanes, Agrarian activity can provide a surrogate urban condenser. Social interaction could be comprehensively associated to food—as a culture rather than the mere purchase of it among many other goods.

Developments structured on useful and productive activity that support the common health and wealth is a compelling vision (and with apologies to the Marxists among us), not least for the marketing of real estate.

THESE ARE THE BASICS:

• Agrarian sociability is based on the organizing, growing, processing, exchanging, cooking, and eating of food—much of it taking place around a Market Square (p. 57). In a post-consumer age, these squares would provide the indispensable "third places"[2] for social interaction that supplement those of home and

---

[1] *The Social Logic of Space* by Bill Hillier and Julienne Hanson
[2] *The Great Good Place*, by Ray Oldenburg

workplace. Third places encourage tarrying in public without the constant pressure to purchase things. The multifunctional agrarian Market Square provides an array of third places perhaps more compelling than the conventional pubs, cafes and clubs that, to be sure, should continue to exist in parallel.

- Certain types of street frontages support social activity. One of the premises of the New Urbanism—based on Jane Jacobs' observation—is that strangers socialize informally when hanging out on stoops and porches, their leisurely presence signaling they are "available to say hello." But the provision of such frontages in practice has proven to be less effective than originally envisioned. As it happens, many people are no longer comfortable publicly displaying themselves in domestic leisure. However, they don't seem to mind being seen in the act or the pretense of working—such as standing in the front garden, leaning on a hoe contemplating vegetables. In such a posture they are likely to become available for engagement with a passerby. To this should be added the casual interaction provided by the vicissitudes of the work itself. A tomato plant may be a vector of conversation no less effective than a baby in a pram or a cute dog on a leash.[3]

- Farming's purposeful obligations lead to extended social networks. Carpooling of schoolchildren is one of the few such catalysts in conventional suburbia. Preserving and preparing produce has a similar effect. All ages can work together to accomplish many of the tasks required to make preserves, flash-freeze vegetables, fill boxes for Community Supported Agriculture, or administer a farmer's market. Celebrating a harvest at the barn on a Saturday night is also possible. All that is required to establish a festival is a meaningful theme with a recurring date and location.[4] Agriculture, with its natural cycles and hard-won successes, provides justification for festivities.

- In conventional suburbia walking and bicycling are considered only as occasional recreation along paths and trails. New

[3] *Edible Estates*, by Fritz Haeg
[4] *The Princeton Journal: Ritual*, by Alan Plattus

Urbanism is more operational, as it is conceives walking and bicy-cling as mandatory and utilitarian—the way to reach daily neces-sities like shops, schools, jobs, and transit. Agrarian activity is a fur-ther extension of this, catalyzed by the commitment to livestock, vegetables, fruits, and herbs. Planting, tending, and harvesting impose a routine that agrarians are compelled to perform (albeit with hired help, as necessary). There is even the youngster's mis-sion of foraging the woodland, fishing, or gathering eggs for a specific meal. For adults and children, this is a disciplined activity with the resulting fitness.

• Hand-tended crops lead to a less toxic environment because the numerous available hands take the place of many carbon-based industrial operations and because weeding replaces weed killers. And any food produced and consumed locally replaces that which would have been shipped, flown and trucked into the community. There are also the direct health benefits of eating the fresh, wholesome foods that result.

• The produce, being hand-tended locally, can be of a kind more delicate and valuable than the tough, travel-resistant foodstuff. Michael Ableman has demonstrated that such specialization can be economically viable, covering the cost of the supporting labor, management and machinery. And remember: the financial model of Agrarian Urbanism also includes the subsidy that is transferred from the debit column of "landscape maintenance."

Habitability is human ecology. Like every ecology it demands its balances ... planning by whatever description must simultaneously embrace urban, rural and wilderness settings.

-Benton MacKaye

CHAPTER 4 – FOOD ALONG THE TRANSECT

A commercial transaction, to be ethical, must be advantageous to both parties—in plain English, "a fair trade." In conventional suburban development, open land is "lost" to a housing subdivision or a shopping center that induces traffic and carbon emissions. This is a downward trade for society, and most opposition to development arises from the intuition that this might be so. With the New Urbanist model, land is typically conserved as a result of compact development, and the proposed community is mixed-use, walkable, transit-oriented, and socially diverse. An open field may have been lost to society, but a village will have been gained in its stead. Although a marked improvement over conventional development, this is not completely fair, either. After all, a village could always be *more* compact and the environmental impacts even less.

To help overcome this discrepancy, Southlands, the Canadian project mentioned in the preface, proposed that one-third of the existing farmland be urbanized, but that the economic value of the food production be tripled. This is clearly a fair trade. It came to be called the Southlands Compact (p. 52). The productivity is achieved by requiring that "all hands" participate in the growing of food. The concept of the rural-to-urban transect (referred to simply as the Transect) enables that participation.

In the natural sciences, a transect is a cut through a geography showing the sequence of habitats. Passing through an area, a transect records the symbiosis of certain kinds of flora and fauna, soils and microclimates. Biologists and ecologists have been using transects to study nature for about 200 years.

With the rural-to-urban transect, New Urbanists have extended the concept into human habitats. As with natural habitats, urban patterns can be differentiated by their character and components on a spectrum from rural to urban. In addition to using the Transect as an analytical tool, it is a method to organize the built environment that can be administered like zoning (p. 41). The Transect is easily applicable to the requisites of Agrarian Urbanism, establishing a framework to allocate the elements of food production, whether physical or cultural.

The Transect of food production allows the exercise of preference in lifestyle in terms of where to live, while establishing a "fair trade" through expectations of food production—and in its most complete ecological manifestation, also energy production, recycling, and composting (p. 42-43). The Agrarian Transect corresponds to the level of mitigation demanded by the amount of land consumed and the consequent carbon-spewing traffic that is generated (p. 75).

Those who wish to live on a large lot will by agreement either farm it or cause it to be farmed. For those who wish to work less or who desire less land, and are willing to live in a rowhouse, the kitchen garden or the roof garden will suffice. Those who live in low-rise apartments could be associated with a community garden and those in high-rises might have a balcony garden or a window box. The more rural the Transect Zone, the more self-sufficient the dwelling on its larger lot can and should become. Even a simple window box can contribute to the fair trade.

T1 NATURAL ZONE
Consists of lands approximating or reverting to a wilderness condition, especially where unsuitable for settlement due to topography, hydrology or vegetation.

T2 RURAL ZONE
Consists of sparsely settled lands in open or cultivated conditions. These include woodland, farmland, grassland, and irrigable desert. Typical buildings are farmhouses, agricultural buildings, cabins, and villas. Roads and trails are common.

T3 SUB-URBAN ZONE
Consists of low-density residential areas and some retail at corners. Home occupations and outbuildings are present throughout. Planting is naturalistic and building setbacks are relatively deep. Blocks may be large and the road pattern irregular to accommodate natural conditions.

T4 GENERAL URBAN ZONE
Consists of mixed-use, but primarily residential, areas. It includes a wide range of building types: shops, houses, rowhouses and small apartment buildings. Setbacks and landscaping are variable. Streets with raised curbs and sidewalks define medium-sized blocks.

T5 URBAN CENTER ZONE
Consists of higher-density, mixed-use buildings with shops, offices, rowhouses and apartments. Streets have raised curbs, wide sidewalks, steady tree planting, and buildings with short setbacks.

T6 URBAN CORE ZONE
Consists of the greatest density and building height, most being mixed-use. It is the setting for civic buildings of regional importance. Blocks may be large to accommodate parking within. Streets have steady tree planting and buildings set close to the wide sidewalks. Only large towns and cities have Urban Core Zones.

41

FOOD ALONG THE TRANSECT

Transect theory identifies and locates aspects of human habitation and natural processes along a rural-to-urban continuum. Each Transect Zone, *once conceptualized, becomes a technical zoning category that may be applied to a complex geographic situation as would a patch in nature.*

| T1 | NATURAL ZONE | T2 | RURAL ZONE | T3 | SUB-URBAN ZONE | T4 | GENERAL URBAN ZONE | T5 | URBAN CENTER ZONE | T6 | URBAN CORE ZONE |

PUBLIC

◄ ROADS & LANES	STREETS & ALLEYS ►
◄ NARROW PATHS	WIDE SIDEWALKS ►
◄ HIGH L.O.S. STANDARDS	LOW L.O.S. STANDARDS ►
◄ OPPORTUNISTIC PARKING	DEDICATED PARKING ►
◄ LARGER CURB RADII	SMALLER CURB RADII ►
◄ OPEN SWALES	RAISED CURBS ►
◄ NIGHT SKY	WHITE NIGHT ►
◄ MIXED TREE CLUSTERS	ALIGNED STREET TREES ►
◄ MORE SILENCE REQUIRED	MORE NOISE ALLOWED ►

CIVIC

| ◄ LOCAL GATHERING PLACES | REGIONAL INSTITUTIONS ► |
| ◄ PARKS & GREENS | PLAZAS & SQUARES ► |

PRIVATE

◄ LESS DENSITY	MORE DENSITY ►
◄ LARGER BLOCKS	SMALLER BLOCKS ►
◄ PRIMARILY RESIDENTIAL	PRIMARILY MIXED-USE ►
◄ SMALLER BUILDINGS	LARGER BUILDINGS ►
◄ MORE PERVIOUS	MORE IMPERVIOUS ►
◄ DETACHED BUILDINGS	ATTACHED BUILDINGS ►
◄ ROTATED FRONTAGES	ALIGNED FRONTAGES ►
◄ YARDS & PORCHES	STOOPS & SHOPFRONTS ►
◄ DEEP SETBACKS	SHALLOW SETBACKS ►
◄ ARTICULATED MASSING	SIMPLE MASSING ►
◄ WOODEN BUILDINGS	MASONRY BUILDINGS ►
◄ GENERALLY PITCHED ROOFS	GENERALLY FLAT ROOFS ►
◄ SMALL YARD SIGNS	BUILDING-MOUNTED SIGNAGE ►
◄ LIVESTOCK	PETS ►
◄ FARMS	GARDENS ►

This chart details the last two elements from page 42, parametrically correlated to Transect Zones. The types of agricultural operations are listed in the upper part, with the types of produce shown below (see also Chapter 8). The primary source for information on the Transect is transect.org.

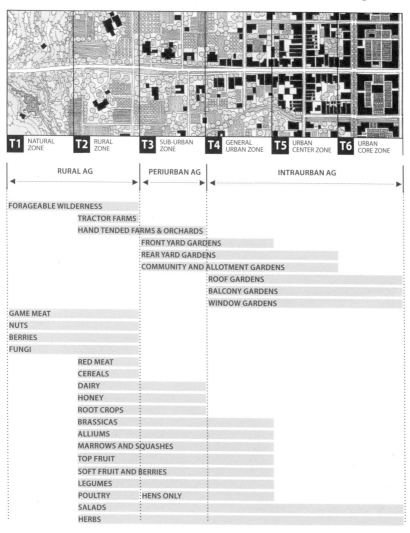

| T1 | NATURAL ZONE | T2 | RURAL ZONE | T3 | SUB-URBAN ZONE | T4 | GENERAL URBAN ZONE | T5 | URBAN CENTER ZONE | T6 | URBAN CORE ZONE |

RURAL AG | PERIURBAN AG | INTRAURBAN AG

FORAGEABLE WILDERNESS
TRACTOR FARMS
HAND TENDED FARMS & ORCHARDS
FRONT YARD GARDENS
REAR YARD GARDENS
COMMUNITY AND ALLOTMENT GARDENS
ROOF GARDENS
BALCONY GARDENS
WINDOW GARDENS
GAME MEAT
NUTS
BERRIES
FUNGI
RED MEAT
CEREALS
DAIRY
HONEY
ROOT CROPS
BRASSICAS
ALLIUMS
MARROWS AND SQUASHES
TOP FRUIT
SOFT FRUIT AND BERRIES
LEGUMES
POULTRY   HENS ONLY
SALADS
HERBS

43

The revolution comes in breaking these long chains in the food system and in the minds of buyers and in building new, tight webs around the centers of communities.

-Will Allen

CHAPTER 5 – A STANDARD DEVELOPMENT

While the village of yore was essentially an apparatus to grow, process and distribute food, circumstances are now different. Then people had little choice but to put shoulder to plow. There are reasons why in the West agrarian life has all but disappeared, and often with a sense of good riddance. The settlements of Agrarian Urbanism may learn from those villages of history, but they cannot be identical.

This new kind of settlement to compete with other attractive options, must assimilate the advantages of an agrarian way of life while mitigating the many disadvantages. It must respond to the expectations of lifestyles in the 21st century. But, because of its benefits, Agrarian Urbanism could easily be idealized to the point that it remains yet another unbuilt utopia. And the opposite: there are always the challenges of promoting innovation in development, a business governed by the rear-view mirror. Nevertheless, Agrarian Urbanism should become a normative "real estate product" (to introduce a coarse professional term).

The only way to induce change at the scale commensurate with the global environmental crises is to engage the same market-oriented system that so efficiently delivered conventional suburban development during the recently concluded century. Within this system, Agrarian Urbanism must join the "19 standard real estate products" that Christopher Leinberger has identified.[1] Agrarian Urbanism can be positioned as the 20th.

[1] *Places* Vol. 17, Issue 2, Christopher Leinberger.

Standardization exists in real estate because financial institutions impose it for their own convenience in packaging loans as abstract "financial instruments." A standard "real estate product" can be inserted without the titanic effort that would be required to dismantle the entire system. To do so, Agrarian Urbanism must follow certain protocols that connect the implied utopia to the efficient techniques of modern development, and the realities of global capital. For this new product to emerge, an unprecedented hybrid is required.

But it is not as difficult as it might have been a decade ago. Agrarian Urbanism would not be seriously contemplated today if the Internet had not already eliminated four of the perennial disadvantages of village life, providing virtual surrogates for: 1. limited social networks, 2. scant entertainment, 3. the threadbare shopping and 4. the absence of medical diagnostics. And there remains easy motorized transportation to reach the real thing! This is not your grandmother's village

But those were not the only problems. Two centuries of intentional agrarian communities reveal that success is elusive. Growing food is an unforgiving endeavor. Cheap labor, real need and good intentions are not sufficient. The erosion of the Israeli kibbutzim, the disarray of the socialist cooperatives, the faded delights of hippy communes, those brave, dead, 19th-century American and British utopias, all occlude the landscape.

History shows there are many reasons for failure, some of which are unique and random, but the recurring ones involve deficient management and the human flaw of sloth. By way of contrast, most of the hundreds of Mormon communities settled between 1850 and 1900 flourished, even in a desert environment. They were distinguished by their expert management and the willing participation of the residents. Agrarian communities must likewise be well-run and inhabited by intentional residents. This is emphatically confirmed by Michael Ableman, consultant to the Southlands and a very successful farmer himself.

Agrarian Urbanism envisions communities based not on coercion, or the backwash of difficult circumstances, but as a competitive market-oriented option. Those participating will have literally bought into the kind of life proposed. This is not today an unusual arrangement. There are similar legal structures in conventional development: the homeowner's association, the co-op, or the condominium. As a condition of purchase there is the agreement to participate in certain activities, as well as to financially contribute to what is usually a rather elaborate and finicky infrastructure. The prospective agrarian residents, like their golfing, skiing and sunbathing equivalents, agree in the contract of purchase to an array of mutual expectations, laid out in clear detail and binding.[2] So it goes for agrarian communities.

[2] *A Legal Guide to Sustainable Development for Planners, Developers, and Architects* by Doris Goldstein and Dan Slone.

Conventional urban boundaries allow only minimal habitation beyond, inadvertently assuming large-scale farming. In nature, transition zones between ecological communities are called ecotones. They contain habitats common to the bordering zones as well as their own. This increased diversity is known as an edge effect. Rather than a tight, linear, prophylactic boundary, Agrarian Urbanism "corrugates" the T3-T2 boundary. This social and agricultural interface has its own edge effect, creating the most diverse and productive sector in the community. Along the complex boundary, dwellings associated with working the land continue to be attached to the "main road." Farms may be large

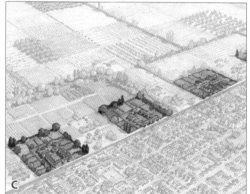

or small, but their layouts are interlocked so that the farmhouses remain physically within society, no less than with the fields being tended beyond. There are: **A.** *large tractor farms;* **B.** *medium hand-tended farms; and* **C.** *small farmsteads.*

• *Southlands (early), Canada 2008*

Agriculture is allocated to each Transect Zone according to the productive potential of the lot size and by the degree of negative impact of its crops and livestock on the nearby residents. Large-scale farming requires motorized machinery and sprays, *generating smells, noise and dust. That takes place on the corrugated rural and periurban edge (p. 43, 48-49). In the intraurban areas, Transect standards determine what can be grown in the interest of social harmony. Within the more urban Transect*

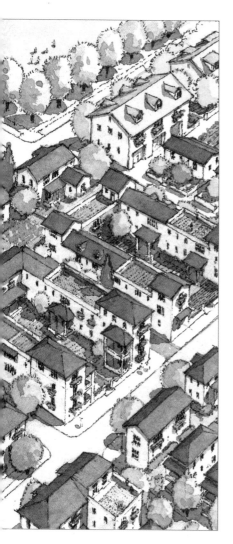

Zones of T4, T5 and T6, the food-growing operations are: **A.** *community gardens;* **B.** *yard gardens; and* **C.** *balcony and roof gardens.*

• *Southlands (early), Canada 2008*

The Southlands Compact states, "Farmland to be developed allocates one-third of the land to be urbanized, one-third is assigned to open space, and one-third to agriculture, with the value of the produce to triple that of the prior farmland." This is achieved by increasing the number of hands dedicated to tending food and hence increasing its market value (for details A-G, see p. 54 and 55).

• Southlands (later), Canada 2008

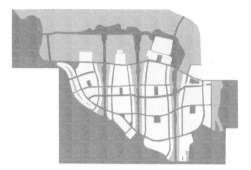

The areas allocated in thirds, according to the Southlands Compact.

Main, principal, secondary and farm roads, the latter being unpaved.

The rural-to-urban Transect Zones.

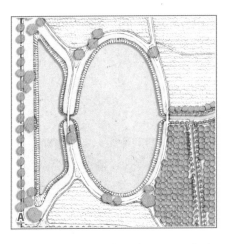

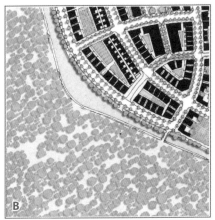

A. The runoff from an uphill suburb is intercepted by the narrow sediment pond and then allowed to flow over a weir to the oval retention pond, from which it is released downhill via the irrigation canals. This is both a water feature and the principal fish pond.

B. The existing woodland on a hillside is preserved and managed for foraging (nuts, berries, mushrooms, and small game).

C. The tractor farms are located beyond the urbanism, where their noise, dust, and smells will not affect the

dwellings. Note the buffer of hand-tended orchards.

D. The corrugated social-agricultural edge, with larger and smaller farms attached to the society of the "main road." Note the typical streets, secondary roads, and farm roads.

E. Extending the corrugated edge, a rural weave burrows deep into the intraurban zone, creating a high proportion of gardens. These agricultural incursions are along the existing irrigation canals, which have been enhanced and widened as functional and visual features. With the

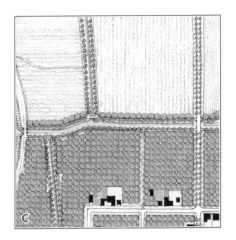

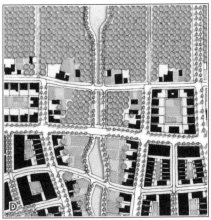

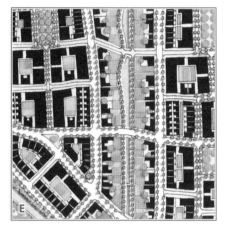

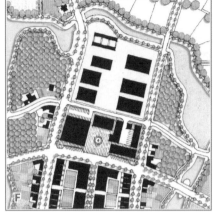

north-south insertion of agriculture into the urban fabric, the Transect also works east-west. Each sector has a rural edge and an urban spine. The squares shown are social, not agricultural.

F. *The Market Square is the locus of agricultural process-ing as well as the social and commercial center of the community (p. 56 and 57). Socializing takes place around food and its consumption rather than being based on recreational shopping.*

G. *Dwellings for support workers are included in the community as affordable courtyard housing. Workers have their own allotment gardens. As they are experts, these gardens are agricultural test-beds.*

H. *For instruction, the school campus is associated with the workers' area. The students have their own gardens, managed by the workers/experts living nearby.*

• *Southlands (later), Canada 2008*

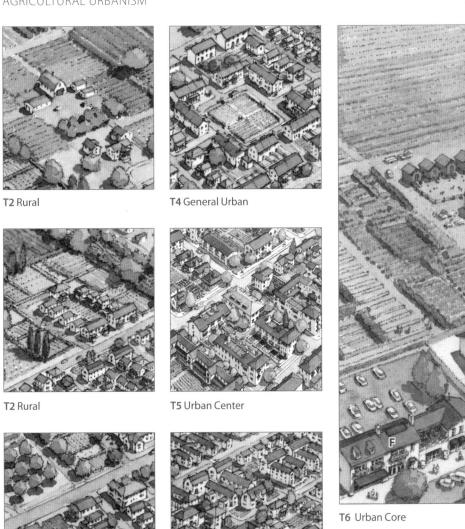

T2 Rural

T4 General Urban

T2 Rural

T5 Urban Center

T3 Sub-Urban

T5 Urban Center

T6 Urban Core

This Market Square is the primary social condenser of Agrarian Urbanism. The strength of its social function is based on its utilitarian role. The market square has several manifestations depending on its context. For Agricultural Retention, a model is shown on page 11. For Urban Agriculture, a model is shown on page 16. The one on this page corresponds to new towns and villages.

• *Southlands (early), Canada 2008*

A. The farmyard, for agricultural operations.

B. The barn, which is also the meeting house.

C. The administrative offices and instruction rooms.

D. The processing areas, grocery store and dining hall.

E. The farmer's market.

F. Shops with dwellings above.

G. Residential buildings.

57

AGRARIAN URBANISM

The acre is a unit of measurement applicable to both the density of urbanism and the yield of agriculture. These diagrams show a range of dwelling types on blocks of one acre. It is possible to calculate the ratio of production and consumption for each of these once the soil and climate is factored.

Note that the buildings tend to be on the northeast portion of their lot, allowing the most sunlight to reach planting areas. Solar access as a physical determinant leads to an urban pattern where streets may be asymmetrical.

A. B. C. Farmhouses that use small tractors. Note the utility wing for machinery and livestock.

D. Cottages in tight layouts must be one-story so sunlight can reach the small yards. This ground-floor living arrangement is recommended for seniors who would enjoy activity in their small yards (see this model fully developed on p. 59).

E. Rowhouses showing either front or rear "kitchen gardens," depending on orientation. Front and back gardens have markedly different social implications. A back garden may be allowed to become very messy, while the front garden provides the opportunity for sociability with passersby.

F. Rowhouses above a certain density offer no prospect for solar access to a garden on the ground, but roof gardens are perfectly workable surrogates, even if they have less social potential.

G. Perimeter apartment blocks may contain allotment gardens within their courts. These are associ-

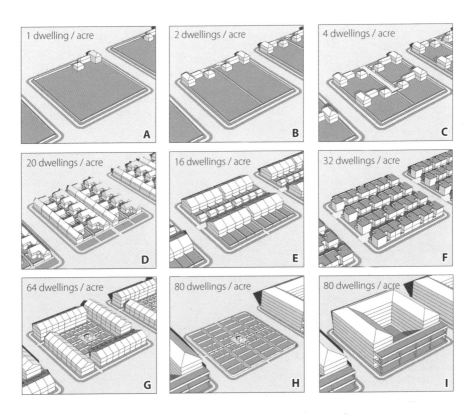

1 dwelling / acre **A**

2 dwellings / acre **B**

4 dwellings / acre **C**

20 dwellings / acre **D**

16 dwellings / acre **E**

32 dwellings / acre **F**

64 dwellings / acre **G**

80 dwellings / acre **H**

80 dwellings / acre **I**

ated to individual dwellings. It is a semi-public variation on the public community garden (H).

H. Apartment buildings cannot usually be directly adjacent to ground gardens because of the shadows cast by the tall buildings. They can be assigned off-site community gardens, which work despite the distance from the dwellings. As they may be shared by residents of other buildings, community gardens also serve as social condensers. When equipped with nice, habitable "garden sheds," they are like weekend vacation resorts (see p. 85).

I. Apartment buildings may also incorporate balcony gardens. One type has the balcony individually associated with each apartment— which is convenient, but has no potential as a social con-

denser. These might be placed on a checkerboard pattern on the façade to increase solar access. Another type, shown here, is the common balcony, which can be much wider and thereby more suitable for efficient food growing, but must be designed for alternate floors to provide extra height for solar access. This pattern is sociable, and even more so if the trajectory from the elevators to the apartments involves the gardens.

The housing shown in the prior diagrams is to be developed by architects into preliminary and then final designs as shown below, by William Dennis.

• Southlands (early), Canada 2008

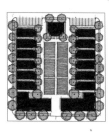
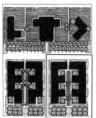
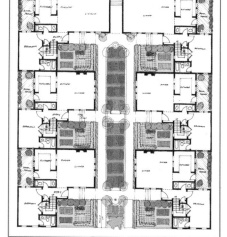
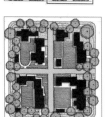
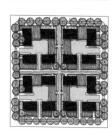
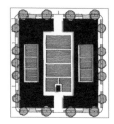

The lawn has been attacked by me and by many others as an environmental hazard. In the end, nothing less than the abandonment of this developed and admired form is required.

-Diana Balmori

CHAPTER 6 – MANAGEMENT PROTOCOLS

A great deal of choice is available today, particularly in the U.S., so developers must be more clever than usual in conceiving projects where agriculture is the principal amenity.

Historically, people had few alternatives. Some towns and most villages were based on food production and distribution as the principal economic and social activity. Other means of livelihood may have coexisted—shoemakers, weavers, shamans, bankers, crafters, builders—but foraging, husbandry and cultivation were paramount. Today agricultural landscapes may still be found adjacent to historic towns, but usually where protected by government policy for reasons beyond their economic viability.

As the outlines of the 21st century become clear, villages again emerge as practical and desirable. But they will proliferate only if their design and management is handled in a thoroughly modern way, which is to say, with a certain idealism present, but not an ideology that would prevent a realistic assessment of the possibilities.

To begin with, these new villages must count on the support systems that subsidize conventional suburbia in general. Among these is the great deal of land, money and labor that is usually expended on ornamental landscaping. In addition to the voluntary work of the private gardener, there is the hired help that does the underlying maintenance of these areas. There are also the municipal budgets for public areas and the surprisingly high fees collected for the semi-public landscaping of suburban developments. Agrarian Urbanism reassigns those public, semi-public and private funds away from ornamental planting to the more demanding aspects of agriculture. Instead of lawns and exotic plants that require constant attention, the fees and salaries would be directed to edible landscapes.

Thus the great difference between Agrarian Urbanism and the moribund communes, kibbutzim, social gardens, cooperative farms and old villages: the really hard work, the demanding schedule, and the boring aspects of agriculture are handled by contract workers. The lighter, more satisfying and pleasant roster of tasks—still a good portion—would be done by the willing residents in their spare time, much as they putter (and sometimes much more) in their own gardens.

To this end, the indispensable tool is the property owner's association or co-op—an administrative arrangement similar to that of any community that has a common facility like a lobby, parking lot, golf course, marina, pool, or security guard to maintain.[1]

Agrarian Urbanism envisions three levels of commitment. The basic one is the decision to be a dues-paying resident in such a community; the next is participation in a loosely organized gardening association; and highest is the agreement to cooperate in planting-to-table activity. Supporting, Associating and Cooperating Memberships might be good names for these three levels.

Those who thrive with purposeful order will belong to the co-op, organizing what to plant and making use of the pool of contract workers to supplement their own labor. The produce of this co-op would be distributed by a C.S.A. within the community or sold outside. Those who cannot tolerate management could belong to a more rudimentary and flexible Association, relying on an informal network for processing and distribution. The Supporters would just commit to buy their

[1] *A Legal Guide to Sustainable Development for Planners, Developers, and Architects* by Doris Goldstein and Dan Slone.

share of the produce that others grow, and pay to mitigate their share of personal labor not contributed. These options would be spelled out and agreed to as a condition of purchase or lease.

There is nothing unusual about such arrangements either in Britain, with its garden clubs and housing estates, or in the United States, with its homeowner's associations, condominiums, and coops. This, after all, is an intentional community, with its conditions fully disclosed. Although it is not for all, there will be takers, as gardening has become the most popular hobby among Anglo-Americans. It is more than a niche, and it is growing.

Then there is the aging Baby Boom generation that will be looking for things to do with the enforced leisure of retirement. And many of the young Millennials, with their green-saturated education, will doubtless find Agrarian Urbanism appealing. But these may not provide the ultimate market for Agrarian Urbanism—cross-generational survivalism may be its future appeal—as discussed in the next chapter.

I don't have to grow or cook. There is enough food out there for a life free of both garden and stove. But I like getting my hands in the soil as much as I like rubbing butter into flour to make pastry.

-Nigel Slater

CHAPTER 7 – TARGETED MARKETING

Like everything (including religion, dating or politics), environmentalism cannot avoid marketing its ideas and wares. Leaders in all fields have learned that virtue can no longer be simply imposed, even if it is necessary for survival. It is not enough that a certain way of dwelling on this earth is sensible—people are not so rational. Lifestyle choices in particular must be attractive to that complex and unforgiving entity called "the customer."

A customer comes into being when there is choice available. Modern real estate seldom exists in a situation of absolute scarcity. In the epic war between New Urbanism and conventional suburban development the existential condition has been between a shopping center or a main street, a house on a cul-de-sac or an urban townhouse, a drive in a car or a ride on a bus. Studies show that between one-third and two-thirds of the market would prefer the New Urbanism/Urban Village model when it is available and competently executed—too rare an occurrence thus far. Likewise, if Agrarian Urbanism is not well presented, customers will continue to choose among the 19 other products (p. 45), despite their negative environmental consequences.

To become one of the widely accepted real estate products, Agrarian Urbanism must access several environmental market niches, which may be individually small but substantial in aggregate. The market can be drawn from all age and socioeconomic groups, except perhaps those who have recently left behind agricultural servitude. The challenge is not only to design the settlements and the procedures as discussed in this book, but to craft a message that is compelling against some very competitive offerings—like the suburban "dream house." To paraphrase the advice of both George Bernard Shaw and Saul Alinsky: If the revolution is not entertaining, no one will show up for the second meeting.

And some will not show up even for the first meeting. The reality is that an intelligent and responsible lifestyle, whatever its manifestation, does not have universal appeal. Developers should be prepared to drop those who know nothing of food or environmentalism, or lack sympathy for community. It is not the developer's job to convert or compel them; there are hundreds of organizations that exist precisely to do so. But among those who are already inclined it is possible to discern four kinds of environmental consumers, provisionally referenced as Ethicists, Trendsetters, Opportunists, and Survivalists.

1. THE ETHICISTS (Because it's the right thing to do): These are guardians of Mother Nature, heirs to the pioneers of the 1960s. One might take heed from that first failure of environmentalism to take hold; perhaps to remember the granola that could break your teeth and the houses that gave you splinters. It is essential to avoid a reprise of that tawdry retreat. Because they are ethically driven, these "green gurus" may still display that tiresome higher morality. Their message can easily become misanthropic or penitential, calling for smaller and more expensive "green" dwellings, dinky cars, owning less "stuff," laundry on clotheslines, and a dwindling population—all of which can seriously limit environmentalism's appeal. However, authentic Ethicists will voluntarily suffer these inconveniences themselves, and their personal example is very compelling. They are our conscience. A dour approach has not heretofore contributed much to easy sales in the English-speaking countries, but they have since learned to compel by tapping into government policy and some have become regulators as well as activists. So compunction might yet succeed. Be on hand for the zero-carbon turnip!

2. THE TRENDSETTERS (Cool greens): These are consumers who will make the more environmental choice so long as it does not involve sacrifice. It is sometimes only "greenwash," but what they adopt is likely to enter the mainstream quickly (local food is a current darling and we assume a long-lived one). They are pleased to eat organically if it tastes good, and they will recycle if it is convenient. They will drive small cars and live in energy-efficient houses so long as they look really good. This is typified by the handsome and popular Prius (few bought the hideous first-generation Honda). This market segment is important because it is mostly young, and their virulent networking will likely provide the critical mass for a tipping point. They are the target audience of the new green trend of the advertising industry, which provides a tremendous multiplier effect to the cause. As happened with smoking, it will one day surely become profoundly uncool to eat processed food.

3. THE OPPORTUNISTS (What's in it for me?): These are pragmatists who thrive on the economics of environmentalism. The two categories of Opportunists are the entrepreneurs creating the green products, and the consumers seeking the savings of those products—like energy-efficient houses. Their message is usually optimistic, trusting that innovation will pull us through. Most are "gadget greens," seeking technological fixes rather than behavioral changes. They are not averse to government tipping the economic playing field their way through subsidy or regulation. Agrarian Urbanism, for example, would typically be developed by Opportunists and marketed to Trendsetters and Survivalists. '

4. THE SURVIVALISTS (Circle the wagons!): They consider themselves the only realists—the ones who understand the inevitability of decline and the troubles to come. These "grim greens" have concluded that it is too late to avoid the tipping point of climate change. In this they are inadvertently supported by the increasingly scary statistics put out by the Ethicists. But unlike the Ethicists' global concerns, Survivalists are resolutely local in

mentality. Having given up on *mitigating* the harm to nature, they will engage in *adapting* to the consequent energy short-ages, food scarcity and social instability. Unlike their bunkered predecessors of the Cold War, the Survivalists depend on com-munity. Indeed, precisely because the global scale is intracta-ble, they believe the only effective response is at the scale of their community (village, compound, family). Their intellectual leader is the formidably prescient James Howard Kunstler, who has pointed out that the lifestyle ensuing from what he calls the "Long Emergency," has its satisfactions—that one could do worse than the simple pleasures of tending to animals, fresh food and physical work.

ALL GREEN MARKETS: Marketing environmentalism is not a matter of ratcheting up frightening statistics or providing more accurate maps of disaster. Rather than tinkering with the science, it requires tinkering with the messages to the various consumers. As Christopher Alexander once said, "We all know what the appliance is ... what we must now do is design the plugs that will connect it to the existing power grids." (Note the plural.)

The Agrarian settlement is presumably always optimized, and it need not be adjusted to these market segments. What must be adjusted is its presentation. Only the purchase-deci-sion protocol needs to be customized.

Take for example the emblematic chicken and its fresh egg. How would each of the market segments best be convinced to adopt what is an additional cost and trouble?

The Ethicists will accept the bother if told that it is the right thing to do. In fact, they might not flinch at the smell and visual blight in their backyards, as those fulfill a penitential streak. Convincing the Trendsetters may require exotic fowl—and a demonstrable culinary improvement. And if the chicken coop is designed by Ikea or Leon Krier, it will become an element of class distinction. The Opportunists need no persuasion beyond the information that it is good value to consume or sell their own eggs. The Survivalists will install their coops, not because they are cool, nor because they are the right thing to do, not even to save costs, but because the protein would be available to bridge the coming supply disruptions of the Long Emergency.

The full range of agriculture could similarly be presented. To the Ethicists, explain that local agriculture is less petroleum-intensive in transport and fertilizer, and therefore harms nature less than either agribusiness or ornamental gardening. For the Trendsetters, who today tend to be foodies, emphasize the aesthetics and culinary pleasures of food. Also pitch the pleasure of a healthy lifestyle that also happens to catalyze socialization for kids and older folk. The Opportunists are the ones who can start food-processing businesses. The techy aspects of the community could also be catalogued for them—after all, Agrarian Urbanism is no less fascinating technically than a carbon-neutral house. The Survivalists will respond to the prospect of food security and toughened kids—like the Israeli Sabras. They are best engaged with the message of self-sufficiency: most ordinary daily needs are to be available within walking distance—implying that this is a fundamental bulwark against adversities to come.

So much for agriculture. What about the rest of the life-style? It's the same method: what goes for livestock goes for solar panels. But, like the tens of thousands who have bought into the original premise of the New Urbanism, don't forget that many will also be attracted by the prospect of community, all too absent in conventional suburbia. Emphasize that old standby when trying to make the sale.

And, as always, make the classic argument of real estate investment: that these communities are likely to hold their value better than the alternatives.

Thanks to my garden, I can take a small stand against everything I find witless, lazy and ugly in our civilization.

-Michele Owens

CHAPTER 8 – GENERAL TRANSECT THEORY

For those whose notion of fulfillment excludes dwelling in dense cities, Agrarian Urbanism provides an underlying theory that mitigates the environmental impact of their desire to live large on the land.

Scientific environmentalism must provide to the important field of real estate development an assessment protocol analogous to carbon exchange for industrial production. If the commons must suffer degradation—natural land, clean air—what might be a theoretical compensatory metric for the proposed impact?

Both biological and economic activities are based on transactions (of chemicals, of heat, of goods or services). A currency must be devised to evaluate what is lost in exchange for what is gained. A transaction is considered physically, economically or politically sustainable if understood to be a fair trade in this currency. Before suburban sprawl, development was generally considered so: a woodland or a farm might be lost, but the village or town gained was good value. But today a suburban housing estate or a shopping center is quite correctly considered a downward trade for the loss of a field or woodland. It is this fraud, this constant loss to society, that has given rise to pervasive public opposition to development and the NIMBY.

To be applicable, an environmental theory must mediate this kind of transaction by deploying formulas in a common currency. In the case of urban development, that could be the concept of *diversity*, which both the natural sciences and the social sciences employ as an index of value.

Levels of social and natural diversity can be measured at points along the rural-to-urban transect. The Transect is a 200-year-old ecological construct that has recently been extended to integrate environmental metrics for habitat management with socioeconomic metrics for urban design. The Transect can blend these specialists, enabling environmentalists to assess the value of cultural habitats and urbanists to protect natural ones. It can analyze the disparate human and natural interchange of complex place-types (p. 41-42).

There are currently four urban theories available to a society that increasingly demands justification for development of any kind, but particularly that on open land. These can be assessed by means of the currency of blended diversity.

1. TRADITIONAL URBAN THEORY relies on the enhancement of land value by inducing a mix of jobs, housing, shops and entertainment in geographical proximity. This social diversity was assured organically within pedestrian sheds until the 1950s when cars became ubiquitous, and broke the discipline of the neighborhood structure. The positive environmental consequences of traditional urbanism are a result of its compactness, completeness, walkability and transit support, all of which result in less transportation-based carbon emission. The major negative consequence is that land must be denatured into a commodity suitable for a continuous urban network. Natural features are effectively impediments to the optimized utilitarian state. Traditional Urbanism manifests good carbon impact metrics, but it cannot be inaugurated or extended without the elimination of natural traces on the land. Analyzing along the Transect, Traditional Urbanism correctly rates the social diversity of *T6 Urban Core* highest. But there is an enormous flaw, as this conceptualization assigns a higher value to the *T3 Sub-Urban* than to *T1 Natural*, which has no value at all (p. 75-1).

2. LANDSCAPE URBANIST THEORY has the opposite problem: By the absolute privileging of natural diversity, it assigns the worst performance to the *T6 Urban Core*, perversely rating it

worse even than *T3 Sub-Urban*. This reveals a serious concep-
tual flaw. Environmentalism, when based on humans being
"other" than nature has no metrics to assess the human or
urban declension of the Transect. With only natural tools available, the social diversity of the *T6 Urban Core* does not register,
except as denatured impervious pavement and "heat island."
As a result, the most urban places are unintentionally rated
with the most negative "ecological footprints." Dense urban
patterns are thereby considered part of the problem and not
part of the solution, which is the irremediable problem of this
theory (p. 75-2).

3. NEW URBANIST THEORY, by measuring a blend of both
social and natural diversity, assigns both *T1 Natural* and *T6
Urban Core* the highest value. This is as it should be. *T3 Sub-Urban* is also correctly shown to be the lowest value, as areas of
suburban single-family house have the worst diversity indices
of both, being usually social and natural monocultures. This
theory thus improves upon the prior two. The New Urbanist
formula is capable of assessing the loss of natural areas and
compensating for them by the relative urbanity to be gained.
However, it has never been able to justify the persistence of
the suburban house in *T3 Sub-Urban*, except as a regrettable
market necessity to implement its mission elsewhere at the
end points of the Transect. This flaw precludes the New Urbanism from becoming an unchallenged paradigm for ecological
performance (p. 75-3).

4. AGRARIAN URBAN THEORY correctly retains the New Urbanism's high natural diversity of *T1 Natural* and high social
diversity of *T6 Urban Core*, but it also radically improves the
performance of *T3 Sub-Urban*. This is done by integrating it
technically into a "green" regime of which Agrarianism is the
most thorough manifestation. The suburban single-family
house is designed and equipped to compensate for the higher
impacts of its land occupation and induced traffic. By also
enhancing requirements for energy generation, water reuse,

recycling/composting, and food production *T3 Sub-Urban* can approach a fair trade for loss of open land. The theory of Agrarian Urbanism thus equalizes environmental performance all along the Transect, while retaining the lifestyle choice that is necessary in a market economy—and essential to human happiness as self-defined (p. 75-4). Side note: Agrarian Urbanism also improves the social aspects of *T1* and *T2*, and the natural aspects of T6. One could legitimately claim it improves the combined diversity of all T-Zones.

SUMMARY: A truly ecological theory proposes that both natural and social diversity be combined and rated in various ratios along the rural-to-urban Transect. The high natural diversity of *T1 Natural* responds to the Landscape Urbanist ideal, while the high socio-economic diversity of *T6 Urban Core* is the ideal for Traditional Urbanism. But each of these two monovalent and lopsided paradigms undervalue the other, while assigning unwarranted value to *T3 Sub-Urban*. The New Urbanist Theory performs better by valuing both the natural and social diversity at *T1* and *T6*, while correctly but problematically devaluing the suburban point of *T3*, which has the lowest indices of both. Agrarian Urbanism mitigates *T3 Sub-Urban* so that all Transect Zones are equalized.

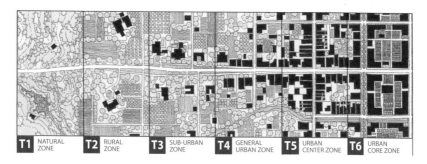

| **T1** NATURAL ZONE | **T2** RURAL ZONE | **T3** SUB-URBAN ZONE | **T4** GENERAL URBAN ZONE | **T5** URBAN CENTER ZONE | **T6** URBAN CORE ZONE |

1 - TRADITIONAL URBANISM - PRIVILEGES SOCIO-ECONOMIC DIVERSITY

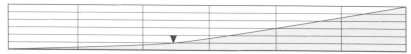

2 - LANDSCAPE URBANISM - PRIVILEGES NATURAL DIVERSITY

3 - NEW URBANISM - COMBINES NATURAL & SOCIO-ECONOMIC DIVERSITY

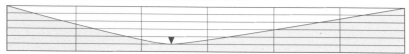

4 - AGRARIAN URBANISM - COMBINES NATURAL & SOCIO-ECONOMIC DIVERSITY AND MITIGATES ALL COMBINATIONS

The underlying theory of Agrarian Urbanism (4) involves an agreement that all residents commit to sustainable practices commensurate with the impact of their residential arrangement. Both for reasons of mitigating their heavier ecological footprint and also because it is better able to do so, the suburban house of T3 is regulated to become a locus of compensatory food and energy production, as well as recycling.

Agrarianism tests success and failure not by projected income statements or by economic growth, but by the health and vitality·of a region's entire human and non-human neighborhood.

-Norman Wirzba

CHAPTER 9 – THE USUAL QUESTIONS

Good developers ask questions. Risk in this business, though inevitable, can be minimized by trying to play out what could go wrong before it happens. The following challenges should be expected:

WHERE HAS THIS BEEN DONE BEFORE? While a complete Agrarian community has never been carried out, its components have been implemented. In those built Agricultural and New Urbanist communities, most aspects of financial practice, infrastructure, management and farming are available for study.

WHAT IS MEANT BY "AMENITY"? An amenity is an asset, extraneous to the dwelling, which adds value. The most desirable amenities are views (shore, golf frontage and mountain); security (gates and guards); prestige (high price range, civic ornaments); location (proximity, accessibility, visibility, climate); activity (skiing, golf, water, clubhouse); and community. The latter is the only amenity that does not entail additional developmental cost. The Agrarian program is proposed as a kind of amenity

CAN IT BE FINANCED? To a lending institution, the numbers should not appear too differently from a New Urbanist community equipped with, say, a golf course. Obviously, a presentation that emphasizes innovation is not going to be compelling to a loan officer. A good slant might be that it is a "green" development of a type that is not yet overbuilt.

WHAT DOES THE BOTTOM LINE LOOK LIKE? This type of development should perform like a typical golf community—and it is likely to be more conservative, as the common amenities cost less to build and are easier to phase. The barn is cheaper than the clubhouse, and the provision of community gardens more incremental than eighteen fairways.

WHO PAYS FOR THE COMMON AMENITIES? The facilities necessary for administering and processing food can be more utilitarian than the typical clubhouse. Furthermore, the expense of the shopping center usually required as a social condenser would simply be replaced by the Market Square.

HOW DO WE KNOW THE MARKET? The depth of the market may be determined by any sophisticated assessment technique—so long as it is based on psycho-demographic research and not the rear-view mirror. Even so, if conservatism is required, even rudimentary research will reveal a large market that overlaps with the overwhelming popularity of gardening.

IF THIS IS NOT FOR EVERYBODY, PLEASE BE PRECISE. Agrarian Urbanism is not for: People who abhor physical activity on their time off; people who do not care about their food or the environment; people who would rather not know their neighbors; people who are class-conscious and get nervous with the presence of "workers"; people who have no disposable income; nor is it for people of anarchistic temperament.

HOW DO WE MARKET THIS? Promote it like any other intentional community, such as those dedicated to skiing, waterfront activity or golf. In other words, organize the usual brochures, sales office and trained staff. In the end, Agrarian communities may even have the advantage of targeted advertisement in the environmental and garden periodicals that now proliferate.

WHO WILL MANAGE ALL THIS? There is no question that Agrarian Urbanism is as management-intensive as a golf community, with which there are rough equivalencies in terms of staffing. Remember that residents have chosen to live in such a place. They don't have to be unduly coerced to comply with the rules.

WHO DOES THE DIRTY WORK? There are always the difficult and boring tasks of maintaining the landscape on a conventional suburban community. The solution is exactly the same: to have a paid staff do the heavy work, with the rest done by the amateur gardener or, as the case may be, the association or cooperative.

WILL IT BE AN UNENDING RESPONSIBILITY? Only to the extent that all development is a residual responsibility for the developer. Unless there are well-written association documents that minimize conflict, preserve the freedom of decision for the developer, and manage a comprehensive hand-over to the owners' association, there will always be problems. But there exist legal structures that successfully extricate the developer, and the ones for Agricultural Urbanism would be but a variant of these.

IS THERE A FUTURE FOR THIS? This kind of development is *all* about the future. Sustainability to the point of self-sufficiency is where the market is going, especially if it becomes apparent that the campaign to mitigate climate change is being lost. If this conclusion seems early, remember that urbanism operates on the time frame of decades. The present is a distortion field that should be examined skeptically.

WHAT IS THE BEST LOCATION? Even where other development models have been overbuilt, Agrarian Urbanism stands a chance of finding buyers. However, a full-fledged Agrarian community with its potential for surplus production should be near a city with a market, hotel and a restaurant culture prepared to consume and pay for the better food. As with most community-supported agriculture, it is primarily a metropolitan model, although there may also emerge a secondary market for survivalist communities distant from the "troublesome" cities.

IS NOW THE TIME? Given the time required to build communities, Agrarian Urbanism is not too terribly futuristic a proposition. With the combination of the Baby Boomers who do not want insipid "retirement villages," the impending family formation of the green Millennials, and of course climate change, Agrarian Urbanism is timely.

CAN I DO A "LIGHT" VERSION OF THIS? Agrarian Urbanism is the complete version of the concept. Agricultural Urbanism, with its separate farm, is an easier version to implement, although a center with shopping would then have to be provided at considerable cost and effort, as the separate agricultural farm would not perform as a social condenser.

WHAT TYPES OF BUILDINGS WOULD BE INVOLVED? The dwellings are the standard types: houses, cottages, townhouses and apartment buildings—with relatively modest internal differences accommodating food and tool storage. There are some rather intriguing variations regarding roof and balcony gardens and solar orientation, but none are unusual or costly. They would require only good, practical design and the real-location of some resources.

WHAT INCENTIVES ARE THERE? A suite of financial incentives from government has not yet been worked out, but it is possible to conceive that with current green and agricultural subsidies, and with public-private partnerships available, a clever developer would be able to make a case based on support of the environment or public health. An immediate incentive might be the ability to gain planning approvals that are otherwise difficult to secure. As Agrarian Urbanism is clearly part of the solution, not part of the problem, it brings along the moral authority of much of the environmental agenda.

ARE THERE BUREAUCRATIC IMPEDIMENTS? There are always impediments to development that is not conventional suburban sprawl. New Urbanist developers have been overcoming such impediments for three decades, and there is a great deal of commiseration available.

WILL THIS FIT INTO "THE SYSTEM"? It depends on the system. The banking protocol that resells mortgages as large bundles of identical "development product" could cause difficulty if the differences were to be emphasized. However, every aspect of Agrarian Urbanism can be presented to a financial institution as conventional. A house with a yard, a townhouse (skip the description of the roof garden), or an apartment building next to a public park (don't necessarily call it the community garden) are not difficult to explain. This has been done for decades with live-work units, for example, where the workplace is labeled the "den."

REMIND ME AGAIN: WHY SHOULD I DO THIS? Well, there is a list of good reasons: 1. Regarding health, Agrarian Urbanism provides recreational and productive physical activity; fresh, humanely raised food; control over food supply and quality; and it preserves open space. 2. Environmentally, with Agrarian Urbanism there is less pollution of water and soil; closed cycles of food-to-waste-to-food; retention and restoration of marginal agricultural land; an intensification of crop yields; and less energy applied to, and pollution resulting from, food transportation. 3. Economically, Agrarian Urbanism efficiently delivers to a variety of emerging economic realities; it positions recreational time as productive rather than consumptive; it saves cost in waste disposal, fertilizers and herbicides; it allows maintenance budgets to be reduced; and it appeals to a large and growing market. 4. Socially, Agrarian Urbanism supplies social gathering places enriched by utility; provides training in a useful craft, meaningful jobs for some, and participation for all, including children and seniors; it fosters cultural traditions based on mutual reliance, and it aggregates individual effort to the level of an economic system—not just amateur performance. In other words, this should be done because there are few better ideas around.

"The vegetable garden, it turns out, is a ripening political force: the best response to the energy crisis, the climate crisis, the obesity crisis, the family crisis and the financial crisis… It will be no small irony if suburbia becomes the locavore's home of choice… and growing backyard veggies could be the answer to the crisis of disaffected suburban youth."

-Dominique Browning

CHAPTER 10 – ADDITIONAL READING

As mentioned in the preface, this book is small because there are so many other good books available that supplement the know-how. Below are some of the better ones.

A good companion is *Civic Agriculture* by Thomas Lyson. It covers the politics and macroeconomics as succinctly as this book covers the social, the design, and the development aspects.

For a description of the dismal prospects confronting the 21st century, there is nothing better than James Howard Kunstler's *The Long Emergency*. The book that alerted so many to the agricultural aspects of the Long Emergency was Michael Pollan's *The Omnivore's Dilemma*.

The best general collection of essays is probably *The Fatal Harvest Reader* by Andrew Kimbrell, which has an essay by Wendell Berry, most of whose books are worth the while. A nicely intellectual collection is the *Essential Agrarian Reader*, edited by Norman Wirzba with a prescient essay by Benjamin Northrup.

For a rather sweet interpretation, try Barbara Kingsolver's *Animal, Vegetable, Miracle*. Then turn to the spartan virtues of the farming life in the personal experience of Roger Scruton. *News From Nowhere* recounts how a most urbane person seriously roughs it.

For technical instructions on food growing, there are two manuals that make it interesting: Rosalind Creasy's *Edible Landscaping* ("Now you can have your gorgeous garden and eat it too") and John Seymour's *The Self-Sufficient Life* ("The complete back-to-basics guide"). For even more specific technical instruction there is *The Garden Primer* by Barbara Damrosch, which describes itself as "The gardener's bible." A version for smaller urban gardens is *Square Foot Gardening* by Mel Bartholomew.

The book that introduced me to the social aspects of urban gardening is Fritz Haeg's *Edible Estates*.

Books that bridge social and agricultural issues are *Agricultural Urbanism* by Janine de la Salle and Mark Holland and *The Next Agricultural Revolution* by Kent Mullinix: All three authors worked on Southlands.

At the scale of Agricultural Retention, there is *Dwellers on the Land* by Kirkpatrick Sale and the more legalistic *Saving American Farmland* by the American Farmland Trust.

For a graceful British presentation, Prince Charles' *Harmony* and also *Highgrove: Portrait of an Estate,* will seem a relief from the Americanisms of this book. For intense Germanic ideas about gardens, see the most interesting *When Modern Was Green* by David Haney. To each his own.

For an encyclopedia that includes not only growing food but environmental living "whole hog," there is Doug Farr's *Sustainable Urbanism*. At the scale of the building, there is the equally comprehensive *Solar Living Source Book* by John Schaeffer.

For fixing the suburban mess—the context within which 21st-century planning must occur, there is the *Sprawl Repair Manual* by my partner at DPZ, Galina Tachieva.

Underlying the New Urbanism is our *Suburban Nation, The Smart Growth Manual*, and *The Lexicon of the New Urbanism*.

The Charter of the New Urbanism, and Leon Krier's *The Language of Towns and Cities* are also essential.

Underlying Landscape Urbanism is Charles Waldheim's *Landscape Urbanism Reader*.

Underlying it all is William Cronon's *Uncommon Ground*.

These are two of the various scales of Agrarian Urbanism: the house on the half-acre farm and the shed on the community garden. Both are in the middle range between the extremes of the tractor farm to the balcony garden. Note that the smaller community garden has variety in production similar to the larger farm. Only the extremes tend to monocultures of cultivation.

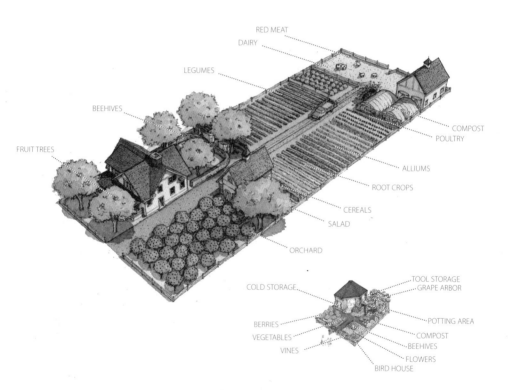

RED MEAT
DAIRY
LEGUMES
BEEHIVES
COMPOST
POULTRY
FRUIT TREES
ALLIUMS
ROOT CROPS
CEREALS
SALAD
ORCHARD

COLD STORAGE
TOOL STORAGE
GRAPE ARBOR
BERRIES
POTTING AREA
VEGETABLES
COMPOST
VINES
BEEHIVES
FLOWERS
BIRD HOUSE

Half the world's food is lost, wasted, or discarded along the chain from farm to shop to consumer to dump.

-London Evening Standard 2-21-2011